PRAISE

NOT A CREATURE WAS STIRRING

"Vintage Christie [turned] inside out . . . *Not a Creature Was Stirring* will puzzle, perplex and please the most discriminating readers."

—*Murder Ad Lib*

PRECIOUS BLOOD

"A fascinating read."

—*Rave Reviews*

A GREAT DAY FOR THE DEADLY

"Haddam plays the mystery game like a master. . . . A novel full of lore, as of suspense, it is bound to satisfy any reader who likes multiple murders mixed with miraculous apparitions and a perfectly damnable puzzle."

—*Chicago Tribune*

The Gregor Demarkian Holiday Series
by Jane Haddam

*Available wherever Bantam Books
are sold*

DEAR

O · L · D

DEAD

Jane Haddam

BANTAM BOOKS
New York · Toronto · London · Sydney · Auckland

DEAR OLD DEAD

A Bantam Book / July 1994

ISBN 0–553–56447–1

Published simultaneously in the United States and Canada

Bantam Books are published by Bantam Books, a division of Bantam Doubleday Dell
Publishing Group, Inc. Its trademark, consisting of the words "Bantam Books" and the
portrayal of a rooster, is Registered in U.S. Patent and Trademark Office and in other
countries. Marca Registrada. Bantam Books, 1540 Broadway, New York, New York
10036.

PRINTED IN THE UNITED STATES OF AMERICA

RAD   0 9 8 7 6 5 4

D·E·A·R
O·L·D
D·E·A·D

P·R·O·L·O·G·U·E

A Hot Night in the
Middle of May

1

There was a banner over the masthead of the New York *Sentinel* that night, a banner in red letters that read,

**YOU COULD BE NEW YORK'S LUCKIEST FATHER!
WIN $100,000 FOR FATHER'S DAY.**

Under the masthead, there was a picture of the president of the United States and the word ***SMASHED*** in thick black letters. Dr. Michael Pride didn't know what the president of the United States had done to deserve the headline, but, he thought, coming down the stairs from the third floor at a run, leaning over to pick the paper off the floor and throw it in a garbage can, the president deserved it a hell of a lot less than the people he was now about to see. Dr. Michael Pride felt that way about a lot of the headlines the *Sentinel* stuck next to the president of the United States, but he wasn't a political man and he wasn't going to complain about it. It wouldn't have done any good. The *Sentinel* was owned—as this clinic was to a large part financed—by good old Charlie van Straadt, the Citizen Kane of his time. Charlie van Straadt liked two-hundred-foot luxury yachts, one-hundred-room apartments in Trump Tower, and conspicuous charity. He also liked Republicans of the Neanderthal variety. This president was a Democrat and a disaster by definition. But Michael had more important things to think about.

There was a copy of the New York *Post* on a molded-plastic folding chair in the corridor as Michael headed for the back of the building and the stairs that led down to the emergency-room door. The headline said, **CAUGHT** and the picture underneath it was of Michael himself. It had been taken two days ago and showed Michael being led to a police car in handcuffs with a group of men who looked as if they could provide a pictorial definition of the word *degenerate*. Behind them, the neon storefront of the place they'd all been in when it was raided said, **HOT BUNS HOT BUNS HOT BUNS.**

Everything in New York takes place in capital letters, Michael thought, and then he was into it, at the bottom of the stairs, in the middle of the action. It was a Saturday night with a difference.

Actually, it wasn't even Saturday night, not technically. It was six o'clock in the evening and still more than a little light. It had been an unseasonably hot day and the heat was lingering. Michael was reminded of the first long summer he had spent in the city. He had been an intern at Columbia Presbyterian. He had been able to afford neither the time nor the money for air-conditioned rooms. He had spent a lot of time sitting on fire escapes, letting the sweat trickle down his neck and dreaming about being a rich-and-famous specialist, with a big house in Connecticut and an apartment off Fifth Avenue and a portfolio full of real estate deals for the Internal Revenue Service to worry about.

He could have been a rich-and-famous specialist.

That was one of the things everyone agreed about, even papers like the New York *Post*. He could have been someplace else. But he wasn't.

He was standing in the middle of the small emergency room of the Sojourner Truth Health Center, which he had founded, just off Lenox Avenue in Harlem. He was standing knee-deep in bleeding teenage boys and frazzled nuns. He was wondering how he was going to get through it all this time. Every once in a while, he caught one of the boys staring at him, proof positive that the pundits were all wrong. These kids could read just fine if they had something that interested them to read. Michael would stand back and the kid would look away, ashamed. Ashamed of what? **HOT BUNS HOT BUNS HOT BUNS.** Michael saw little Sister Margarita Rose going by with a tray of instruments and grabbed her by the wide end of her sleeve. Sister Margarita Rose came to an abrupt and panicked stop and only relaxed when she saw who had hold of her. She wasn't going to last long, Michael thought. She'd only been here since the first of the year, and he wouldn't give her another three full months.

"Oh," she said, when she saw who was holding her. "Oh, Dr. Pride. Excuse me. I was on my way to get these sterilized."

"Stop and talk to me for a minute," Michael said. "What's the situation? Has anybody got any news from out there?"

"News?" Sister Margarita Rose said.

"I've got news," Sister Augustine said. Unlike Sister Margarita Rose, Sister Augustine was neither young nor delicate, and she didn't wear a habit. Sister Augustine was somewhere in her fifties, five feet tall, a hundred and forty plus pounds, and fond of velour sweatsuits. She was wearing one now in bright purple, with a little black veil on the back of her head.

Michael let Sister Margarita Rose go. "Hello, Augie. I haven't seen you all day."

"I had four deliveries today," Augie said. "Never mind about that. The Blood Brothers have the block between One Forty-fifth and One Forty-sixth streets on Lenox blocked off. The Cyclones staged a raid over there about five thirty. The casualties are just starting to come in. The Cyclones have assault rifles."

"Bad?"

"Two police officers dead over at Lenox Hill Hospital not more than five minutes ago. A two-year-old boy dead on arrival here about quarter to six. What do you mean, bad?"

"Right," Michael said. He looked around the emergency room. People were tense and bustling, but they weren't really busy, not yet. That would come when the sirens he could hear in the distance were no longer so distant.

"Okay," Michael said. "We better assume a full disaster and set up to process to Triage. Can you get me six nurses down to OR in five minutes?"

"Sure."

"I'm going to need both Jenny Kaplan and Ben DeVere. Jenny's supposed to be having the day off. You'll have to find her."

"I already have."

"Find Ed Marchiano, too. I know he's only a medical student, but we'll just have to fudge a little. It's that or watch people die on the floor. He's supposed to be teaching a health class to the mother's group at six thirty. You can find him there."

"I'll send Sister Margarita Rose."

"Right," Michael said. Then he looked around and shook his head. "Are we ready for this? Didn't we promise ourselves the last time that we'd be more ready for this? What's happened to New York?"

"Oh, New York." Sister Augustine was dismissive. "This hasn't been New York for years. This is Beirut. Are you all right, Michael?"

"I'm fine."

"Newspapers haven't been bothering you?"

"I'm fine, Augie. I really am."

"I don't care if you get arrested, Michael, but if you keep this up, you could get AIDS. Or just plain killed."

Michael was about to tell her that it didn't make any sense to practice safe sex through a glory hole, just to see if she knew what that was, just to see if he could shock her—but he knew he couldn't. He didn't because the bell started to go off and the staff started to run in from everywhere at once, pulling back the double doors to let the stretchers in, standing back while one white-sheeted casualty followed the other in a confusion of sterilized cotton and stainless steel. Michael grabbed a box of disposable surgical gloves from the nearest shelf and started heading for the OR.

"Demerol," he shouted back at Augie over the crowd. "I need Demerol for post-op."

"Coming," Augie shouted back.

Michael saw Sister Margarita Rose and thought it might be a lot less than three full months. The little nun looked paralyzed. She looked as if she wanted to be dead.

Michael himself felt fully alive for the first time all day—for the first time in weeks, really, in spite of that ill-fated excursion down to Times Square. He felt alive and clear and healthy and energetic and smart and beautiful and perfect. It was as if he had been taken completely out of the world and transformed and returned to it. It was as if he had reached that state desired above all others by every graduate of the Harvard Medical School: the state of being able to do no wrong.

He smashed through the double swinging doors to the back hall where the OR was and started to jog. He passed nuns and center volunteers and surgical nurses in OR green who stopped to stare at him. He knew what they were all thinking and he didn't care.

He could see himself, a tall, cadaverously thin man with a face too lined for his forty-six years, beginning to lift up off the floor and swim with effortless grace through the air.

2

Charles van Straadt knew, almost as soon as he sat down in Michael Pride's office, that he had come down to the center at a bad time. That he had come down to the center at all he thought was perfectly understandable. Charles van Straadt was a very rich and a very powerful man, and a very old one. He had reached all three states on his own and by virtue of superior cunning. He had never given himself credit for superior intelligence. Charles van Straadt was no Michael Pride, and he knew it. He could never have graduated from high school at fifteen or MIT at eighteen. He could never have made it into the Harvard Medical School, never mind out with a *summa cum laude* and an internship at Columbia. What Charles understood was much more basic. Charles knew why the New York press was dying and what to do about it. He knew what people everywhere were willing to pay to hear. He understood populist politics, local television, working-class aesthetics, and the art of the headline. He understood these things so well that he was now the major newspaper player in sixteen cities across the world, from London to Melbourne, from New York to Milano, from Miami to Athens. He was seventy-eight years old and still in excellent health. He attributed his longevity to red meat and fried potatoes and owned a steak house in every city where he owned a newspaper. He made the covers of gossipy magazines in pictures that showed him smoking a big cigar and scowling into the camera. He was an eccentric of the first water and getting more eccentric all the time—but he understood that, too. It had been a long, hard life, but he had loved every minute of it. Lately, he had been expecting to find out he was immortal.

Now he sat in the big plastic-covered easy chair Michael kept just for his visits and looked around at the usual mess, at the papers strewn everywhere, at the charts tacked haphazardly to the wall and notes stuck to the side of the telephone with messages like *"call Augie @ cattle cultures"* written across them. Charles van Straadt had decided to provide major funding for the Sojourner Truth Health Center seven years ago, and in those seven years he had scrupulously kept his promise to Michael Pride not to interfere in operations, with one exception. Charles van Straadt paid for Michael Pride's secretary, and paid well. He couldn't stand the thought of the chaos to which Michael's life was reduced when Michael was left to organize it alone.

Charles's granddaughter Rosalie—his favorite one, the one he kept around him all the time—was standing on the other side of the office, looking out the windows onto the street. She wore a black turtleneck sweater and black slacks, like a Beatnik girl from the 1950s, and it was a measure of just how pretty she was that she looked good in them. Her dark hair was pulled up on her head in a knot. Her fingers were full of gold and silver rings.

"I don't think you're going to get to see Michael today," Rosalie said. "There's some kind of emergency going on down there. I wonder what could have happened."

"Gang war," Charles said.

"Do you think so really? It just seems so odd that people would go to all that trouble. To have a war, I mean. Why bother?"

"If you're asking me what the issues are, I don't know."

"I passed Martha downstairs while I was coming in. She isn't speaking to me. Ida and Victor aren't speaking to me either. I don't think any of them will ever speak to me again."

"I wouldn't worry about it."

"I don't worry about it, grandfather. I just get annoyed by it. It's so unnecessary."

"Is that what it is?"

"You could have gone about it differently, you know. You could have set it up in secret and not let anyone know until it was over." Rosalie's voice was accusing.

"I can't do anything in secret," Charles van Straadt said. "That's why I own a lot of newspapers."

Actually, he owned a lot of newspapers because newspapers were what had been available for him to buy, all those years ago, and had been what he knew, too—but telling that sort of thing to his grandchildren was like trying to explain the intricacies of oil painting to a blind person. Rosalie was good with money, but she had no ear for the business. Martha and Ida and Victor weren't even good with money. Charles looked around the office one more time and came up blank. Either Michael hadn't read the newspapers today or he'd gotten rid of the ones he had read.

Charles took a cigar out of his inside jacket pocket and lit up. What he lit up with was a twenty-two-carat-gold cigarette lighter he'd had custom made for himself at Harry Winston. Like the custom gold cufflinks on his shirts and the custom gold buckles on his John Lobb loafers, the cigarette lighter was part of Charles's legend. He reached over to Michael's desk and extracted the black plastic ashtray from under a stack of forms that would have brought Michael a fair amount of money if he'd ever decided to file them with Medicaid. Michael would never decide to file them with Medicaid. Michael said that taking government money made you far too vulnerable to government regulation.

Charles put the black plastic ashtray in his lap and tapped a thin stream of cigar ash into it.

"Did you walk around the building?" he asked Rosalie. "Did you check out what I asked you to?"

"Yes I did."

"And?"

"The gay rights protesters are gone, maybe because of all the stories this morning. The guy from the Holly Hill Christian Fellowship is still there, carrying the same old sign. Maybe he doesn't read the papers any more than Michael does."

"That's unlikely. And there was a lot of television play. Nobody else?"

Rosalie shook her head. "It's really spooky up here. It feels dangerous just to breathe the air. Maybe people are afraid to come up and harass him."

"Well, they're certainly harassing us," Charles said. "I

checked with the *Sentinel* office before we came down here. We're getting fifteen calls an hour on how we're covering up for Michael Pride. We're not going to be able to hold off on this story forever."

"I don't understand why we're holding off on it at all," Rosalie told him. "I mean, it's not like it really matters. This is a privately funded foundation. There isn't some bureaucrat someplace who could get Michael fired. The only person who could force him out of here is you, and you don't want to."

"True."

"I don't see what difference it makes if he does patronize ... glory holes. I think it's gross, but I don't see what difference it makes. Why shouldn't the *Sentinel* make just as much of a fuss about it as everyone else?"

"Well," Charles said mildly, "we owe Michael something, you know. The whole city of New York owes Michael something."

"What?"

Charles van Straadt cocked his head. Was it possible that Rosalie didn't understand what was going on here? Was it possible that his granddaughter didn't realize how incredible it was, that a doctor of Michael Pride's training, ability, and stature should be spending his life in this place, bringing medicine to people so poor and so poorly educated, so defeated and so paranoid, that the rest of the country had given up on them all long ago? The disturbing thing was that Rosalie probably didn't understand—and that Martha and Ida and Victor wouldn't understand, either. They lived in a fog, these children. The world was not what it had been when Charles van Straadt was young.

Charles took a long deep drag on his cigar and sighed.

"Do me a favor," he said. "Go downstairs and get me one of those fudgey ice lolly things from the cafeteria. I'll wait here for a while and think through what I want to do."

"Do you think it's safe?"

"Your going or my staying?"

"Your staying, of course. It's so—deserted up here."

"It's deserted up here because there's an emergency down there," Charles said. "Take off now, I'll be fine. I promise."

"All right," Rosalie said, reluctantly.

"Take off now."

Rosalie hesitated a moment longer. Then she shrugged her elegant shoulders and strode out of the office, not looking back.

"Try not to get yourself mugged," she told him as she slammed the door behind herself. It popped open again, refusing to catch.

Charles van Straadt took another drag on his cigar and got out of his chair. Michael's phone was covered with Post-It notes, but it was otherwise free of debris. Charles sat down in Michael's chair and picked up the receiver.

"I would like to speak to Martha van Straadt," he told the house operator. "I believe she's on duty in post-op this evening."

The operator said something inane in half-Spanish, half-English and Charles chewed at the end of his cigar.

Crises, crises, crises, he thought.

There never seemed to be an end to crises.

3

Unlike practically everybody else in the city of New York—or at least, practically everybody else who didn't work at the Sojourner Truth Health Center—Father Eamon Donleavy had not been surprised to open his copy of the *Daily News* this morning to find Michael Pride splashed all over the front of it. He hadn't even been surprised at the occasion for the story, which was the fact that Michael had been caught in the raid of a particularly nasty gay porno house off Times Square. Eamon Donleavy and Michael Pride had known each other all their lives. Their families had had practically identical six-room ranch houses next door to each other in Kickamer, Long Island, and they had gone straight through high school together, with Eamon two years older and more or less on track, and Michael not even old enough to drive on the day he graduated. After that, Eamon and Michael had parted. Eamon had gone on to the seminary and Michael had gone on to MIT. It had surprised neither of them when, running into each other much later, it had turned out that they had a lot in common. It had surprised Eamon not at all that Michael was "gay." Eamon always put quotes around that word because, in Michael's case, the situation was somewhat complicated. Eamon knew dozens of gay men. It was impossible not to, living in New York. Michael was something different, an original, a law unto himself. Michael wasn't so much definitely gay as he was definitely crazy.

Eamon Donleavy had the newspapers spread out across his desk: the *Post*, the *Daily News*, even *The Times*. The only paper that hadn't played up the story of

Michael's arrest was the *Sentinel*, and that was Charles van Straadt shielding his personal saint. Eamon didn't know how long the *Sentinel*'s silence could possibly last. He didn't know what was going to happen next, either. The center couldn't operate without Michael. The center was Michael. Eamon didn't think Michael could operate without the center. It was getting as crazy as Michael's personal life.

Eamon Donleavy served as chaplain to the nuns who worked at the Sojourner Truth Health Center, and offered Mass once a day to anyone who wanted to attend, and gave classes in reading and religion to anybody who wanted to show up. He was really here to ensure that the Archdiocese of New York did not get into any serious trouble through the fact that they provided the Sojourner Truth Health Center with a good deal of money and resources. This was a tricky maneuver, because the center quite definitely did abortions (for free) and gave abortion counseling. The official position of the Archdiocese on that was that the Catholics at the center had nothing to do with abortion or birth control in any way and the money the Archdiocese sent was used for a children's lunch program and the provision of school supplies like pencils and notebooks to children who could not afford their own. As a policy position it left a lot to be desired, as had been pointed out in everything from *The National Review* to *The New Criterion*. The Archdiocese was getting away with it because the present Archbishop had the reputation of being a conservative hard-liner. It was difficult to accuse the man of liberalism when he'd just delivered a speech on the evils of R-rated movies and nonprocreational sex. Still, it was a balancing act—and now there was this. The Archbishop had known about this long before the papers had, just as Eamon had. It didn't make the stories any easier to take.

Eamon's office was right across the hall from Michael's own. Through his open door, Eamon could see Charles van Straadt making calls on Michael's phone. Eamon didn't like Charles van Straadt. He thought the man was dangerous. Eamon especially didn't like the way Charles sent his grandchildren to volunteer at the center. To Eamon, Charles van Straadt's grandchildren looked very much like spies.

"We've got to start working on some kind of contingency plan," the Archbishop was saying in Eamon's ear. "We've got to think of a rationale. That is, unless you want us to pull all the nuns out of there, which I don't."

"No, Your Eminence. Of course I don't."

This Archbishop was also a Cardinal. The Archbishop of New York was always a Cardinal. In Eamon's experience, there was something about making a man a Cardinal that rendered him incapable of making a short phone call. This call had lasted half an hour so far, and it was beginning to look like a real marathon.

"How's Michael?" the Archbishop said. "Is he keeping his mind on his work?"

"I don't think Michael's noticed the fuss at all, Your Eminence."

"How could he avoid it?"

"By working."

"Well, yes, Eamon, of course, by working, but—it's all over the place. He couldn't go to the corner for a cup of coffee without finding a newspaper staring him in the face."

"You don't go to the corner for a cup of coffee in this neighborhood, Your Eminence. At least, you don't if you're Anglo. Michael might be able to get away with it just because he's Michael, but I don't think he'd count on it."

"People must have said things to him. There must have been phone calls."

"The phone's been ringing off the hook all day, Your Eminence. Augie—Sister Augustine has one of those Benedictines that came in from Connecticut answering the calls. She's very polite and very noncommittal and she doesn't let anything get through to Michael. There have been a few reporters hanging around, too, of course, but fewer than you'd think. This isn't a neighborhood up here, Your Eminence. This is a war zone. It's not safe."

"No. No, Eamon, of course, it's not safe. But what about Michael himself? What about the arraignment? Is there going to be a trial?"

"Well," Eamon said drily, "it seems that the New York City Police Department has neglected to file charges—"

"What?"

"Michael hasn't been charged, Your Eminence, and he's not going to be. Not for something like this."

"I see. Yes, Eamon, I see. What about his health? Not just his psychological health. His physical health."

"I don't know," Eamon Donleavy said.

There was a lengthy pause on the other end of the line. Eamon Donleavy could just imagine what the Archbishop was thinking. It was what Eamon himself thought, when he let himself think, about the medical indications of Michael's periodic bizarre behavior. A glory hole was a hole in the wall of a stall in a gay porno theater. A client entered the stall, paid his quarters for the movie, and then, if the whim took him, either stuck his own private parts into the hole for the man in the next stall to service, or serviced whatever was sticking through the hole in his own stall. The very idea made Eamon Donleavy physically ill. For Michael, in this age of AIDS, it was a death wish. For the Archbishop, it was undoubtedly more incomprehensible than genocide.

There was a cough on the other end of the phone. "Eamon? Are you as worried by all this as I am?"

"I'm worried about Michael, Your Eminence."

"I'm worried about Michael, too. Will he be able to withstand all this publicity?"

"It depends on what the van Straadt papers do. If they pull out all the stops, he could be in trouble. Maybe not, but he could be."

"Will they pull out all the stops? Don't they fund most of the center's operations?"

"Yes, they do. And the old man professes to like Michael."

"Only professes?"

"I don't know, Your Eminence. I don't seem to know much of anything today."

"You know as much as you need to know. All right, Eamon. I'd better let you off the phone. We're getting reports of a full-scale gang war going on up there."

"Yes, Your Eminence. There's something like that going on. We have one or two of these every summer."

"It's not summer, Eamon. It's barely spring."

"Excuse me, Your Eminence."

"Take care of Michael, Eamon. As much as he'll let you. God bless."

The Archbishop hung up. Eamon Donleavy hung up, too, and stared through his still-open door at Charles van Straadt sitting across the hall. Charles van Straadt was still on the phone, talking to God knows who, doing only God knows what. No, Eamon thought, I don't like him. I don't trust him. I don't want him slithering around on the edges of our lives.

If I were a man of courage, Eamon thought, I'd do something about him.

4

Sister Augustine had been seventeen years old on the day she entered her order, stubborn and exhilarated and panicked all at once. Those were the days when nuns wore tight white wimples fastened around their throats and so many skirts it felt like wading in water just to walk down a hall. Those were the days when Sisters barely spoke except to ask Sister Anne to pass the salt to Sister Josepha at breakfast. Those were also the days when nuns were never allowed to ask for anything for themselves. Sister Augustine remembered it all without regret. She was not a radical. She didn't care if women were ever ordained into the priesthood or not. She felt no urge to think of God as a goddess or to call her Heavenly Father "She." Sister Augustine simply preferred to spend her days in sweatsuits and sneakers rather than habits and nun shoes. She also preferred to be called "Augie." Sister Augustine had been born Edith Marie Corcoran, which she hated. She had been named "Mary Augustine" by the Mother Superior of her order on the day she received its habit. She had first been called "Augie" here, about ten years ago, by one of the girl junkies in the refuge program. The street kids all thought she was cute. It annoyed her sometimes. She tried not to show it.

Sister Augustine regretted nothing of the passing of the old order after Vatican II, except this: Before the changes, there always seemed to be hundreds of people milling around, willing to do everything and anything and willing to do it for free. That wasn't true, of course, not really. Augie knew her own selective memory when she caught it in the act. Even so. Her order used to run two dozen elementary schools, paid for by their parishes and provided to parishioners for free. These days, with no nuns to speak of and lay teachers having to be paid just like public school teachers and provided with benefits besides, it was a miracle if a parish school's tuition wasn't just as high as the tuition of the fancy private school down the road. And then there were the hospitals . . .

Sister Augustine looked out the window of the emergency-room nurses' station at the man with his cardboard sign walking back and forth on the sidewalk outside and shook her head. In a minute she would have to go out there again, where all hell was breaking loose. In a minute she would have to pretend she was competent and wise and no more prone to hysteria than anybody else. For just this second she could contemplate the center's most faithful protester and wonder to herself what had happened to all the nuns. Even if the habits had disappeared and church discipline had been relaxed—why should that make a difference? Doing good was doing good, no matter how you justified it to yourself. Doing good didn't become less important than climbing the corporate ladder to vice president in charge of operations for IBM just because the Mass was being said in English.

The door to the nurses' station opened. Augie turned around to see Sister Kenna Franks coming in with a large tray of cafeteria food. Sister Kenna Franks was a Franciscan from an order in Boston, an order that, like Augie's own, had almost no nuns left in it. Back in the old days, Augie might have been assigned to a place like the Sojourner Truth Health Center, but the Sisters under her direction would all have been Sisters in her own habit. These days, they took any nun whose order was willing to sponsor her for a year or two, they took nuns the way they took acts of charity from rich old men whose anti-Papism was only just beneath the surface. Augie had quite a lot of nuns on her staff. She had many more nuns than any other Catholic medical facility in the city. Only one of them was a nun of her own order.

Sister Kenna Franks wore a loose black cowl-necked robe tied at the waist with a rope. It fell to her feet and covered up the fact that she was wearing socks and sandals. Sister Kenna Franks was very young and very thin and never ate much of anything at all. She put the cafeteria tray down on the desk and cocked her head.

"We figured you were hiding out," she said. "Is there something interesting going on out there on the sidewalk?"

"What's his name with the sign," Augie told her.

Sister Kenna Franks went to the window and looked. "Oh, him. The others are gone, you know. The ones from that group that wants civil rights for homosexuals. Sister Victoria said this morning at breakfast that that was because of all the stories in the newspapers."

"They'll be back," Augie told her.

"Really?" Sister Kenna sat down at the desk and looked over the tray of food. "You really ought to sit down here and get something to eat. Mrs. Angelini sent up all the things you like best. And you need your strength. Dr. Pride is down in OR bellowing for you right this minute."

"OR being kept busy?"

"Oh, yes. All three theaters. We've got those back-up doctors Dr. Pride set up last summer, you know, those men he used to know in medical school who said they'd come down if there was ever a real emergency. Two of them who said they would wouldn't, but the other three are here. It's a good thing, too, because it's all very bad out there."

"Any news as to how soon it might get better?"

Sister Kenna shook her head. "I haven't had time to watch the news, but the television set is turned to Channel two down in the cafeteria and people report when they have a chance. There seems to be some kind of impasse, but there hasn't been an end to the shooting. Three police officers are already dead."

"Wonderful. It's drugs, I take it."

"I think so."

Augie went over to the desk and looked at the cafeteria tray. A hot turkey sandwich, piled very high with turkey and gravy on white bread. An enormous slice of Mrs. Angelini's killer chocolate pie, with whipped cream and a cherry. A cup of coffee. Augie got a chair from near the window and sat down to eat. It was embarrassing how accurately Mrs. Angelini had her pegged. It was embarrassing how much of a rut she'd let herself get into. Back on the day she had entered the convent she'd told herself, secretly, that it would be good for her figure. She would become an ascetic and a saint and live on Holy Communion wafers and air, like Saint Catherine of Siena. Instead, she'd become thoroughly addicted to chocolate and even rounder than when she'd started out.

Mrs. Angelini had included four little cups of cranberry sauce. Augie picked up the closest one and began eating that.

"Tell me," she asked Sister Kenna. "How are the Sisters taking all the newspaper stories? What are they saying about Dr. Pride?"

"Saying?" Sister Kenna looked confused. "They're not saying much of anything, Sister. Just that it's a shame."

"A shame that he did it or a shame that he got caught?"

"I don't know. I don't know what to think of it myself, Sister. I mean, Dr. Pride is a kind of saint, isn't he? Starting this place and working here. He could have been a doctor in private practice and made a lot of money. He wasn't just stuck with a situation like this."

"True."

"And then there are these—these glory holes. Do you know what a glory hole is, Sister?"

"Yes, I know."

"Well, I don't, and most of the other Sisters don't either, but some of the girls in the refuge program—they know. And they laugh."

Augie winced. "I'm sure they do. Are they upset about all this?"

"No," Sister Kenna said. "No, they're not. One of them, Julie Enderson—do you know Julie Enderson, Sister?"

Augie knew Julie Enderson. Julie was a prostitute who claimed to be eighteen years old. Augie was fairly sure she was no more than fourteen. Julie was the great good hope of the refuge program at the moment. She was bright and energetic and good at schoolwork when she put her mind to it. She had a chance to make it out of this place if she really wanted to. Everybody at the center knew Julie Enderson.

"I hope Julie isn't off her stride," Augie said carefully. "That would be unfortunate."

"Julie says it's just like Dr. Pride, that he'd pick a vice where there was no question whatsoever that he wasn't forcing anybody else into anything. And the other girls agreed with her."

"Well, that's one way of thinking about it," Augie conceded. "It wouldn't have occurred to me, but that's one way of thinking about it. Anything else going on over there?"

"Not really." Sister Kenna stood up. "But I do think you ought to talk to the girls about Mr. van Straadt, Sister. I mean, I don't like him either, but the things they say about him—and he does give us so much of our money, and we need the money, don't we?"

"Yes," Augie said. "We need the money."

"I'll leave you here with your dinner," Sister Kenna said. "You eat up and then come down to OR and calm Dr. Pride. There's talk that the police are going to send in a whole set of SWAT teams this time. The last time they sent in one and it didn't work. But you know what that means. It's going to get even worse around here than it already is."

"Yes," Augie said. "Yes, I do know."

"Fine," Sister Kenna said. She went to the door, opened it up, and looked outside. Augie caught a sudden rush of noise, made up of the groans and screams of injured people and the hard clang of metal instruments being used with too much haste and too much force.

"See you later," Sister Kenna said, and slipped outside.

The door closed again and the station was silent. Augie thanked God for the decision, made three years ago, to get this station in the emergency room soundproofed. They'd done that because the nurses were finding it impossible to do the necessary work on dosages and diagnoses in the middle of crises like this one. Augie stood and went back to the window, taking the chocolate pie with her. There were a pair of ambulances pulling up outside. The attendants jumping out the backs of them looked worse than strained. The picketer had stopped his pacing to watch the action. He had his sign up over his shoulder, resting on his collarbone, so that the ambulance men could read it. **THIS CENTER IS A DEATH CAMP,** his sign read. The ambulance men weren't paying any attention.

Augie went back to the desk and began to attack the hot turkey sandwich. Sister Kenna was right. She had to get moving and be a help to Dr. Pride. She had to be a help to somebody.

As for the rest of what Sister Kenna had said—

Augie put her fork down and stared out across the desk. She knew exactly how the girls felt about Charles van Straadt. She knew better than they did why they felt that way. The man was a snake, that was the truth, sneaking around Michael the way he did, insinuating himself where he didn't belong, stocking the center full of his own grandchildren and expecting the rest of the volunteers to put up with them. There was something . . . sly about this whole operation, something *wrong*. She only wished she knew what it was.

In the absence of knowledge, Sister Augustine wished she had the guts to poison the man's tea.

5

When Victor van Straadt first heard that his grandfather was thinking of changing his long-standing will to one that left virtually everything to Victor's cousin Rosalie, he panicked. It wasn't the loss of the money itself that bothered him—although that did, of course, bother him. He got mixed up whenever he tried to think about it. No, the real problem was time, his own time, the way he would spend it and what it would mean to the dozens of people who knew him, but not very well. Victor never allowed anyone to know him very well. Victor was twenty-two years old and very good-looking, in a cover-of-a-J. Crew-catalog sort of way. He looked best in cotton crewneck sweaters and baggy khaki pants and the kind of overly expensive sun visor that litters the slopes of Aspen at the end of every season. The adjective *preppy* might have been invented to apply to him. Beyond what he looked like, though, he had very little. He had graduated from Yale with a bachelor's degree in classics, but his grades had been no better than mediocre and classics wasn't good for anything. He had done his grandfather-mandated eighteen-month stint at the Sojourner Truth Health Center, but he had done it with such a commitment to laziness, he hadn't got much out of it. Now he had a job at the New York *Sentinel*, but it wasn't much of a job. They had started out trying to train him as a reporter, but that had been impossible. Now he ran the contests the paper was so fond of, like the Father's Day contest it was red-bannering over the masthead daily now—except he didn't. Victor never did his own work if he could help it. He got his sister Ida and his cousin Rosalie to help with the contests, because they were both so much smarter than he was and so much better with money. Sometimes he got his cousin Martha to help, too, but he didn't like Martha very much. Victor didn't like much of anything that required a lot of work, and work was what he would have to do if grandfather changed his will. Victor thought he really had to do something about that. His parents were both dead. Who would support him? If he never accomplished another thing in his life, he had to stop his grandfather from handing eight hundred and fifty million dollars into the hands of dear cousin Rosalie, that world-class bitch.

Victor's appointment to meet Martha and Ida for dinner at the Sojourner Truth Health Center had been set up over a week ago. If he watched the news on television or listened to any radio station besides the all-music Rock Bop on 107.7 FM, he would have known not to come. If he had bothered to look around his own newsroom, he would have known not to come. But Victor had spent the entire day in his office, his Walkman earphones glued to his head, listening to the Beach Boys moan peppily about hot cars and tanned girls and places where it never, ever got any snow. No one had bothered him, because no one ever bothered him. The people he worked with had long ago realized that Victor was useless.

If Victor had had to take a cab uptown, he would never have gotten there. The cabdrivers were listening to the news, even if he wasn't. Victor didn't take a cab because he had learned from previous forays into Harlem that cabs didn't like to go there. It was easier on the nerves to take his very own car and his very own driver, which is what he kept a car and driver for. Victor's driver didn't listen to the news any more than Victor did. He couldn't. Victor's driver was from an obscure little town in Brazil. He spoke ten words of English and a dialect of Portuguese so rarefied he shared it with no other person in the city of New York.

Victor's driver took the car to the front door of the Sojourner Truth Health Center, around the corner from the emergency-room door and more or less out of the fray. It was only more or less because everything up here was in the fray now. The crisis had gotten so large, there was no real way to avoid it north of 140th Street. Even from inside the car, Victor could hear gunshots. He could have heard the sirens if he'd been dead in a coffin in the back of a hearse. He scooted over to the side of the car closest to the curb and looked out.

"What do you think is going on around here?" he asked.

He could have asked the air. The driver didn't answer. Victor opened the door and got out. Most nights when he came up here—which was not often; he hated coming up here—there were bag ladies in little clusters around the front door and kids in torn jeans cluttering up the sidewalk, but tonight there was nobody. He climbed the steps and rang the bell and looked around again. If it wasn't for the light spilling out from the front windows, he would have thought everybody had disappeared. Yes, disappeared. Just like in one of those old *Twilight Zone* episodes. Victor often felt as if he were in one of those old *Twilight Zone* episodes.

It took forever for someone to open up. The doors to the center were never left unlocked. The young woman who let him in seemed distracted and upset. Instead of asking her what was wrong, Victor asked her where his cousin Martha was. The young woman repeated "Martha" a couple of times, then went off shaking her head.

Victor was just about ready to decide that he was going to have to go wandering around looking for Martha himself, when Martha herself showed up in the dimly lit foyer, looking as frazzled as the young woman had. Victor did not put a great deal of stock in this. Martha always looked frazzled. Martha always looked undone. She was pudgy in that depressed-teenage-girl sort of way adolescents got around the time of their parents' divorce, and her skin always seemed to be on the verge of sprouting out in pimples. Victor had never known her actually to have a pimple, but that was something else.

Martha was wearing a long black jersey jumper and a short-sleeved shirt. She looked like the least popular girl in camp.

"I can't believe you're here," she said as soon as she saw him. "Don't you realize what's going on around here? We're in the middle of some kind of war."

"War?"

Martha looked impatient. "Never mind, Victor. Let's just say that dinner is off, all right? Ida can't make it. She's all tied up in the emergency room."

"Medical school." Victor made a face. "Can you imagine medical school? Why would she do something like that when she doesn't have to?"

"Maybe because she doesn't want to be bored. I really think you ought to get out of here, Victor. Grandfather is up in Dr. Pride's office and Rosalie is stalking through the building. I keep running into her in the oddest places. You don't want them to catch you here."

"Why are they here?"

"Grandfather comes up to check things out every once in a while. I suppose he's here tonight because of all that publicity about Dr. Pride. You have seen something of the publicity about Dr. Pride?"

Victor had seen it. More to the point, he had heard a violent argument between the city editor and one of the *Sentinel*'s top reporters about the fact that the *Sentinel* was not reporting any of the news about Dr. Pride. This, he was caught up on.

"That explains why grandfather's here," he said, "but it doesn't explain why Rosalie's here. Is she going everywhere with him these days?"

"Something like that."

"One of us should have gotten a degree in accounting. I should have. We're going to have to meet on this sooner rather than later, Martha. We can't wait on it forever. Eventually he's going to stop talking about changing his will and actually go do it."

"It's not that I want any more money than I've already got," Martha told him. "It's just that I don't want to see it all go to *her*. God, she's a poisonous woman. She was a poisonous child."

"If you had all that money, you could start your own clinic like this," Victor suggested. "You could be Mother Teresa with your own funds. That would have to be more amusing than sleeping on a board. Isn't that what Mother Teresa does? Sleep on a board?"

"I don't know. What are you talking about?"

Victor hadn't the faintest idea. He was babbling. He often babbled. "Look," he said, "as long as I'm here, I might as well get a cup of coffee or something. I gave my driver two hours off. I can call him back, of course, but he really hates that. He gets sullen."

"I don't have time to have a cup of coffee. I have work to do." Martha sounded irritated.

"I know, I know. It's all right. I'll go down and get a cup on my own. I know where the cafeteria is."

"Rosalie—"

Victor put on a brave smile. "So, maybe I'll run into Rosalie. Maybe that would be a good thing. Maybe she'll go back and tell grandfather that I'm finally taking an interest in the family charity."

"Don't be an idiot."

"I'm not. Maybe it would be a good thing if Rosalie did get the idea that we were plotting something. Maybe it would be a good thing if grandfather got that idea, too. Why not? The old man's a paranoid. He'd probably be terribly impressed that we'd suddenly acquired so much practical intelligence. It couldn't hurt."

"Don't be an idiot," Martha said again, but she was beginning to smile, faintly, and that made Victor feel better. Getting Martha to smile was as easy as convincing Newt Gingrich that Mikhail Gorbachev would make a good president of the United States.

"Look," Victor said to her, "try to see it in the best possible light. You know what this place is like. Maybe one of the juvenile delinquents they have roaming through the halls around here will stumble over grandfather on his own, and mug him."

6

Robbie Yagger was not a very intelligent man. He wasn't even a streetwise smart one, like some of the boys he had grown up with out in Queens, where the same child who failed miserably at every mathematics test could compute the odds on fifteen different horses in a Monmouth Park trotter race in his head. Robbie Yagger had been the kind of earnest, dim young boy who works very hard to get nowhere and works harder to get half a step ahead, only to be squashed flat the first time he stops to take a rest. For Robbie Yagger, thinking was like swimming through a polluted river in a fog. It was hard to do. It didn't get him very far. It made him feel awful. He only went on doing it because he felt that he had to.

It was now seven o'clock in the evening and, May or not, it had started to get cold. Robbie stopped watching the ambulances unload—what the hell went on up here, anyway? It was like one of those war movies he used to like to go to see before the old Majestic Theater closed—

and rested his sign down against the side of the building. The sign made only peripheral sense to him. He knew something about the Nazis and the death camps. He'd learned a little about them in school, and he'd seen dozens of movies in which the Nazis were the enemy. He even knew that the Nazis had tried "to kill all the Jews," as he put it to himself, and that that attempt was what was called "the Holocaust." He had learned that much at pro-life meetings, where the connection between abortion and the Holocaust was made at least twice in any important speech. Robbie tried not to think too hard about it, because it got him confused. For one thing, he didn't quite believe that the Nazis really had tried to kill *all* the Jews. That was like saying you were going to walk to the moon. Robbie knew it wasn't possible. Maybe they were only trying to kill as many Jews as they could get their hands on. Maybe it had all had something to do with sex. In Robbie's experience, practically everything had something to do with sex. You saw that in the movies, and on television, too, these days, now that television had gotten more honest and more decadent. Robbie didn't know. The only thing he was absolutely sure of was that he was doing the right thing to be here with this sign.

He had his light spring jacket tied around his waist by the arms. He untied it and put it on, looking up as yet another ambulance arrived from uptown and wound its siren down to a blipping moan. The ambulance's back doors shot open and four men in white jumped down to the pavement. Robbie could see four stretchers crammed into the space that had been meant only for two. He reached into his pocket and found his pack of cigarettes, the only pack of cigarettes he would be able to afford this week. It was half empty already. He took out a cigarette and lit up against the wind. He smoked very high tar and nicotine cigarettes these days. All cigarettes cost the same, whether they were high tar and nicotine or not. When he could only afford a pack a week, he wanted to get as much kick for his dollar as he could.

One of the white-coated men from one of the earlier ambulances—they were all parked out there together; it looked like an ambulance parking lot—came out of the emergency room and got out a cigarette of his own. He looked at Robbie and Robbie's sign and seemed to shrug. Robbie could feel himself blush.

The ambulance man was young and very Brooklyn, as Robbie saw it. He was dark and hip and cool and smart and all the other things Robbie was always imagining himself to be, except that as the years went on Robbie no longer believed he was ever going to achieve any of those things. The ambulance man was looking at Robbie's sign again and frowning.

"I don't get it," he said. "What's that supposed to mean?"

This was a new one. Robbie almost never ran into people who didn't understand what his sign was supposed to be getting at.

"It's about abortion," he said. "They do abortions in that place."

"In the emergency room?"

"You go through the emergency-room door to get to the family-planning clinic. I used to picket right in front of the family-planning clinic, but they threw me out. It's private property."

"Are you from those clinic-closer people? Operation Rescue?"

"Oh, no." Robbie blushed again. He had tried Operation Rescue once, but he hadn't liked it. It was too military for him, too organized and controlled. All the people he met always seemed to be talking right over his head. It was just like school. "I come up here on my own," he told the ambulance man. "I've been coming for months. Ever since I got laid off."

"From what?"

"Maintenance. I was a janitor. At the Trade Center. Then that bomb went off down there, and they closed the towers and—here I am."

"Abortions," the ambulance man said. "They can't do abortions in there. The place is full of nuns."

"Parts of the place are full of nuns," Robbie corrected, "but the rest of the place is operated by a private foundation. Run by Dr. Michael Pride."

"I know who Dr. Pride is."

"He's a devil," Robbie said solemnly. "He's an agent of evil. And he's slick, too. He makes everybody think he's a saint."

The ambulance man looked skeptical. Robbie's cigarette had burned halfway down. No matter how careful Robbie tried to be with his cigarettes, they always burned down much too fast for him. The ambulance man's cigarette was entirely gone. He threw the butt on the pavement and stamped it out with the heel of his boot.

"Michael Pride isn't a devil," the ambulance man said. "He's just a poor godforsaken poof is all. But he's a good doctor. Now you want a devil, you should pick on old Charlie van Straadt."

"Who's Charlie van Straadt?"

"He's the guy who puts up most of the money for this place. The guy who owns the New York *Sentinel*, you know, and that television station the Morty Grebb talk show is on."

"Oh," Robbie said. Something was coming to him dimly, some lecture he had heard at a pro-life meeting down in Queens. There had been quite a lot of talk about Charlie—no, *Charles* van Straadt, and all the money he put into various things, and how he supported all the parts of this center the church wouldn't. Robbie hadn't paid too much attention, because it was just the kind of thing that aggravated him.

Robbie's cigarette was burned to the butt. He dropped the filter on the ground regretfully and ground it into the pavement with the edge of his shoe. He wished he had thick lace-up boots like the ambulance man, but he knew they were much too expensive. The ambulance man must be some kind of paramedic. Robbie couldn't have afforded boots like those even when he was working.

Robbie put his hands in the pockets of his jacket and looked away. "Do you think I could bum a cigarette from you?" he asked. "I seem to be—out."

The ambulance man took out a pack of Winston regulars and handed them over. Robbie very carefully took only one and lit up again. Then he looked at the tops of his shoes and sighed.

"It's terrible what's been going on in there today. There must have been a dozen ambulances driving up to this door in the past hour. I've never seen anything like it."

"Gang war," the ambulance man said curtly. "Big shoot-out going on uptown."

"It's the culture of violence," Robbie said, struggling through the fog in his mind to remember what he had heard about all this. "That's what abortion is, the foundation of the culture of violence. The United States is turning into a third world country now. Life is cheap."

"Life is certainly cheap up here," the ambulance man said.

The doors to the emergency room opened and another ambulance man came out, dressed in whites, in a hurry. The first ambulance man saw him and straightened up.

"We're out of here," he said to Robbie. "You want the rest of my open pack? I've got a carton in the van."

"Oh," Robbie said. "Yes. Thank you."

The first ambulance man handed Robbie the Winstons and began jogging toward the parked ambulances and his friend. The pack was missing only the two cigarettes Robbie and the ambulance man lit up out here. Robbie put the pack into his jacket pocket and picked up his sign again.

The culture of violence. The Holocaust. The destruction of the American family. People in the pro-life movement talked and talked and talked—and from what Robbie had been able to see, the other side talked and talked and talked, too. And it was all useless, because they were never going to convince each other. They were never even going to listen to each other. For Robbie, it was all much more simple. It had started on the day when he realized that a woman could have an abortion because the child she was carrying was mentally retarded. He didn't know how she found out that the child she was carrying was mentally retarded. He was never too clear on the details. What he did know was that if the option had been available when his mother was carrying *him*, he would never have seen the light of day. Isn't that what she'd told him, over and over and over again, all the time he was growing up. "Stupid retard," she'd called him.

Robbie left metaphors and strategies and all the rest

of it to people who understood those things, which he didn't. As far as he was concerned, what he was engaged in was an act of self-defense.

The wind was picking up. Robbie zipped his jacket closed and hunched his shoulders against the growing cold, wondering what it was like in there, deep in there, in the places he'd never been. What would happen to him if he went inside? What would they do to him if he got Dr. Michael Pride into a corner and told him the truth about what this center was doing?

Then Robbie remembered. It wasn't Michael Pride. It was the other one. Van Straadt. Was van Straadt in there? What would happen to the center if van Straadt was no longer around to give it money? What would convince van Straadt?

If Robbie hadn't hated the center and everything it stood for, he could have used it. The center provided medical services to anyone who showed up at the door, no questions asked. Maybe he could just walk right inside and then walk right—

Where?

And then what?

He didn't have the ghost of an answer to that. He only knew that the soles of his feet itched.

7

Julie Enderson had been in the refuge program for three months now, and in all that time—the only time in her life she could remember not being high for more than a couple of hours at a stretch; the only time in her years she could remember not having a pimp—she had never broken the rules of the center or the program even

once. Julie had no real idea why she was being so careful. She knew that no one on the staff here was overly
strict or too much of a purist about rules and regulations.
Friends of hers had been caught drinking beer in the
boiler room and sneaking boys into the utility shed out
back and even shoplifting a little. No one had thrown
them back onto the street. Julie didn't want to risk it. She
had told everyone here that she was eighteen years old.
Sister Augustine suspected she was fourteen. Julie was,
in fact, sixteen. The subterfuge was necessary, because
Julie had had a very strange and checkered life. She
knew much more about some things than the nuns did.
Julie's mother had been a black prostitute. Her father
had been a white john. When Julie was eleven years old,
her mother's live-in boyfriend had sold her to a pimp for
the drug money he never had enough of. Her mother
had noticed only enough to register the fact that there
was now a little decent dope in the house. Three weeks
later, Julie had found herself out on the street, feeling
numb and crazy and weak. It was the middle of February
and the wind was blowing up Tenth Avenue, making her
legs cold. That was what she remembered forever
afterward—what she remembered with perfect clarity
once she came to the center and started to dry out—
streetwalking made her legs cold. Maybe it was because
she was always wearing hot pants or very short skirts.

At the center, Julie wore baggy jeans and T-shirts and
big cotton sweaters, even in summer, as if the point of
being here was to claim her body for herself. When the
temperatures began to fall this night in May, even though
they didn't fall very far, she put on a turtleneck to cover
up her throat. Then she got her friend Karida and
headed for the bridge that led from the west building to
the east one. That was how the center had been

built—or, rather, renovated into existence. Dr. Pride hadn't had the money to put up a big new building. Hospital corporations ran fund-raisers for years and took money for the government to do that. Dr. Pride had had only his own money and some seed money. He'd bought the two tenement buildings on this block when they were abandoned and condemned. Then he had gone to work to make them habitable and suitable for the center he envisioned. What construction work had been done here was minimal. There was the emergency-room complex and the OR. Those were state of the art because they had to be. There was the interlocking security system. That was better than the one the CIA had at Langley. There was this bridge. The bridge was made of steel and stone and lined with windows on either side. The windows were great glass squares tinted smoky gray. Standing here you could look out over the tops of half the buildings in Harlem. Standing here, you could see the world.

One of the absolute rules of the center was that no one from the refuge program was supposed to cross the bridge to the medical building without permission. Because going into the medical building almost always meant running into either your own old pimp or someone who knew him—the girls got hurt more often than the pimps but the pimps got hurt enough; Julie had been amazed to come out of her drug-induced distraction and discover how much time the people she knew spent bleeding—permission was almost never given except in a medical emergency. Julie rationalized what she was doing now by telling herself that this was a medical emergency. It just wasn't *her* medical emergency. Then she asked herself why she still cared. All right, all hell was breaking loose out there. It happened every once in

a while. All right, her mother had last been heard of
serving as a kind of house mother to the Blood Brothers.
That was the kind of thing her mother would do. Julie
wasn't sure her mother would remember she was actually
a mother, of the biological kind. Why was it so important
to go over to the emergency room and find out if she had
been hurt?

Karida only wanted to get out of the west building
and see some excitement. She had a look Julie recognized, the look of a girl who doesn't last long in the refuge program or anywhere else. Karida had had a good
scare a month and a half ago. A john had turned violent
and broken her arm, and then, when she'd gotten out of
the Lenox Hill Hospital emergency room, her pimp had
beat her bloody for letting herself get put out of commis-
sion. Karida had ended up at the center. When she'd
been offered the refuge program, she had taken it. It
wasn't going to last. In the last three months, Julie had
seen two dozen girls disappear back onto the streets and
only three go on to the next step on the way to regular
lives. She was beginning to know the signs.

It was Karida who knew how to get the bridge door
unlocked. She had worked it out the very first day she
was on the refuge program dormitory corridor. Julie
watched with amusement while Karida jiggled and rattled the door knob, muttering under her breath. It was as
if Karida were performing a form of voodoo, and the
hocus-pocus spell mattered as much as the physical ma-
nipulation.

"There we go," Karida said. "I can't believe you've
never done this before."

"It's against the rules."

"So what?"

"So I don't want to be thrown out of here."

"They're not going to throw you out of here. And how long can you stay? Aren't you getting nuts?"

"Not really." Julie walked to the center of the bridge and looked first downtown and then up. Uptown she could see spurt-flashes in the dark, what she knew must be gunfire. Julie had been in a few gang wars in her life, but this was something special. "I'm going to take the test of the academy next month," she said carefully. "Augie says I probably won't pass it this time, but I can take it as many times as I want, so I might as well get started. Then after I see what I don't do so—so well on, I can study those things and take the test again."

"You've got to be crazy," Karida said.

"Why?"

"Because it is crazy. What do you think you're doing? I'll bet they've never had a single black girl up at that academy."

"They've got Hiram Corder's daughter."

"Who's Hiram Corder?"

"He plays with the New York Giants."

"I mean black girls like us."

Julie turned away from the windows and started walking down toward the other end of the bridge. "Augie says the world is a hard place and it's full of jerks but every once in a while there's a window of opportunity, and when you find one of those, you should go through it. That's what I'm trying to do. Go through it."

"To what?"

"I don't know."

"What do you think is going to happen to you?" Karida insisted. "You think you're going to turn into some kind of actress or model or what?"

"No. No, nothing like that. That kind of thing would be too much like whoring, you know what I mean."

"No. I don't know what you mean."

Julie sighed. She didn't blame Karida, really. She didn't know what she meant herself, not completely. It was a feeling she had. All those models and actresses, what did they do? They showed their bodies around for money. They had very valuable bodies, so nobody was allowed to touch, but what difference did that make? Didn't they do exactly the same thing whores did, except in a classier way? Sister Augustine had a picture of herself on the desk in her office, dressed in the long veil and floor-sweeping habit her order had worn in the old days. When Julie dreamed herself into the place she called freedom, that was how she saw herself dressed. Completely covered up. Completely hidden from the world.

Julie tried the door at the east end of the corridor, expecting it to be locked. It wasn't. She stood back and looked through into the corridor beyond. The corridor reminded her of the hallways in the old apartment buildings in the neighborhood. It was dark and painted green and ringed with nearly black wood doors. Julie wondered what went on up here. These couldn't be apartments for the staff. The staff had rooms in the west building. Even Dr. Pride had his main residence in the west building, in spite of the fact that he spent half his nights sleeping in his office. At least, they had thought he had. Julie thought about all the newspaper stories and felt as if she wanted to cry. She didn't care what Dr. Pride did for sex in his free time, as long as he didn't patronize a prostitute. She did worry that he would get the kind of disease there wasn't any cure for. She worried more that he would get knocked out of the center by Them. Julie didn't have a coherent definition of Them. She couldn't have described Them in concrete terms if her life depended on it. She just knew Them when she saw Them.

"This is where they have the day-care center in the mornings," Karida said, coming onto the corridor past Julie at the door. "They open all the doors and stick a gate thing in the stairs and let the kids wander around. Sister Kenna set it up. It's kinda neat. All the different rooms are different ideas. One of them's a jungle room. One of them's supposed to be a castle. Skeera Hoyt and I came over here one night and got all the doors unlocked and looked around."

"You had to be crazy."

"Not everybody thinks like you," Karida said. "Not everybody just smiles and croons whenever some nun says she's done a good day's work. I don't like those nuns. I think they're weird. I mean, no sex, for God's sake. It's got to do something awful to your insides."

"What?"

"I don't know what. I just know it's got to do something awful."

There was nothing blocking the stairs now. Julie came onto the corridor and let the bridge door close behind her. She went to the stairs and started down. Beneath her in the stairwell, she could see the harsh lights of office overheads. They were just like the office overheads in the west building, probably because the center bought all its light bulbs in bulk. Julie stopped a little way down the stairs and listened. There was a man down there somewhere, talking. She couldn't hear anyone talking back, so she supposed he must be on the phone. Whoever he was was pacing as well as talking. She could hear the scuffle of shoes on carpet.

"There's someone down there. What's on that floor?"

"Offices," Karida said promptly. "All the really important offices. Father Donleavy's. Dr. Pride's."

Julie listened again. "It's not Dr. Pride. It's not Father Donleavy, either. Who else is down there?"

"I don't know. I don't know everybody who works here."

Julie went a little way farther down the stairs. What she really wanted was to turn right around and go back to her own dormitory room. She had a history book there she hadn't finished reading. She had some work to do she had promised Sister Augustine to finish before morning. Her mother had never given ten seconds thought to what happened to her. Why should Julie give ten seconds thought to what happened to her mother?

Julie went down more stairs, almost all the way to the bottom. The corridor there was much better lit than the one on the floor above. Most of the doors that opened onto it were in fact open, with more light spilling out of them from desk lamps and auxiliary reading lights. Julie stepped off the bottom stair and edged her way toward the voice. It was coming from the door of the office she could now see was clearly marked as Dr. Michael Pride's—there was a big sign on the wall next to the door jamb, ragged enough to make Julie think it had been hand stenciled by someone at the center—but the voice was most definitely not Dr. Pride's. That's an old man, Julie thought, and then wondered why the sound made her so uncomfortable. She was having a very hard time making herself not squirm.

"Hey," Karida said in an exaggerated whisper. "What are you doing? You're going to get caught."

"I just want to see who it is."

"Who cares who it is?"

This, of course, was perfectly sensible. Julie knew it. She couldn't stop herself. She edged closer and closer to the door.

"I want you to have it ready for me to sign tomorrow morning," the old man was saying. "I've pissed around with this long enough. I'll be at your office at eight fifteen—"

Pause. Pace. Breathe.

"—Yes, I know—Yes, it's early—I don't really care about the trains coming in from Larchmont, Felix, they're not my responsibility—Yes—"

I should do what Karida wants me to do and keep on going down the stairs, Julie thought. That's what I should do.

Whoever that is in there doesn't work at the center. If he did, I would know the voice. He won't know that I'm not supposed to be here. There's no reason why I shouldn't walk right up there and look right in.

"Hey," Karida said again. "Julie, we've really got to—"

That was when Julie realized that the old man had stopped talking. She hadn't even heard him hang up the phone. He had stopped pacing, too. She wondered what he was doing. She wondered why he was in Dr. Pride's office. Maybe he wasn't supposed to be there. Maybe he was dangerous. There was a clock on the wall of the office just across the corridor. Julie could see through its open door to read the time. The time was 7:22.

"Julie," Karida said urgently. "Come *on*."

Julie took a step toward Dr. Pride's door just as the man came out of it. He was a big man and he was moving quickly, but that wasn't what startled her. It wasn't even that he appeared when she wasn't expecting him. Julie could have taken all that in stride. She had been on the streets a long time.

What startled Julie Enderson was that this old man

wasn't someone she didn't know after all. In fact, he was someone she knew quite well.

The last time she'd seen him, he'd been in a very different kind of place.

8

Ida van Straadt Greel was nothing at all like her brother Victor. For one thing, she wasn't as pretty. In the way of genetic practical jokes from Irkutsk to Antarctica, where Victor had gotten all their mother's most distinctive features, Ida had gotten their father's, and their father had been a small, gnomish, distinctly ugly man. Ida was five feet two inches tall and as gnarled as the sort of tree trunk that ends up polished as a coffee table in the living room of a country house of a lawyer from Manhattan. She had the kind of body that never gained weight, no matter how much she put into it, but other women didn't envy her for it. She looked nothing at all like a fragile fashion model and everything like the girl voted most likely to succeed at competitive sports by her high school graduating class. Nobody would ever mistake her for the cover of a J. Crew catalog. When people discovered who Ida was, they were often both surprised and resentful. The American rich were supposed to be different from this, at least if they were women.

Very few people discovered who Ida van Straadt Greel was, because unlike her brother Ida hadn't dropped the "Greel" from her name as soon as she turned eighteen and unlike her brother and her cousin Martha she made an effort to keep her identity hidden. Of course, at the center Ida had no real privacy. Martha was there and Martha would talk, and Ida owed her position to her grandfather. At least, she half owed it to him. When Ida was Martha's age, she had come down here to volunteer for the obligatory two years—the center insisted on two years—and her acceptance in the volunteer program had definitely been a result of her connections. Since then, however, she thought she'd made it on her own. Ida Greel was very good at what she did. She made a point of it. She had gone through Yale with an unblemished straight-A average, made Phi Beta Kappa and gotten herself admitted to the Albert Einstein College of Medicine. She had spent her summers first getting her paramedic training and then serving at the center as a paramedic. She had every intention of ending up twentyfive years from now more famous than Dr. Christiaan Barnard. It was a matter of honor. Ida had spent so much of her childhood hearing about how impossible she was, and how much of a blot on the van Straadt family name (*can't you* do *something about yourself?*), that she had a lot to prove to practically everybody.

She was laying sterile instruments out on a tray when Martha came to the door and waved through the small square of glass at her. Ida waved back and checked her work over one more time before going out. It was seven thirty-five. The shoot-out or whatever it had been—Ida hated rumors, and rumors were all you ever got around here in the middle of a crisis—was over, and the last of the casualties were just coming in. Ida had been feeling a slackening in the tension for a good fifteen minutes. There was no reason why she shouldn't talk to Martha now. She had her work done. Ida hated to let Martha or Victor or her grandfather or anyone else in her family know she had any free time at all. As soon as she let them know that, she lost control.

Ida checked her instruments for the third time. Then

she admitted that there was no further excuse for standing where she was. She went through the swinging fire doors to the hall and wove among the stretchers to where Martha was standing. Half an hour ago, this hall was full of people. Now there were only a nurse and a cleaning woman, both heading someplace else. All the action for the rest of the night was going to be in Admitting or in OR.

Martha was leaning against the far wall, looking tense. Martha always looked tense. Ida thought of tension as Martha's occupation.

"Why do you always take so long to do everything?" Martha demanded, when Ida was close enough to hear. "You're always puttering around at something. It's maddening."

"I had work to do. Now it's done."

"That's nice. Victor is here, in case you didn't know. You might not remember, but we had an appointment to have dinner and talk about the will."

"Oh, I remember. I just can't believe he came. Doesn't he listen to the news?"

"No."

"I suppose he doesn't." Ida was wearing surgical gloves. No one was allowed to handle sterile instruments except in surgical gloves. Ida peeled these off and dropped them in the nearest waste container. It was a red waste container, which was silly—the gloves hadn't been near any blood or feces, just handling steel in a perfectly clean instruments' room—but she didn't feel like walking across the hall again to throw them in a white one. She shoved her hands into the pockets of her lab coat.

"What about you?" she asked Martha. "What are you

doing down here? Don't you have work in the other building?"

"Nobody's doing anything in the other building. We're just sitting around staring at each other and saying what a shame it is. I don't know if it is a shame."

"I don't think of things in terms like that. Where's Victor?"

"Still down in the cafeteria. I couldn't stand him any more. He was going on and on. What's wrong with Victor, anyway? We have to get something done and he just . . . dithers."

"Maybe he doesn't care about the money," Ida said. "I don't care about the money. Not very much."

"We all care about the money," Martha said sharply. "No matter what we say. And we all care about Rosalie. Have you seen her lately?"

"I saw her down at the bank last week. I was coming in and she was going out. She looked the way she always looks, Martha."

"She looks like the daughter of Dracula," Martha said firmly. "That getup she's always wearing these days. What does she think she's trying to do, audition for a beatnik movie?"

"I suppose she thinks she looks good that way. She does. Rosalie is very pretty."

"Victor thinks she's pretty, too. Pretty. It makes me want to spit. She looks like a cat with poisonous claws."

"There are no cats with poisonous claws."

"Maybe Rosalie will invent one. Maybe when she gets all our money, she'll open a genetic engineering lab and concoct all kinds of creatures for herself. Like koala bears that kill on command."

"Would you feel this way if Rosalie weren't getting all our money?"

"But she is getting all our money, isn't she? Or she will if we don't find some way to stop her."

"It's not our money anyway," Ida said. "It's Grandfather's. He made it."

"Did he? Maybe he stole it from the Indians. Maybe he conjured it up out of a cauldron he keeps in his basement and feeds the flesh of virgins to. I think this whole family is foul, Ida, honestly. I really do."

Ida was tempted to say that if the whole family was foul, then Martha herself was foul. The drawback to that was that Martha might agree to it. Ida was not subject to guilt, liberal or otherwise. Her grandfather's money and her own trust funds seemed to her to be as much matters of chance—and as neutral in terms of morality—as the strange shape of her body and the plainness of her face. Martha felt differently, as Ida had good reason to know.

"If Victor is down in the cafeteria, maybe we should go join him," Ida said. "God only knows I'm hungry, and I don't have anything I have to do for the next half second. They can always page me if they want me."

"They want you too much. You should stick up for yourself."

"There are people dying all over the building, Martha. Myself can wait until all that's under control."

Ida went down to the end of the corridor and opened the set of fire doors there. Martha passed ahead of her and Ida let her go. The cafeteria was just at the bottom of this flight of stairs. Ida could smell the cardboard food and hear the clink of silverware and the hum of voices. The hum was low, meaning that the television was tuned to something most people wanted to hear. Ida was sure it was press reports of the shoot-out. There wouldn't be too much in the way of press reports. The New York City press treated gang wars in Harlem on about the level it treated a bunion on the mayor's toe.

Ida went in through the cafeteria doors, picked up a tray and put it on the metal runners. She took a fork and a knife and a spoon out of habit, in spite of not knowing what she wanted to eat. She looked out across the sparse crowd and found Victor sitting at a table almost exactly in the center of the room, plowing through a copy of the New York *Sentinel*. There were always stacks of copies of the New York *Sentinel* in the cafeteria and the common rooms of both the east and west buildings, given out free. It was one of the things Charles van Straadt did for this place.

"There's Victor," Ida told Martha. "He's actually reading something. The stars may fall from the heavens."

"Did you know that Rosalie was here?" Martha asked. "Rosalie and Grandfather both, but you know Grandfather. He gets himself to where he wants to go and then he stays put. Rosalie is wandering around."

Well, Ida thought. That's just like Martha. That's *just* like Martha. She takes the only important piece of news she has, and she treats it like waste paper.

"Bowl of duchess," Ida said to the young woman behind the counter. The young woman was vaguely familiar from around the center, but not familiar enough for Ida to know her name. The soup was passed over the high end of the counter and Ida said, "Thanks."

"Now," she said to Martha, "go back to the beginning on this. Rosalie and Grandfather are here at the center."

"That's right."

"Why?"

"The usual thing. Probably because of all that news about Michael, don't you think? Don't you think it's disgusting? What is it with men, anyway?"

"I don't know." Ida hadn't known many men. That is, she hadn't known them intimately. The only reason she wasn't a virgin was that she had made a point of losing her virginity. "When did Grandfather and Rosalie get here?"

"I don't know. I saw Rosalie wandering around just after six. And Grandfather's been trying to call me. He's probably been trying to call you, too."

"Probably. What do you mean, been trying to call you?"

"Well, I haven't been taking the calls, have I? I mean, why should I? I mean, he's being such a pain in the ass about all this stuff. Why should I hop to it every time he wants to tell me what an idiot I'm being for not getting my hair cut at a good salon."

"Does he lecture you about that?"

"About that kind of thing. All the time. My clothes. My hair. Why I don't wear makeup."

"Maybe he thinks I'm hopeless," Ida said. "He never talks to me about that kind of thing at all."

"You want beef, fish, or chicken?" the woman behind the main-course counter asked.

"I want two grilled ham-and-cheese sandwiches," Ida said. Then she turned around and looked at Victor, still oblivious to everything behind the pages of his paper. Maybe he was reading out loud under his breath. Maybe he was spelling everything to himself to decode the words. Maybe she should stop being so nasty about Victor.

The counter woman handed her two grilled ham-and-cheese sandwiches on two separate paper plates. Ida put them on her tray and reached into the pocket of her pants for some money.

"Look," she said to Martha, "do me a favor, will you?

Pay me out and bring my tray over to the table. My colitis is acting up."

"What does that mean?"

"That means I have to go to the bathroom. I have to go now. Will you do this for me, please?"

"Well ... I suppose so. Are you going to be long?"

"How the hell should I know? It's a tension thing. Please, Martha, I've got to go *now*."

"Well." Martha looked mulish. "All right."

Ida threw the money on the plastic tray and bolted, back down the line, back through the doors, out into the stairwell again. She did not, however, go to the ladies room. She went up the stairs instead.

One of the few things Ida Greel had always liked about her body was her legs, because they were strong, and because they were fast. Right now, she wanted to be very, very fast.

9

It was after eight o'clock by the time Dr. Michael Pride got a chance to breathe again, and by then he was so tired it felt like too much effort to draw breath. It felt like too much effort to take off his gloves and his mask and sit down. It felt like too much effort to think about what he was going to have to do next. He was going to have to do a great deal. He had just performed two very difficult operations, because those two had been the two least able to wait. Over the next twenty-four hours, he was going to have to perform half a dozen more—and that was assuming that his emergency help didn't wimp out on him, which they probably would. Michael was very good at getting fancy high-paid physicians to come down to the center and do some work, but those physicians defined work in their inimitable Park Avenue way and not in the way anyone on staff at the center was forced to define it. Michael would start to consider himself overworked when he had done three more surgeries back-to-back and without sleep. His two friends probably thought they were about to collapse from exhaustion already, having each performed one.

Paragon of workaholism or not, though, Michael had to admit he needed a break. If he went right back into OR the way he was now, he would make mistakes. He refused to make mistakes. He knew the way these people lived. They were the guinea pigs for every new procedure, the victims of every quack, the client lists of every half-qualified pretender who squeaked through the boards with a crib sheet. Michael's whole point in starting the center was to give them better than that.

I'd better go upstairs and drink coffee in peace, Michael told himself. He looked around for Augie but couldn't find her. The hall outside OR was full of people in white coats, people he knew, but he was tired enough so that they didn't look familiar. He stuffed his used surgical gloves into a red waste disposal and headed for the stairs. Everybody was calming down now. He could feel it. The shooting must have stopped.

Halfway up the stairs to his office, he passed Sister Kenna coming down. She was looking frazzled but relieved. She held her long habit up so she wouldn't trip on it.

"Oh, Dr. Pride," she said. "There you are. People have been looking for you everywhere."

"I've been operating."

"That's what Sister Augustine said. When you have a chance you should try to find that granddaughter of Mr.

van Straadt's, the pretty one. You know, the one who doesn't work at the center."

"Rosalie."

"That's the one. I just saw her upstairs. She's looking for you."

"I'll check her out as soon as I get a chance."

"Thank you, Dr. Pride. I'm sure it must be something terribly important."

Michael thought it must be something terribly important, too, meaning his arrest, or maybe just the publicity resulting from his arrest. He knew he didn't want to talk about any of it, not now and not later, not ever. God, what a mess all that was.

He went the rest of the way up and looked into Eamon Donleavy's office. It was empty. He looked across the corridor at his own door and sighed. His door was closed, and he never closed it when he was still in the building and available for work—meaning he never closed it, except once or twice a month when he made a point of going into the east building and spending the night, just so that the nuns would stop fussing at him. If his door was closed now there could be only one reason for it, a reason he should have suspected as soon as Sister Kenna said she'd seen Rosalie in the building looking for him. Old Charlie van Straadt was here and ready to talk, whether Michael was ready or not.

"Crap on crap," Michael said to himself. "Just what I need."

Then he got ready to read old Charlie the riot act. Michael was good at reading people the riot act. He'd turned the process into an art form.

He grabbed the knob of his office door, got ready with his opening sentence—*I don't care how important you think it is, Charlie, we've got thirty-two gunshot cases*

needing attention down in Emergency right this minute—
and vaulted himself into his office. He was halfway across
the room to the desk when the scene inside made any
impression at all.

The scene inside was pretty grim.

Charles van Straadt was sitting in the chair behind
Michael's desk just as Michael had expected him to be,
but he wasn't sitting still.

He was rearing and bucking in a series of convulsions
that could only have been caused by strychnine, and that
made him look as if he had hold of one end of a live
wire.

P·A·R·T O·N·E

The Cardinal Archbishop of New York
Has a Suggestion to Make.
Just a *Little* Suggestion

O·N·E

1

Always before, when Gregor Demarkian had come to
New York, it had been winter. "New York is cold," he
told friends who asked him how he liked it. Cold was
what he thought of when he stood in his apartment in
Philadelphia, packing a single large suitcase to take with
him on the train. Philadelphia was not cold, at the moment. It had been an unseasonably warm May, and now,
at the beginning of June, green buds had blossomed into
leaves on all the trees and house fronts had blossomed
into red-and-white streamers. At least, the houses on
Cavanaugh Street had. Donna Moradanyan, the young
woman who lived with her small son in the fourth-floor
floor-through apartment in Gregor's brownstone, was
making up to the neighborhood for the funk she had
been in for Valentine's Day. Gregor didn't remember Father's Day being a vigorously celebrated holiday. He
didn't remember ever having taken notice of it before in
his life. Mother's Day, that was another story. Mother's
Day was on a par with Easter on Cavanaugh Street. People around here said "my mother" the way twelfth-
century religious fanatics had said "my God." Fathers had

always seemed to be superfluous. Now Ohanian's Middle Eastern Food Store had a Father's Day poster taking up most of its plate-glass front window, and the Ararat restaurant was offering "the Father's Day Breakfast Special," meaning pancakes in the shape of knotted ties. The children at the Holy Trinity Armenian Christian School were getting ready to hold a Father's Day pageant. The choir at Holy Trinity Armenian Christian Church had announced its intention of holding a benefit concert for the Armenian refugees in the church basement on Father's Day proper, made up entirely of hymns with the word *Father* in the title. Even the Armenian-American Historical Society had gotten into the act. They had taken St. Joseph, Foster Father of the Holy Family, as their patron saint.

"That's Catholic, that bit about St. Joseph the Foster Father," Gregor told Bennis Hannaford as he threw balled pairs of black socks into his suitcase. "And it's all my fault, too. I had that little booklet Sister Scholastica gave me after the mess in Maryville and I gave it to Sheila Kashinian. That was all it took."

"It never takes much of anything with Sheila Kashinian," Bennis said.

Bennis Hannaford was sitting cross-legged on Gregor's bedspread, looking curiously into his suitcase without offering to help. She had an ashtray in her lap and one of her standard Benson & Hedges Menthols in her right hand. Her thick black hair was pinned to the top of her head with scrunched-looking amber metal things that looked ready to fall to the floor. Gregor knew she had to be nearly forty, but she didn't look it. Bennis had the second-floor floor-through apartment in this building. Gregor often felt sandwiched between her and Donna Moradanyan, cream cheese filling between slices of date nut bread. Any minute now, somebody was going to come along and squash him flat.

Socks, ties, shirts folded around cardboard from the laundry: Gregor had no idea how to pack a suitcase. When his wife, Elizabeth, had been alive, Elizabeth had packed his suitcases for him. When Elizabeth hadn't been around to help, he had usually had an assistant. That was all gone now, of course. For the twenty long years of his professional life, Gregor Demarkian had been an agent of the Federal Bureau of Investigation. For the last ten of those years, he had been the founding head of the Behavioral Sciences Department, the arm of the Bureau that helped track the interstate progress of serial killers. That had amounted to being an Important Personage, as government bureaucrats go. That had meant getting his name in *Time* and *Newsweek* and being asked to explain the interior motivations of psychopaths on network television. It was odd, Gregor thought. Since he'd left the Bureau, he'd become much more famous than he'd ever been while he was in it. He spent much more of his time seeing his picture in magazines and being asked to show up for talk shows and generally being hounded by the press. He still couldn't get anyone to pack for him. It was as if packing were the worst job on earth, worse than cleaning toilets. He had a cleaning lady who came in and cleaned his toilet every week. Either that, or the people on Cavanaugh Street didn't like to see him go away.

Bennis dropped her cigarette butt in the ashtray, got another cigarette from her pack, and lit up again.

"So how long do you expect to be gone?" she asked. "I've promised Donna a dozen times that you'll be back before the twentieth, but I was making it up. For all I know you're going to be away for months."

"I take it the twentieth is Father's Day."

"That's right."

"Unfortunately, I should be back home in plenty of time. This isn't a major project, Bennis. It isn't even a case. The New York City Police Department is neither willing nor able to be helped by me."

"Some people would say the New York City Police Department is neither willing nor able to be helped by anybody."

"I'm not even going to consult with the police department," Gregor went on, ignoring her. "It's the Archbishop I'm supposed to see. It's the church I'm dealing with."

"The Cardinal Archbishop of New York called the Cardinal Archbishop of Colchester. The Cardinal Archbishop of Colchester called his friend Father Tibor Kasparian. Father Tibor Kasparian called you."

"Something like that."

"Father Tibor isn't Catholic, either. This is always the explanation you give me when these people get hold of you, Gregor. It never makes any sense to me."

"You come along when you're asked."

"That's different."

Gregor's two pairs of casual slacks were hanging folded over the bottom bars of wooden hangers suspended from the top of his bedroom door. He got them down and tossed them into the suitcase with everything else. He knew he ought to hang them up in a suit bag and put his shirts in the suit bag, too. He hated suit bags with a passion. Running through airports and train stations, they slapped heavily against his legs and made his knees ache.

Gregor flipped the top of the suitcase over and zipped the case shut. This suitcase was of the very soft leather variety, a black shiny expensive amoeba that allowed itself to be molded by the clothes inside it. He went to his bureau and found a thick wool V-neck sweater to wear over his shirt and under the jacket of his coat. He got himself put together and looked into the mirror. Gregor didn't like looking into the mirror. He couldn't help feeling that he was supposed to see something significant there, and he never did.

"What time is it?" he asked Bennis. "I'm supposed to catch the two forty-five train."

"It's only half past one. Are you sure you want to wear that sweater?"

"Yes."

"Aren't you hot?"

"I'm hot here," Gregor said, "but I'm always cold in New York. Do I have everything I'm supposed to have?"

"Your briefcase is on the kitchen table. Are you going to take it?"

"I'm going to have to. The Archbishop sent me all kinds of things, press clippings, the transcript of a radio show, pictures. I suppose I'd better have them on me if I want to look even halfway competent. Not that they were any use to me."

"It seems so odd that no one's been able to solve that murder," Bennis said. "It seems so odd that there's any kind of murder to solve. Don't you read the reports and think it was just some kind of mugging, some stray lunatic and Charles van Straadt was in the wrong place at the wrong time?"

"A mugging done with strychnine?"

"You know what I mean," Bennis said in exasperation. "I mean it didn't happen in the high-rent district, did it? It happened in a medical center full of hard cases, psychopaths, and loonies all over the place—I mean, all right, strychnine might be pushing it a bit, but so what? There was probably a ton of strychnine in that place. Aren't there medical uses for strychnine?"

"One or two."

"So there."

"So there?" Gregor got the suitcase up off his bed and put it on the floor. Bennis was exasperating him a little. The tone in her voice was so stubbornly superior. It was as if she thought any damn fool ought to be able to see this thing the way she saw it—and what was most annoying about that, Gregor admitted to himself, was that he had to agree with her. There were undoubtedly facets of this case he knew nothing about. If he had been dealing with John O'Bannion, Cardinal Archbishop of Colchester, he would have expected full disclosure. Instead, he was dealing with an unknown quantity. There were holes in the report the Archdiocese of New York had sent him. As long as those holes were not filled in, Bennis had more than a point. Why *weren't* the police assuming that the murder had been committed by one of the myriad misfits and crazies that infested a neighborhood like the one Sojourner Truth Health Center was supposed to inhabit?

Of course, maybe they were.

Gregor took his suitcase out of his bedroom, down the hall, across the living room and into the foyer. He dropped it next to his front door and went into his kitchen. His briefcase was indeed lying on the table there, open and organized. Gregor's briefcases were always organized. It was his life that was a mess.

Gregor snapped the briefcase up and stood it on its end. Bennis was leaning against the door jamb with her bare feet comfortably on his kitchen floor tiles. She was shaking her head dolefully and rhythmically, as if he were a small child about to embark on a patently stupid adventure.

"I think you're kidding yourself," she said. "I think you're going to get to New York and find yourself in the middle of an absolute firestorm of publicity. I think the police commissioner is going to be ready to kill you. I think the *Daily News* is going to be on the commissioner's side. I think—"

"You think too much," Gregor interrupted. "I've been asked to do the Cardinal a favor. I'm going to do the Cardinal a favor. You should try to relax."

"I should come with you to keep you out of trouble."

"Bennis, when you come with me, you never keep me *out* of trouble."

Bennis pushed herself away from the kitchen door. Then she turned around and walked back out toward the foyer, clucking to herself. Gregor heard his own front door open and close and more clucking going on out in the hall. Bennis's clucks could be as loud as a jackhammer when she wanted them to be. Gregor waited until the clucks had died away. Then he went into his living room and looked out on Cavanaugh Street.

Years ago—so many years ago now, he didn't want to remember; my God, he was nearly sixty—when Gregor Demarkian had been growing up, Cavanaugh Street had been just another Philadelphia ethnic neighborhood, a few ramshackle blocks of tenements dotted here and there with groceries and shoe stores, dry cleaners and religious supply shops. Back in the 1960s, when Gregor first joined the Bureau, it had begun that characteristic slide of American urban neighborhoods, that descent into carelessness and decay. Gregor remembered coming back for his mother's funeral. The steps of Holy Trinity

Church were crumbling. The gold paint on its double front doors was chipped and peeling. The building where Gregor's mother had lived was in fairly good repair, but the building next to it was abandoned on the top two floors. Pacing the sidewalks on the night of the wake, getting away from the endless stream of condolences delivered to him by people he didn't know any more, Gregor had accidentally turned the wrong corner and found himself face to face with a porno bookstore. Porno bookstores hadn't been then what they became later. Decadence hadn't been fashionable enough then. Gregor knew that porno bookstore was a sign, the mark of the beast, the beginning of the end.

Gregor had no idea what had happened between then and the time, three and a half years ago now, that he had come back to live in this place. He had seen urban neighborhoods turn around before. The Upper West Side of Manhattan had gone from Mostly Undesirable to Very High Rent in no time at all. Cavanaugh Street was the only urban neighborhood he had ever heard of that had turned itself around on purpose. Urban renewal failed. Enterprise zones were less than useless. Revitalization projects shot themselves in the foot. Here, the grandmother had wanted to stay and the grandchildren had decided to help them. The tenements had been torn down and replaced by neat brick replicas of Federal houses. The brownstones had been converted either into floor-throughs, like the one he lived in, or one-family town houses with living rooms that took up their entire second floor. There was still a grocery store—Ohanian's Middle Eastern Food Store—but it sold as much to tourists coming in from the Main Line as it did to people in the neighborhood. People in the neighborhood liked Armenian food, but they also ate their share at Burger King and McDonald's. The religious supply store was gone. If you wanted an oil lamp or a picture of the Virgin, you had to talk to Father Tibor Kasparian and listen to a lecture on why you really ought to give that money to the poor. Even Holy Trinity Armenian Christian School was less insolently ethnic than it appeared. Its students were mostly refugees who had come to America from Armenia after the collapse of the Soviet Union. Its stated purpose was to get those students ready to take their places beside their thoroughly Americanized cousins at Groton and The Hill.

From the window of his living room, Gregor could see across the street into the living room of Lida Arkmanian's town house, which was on the third floor instead of the second. When they were growing up, Lida had been the prettiest girl on Cavanaugh Street, and Gregor had been in love with her. Now he looked down to the street and saw Donna Moradanyan and her son, Tommy, coming out of Lida's front door. They were being met on the stoop by Russell Donahue, Donna's steady "friend" and seen off by Lida herself, looking magnificent in something bright red and flowy. Cavanaugh Street always looked best in this kind of weather. It was a place of bright emotions and happy thoughts, like the world seen through fairy dust in *Peter Pan*. It never seemed suited to the nasty darkness that made up so much of Philadelphia's climate.

Lida Arkmanian's town house was decorated in the same kind of red-and-white streamers Gregor's own town house was decorated in. Donna Moradanyan had been active over there, too. Gregor tilted his head and looked down the street. There was a Saint Joseph display on the steps of Holy Trinity Church, and red-and-white streamers wound around every lamppost from here to there. Donna was definitely outdoing herself this time. Gregor

wondered if Tommy Moradanyan was going to buy
Russell Donahue a Father's Day present, and if so,
what that would mean. God only knew, he was as anxious
as any of the old ladies on the street to see Donna
Moradanyan married to a responsible man.

Gregor backed away from the window. He went to
the kitchen phone and called a cab. He had to watch
himself around this place. It was too easy to turn into a
matchmaker on Cavanaugh Street. It was too easy to turn
into a gnome who thought the most important thing in
life was who married who and what they wore when they
did it. It was maddening.

The kitchen clock said it was two, on the nose. The
cab company said it would take ten minutes to get a taxi
to Gregor's front door. Gregor said fine and hung up.

It was past time for him to take a little trip, that was
the truth. He was getting something worse than stale.

Gregor opened his briefcase again. Press clippings,
magazine stories, the transcript of a radio program—lots
and lots of paper, but not a single piece of information he
couldn't have gotten on his own in one long day at the
main branch of the Philadelphia Public Library. Gregor had
the feeling that, unlike John O'Bannion, the Cardinal Archbishop of New York was something of a conspiracy theorist.

And that could mean nothing but trouble.

2

An hour and a half later, sitting in first class on the
Amtrak train speeding toward New York City—why he
bothered to travel first class for this short a trip, Gregor
didn't know—Gregor opened his briefcase again. Bennis
was right about more than the fact that this murder

should have been put down to random violence and the investigation abandoned at least a week ago. She was right about the kind of snake pit he was about to land himself in. Gregor had put a brave face on it back at the apartment, but he knew the truth. Unless the Archdiocese of New York was willing to smuggle him into this case trussed up in feathers in the back of an armored car, there was going to be no way to keep his presence in New York and his connection to the ongoing inquiry into the death of Charles van Straadt secret. The NYPD was going to be pleased at his arrival only for public consumption. When you were failing miserably at making headway in a high-profile crime, it was to your advantage to seem as if you were willing to accept any help you could get. In private, Gregor knew they were going to be ready to shred him with their teeth, and he didn't blame them. Things were bad enough as they stood. New York City Homicide didn't want a man who was now—no matter what he might have been before—an amateur coming in and making them look like fools. Unfortunately, on one or two occasions, Gregor had made the men of one police department or another look like fools.

He went through the mass of press clippings, came to the one he wanted, and pulled it out. This was the one that worried him. He looked down at a grainy black-and-white picture of a tall, thin man in hospital whites, surrounded by a sea of faces so ethnically diverse they could have served as a public relations poster for multiculturalism in New York City. Underneath the picture, a caption in thick italic lettering read,

Dr. Michael Pride, standing on the steps of the Sojourner Truth Health Center, the morning after Charles van Straadt's body was found in his office.

Gregor picked the picture up and put it down again. He looked into the face of the tall, thin man and discovered nothing. He looked into the faces of one or two of the others and found only that they hadn't been looking at the camera. It was impossible to find out anything serious from a photograph, except for the kinds of photographs taken by security systems in banks.

The reason this clipping worried him had less to do with the clipping itself than with something the Cardinal Archbishop of New York had said to him on the phone, the first and only time they had talked. Gregor hadn't liked the Cardinal Archbishop's voice. It wasn't like O'Bannion's voice, or like this Cardinal Archbishop's predecessor's. There was something smooth and hard about it that reminded Gregor of political appointees in the Department of Justice. Besides, the Cardinal Archbishop was in no way a New Yorker. The Cardinal Archbishop had been trained in Catholic seminaries and canonical universities from Los Angeles, California, to Rome, but he still had the Mississippi drawl in his voice. It was faint but unmistakable, like a fashionable woman's mist of perfume.

"What do you know about Dr. Michael Pride?" the voice had asked him—and Gregor hadn't been able to shake the feeling that he was being asked to rat to the Inquisition, in spite of the fact that he'd never met Michael Pride in his life. "I suppose they've heard of Michael even out there in Philadelphia," the Archbishop had said.

They had certainly heard of Michael Pride in Philadelphia. They had heard of him in Calcutta and Madrid and São Paulo, too. The question was ingenuous. Gregor thought the Cardinal was trying to ask something else but was not willing to put that something else into words. Did it matter who had heard of Michael Pride? All the same people had heard of Charles van Straadt.

"Of course I've heard of Dr. Pride," Gregor said. "It would be difficult not to."

"I suppose that's true. Have you been aware of any . . . news about him lately?"

"I've been aware of his connection with this murder, Your Eminence. I could hardly have avoided it. This is a national story."

"Yes. Yes, I know. You may not be aware of it, Mr. Demarkian, but Michael Pride has a long association with this Archdiocese. A very long association. The Sojourner Truth Health Center was a special project of my immediate predecessor's. He was very fond of Michael. And very involved in the center's activities. Much more involved than simply signing off on the money the Archdiocese donated to help with the center's operations. And then, of course, there are the nuns."

"I remember reading somewhere that there were nuns who work at the center, Your Eminence."

"Yes. Yes, there are several. Not a single order, you understand. The center isn't the project of any single order, the way Covenant House is with the Franciscans. But there are a number of nuns who do nursing and social work there."

"They probably work cheap," Gregor suggested.

"They probably do. I will admit something to you, Mr. Demarkian. If it had been up to me, if I hadn't arrived on the scene here to find that the bonds of connection between the center and this Archdiocese were so firmly established, I do not think I would have allowed such bonds to grow up. I'm not saying that I wouldn't have allowed the Archdiocese to come to the aid of the center. I'm not saying that. I'm just saying that I wouldn't have allowed the association to become so strong and so close."

"I take it there are things going on at the center that you don't like."

"A number of things, Mr. Demarkian. The fact that part of the facility dispenses family-planning information, including abortion information, and that the gynecological department performs abortions through the second trimester. This is the Roman Catholic Archdiocese of New York. I do have a stand my people in Rome expect me to take. Even the most liberal of the bishops in this country don't use church money to fund abortion clinics."

"No, Your Eminence. I can see that."

"Did you know that Michael Pride was a homosexual?"

Gregor had been taking this phone call in his kitchen, sitting in the chair at the kitchen table closest to the wall phone, picking at a plate of *yaprak sarma* Lida Arkmanian had left him just that morning. Now he stood up and began to pace.

"Is that really relevant, Your Eminence? That Michael Pride is a homosexual?"

"No," the Cardinal said. "In and of itself, it's not relevant at all. In spite of all the fuss we've had out here with the St. Patrick's Day parade and ACT-UP and all the rest of that nonsense, the church is likely to leave matters of sexual orientation or sexual preference or whatever you want to call it strictly alone, unless she's pushed. You know, before 1985, I don't think I ever heard a discussion of homosexuality in any Catholic facility anywhere, except for three days in the seminary when it was covered under sexual morality and the moral law. As I remember it, the word was used in a long list of words meant to detail practices considered to be contrary to full fruitfulness. I came away with the distinct impression that practice of homosexual sex and the use of a diaphragm were more or less on a par where sin was concerned. I definitely got the impression that knowingly receiving communion on less than four hours fast was worse than both. I suppose that was a more innocent age."

"Maybe."

"The problem with Michael isn't that he's a homosexual. The problem with Michael is that he's a homosexual the way he is everything else. Michael Pride is a man who doesn't know how not to go to extremes."

"Do you mean that he's effeminate?" Gregor ventured. He was mystified.

"No, I don't mean that he's effeminate. He's anything but. I mean that he's outrageous. Of course, that's not an entirely negative trait, is it, Mr. Demarkian? A project like the Sojourner Truth Health Center would never get started, and would never go on running, if there wasn't someone behind it who was willing to do anything, no matter how insane, no matter how bizarre, to make it real. Do you know how the Archdiocese first came to be involved with the center?"

"No."

"Michael ran out of money about year three of the operation. He couldn't go to the state. One of the avowed purposes of that center is to keep its clients out of the clutches of social workers, and I don't blame either the center or the clients. He didn't have enough money to run a mail-order fund-raising campaign, either. When I say they were broke, I mean they were broke. So Michael looked around for someone who might have some cash, and he found us. He tried the usual way to get money out of us at first, and he didn't get any. For obvious reasons. So he decided he had to talk to the Cardinal himself. This is old Cardinal Hessart we're talking about here. It was the last three years of the Cardinal's life. Do you know what Michael did when Hessart wouldn't see him?"

"No," Gregor said again.

"He set himself up on the steps of St. Patrick's Cathedral and held a tag sale of all his worldly goods. And I do mean all of them. He had his medical degree from Harvard in a nice frame priced at one ninety-five. He had his underwear in little piles. I was assigned to the chancery here that year, and I went down to see it. It was incredible. I suppose these days we wouldn't think anything of it, but then—good heavens. The fuss it made. And Cardinal Hessart met with him, of course. And they worked out an arrangement. And the arrangement is still in force."

"Dr. Pride sounds like an interesting man."

"Oh, Michael's interesting enough, all right, but he isn't sane. He isn't sane at all. That's what we really want you to help us out with."

"I don't think I could do anything about a man's sanity, Your Eminence. I don't have much expertise at anything except solving murders."

"If you solve this murder, you'll do a great deal for my sanity, Mr. Demarkian. You'll do a great deal for Michael's sanity, too. Of course, the police think he did it."

"Because the body was found in his office," Gregor said.

"No, not because of that. If that was all there was, I wouldn't be worried. I'll see you up here on the first of June, Mr. Demarkian?"

No, Gregor thought now, stuffing clippings back into the leather pockets of the briefcase's interior, as the landscape whizzed by, he most certainly did not like the present Cardinal Archbishop of New York. He didn't like him at all. If it hadn't been that the case itself was so interesting—and that Tibor was so insistent—he might have turned this project down on personal antipathy alone.

He dropped his briefcase onto the seat beside him, put his head on the backrest and closed his eyes.

If he had any luck, the Cardinal Archbishop would assign a subordinate to shepherd Gregor around, and Gregor would never have to deal with the man in charge at all.

T·W·O

1

"Look for a priest carrying a copy of the New York *Sentinel*," the Cardinal's secretary had said. It wasn't until he was arriving at Penn Station that Gregor realized how ludicrous that was. "A priest" could mean a man in a Roman collar. Religious dress was one of the things about which the Cardinal was rumored to be a hidebound traditionalist. The New York *Sentinel* was something else. Any number of priests could be carrying the New York *Sentinel*. It was a very popular paper.

Gregor got off the train and looked around. This part of Penn Station was relatively clean and relatively empty. Gregor saw one old woman who might have been a bag lady, but might just as easily have been a tourist from Wilmington struggling home under an unusually large load of packages. He saw a slender young woman in jeans carrying a baby on her back in a sling. The young woman read compulsively through her ticket, frowning. The only male Gregor could see besides the ticket takers was reading a New York *Sentinel*, but he didn't look anything like a priest. No Roman collar. No sober black suit. This man was wearing a crumpled tan linen jacket with sleeves pushed up his bare arms to his elbows, over a bright orange T-shirt and a pair of ancient jeans.

The headline on the New York *Sentinel* read, "FOILED AGAIN" in letters so large Gregor couldn't imagine their type size. At the bottom of the letters was a small picture of President Clinton looking forlorn. It always surprised Gregor how easily the tabloid press could come up with morose pictures of Bill Clinton, when in real life the man was always smiling. Gregor walked up to the man and cleared his throat.

"Excuse me," he said. "You don't happen to be here from—"

The man folded up his paper immediately and tucked it under his arm. "Mr. Demarkian? Excuse me, please. I was daydreaming. About the Mets."

The Mets were a baseball team. Gregor knew that. He cleared his throat again. "You're Father—"

"Father Donleavy. Eamon Donleavy. Please let me apologize again. The Mets are winning all of a sudden. Never mind. Let me take your bag."

Gregor let Eamon Donleavy take his bag. He looked the father over a little more carefully. The loafers were soft calf ones with the distinct look of a custom British shoemaker, but they were old. The watch was plain stainless steel and said "Timex" on its face. Interesting man, Father Donleavy.

"Excuse me," Gregor said, "but if you don't mind my saying so, you don't look the way I'd expect the emissary of this particular Cardinal to look. You don't even look like somebody I'd expect him to tolerate."

"No?" Eamon Donleavy laughed. "Well, you're almost right. I'm not the Cardinal's emissary except in the most peripheral way. I don't work at the chancery, I work at the Sojourner Truth Health Center. As for the rest of it,

the Cardinal baptized not only me but all six of my
brothers and sisters, and he's so glad we all remained in
the church, he puts up with us. I have a sister who's a
nun in one of those orders where they wear jumpsuits
and picket for world peace. The Cardinal doesn't know if
he should count that as staying in the church or not.
There's a cab stand up around here. I know a couple of
the drivers. We'll be able to get uptown."

"Uptown?"

"To the Sojourner Truth Health Center. The Cardinal
says you'll do better if you're right on the spot."

"Mmm," Gregor said.

"No?"

"There's no reason not to be on the spot," Gregor
said, "but if you ask me, your Cardinal is being smart. I
take it the Archdiocese is making some attempt to keep
my presence here on this errand unpublicized?"

"Oh, yes, Mr. Demarkian. These days, they're all running around the chancery behaving like extras from a
cold war domestic spy movie. The Cardinal probably
thinks he's John Wayne."

"It might be better for secrecy purposes for me to arrive at the center than at the chancery, you see. It's less
likely I'll be spotted. That is, assuming that the New York
papers still stake the chancery out on a regular basis and
don't stake out the center. With all the trouble up there
lately, I might have it all backward."

"The trouble was two weeks ago," Eamon Donleavy
said. "And the center's hardly the place you'd expect to
be trouble-free. Do you know what was going on up
there, the night Charles van Straadt was killed?"

"Something special?"

"It was definitely something special, Mr. Demarkian.
That's Harlem we're talking about now. Spanish Harlem.

The center averages, oh, about five knife wounds a night."

"Wonderful."

"Definitely wonderful. It's been worse than that, of course. It gets terrible. Anyway, the night Charlie was killed, we were in the middle of a gang war. Big time. Two rival gangs had taken over opposite sides of an entire city block uptown and they were blasting away at each other with assault rifles. We were getting thirty or forty admissions every ten minutes for a while."

"The place must have been a mess."

"Oh, it was, Mr. Demarkian, it was. Everyone was running around going crazy. And of course Charlie showed up at just the wrong time, itching for a confrontation with Michael. Charlie had the kind of timing that ought to have been bottled and studied at MIT. Anyway, there we were in the middle of a war, and there Charlie was in the middle of a snit."

"Why?"

"Over here, Mr. Demarkian. This is Juan Valenciano. He'll take us uptown."

Juan Valenciano was leaning against the side of his cab, pulled up at the curb out of the rank and with his "off duty" light lit. When he saw Eamon Donleavy and Gregor he straightened up and smiled, opening the back passenger door with a flourish. Gregor let himself be shepherded toward the waiting vehicle. He didn't flinch at all when his suitcase was whisked away from him and into the trunk, or when Juan Valenciano took his briefcase and chucked it into the front passenger seat. Usually Gregor hated being parted from his things. One of the first things he had been taught as a rookie agent was never to allow that to happen. Once your suitcase or your briefcase was out of your hands, you never knew what was going to happen to it. It could be searched. It could be destroyed. It could be lost, taking all the work you'd done for the last three months with it.

Gregor climbed into the cab and let Eamon Donleavy climb in beside him. Eamon Donleavy said a few things in Spanish to Juan Valenciano and slammed the cab door shut. Juan Valenciano turned his "off duty" light off, put his "in service" light on, and pulled out into the street.

"There," Donleavy said. "I'm sorry, Mr. Demarkian. I interrupted you. I didn't mean to be rude, but it's practically impossible to get a cab as far up into Harlem as we're going. It's not supposed to be. The city ordinances are quite specific. Medallion cabs are supposed to go anywhere in any of the five boroughs they're asked to go, but it doesn't work like that in real life. If they don't want to go, they just refuse to take you. Juan here lives up in Spanish Harlem and he knows practically everybody at the center. We use him all the time when we need to bring somebody uptown."

"You're lucky to have him. New York looks—shabbier than I remember it being."

"New York is a mess."

"New Yorkers are always saying that."

"Maybe we are. Let's see, Mr. Demarkian. What were you asking me? Oh, yes. You were asking me why Charlie van Straadt was having a fit."

"Answer something else first. You've just described what sounds to me like a very chaotic situation."

"That's putting it mildly enough."

"What I want to know is, in such a situation, why didn't the police—and the papers and everybody else— why wasn't the first assumption simply that Mr. van Straadt had been killed by a stray loony or a gang member or some nut in off the street? How did this turn into a murder mystery?"

Eamon Donleavy looked uncomfortable. "Well," he said, "the papers are treating it as if it were some loony or a gang member."

"Nobody else is."

"I know that. There was the strychnine, Mr. Demarkian. Stray loonies don't usually poison their victims with strychnine. Gang members use Uzis and knives."

Gregor was impatient. "Stray loonies do use strychnine, Father Donleavy. They use it all the time. Under ordinary circumstances, it would be difficult for a bag lady to get, but we're not talking about ordinary circumstances. The center is a fully equipped medical facility, isn't it?"

"We're not Mass General, Mr. Demarkian. We do have a fully equipped emergency room—one of the best and most up-to-date in the country, as a matter of fact—because we have to, and we do a lot of obstetrics because the neighborhood needs it. I suppose we're at least as good as a small-town hospital. Maybe better."

"Fine," Gregor said. "Then there must have been strychnine around. There must have been strychnine available."

"There was some. It was locked up."

"I'm sure it was locked up, Father Donleavy. My point is that locked up or not, someone could have gotten to it."

"The police thought of that. And they checked. Sister Augustine even had them walking through the center with clipboards, checking off our entire inventory of the stuff, which wasn't much. There wasn't any missing."

"You mean as far as you know somebody brought that strychnine in from the outside?"

"No. I should have said none of it was missing except the strychnine that had been suspected all along of having killed Charles van Straadt. We do call him Charles in public, Mr. Demarkian, not Charlie. The family gets very upset with us when they think we're being snide."

"Go back to the strychnine," Gregor said. "What strychnine had been suspected all along of killing Charles van Straadt?"

Eamon Donleavy rubbed the palms of his hands against the knees of his jeans. He was staring straight at the back of Juan Valenciano's head.

"Well," he said carefully. "Michael's strychnine."

"You mean Dr. Michael Pride's."

"That's right."

"What do you mean by saying it was his strychnine?"

"It was the strychnine from his office medical cabinet. His office downstairs. Not the one Charlie died in."

"Dr. Pride has two offices?"

"Michael has an office on my floor—that's the third—for administrative purposes and a private examining room-office kind of thing off the emergency room to see patients in. The medical cabinet is down there. The other two doctors on staff have arrangements like that, too. They have their own medical cabinets."

Get this straight, Gregor told himself. This is simpler than it seems. "Let me go over this from the beginning. Charles van Straadt was found dead in Michael Pride's third-floor administrative office."

"Right."

"Poisoned with strychnine that had to come from the locked medical cabinet in Michael Pride's—is it a first-floor or a basement office?"

"First floor."

"Are you absolutely sure that the strychnine came

from this office?" Gregor asked. "The center is essentially a hospital, isn't it? There must be strychnine everywhere. If I remember correctly, strychnine is used in dozens of medicines and household products as well."

"Oh, it's used, and we have it," Eamon Donleavy said carefully, "but it wasn't missing. We have a whole canister of rat poison in the basement—we've been having a rat problem; you do in basements in New York City—but the canister down there on the night Charles van Straadt died was new and it had a seal on it and the seal hadn't been broken."

"Go back to Michael Pride's medical cabinet," Gregor said. "Are you sure this medical cabinet was in fact locked? It hadn't been left standing open during the emergency?"

"The medical cabinets can't be left unlocked," Eamon Donleavy answered. "The drug cabinets can't either. They lock automatically when they're shut. They can only be opened with a key."

"Weren't there people in Michael Pride's examining room that night? Where was Michael Pride?"

"Michael was in OR most of the time—you know, performing surgery. I don't know how many bullets got extracted that night. There were a lot of them. It was one of those nights, Mr. Demarkian."

Gregor was beginning to feel as if he were having one of those days. Why was it that providing some help to the Catholic Church always ended up making him feel as if he had migraines?

They were up by Columbus Circle now, threading their way impatiently through even more impatient traffic. The late afternoon half-light made the broad plate-glass windows on the storefronts around them look tinted green.

"Is Michael Pride the only person with a key to that medical cabinet?" Gregor asked.

"No," Eamon Donleavy told him. "Sister Augustine has one."

"Does Michael Pride carry his keys with him wherever he goes?"

"He leaves them in the center drawer of his desk."

"What desk? In which office?"

"The desk in his upstairs office."

"Was that desk accessible to anyone except Michael Pride on the night in question?"

Eamon Donleavy looked amused. "Well, Mr. Demarkian, it was wide open all night because it's wide open every night. All of our office doors are. But if you're thinking someone sneaked in there and stole Michael's keys and ran downstairs and got the strychnine and then ran upstairs and all the rest of it—I must inform you that there's one catch."

"What's that?"

"Well, no one knew that Charles van Straadt was coming that night, right?"

"That's arguable," Gregor said, "but I'll let it stand for now. So what?"

"So there was somebody in Michael's office from the time Charles van Straadt arrived at the center until the time his body was found—Charles van Straadt was in the office. I know. I was talking to the Cardinal that night, sitting at my desk right across the hall, and I could see him."

"That's interesting. And he never left?"

"Not once while I was there. Which was for nearly an hour. That granddaughter of his went in and out."

"Granddaughter?"

"Charles had four grandchildren. Two of them volunteered at the center. This was one of the ones who didn't. Rosalie. Anyway, Rosalie went off getting coffee and whatnot from the cafeteria, running errands for the old man. The old man stayed put. He usually did."

"That's *very* interesting." Gregor looked out his window at a low stone wall and a profusion of trees. They were on Central Park West now, the great old apartment houses marching uptown on their left, Central Park on their right. This was New York as Gregor used to know it, a place suffering from too much money, not too little.

"You know," Gregor said, "whether you realize it or not, you seem to be implying—maybe subconsciously insisting is what I mean—that Michael Pride and only Michael Pride could have killed Charles van Straadt."

Eamon Donleavy shook his head. "There's nothing subconscious about it. Everybody's been insisting that very thing, Mr. Demarkian. The police. The volunteers at the center. Even the Cardinal."

"There's only one thing missing," Gregor told him. "Motive. And as far as I know, Michael Pride founded the Sojourner Truth Health Center and Charles van Straadt contributed generously to it. Other people also contributed to it. Mr. van Straadt wasn't on some kind of board that could have removed Michael Pride as head of the center?"

"There is no such board. There's just Michael."

"Well then, you see what I mean. This is not the kind of relationship that usually results in homicide."

Eamon Donleavy was a tall man. His legs were folded hard against the seat in front of him, as Gregor's were, since Gregor was even taller. Eamon Donleavy shifted so that he was leaning toward the door and looking out on the apartment buildings. The buildings were just as big as they had been twenty blocks south, but no

longer so well cared for. Gregor could almost feel what
was coming.

"Michael," Eamon Donleavy said carefully, "doesn't
think like other people."

After that, Eamon Donleavy wouldn't say anything at
all.

2

Five minutes later, Juan Valenciano's cab pulled off
Lenox Avenue and up to the front door of the Sojourner
Truth Health Center. Gregor had changed his mind about
his premonition down on CPW. He had not been able to
feel what was coming. In spite of everything he had
heard and seen and read. In spite of twenty years in the
Federal Bureau of Investigation. In spite of dozens of
hard-boiled private-eye novels and more than enough
forays into *film noir*. Gregor had not been prepared for
this. This was not the Harlem you saw sitting on the train
at the 125th Street Station. This was not the Harlem you
saw making forays off the main campus of Columbia University in Morningside Heights. This wasn't even the
Harlem you saw on the six o'clock news. This was—
Gregor had no words to describe what this was. There
seemed to be a tape playing through his head saying over
and over again: *How the hell did we ever let it get like
this?*

The street the Sojourner Truth Health Center faced
was not empty, although the buildings on it were mostly
abandoned. Gregor saw an ancient black woman with a
shopping cart full of worn brown grocery bags. The grocery bags were stuffed full and folded over at the tops so
that no one could see what she had inside them. Sitting

on the stoop of the abandoned building directly across
from the center's front door were three young men, all
stoned into immobility, all laid out as if they were dead
and ready for their own wakes. The steps on the stoop of
that building were made of marble. Gregor recognized
that even from inside the cab. He turned around and
looked toward the center. The front doors were open and
covered with signs in English and Spanish. Gregor could
read only one of them clearly, the one that said, "**IF YOU
ARE DEAF, PLEASE INFORM A NUN.**" Incredible.

"There's Sister Augustine." Eamon Donleavy pointed
up the center's steps to a middle-aged woman in bright
red sweats coming out the front doors. The middle-aged
woman was also wearing a veil, so Gregor supposed she
could be "Sister" somebody. "She's probably been hanging out of her office window waiting for us to show up
for the last hour. She's very interested in meeting you,
Mr. Demarkian. Augie's a big fan of Michael Pride's."

Gregor opened his door and got out. The nun in the
red sweatsuit had stopped at the bottom of the center's
stoop. When Gregor was safely on the sidewalk, she advanced.

"Mr. Demarkian? Mr. Gregor Demarkian?"

"That's right," Gregor said.

The little nun beamed. She really was little, too.
Gregor thought she was barely five feet tall. She was at
least significantly shorter than Bennis Hannaford, who
was five feet four. Unlike Bennis Hannaford, the little
nun was very round, a composition in globes and circles.
She was wearing bright white sneakers with green glow-
in-the-dark patches on the heels and toes.

"Mr. Demarkian," she said. "You don't know how glad
I am to see you. I'm Sister Mary Augustine, but everybody calls me Augie. It's so much easier."

"How do you do," Gregor said.

Eamon Donleavy was out of the cab now, too. The cab was pulling slowly away from the curb. Gregor guessed it was about to head straight downtown. He didn't blame Juan in the least.

"I hope everything's been okay up here while I've been away," Eamon Donleavy said to the little nun. "No hysterical calls from the Cardinal. No last-minute emergencies that require me to call the chancery immediately."

"The Cardinal's been as silent as the dead," Augie said. "We haven't had any trouble from that quarter at all. It's other people you ought to be worried about."

"Did we have a raid?" Eamon Donleavy looked worried.

"What kind of raid?" Gregor asked.

"No raids," Augie said. Then she turned to Gregor Demarkian to explain. "We run something here called the refuge program. We take girls—at their request; we don't coerce anybody into anything here—we take girls who are prostitutes and want to quit and place them, well, anywhere we can place them. The most important consideration is to get them as far away from here as possible, so we try to put them in boarding schools and halfway houses far out into the country. We have a number of orders who will take our girls and young women free of charge, but there aren't always enough places ready when we need them, so for a while we sometimes have to keep them here. It's not the best solution, I know, but there it is. And, of course, the pimps don't like it. So they raid."

"Oh," Gregor said.

"Julie Enderson's pimp showed up DOA at Lenox Hill night before last," Augie said to Eamon Donleavy, "so what I was most worried about in that direction is just not going to happen. I only found out about it by accident, though. We've got to do something about the way we communicate with people around here."

"We're trying," Eamon Donleavy said. "We've been trying for a decade. Didn't you say you had trouble?"

"*You* have trouble," Sister Augustine said. "It doesn't have anything to do with me. Rosalie is here."

"Do you mean Rosalie van Straadt?" Gregor asked.

Augie nodded vigorously. "That's exactly who I mean. And she's blowing a fit—well, you'll have to see it to believe it, if she hasn't calmed down by the time you get in there, which she may not have, because I don't think she wants to calm down. I don't think that's her idea at all."

"What does she want?" Eamon Donleavy asked.

"She wants Michael, of course. She wants what everybody else wants. We haven't let her get at him, though. We're smarter than that around here, even if she is a van Straadt."

"Get Ida," Eamon Donleavy said tensely. "Let her take care of it."

"Oh, we've got Ida, Father E. We've got half the staff, too, and some of the girls from refuge. The next thing you know, we're going to have the United States Marines. I think—"

"Sister Augustine!" someone shouted. "Sister Augustine, Sister Augustine. Come quick."

Gregor looked up to the center doors just as a nun in a calf-length brown habit came rushing out of them, her veil bobbing precariously on her head, her eyes wild. She saw the little group of them standing together on the pavement and rushed down to them, holding on to her veil with one hand and her heart with the other.

"Oh, Augie," she gasped when she reached them,

"and Father E. I'm so glad I found you. You've got to come right along. You don't know what's going on in there."

"Is Michael all right?" Eamon Donleavy demanded.

The nun looked bewildered. "I don't know where Dr. Pride is. Is there something wrong with him?"

"Never mind," Sister Augustine said crisply. "Just tell us what happened. What is going on in there?"

"This is Sister Kenna," Eamon Donleavy said, to Gregor, in an off-hand tone. "She works in the refuge program."

Sister Kenna was taking great gulping breaths. "It's Rosalie van Straadt. She was going on and on and on about how it was all Dr. Pride's fault, and then she just seemed to lose it. She began picking things up and throwing them on the floor—and she's in Dr. Pride's office, you know, and there's a lot of equipment in there and medicine and now there's glass everywhere on the floor and I just don't know what to do—"

"I know what to do," Sister Augustine said firmly. She grabbed Sister Kenna by the elbow and began to propel her back up the stairs to the center's front doors. "I've been dealing with temper tantrums for thirty years. I can deal with one more. Trust me."

Eamon Donleavy sighed. "Come on in," he said to Gregor. "This isn't exactly the first impression I wanted you to get."

Gregor Demarkian didn't suppose it was, but he wasn't unhappy about it. First impressions that came off the way they were supposed to almost never told him anything.

T·H·R·E·E

1

The west building of the Sojourner Truth Health Center was six stories high—five plus the basement level—and on the sixth floor there was a small square space that looked out on the street, furnished with an old black couch and three worn chairs and an ashtray. This floor contained administrative offices. Dr. Michael Pride thought of it as providing a commentary on what he thought of administration. The Sojourner Truth Health Center was committed to getting all the necessary paperwork finished and filed. It was determined to see that both the city and state of New York got exactly what they asked for. It just couldn't bother to waste valuable space in more convenient parts of the building to get it all done. We should have put in an elevator for staff use, Michael thought now. It would have made things easier. It would also have made things more expensive. Back when the center bought the west and east buildings and renovated them, the staff had decided on two stretcher elevators, period, no conveniences provided for people who could walk. It had saved them God only knew how much money. It had been a very good decision. The problem was that here was Michael on the sixth floor, tired as hell and knowing he had to start on down. The problem was that even after all this time, there were days when Michael didn't want to make the right decision.

Michael had been standing against the windows here when Eamon Donleavy had driven up with Gregor Demarkian. He had seen Augie and Sister Kenna and all the commotion. He knew exactly what was going on downstairs. He had been avoiding it all morning. People at the center thought he was an absentminded professor, an Albert Einstein type—except for the periodic forays into some of the stranger establishments in the side streets off Times Square; only Eamon Donleavy ever talked to him about those—but it wasn't true. Michael had excellent radar. He had even had excellent radar on that night the establishment he was in had gotten raided. He just hadn't been inclined to listen to it.

The street was empty now. Everybody had come inside. Michael pushed himself away from the window and wandered back into the hall. This was an old apartment building. The doors that opened off the central corridor opened onto suites, no single rooms. The suites were small and cramped and being drowned in paper. The doors were all open, because with the doors shut the people in the suites couldn't breathe. Michael said hello to Betsey in Processing and good afternoon to Aramanda in Permanent Files, and laughed a little to himself. If he'd ever described the situation here in just that way to someone who knew nothing about it—to one of his classmates in the Harvard Medical School class, one of the ones who had gone on to make a million dollars a year doing plastic surgery in Beverly Hills—it would have sounded as impressive as hell. There would have been no way for his listener to tell Betsey was one of only two people in Processing or that Aramanda had to do the Permanent Files by hand because the center's computer system consisted of three Macintosh PCs, all kept in Augie's office downstairs and used to sort out the medical backgrounds of emergency cases. They needed computers to sort out the medical backgrounds of emergency cases because they got a lot of repeat visits by people who couldn't remember they were making repeat visits. Michael found it absolutely incredible what crack could do to a human brain. He found it even more incredible that kids in these neighborhoods, having seen what crack could do to a human brain, started taking it anyway. Sometimes he thought his cats had more sense than half of the people he knew.

He reached the fifth floor and the day-care center. Forty children between the ages of two and five were running back and forth across the central corridor, into one room and out of another. A cluster of six children around the age of three were sitting in a semicircle around Sister Rosalita, singing the alphabet song. The stairway down was blocked. Michael waited while Kanistra Johnson came over and removed the block for him.

"You going down to see the great detective?" Kanistra asked.

"Something like that."

"Sister Joan Kennedy was up here a while ago saying that that Rosalie was downstairs having a fit."

Michael smiled wanly and continued down the stairs. He passed four without stopping. He stopped on three just long enough to make sure that his own and all the other offices were empty. He stopped on two to check out the room of one Carmelita Gomez, who had given birth the night before under what could only be described as seriously bizarre conditions. Her grandmother—a full-blown schizophrenic who was just cunning enough to appear placid any time she got in front of a social worker—had decided that the baby was taking too long, it was bottled up in there, they had to release it. Then she had gotten a great big kitchen knife and stabbed Carmelita in the top of the abdomen.

Carmelita wasn't in her room. She was supposed to go in for a new set of x-rays today. Maybe she was down there. Michael stopped at the nursery and saw that Carmelita's baby was well and sleeping comfortably. Amazingly enough, it had not been damaged at all, at least that he could see, by the insane circumstances surrounding its delivery. The baby was a boy, whom Carmelita had named Juan, after her grandmother. Carmelita's grandmother's name was Juanita.

There's really no way I'm going to be able to get out of this, Michael thought. I'm going to have to go down there and do something about it. Augie and Eamon Donleavy did their best to shield him from annoyances. They meant well and they often did him a service by affording him protection. Sometimes they were attempting the impossible. And much as he didn't like the idea, he was going to have to meet the Cardinal's private detective eventually. No, Michael didn't like that idea at all. Ever since he'd first heard Demarkian was coming, he'd been having a very difficult time calming down. It was a bad idea, bringing a man like that to a place like this. It was an especially bad idea to bring a man like that into a life like his. Michael Pride had no illusions about himself. Other people called him a saint. He knew he was a fanatic with a socially approved obsession. His other obsessions weren't socially approved at all.

As soon as he got to the first floor, he could hear it:

the breaking of glass; the sound of voices coming from his office, raised in anger. The stairs rose against the back wall of the building. When these buildings had originally been built, they had each had another set of stairs at the front, off the little vestibule with the mailboxes in it. In the east building, these stairs were still standing. In this building, they had been removed to provide space for one of the elevators. Michael's office was at the center of the floor along the east side, near the main emergency examining rooms and only a step or two from the elevators. It was one of the smallest rooms on the floor, but also one of the most conveniently located. The door to Michael's office was open. Staff people were spilling out of it—or maybe crowded into it would be a better description. Patients were indulging their curiosity, too. A man with his arm in a sling edged closer and closer to the back of the crowd in the door even as Michael watched him. A very pregnant young woman was sitting on a gurney swinging her legs in the air, taking in every word.

Michael went up to the two women at the very back of the crowd—Sarah Cavanieri and Judy Hedge, both nurses—and nudged them aside. They both blushed bright red when they recognized him. Judy Hedge tapped the woman in front of her. The woman was not somebody Michael knew, but she was somebody who knew him. She blushed too and moved aside just as quickly as the other two had. This was what it meant to have charisma, Michael decided. You could part crowds the way God parted the Red Sea.

Up at the front, the principals were much too interested in Rosalie van Straadt's fit to take any notice of Michael. Michael stopped one layer of people short of the front to take it all in. There was Eamon Donleavy in his damned orange T-shirt, furious. There was Sister Augustine, proving once again that being a nun had less to do with what you wore than with what you were. Bright red sweatsuit notwithstanding, Augie was radiating all the authority of the Reverend Mothers of Michael's dim childhood memory. He'd always thanked God and the devil that he hadn't been born Catholic whenever he ran into one of those Reverend Mothers. The tall, heavy man in the suit and sweater Michael thought must be Gregor Demarkian. He had seen pictures of Gregor Demarkian in newspapers and magazines, but those didn't count. Michael could never recognize people from magazine photographs. He had once stood next to Christie Brinkley for fifteen minutes in the Pasta and Cheese on East Sixty-first Street and not known who she was. Gregor Demarkian did not look formidable, but Michael wasn't fooled by that. Stephen Hawking did not look formidable. Niels Bohr had been a small round man whom strangers often mistook for a shoe salesman. Michael wondered for a moment if this Demarkian man wasn't hot—why the sweater?—and turned his attention to Rosalie.

Rosalie was quicker than the rest of them. In Michael's experience, Rosalie always was. She had made a royal mess of the office—at least, Michael assumed it was she who had made it—and she was now intent on making that mess ever more magnificent. All Michael's lab beakers were shards of glass on the floor. Fortunately, he only used the lab beakers to grow oregano in when he had the time, and he hadn't had the time for months now. She had overturned his looseleaf desk calendar and scattered the pages on top of the glass shards. She had dumped the ancient brown liquid in his coffeemaker onto his carpet. She had a tray of surgical equipment in

her hands and was about to send it crashing to the floor.
Unlike everybody else in the room, however, she was
paying attention.

Michael caught the moment when Rosalie recognized
him. Her gaze was roving back and forth across the
crowd, checking out her audience. Sister Augustine was
talking to her, but Rosalie was paying no attention.
Rosalie's eyes kept darting back in the direction of
Gregor Demarkian, as if he were the one member of the
crowd she had to convince. Michael wondered what it
was Rosalie was intent on convincing them all of, this
time. Then Rosalie's head swung in his direction, and
stopped. She was holding the tray of surgical equipment
above her head. She froze it there. Then her beautiful
eyes widened and she began to smile.

"Well," she said. "If it isn't the son of a bitch."

That was when she did what Michael had been expecting her to do, ever since she got that tray into her
hands. She raised it just a notch higher in the air. Then
she whirled around and brought the tray down on the
edge of his desk, so hard it clanged like a monster gong.
Surgical instruments jumped into the air and flew everywhere. A scalpel stuck point-first into the side of his desk
and stayed embedded there. Rosalie whirled around,
crossed her arms over her chest and stuck out her chin.

"You son of a bitch," she said again. "I've had the police in my apartment all week and it would never have
had to have happened if you'd had the simple honesty to
do what you ought to do and confess."

2

For Rosalie van Straadt, the day had started to get rotten as soon as she opened her eyes. Either her alarm clock was on the blink or she had forgotten to set it. Whatever the reason, she hadn't made it out of bed until after ten o'clock. That was a disaster. She'd had an important appointment at the bank at nine. She didn't like the idea of making her bankers upset with her. She'd had to reschedule the appointment, and that had been embarrassing. She'd apologized to Harry Stratford himself, but even over the phone she had picked up the dry coldness of disapproval in Harry's voice. She could hardly blame him. Her head ached and she wanted to smoke. She had quit smoking nearly six years ago.

The day got worse when she got her copy of the New York *Sentinel* from the hall outside her apartment door and saw the headline. It was the same headline the paper had had since four days after Grandfather had died, and it was maddening.

POLICE STUMPED: Still No Break in
van Straadt Murder.

Well, that was true enough. All the news had been no news for most of the last two weeks. So what? The other tabloids had moved on to fresher stories. *The New York Times* restricted itself to publishing tempered speculations on the future of Van Straadt Publications in the business section. Why did the *Sentinel* have to go on and on like this, killing its own circulation?

That was when Rosalie had decided to get away from

it all, and picked up the phone to call her old friend Sharon Leigh. Halfway through dialing the number, she stopped. The last time Rosalie had talked to Sharon Leigh, just a few days ago, the conversation hadn't gone too well. Sharon had seemed . . . distant, somehow. Standoffish. Sharon had been willing enough to talk. At points during that call, Rosalie had even suspected that Sharon was keeping her on the phone as long as possible. What Sharon hadn't been willing to do was meet. Rosalie had suggested lunch at the Hard Rock Café. Sharon had given an excuse that had sounded lame even at the time. Thinking back on it, it sounded lamer. Rosalie had hung up and stared at the push-button dial. Over the headline on the *Sentinel* was one of those red banners.

COUNTDOWN TO FATHER'S DAY,

it said.

WIN A HUNDRED GRAND
AND REALLY CELEBRATE.

Father's Day, for God's sake. *Father's Day*. Rosalie had despised her own father with every cell in her body. Grandfather had despised him, too. Fortunately, he had smashed himself up at the age of forty-two. Rosalie had been ten at the time. Rosalie's mother had been distraught. Rosalie's mother had always been distraught. She had been a complete bimbo. Maybe she still was. Rosalie had minimal family feeling, and what she had had to do with money.

On the square marking next Thursday on the wall calendar in Rosalie's kitchen were two exclamation marks and the words *the lawyers* in purple felt-tip pen. Other than that, there was nothing on the wall calendar at all. Of course, Rosalie had work to do. She had investments she managed and charities she supported. She put a lot of time into the Smith College Alumnae Association. Still, if something didn't happen soon, what would she do? This could go on forever. She was as sure as she could be that Michael Pride had murdered her grandfather. She was just as sure that nobody would arrest him for it unless they had to, because nobody at all wanted to see Michael Pride arrested. That was how he'd gotten out from under that raid he'd been caught in the day or so before grandfather died. Rosalie had thought she'd had it all set up, and it had done nothing for her at all. And now—

Now she sat down on the edge of Michael Pride's desk and looked around the office. It was just as much of a mess as she had hoped she was making it. The witnesses were numerous and shocked. Rosalie didn't care that Eamon Donleavy was furious or that Sister Augustine was exasperated. She did care that Michael Pride seemed to be amused, but she shoved that to the back of her brain. What Michael Pride felt or thought or did mattered not at all in this case. Rosalie had her eye on Gregor Demarkian, and in that direction she thought she had made a hit. She knew who Gregor Demarkian was because she had read about him in *People* magazine. She knew what he was doing here because there had been rumors about his coming for a week. It was impossible to keep anything secret in the center from anyone who really wanted to find out. Eamon Donleavy had been talking about Demarkian with the Cardinal for Rosalie didn't know how long. It hadn't occurred to Rosalie that Demarkian might actually be here when she showed up. She thought it was a very good thing for her that he was.

He was supposed to be an independent investigator. He would have to take her seriously.

Rosalie was wearing a little black dress today, instead of her customary slacks and turtleneck. It was too hot for slacks and turtleneck. In this dress she couldn't tuck her legs up under her without showing off her underwear. That was a scenario with possibilities—Michael wouldn't care, but Eamon Donleavy would spit—but Rosalie was afraid it would also make Gregor Demarkian think she was a jerk.

Rosalie crossed her legs at the ankle instead. She said, "Well, now. Are all of you people willing to listen to what I have to say for once?"

For a moment Rosalie thought Eamon Donleavy was going to lunge at her. She even flinched. He moved only to flex the muscles on his arms. "No," he said. "Nobody is willing to listen to what you have to say."

Farther away, Gregor Demarkian coughed. "Excuse me," he said. "My name is—"

"Gregor Demarkian. I know. I'm glad you're here. I'm Rosalie van Straadt."

"I understood that, yes," Demarkian said.

"It was my grandfather that was murdered," Rosalie said. "And of course they're all trying to cover it up. That's why I'm here."

"That's not why you're here," Michael said.

Rosalie ignored him. It was true, of course, but everything she had to say was true, too. That was the point.

Michael came fully out of the crowd and crossed to Gregor Demarkian. He held out his hand.

"How do you do, Mr. Demarkian. I'm Michael Pride. Welcome to the Sojourner Truth Health Center."

"Thank you," Gregor Demarkian said.

Sister Augustine hissed. "Rosalie, get down off that desk. What will Mr. Demarkian think of us?"

Rosalie had no intention of getting down off the desk. She wasn't very tall. She would be swallowed up by the crowd. She started to swing her legs in the air instead.

"They are covering it all up," she said, in as reasonable a tone as possible. "They've been covering it up since it happened, just as they cover up everything else Michael does. Did you know that the strychnine my grandfather swallowed came from the medical cabinet in this very office?"

"Yes," Demarkian said.

"Did you know that the cabinet was locked? And that only Michael and Sister Augustine had keys?"

"I knew that, too. Yes."

"Well, they've been much more forthcoming than I thought they'd be. But I bet there's something you don't know. I bet you don't know that Michael was arrested two days before my grandfather died. Arrested on a morals charge."

"It wasn't a morals charge, Rosalie," Michael said. He sounded so damn patient. "It was a vice charge. There's a difference."

"What difference?"

"On a vice charge, you weren't corrupting the morals of a minor. Don't tell me you pulled this entire stunt just to make sure Mr. Demarkian knew I'd been picked up using a glory hole in Times Square."

Rosalie looked away. He was so damned casual about it. How could he be so damned casual about it? It wasn't like telling people you were gay. Lots of people were gay. This was more like confessing to a *disease*.

"You wanted him dead," Rosalie said, carefully, still

looking away. "You know perfectly well you wanted him dead."

Michael shook his head. "No I didn't, Rosalie. Why would I have wanted him dead?"

"If he hadn't died, he would have put all that stuff about you in the *Sentinel*."

"So what? It had already been in every newspaper in town. It had already been on the local television news. What difference would a story or two in the *Sentinel* have made?"

"He would have forced you out of here, out of the center. He would have made you quit."

"He couldn't have. He didn't own this place. I own this place. I've got better than fifty-three percent of the stock in the parent corporation. Nobody can force me out of here."

"He would have withdrawn his money if you didn't leave. The center would have had to close."

"The center survived before your grandfather started giving us money. It will survive now that he's no longer around to give it."

"It will have to, won't it?" Rosalie said. "I'm not putting a penny into this place."

"I didn't think you would. But Rosalie, dearest, you've just scuttled your own case. I couldn't have murdered your grandfather to stop him from cutting off his funding, because by murdering him I would have cut off his funding."

"Oh, don't be so damned logical," Rosalie snapped. "You're always so damned logical. How can you do this to me?"

"How can I do this to *you*?"

"You're rigging this whole thing," Rosalie said, appalled to realize that she was very near tears. "You're switching everything around. You're doing it on purpose."

"I'm doing what on purpose, Rosalie?"

But there was no answer to that. Of course there was no answer to that. Rosalie's head hurt. The muscles in her back and shoulders ached. What had she meant to accomplish by coming down here? What had she done now that she wouldn't be able to take back?

She eased herself carefully off the desk. She stepped into paper and glass. Everybody around her was dead quiet and watching. Gregor Demarkian hadn't moved. Rosalie felt as if she were transparent, like one of those jellyfish, an undifferentiated ooze of clear membrane you could see the whole of the ocean through.

"I'm going now," she said, making herself sound as stubborn as she could. As righteous. "I can see I won't get anyplace around here. None of you people is going to listen to me."

"We've been listening to you," Eamon Donleavy said.

Rosalie advanced toward the door, steadily, not altering her pace. People moved away as she came, still silent, still watching. This was impossible. She stopped at the door and turned back to look at them all.

"You won't be able to go on with this forever, you know. You won't be able to get away with it. My grandfather was murdered and he was a very rich man. We won't let you hide his murderer and mess the rest of us up. We won't let you."

What was she talking about? The hall behind her was clear. God only knew where all the people had gone. Michael was staring at her, impassive. He was always so damned impassive. Her head was about to explode. She should have eaten something this morning. She wanted to heave and she hated doing that with nothing in her stomach. She wanted to run.

Actually, running was the easy part. The way was clear. The front door was right in her line of sight and temporarily clear of traffic.

Rosalie took one more look at Michael Pride's face, and then took off.

3

Robbie Yagger was standing right next to the Sojourner Truth Health Center's front door when Rosalie van Straadt came running out. As soon as she burst through the doors, he stood up a little straighter and stared, hard. She looked a little familiar, but not familiar enough. And she was nothing at all like that girl he had seen the night it all happened. Robbie had very distinct memories of the night it had all happened, the night of the gang war shoot-out and the newspaper stories about Dr. Pride and the murder of Charles van Straadt. He woke up in the night sometimes, imagining himself walking through the corridors around the emergency room, looking in at bleeding people and wondering what he thought he was doing there. That was when he had seen the girl, or woman, or whatever she was. It was so hard to know what to call female people anymore. It was so hard to know anything.

Robbie Yagger was smoking a cigarette when Rosalie van Straadt came out. He had his sign leaning up against the handrail of the stoop and his hand cupped around the lit end of his butt. The wind was the same as always up here, meaning ferocious. His cigarette always seemed to burn down to the filter too fast. He took a drag, blew out

smoke, took another drag. He looked at the doors of the
center and wondered what he should do.

Robbie Yagger might not be very bright, but he was
honest, painfully honest, and he always had been. In the
two weeks since Charles van Straadt had been murdered,
he had been feeling unrelievedly guilty. He *had* been in
the center, that night, after all. He *had* been wandering
in and out of the rooms on the first floor. He had—well,
seen things, maybe. The problem was, he wasn't sure
what it was he had seen, or if it was important, or what
would happen to him if he told the police or anybody
else official about it. He'd said so many things about the
center and the abortions that went on there and about
Dr. Pride. The man who was killed was the center's big-
gest benefactor. Maybe the police would think that
Robbie had killed Charles van Straadt himself, to stop
the van Straadt money from going to abortions. Maybe
they would think Robbie was the kind of suspect they
would really like to have, meaning somebody not very
important, somebody expendable. Robbie Yagger always
felt expendable.

He finished his cigarette and picked up his sign
again. It felt futile, carrying it back and forth when nobody came up here except the center's clients and half of
them couldn't read English. More than half of them
couldn't read.

I'm going to have to do something about this, Robbie
told himself, shouldering his sign bravely, beginning to
pace back and forth in front of the center's front door in
the wind.

I'm going to have to think of some way to tell somebody what it was I saw.

F·O·U·R

1

Gregor Demarkian had always had the cooperation of the local police in his investigations of what he thought of as extracurricular murders. He had always had it in his investigations with the FBI, too. He preferred to run his life that way. Cooperating with the local police had advantages beyond the obvious one, meaning aside from the fact that it kept you from getting arrested for one reason or another. There was the question of feasibility. The Cardinal Archbishop of New York was a good source. He had come through with copies of all the police lab reports. Gregor didn't know how he'd gotten them. He wasn't going to ask. They were both helpful and necessary. They just weren't enough. He would have given a great deal to be able to sit down with the technicians or the medical examiner (was it a coroner in New York City?) and go over the details, especially after everything he had heard today on the subject of where the strychnine had been and what it had taken to get to it. Then there was the question of information. Gregor already had a lot of information about this case, but all of it was from secondary sources. He had read the Cardinal's report. He had read a slew of magazine and newspaper articles, pulled together from a two-day search of the reading room of the downtown branch of the Philadelphia Public Library, both on the murder itself and on Charles van Straadt. He had been able to find much more on Charles van Straadt than on van Straadt's murder, in spite of the fact that the death of a man that rich was always international news. Reporters didn't know what questions to ask. They thought in terms of headlines instead of solutions. Standing in the middle of Michael Pride's first floor examining room-office, Gregor thought that they weren't even very good at thinking in headlines. Rosalie van Straadt was the murdered man's granddaughter. She was obviously extremely upset about something. There hadn't been a word of what she might be upset about in any of the press reports Gregor had read.

There was a frozen moment after Rosalie left the room, but it was only a pause for breath. The red sweatsuited nun exploded almost immediately.

"That woman," she said. Then she spun around and looked into the crowd. "Sister Karen Ann? Get a broom, Sister, and get Mindy and Steven and clean this mess up. You're going to have to go somewhere else for the next hour or two, Michael. I'm very sorry. All the rest of you get out of here. Out of here. You'd think you'd never seen blood on the floor, the way you rubberneck."

There was no blood on the floor, but Gregor wasn't going to be picky. He started to drift out at the back of the crowd. The crowd was dispersing with uncanny quickness and unnatural quiet. That's what the authority of a real old-fashioned nun could do, sweatsuit or no sweatsuit. Gregor supposed they'd all start gossiping like crazy as soon as they got out of Augie's earshot.

"Wait a minute," Augie said, when Gregor was almost

out the door. "Mr. Demarkian. Don't disappear on us now. We need you."

"Augie," Michael Pride said in a warning voice.

"We do need him," Augie said stubbornly, picking her way across the rubble to where Gregor was standing. "What's the point of the Cardinal having brought him if we're not going to talk to him?"

"I didn't say you shouldn't talk to him," Michael said calmly. "I just meant—"

"I know what you meant." Augie turned to Gregor and sighed. "He feels sorry for her. For Rosalie van Straadt. He thinks she only does these things because she's pining for love for him."

"Now Augie."

"It's true. Well, Mr. Demarkian. You tell me. Would she be behaving the way she has been only since the murder if she's doing it because she's pining for love for Michael? Why wouldn't she have been behaving this way before the murder? She couldn't have had him then any more than she can have him now."

"Augie," Michael said again. He had managed to make his way back to the door from the desk. Three people—two young women, neither of whom looked anything like a nun to Gregor, and a teenage boy—were just coming in with brooms and brushes and one of those gray metal dustpans on the end of the handle all janitors everywhere seemed to have. Michael moved out into the hall and pulled Gregor and Augie with him. There was an empty office next to his own and he drew them into that. Then he shut the door.

"Let's at least not broadcast this to the entire center," he said. "After all, it isn't any of their business."

"The man was murdered in your own office, Michael.

Of course this is our business. And it isn't like it's any big secret around here anyway."

"It isn't like it's a fact, either, Augie. It was just a rumor."

"I believe in rumors," Sister Augustine said. She crossed her arms over her chest and set her jaw and turned to Gregor. For an hallucinatory moment, Gregor thought she was going to lecture him on how he shouldn't bite his nails. He hadn't bitten his nails since he was ten. That was the year his mother was so sick, and there wasn't enough money for a doctor.

"Let me tell you what the rumors have been, Mr. Demarkian, because they've been very interesting. Charles van Straadt left a lot of money, you know."

"Close to a billion dollars," Gregor said. "I read that somewhere."

Augie waved it away. "The billion is a total figure. Most of that's the businesses and whatever. It doesn't come directly to the family. It's tied up in corporations and I don't know what. He's supposed to have left nearly eight hundred million dollars in personal assets. That's the money I'm talking about."

"That is a lot of money," Gregor said.

"You don't know how much money it is," Michael put in, "because the will isn't being read until Thursday and nothing is official until then."

Augie sighed. "I got my information from Ida, Michael. Ida is perfectly trustworthy." She turned to Gregor again. "Ida is Ida Greel, another of Charlie van Straadt's grandchildren. Oh, I shouldn't go on calling him Charlie. He hated it. Anyway, Char—Charles had four grandchildren. Rosalie you just met. In a manner of speaking. Ida is a medical student who works here on her free time, vacations and weekends, that sort of thing, as much as she can while she's studying. Then there's Ida's brother, Victor. Victor calls himself van Straadt and works at the New York *Sentinel*. Then there's Martha, who's a little older than Ida but she's volunteering here in our two-year resident staff program. All Charles's grandchildren volunteered like that, he required it. Even Rosalie was here for two years."

"We could have done without Rosalie," Michael said.

Augie sailed on. "It was Ida who told me how much money there was supposed to be," she explained, "and she told me something else, too. What I call the interesting part. On the night Charles van Straadt died, he had just made up his mind to change his will."

"Augie, for God's sake," Michael said. "You sound like *Murder, She Wrote*."

"Why shouldn't I sound like *Murder, She Wrote*? It's all true. On the night Charles van Straadt died, his old will was still in force. That will left his personal fortune to be divided into equal shares among his four grandchildren. Victor, Ida, Martha, and Rosalie. If Charles had lived another twenty-four hours, that would have been changed. There would have been small bequests to Ida and Victor and Martha, but the bulk of the money would have gone to Rosalie. And Rosalie knows it. That's why she's fit to spit."

Gregor thought about this. About Rosalie throwing glass. About a rich man playing favorites. He wished he had known Charles van Straadt. For some reason, this scenario didn't ring true.

"Why?" he asked finally.

"Why what?" Augie looked as confused as Gregor felt.

"Why Rosalie? Why not one of the others? Are the others even less stable?"

"Hardly," Augie said. "Ida's the stable one. She's the only one with the brains God gave an amoeba."

"Then why would Charles van Straadt want to leave the bulk of his fortune to Rosalie?"

"That's exactly what I was always asking," Michael put in. "This rumor has been going around for weeks, Mr. Demarkian, since long before Charlie died, and now that Ida has confirmed it, I suppose it must be true. But it never made sense to me. Not that Charlie ever made sense to me in any respect."

Augie dismissed sense. "Rich men can be as crazy as loons and nobody thinks anything of it. Charles van Straadt took Rosalie with him everywhere, Mr. Demarkian. For the last six months or so, they've been attached at the hip. And Rosalie worked for him, of course, as a kind of personal secretary."

"She shuffled his papers around and got him coffee when he didn't want to move," Michael corrected. "I always used to think she exasperated him beyond words, but maybe that was because she exasperated me. The fake beatnik clothes and all the pretensions."

"She was here on the night her grandfather died," Gregor remembered. "That was in the report the Cardinal gave me. If she was attached to her grandfather's hip, as you put it, where was she while he was in the middle of being murdered? She wasn't even the one who found the body."

"I found the body," Michael said.

"Maybe saying they were attached at the hip was going too far," Augie conceded. "They were always together, but Rosalie would run errands for Charles. It's just like Michael said. She was all over the place the night her grandfather died. I kept bumping into her in the most outrageous places."

"Only authorized personnel are supposed to be in the emergency-room examining areas during major emergencies," Michael explained, "along with the patients, of course. I don't know if anybody's told you, but we were in the middle of a major battle in a major gang war that night. Not that Rosalie ever paid much attention to the rules."

"Rosalie likes to pretend she doesn't pay much attention to the rules," Augie corrected, "but she's not anywhere near as unconventional as she wants people to think she is."

"The problem is, I don't see what good it's going to do us if Rosalie was prowling through the building in the middle of a gang war while her grandfather was being killed, because although that gives her plenty of opportunity to do absolutely anything, there's still the question of why she would have wanted to do anything at all." Michael looked triumphant. "After all, Mr. Demarkian, if you were Rosalie, and all you had to do to inherit the bulk of eight hundred million dollars was to wait twenty-four hours before you committed murder, I ask you, wouldn't you wait?"

"Yes," Gregor said. "I most definitely would wait."

"So would I." Michael nodded happily. "And I'm willing to bet that neither one of us is anywhere near as venal as Rosalie. No, if it's one of the grandchildren who killed Charlie, it's much more likely to be one of the other three. The problem with that being that at least two of the three of them didn't have the opportunity to do it, and the third one didn't have the psychological—I don't know the word for what I want to say."

"I do," Augie said. "I think you're much too naive, Michael. I think Martha van Straadt is just as capable of murder as anybody else."

"Martha's name used to be Bracker," Michael told Gregor. "She changed her name to van Straadt as soon as her father died. She's like Victor in that respect. The old man asked. The old man got. Ida's the only one who wouldn't budge. Victor's got a spine like wet spaghetti."

"Rosalie was born a van Straadt?" Gregor asked.

"Oh, yes," Augie said. "Rosalie's father was Charles's only son. He was dead before I ever came here— Rosalie's father, I mean—but I've heard about him. One of those cases, you know, where the father is such a strong personality the son just wilts. He drank, from what I heard."

"Never mind all that," Michael said. "Ida was on duty that night. We had her running all over the place from six o'clock on. I think she took a fifteen-minute break to get some coffee, but that was it. She didn't have time to murder anyone. She certainly didn't have time to get my keys, get the strychnine out of my cabinet, go upstairs— all of that. And as for Victor, he was sitting in full view of fifty people in the center cafeteria from about seven or so, and before that he was either at work, in his car with his driver, or over in the other building visiting with Martha."

"Ida says they meant to sit down and talk about the will change," Augie said. "They couldn't know there was going to be a gang war. And Victor never listens to anything on the radio except the all-music stations and he never reads the newspapers at all, so—" Augie shrugged.

"No matter what Augie here says, I don't think Martha could have done it." Michael was firm. "Martha's an extremely unpleasant young woman in many ways, but she's one of those people who writes angry letters to the president of the United States because she thinks the air force training exercises are disturbing the sleep of the spotted owl. I know animals rights activists have been known to resort to violence more than occasionally, but Martha—" Michael Pride shrugged.

"I think this is exactly Martha's kind of murder," Augie argued. "Put the strychnine in the coffee. Hand the coffee to grandfather. Get the hell out of there before he takes a sip of it. That's the way Martha would go about it. So that she didn't have to look."

"Augie, I think in the old days, when they still had chapter of faults, you must have spent your time declaring faults against charity."

"Oh, charity," Augie said.

The red light over the top of the door to the hall went on and a low bonging sound began to come through the loudspeakers.

"That's a delivery." Augie straightened up a little. "Who's on call this afternoon, Michael? Jenny or Ben?"

"I am," Michael told her. "Jenny needed the afternoon off. It's the only time they could give her to go in for her mammogram. Go on out. I'll be with you in a minute."

"Don't you let him hand you any romantic nonsense," Augie told Gregor. "He's much too trusting."

"I'm going to ask him if he knows anybody who would be willing to donate us a mammogram machine. We sure as hell could use one."

"Don't use the word *hell* like that, Michael. It doesn't shock me."

The two men watched the small, round woman leave. Gregor caught an expression of honest affection on Michael Pride's face. It was—endearing, somehow. It made Michael Pride more human than Gregor had found him to be so far.

"Look," Michael Pride said, when Augie was gone.

"I've got work here to do for the rest of the afternoon, but Jenny will be back at six. I'll have at least a couple of hours then. Why don't you meet me downstairs in the cafeteria and we'll have dinner? There are some things you ought to know nobody else is going to tell you."

"Does everybody around here keep secrets as a matter of course?"

"About me they do. Cafeteria at six?"

"How about the Four Seasons at seven?" Gregor asked.

Michael Pride laughed. "The Four Seasons. For God's sake. Not only can't I afford it, I can't even afford to think about it."

"I can. I'll buy."

"That'll come to three or four hundred dollars. Why don't you just donate that money to the center?"

"The center doesn't take credit cards."

Michael Pride laughed again. "You're right. We don't. All right, Mr. Demarkian. The Four Seasons. Seven o'clock. I'll be there. But now I've got to go."

Michael Pride went.

2

Late afternoon is not a busy time in big-city emergency rooms, except for unexpected infant deliveries and household accidents. When Gregor left the office in which he had spent so much time with Michael Pride and Sister Augustine, he found the corridors mostly clear and the atmosphere quiet. Whatever emergency the doctor and nurse had been called to was evidently under control. Gregor stopped a young black girl in a candystriper's uniform and asked for directions to the cafeteria. She gave them in a clear sharp voice with no trace of a New York City accent in it. Gregor introduced himself and thanked her.

"Tell me a couple of more things," he said. "Do you have a minute?"

"I have a minute, yes."

"There are elevators here, aren't there?"

"One at the front and one at the back."

"Where do they go? I take it I can't use one to get to the basement, for instance. Otherwise you would have told me to take one to get to the cafeteria."

The girl had been looking confused. Now her face cleared. "Oh, these aren't ordinary elevators, Mr. Demarkian. They're extra wide ones, for stretchers. They only go from here to the second floor, where the wards are. We don't have much in the way of wards. We're very small."

"I couldn't use these to get up to the third floor offices, for instance?"

"Oh, no. You'd have to take the stairs."

"Thank you," Gregor said.

The girl said "you're welcome" in her clear, firm voice and continued toward the front of the building, where she'd been headed when Gregor stopped her. Gregor followed her directions and made his way to the basement and the cafeteria. It was an involved and frustrating walk. If he had known what he was doing, it wouldn't have been so involved. Most of his feelings of confusion came from the fact that he was in unfamiliar territory. The frustration, he thought, would have been with him no matter what. This building had not been built to serve as a hospital. It had been renovated as well as it could be, but renovations always left something to be desired. What these renovations hadn't managed to accomplish was an adequate amount of storage space. Gregor kept bumping into packing boxes and newly delivered crates. On a hunch, Gregor began to read the descriptions on the outsides of the boxes. It was a useless hunch. The boxes said things like "500 rolls sterile adhesive tape" and "15 lb sterile cotton net." Nothing had been left lying around that could be even imagined to be dangerous. Gregor supposed that if a murderer were really determined, he might be able to use a length of sterile cotton net to strangle someone, but that was pushing it. Gregor missed Bennis Hannaford. Bennis was very good at pushing it.

Gregor got down to the basement and looked around. The way the stairwell was positioned next to the cafeteria doors, it looked as if the cafeteria took up almost every square foot on this level, with just a small cushion of space for men's and ladies' rooms and for the stairwell and entryway. Gregor knew that couldn't be right. There had to be storage space down here, too. He wondered how you got to it.

He went into the cafeteria and looked around. It was standard hospital issue, small but otherwise indistinguishable from its counterparts at every hospital in every city in the United States. There was a food service line with silverware and paper napkins at one end, everything from evil-looking fruit in gelatin-molds to wilted-skinned chicken legs to cardboard apple pie in the middle, and packets of Sweet'n Low and pats of butter near the cash register. The shelf made of stainless-steel tubing to push your tray along on, so that you didn't accidentally drop it, even though four or five people a year would drop their trays anyway. There was a ferocious looking woman in a cap and apron standing at the cash register, looking bored while a shriveled young man counted pennies to pay for his coffee. The young man looked decidedly down at heel, and ashamed of it, too. It was the shame that piqued Gregor's interest. This was Harlem, and the young man was not only white but practically Nordic. He had none of the casual assumption of belonging that would have marked him as a center volunteer. He didn't look sick, except in the sense that he looked hungry. Gregor put a Danish on his tray and moved up the line. That was when he saw that the young man had more than coffee. He had a jelly doughnut on a round paper plate. While Gregor watched, he counted his change twice, sighed, and then put the doughnut on the stainless-steel counter next to the Sweet'n Low. The woman at the cash register looked bored.

"If you're not going to take the doughnut," she said, "you ought to put back the doughnut."

"Right," the young man said.

Gregor was still coming up behind him, but the young man didn't notice. His face was bright red. Shame was too calm a word to put on what he was feeling. This was a form of agony. The young man had the paper plate with the doughnut on it in his hand. It was a small enough doughnut, oozing jelly at one end. Under the cover of slightly lowered lashes, the young man was eyeing it with desperation. It hurt Gregor just to look at him.

"Stop," he said, when the young man reached him. "Turn around."

The young man looked up and blinked. "Excuse me. I have to put this doughnut back."

"Never mind. Go back to the cash register. I'll buy you a doughnut and a cup of coffee. I'll buy you two doughnuts."

"Oh." The young man blushed harder. And harder. Gregor thought the color in his face was going to go right off the red spectrum into orange. "Oh," the young man said again. "Thank you. But I can't. I really can't. I mean, I'm not hungry."

"Take three doughnuts," Gregor said. "Never mind the doughnuts. Eat lunch."

"Oh," the young man said. "But—"

"Chicken or roast beef?"

"Chicken. I mean—"

"The gentleman wants chicken," Gregor said to the girl behind the counter.

Down at the cash register, the old woman snorted. "I don't know what you're helping him out for," she said. "He doesn't help us out any. He's been working overtime for months now, trying to get us shut down."

"That's not true," the young man said quickly.

"Keep the doughnut," Gregor told him. "What kind of potatoes do you want?"

"Fried." The young man was looking dazed.

"Take a couple of desserts, too."

The girl serving main dishes was smiling pleasantly, but the woman at the cash register was scowling more fiercely than ever. Gregor went up to her and took out his wallet.

"How much do I owe you?" he asked her.

"You ask me, you owe me a lot more than you're gonna be able to pay me. Pro-life, that asshole calls himself. Pro-himself is what I say. He's just after the publicity."

"What publicity?" Gregor asked.

The young man came up to the cash register with two pieces of chocolate layer cake as well as the rest of the food. Gregor was glad he had finally gotten into the spirit of the thing.

"There isn't any publicity," the young man said sadly.

"Nobody ever notices me out there. I picket this place. With a sign."

"A sign about what?" Gregor asked.

"About the abortions they do here. I don't know if you knew they did that. I mean, you probably did. But I picket about it anyway."

"Because you're opposed to abortion," Gregor said.

"What? Yeah. Yeah. It's more complicated than that. Thank you for all this. I don't even know who you are. I'm Robbie Yagger."

"I'm Gregor Demarkian. What do you mean when you say you picket this place? You mean you walk up and down in front of it?"

"All the time," the woman at the cash register said. "Day and night."

"Were you picketing here the night Charles van Straadt died?"

Robbie Yagger nodded. "Oh, yeah. Except, I don't think of it like that. I think of it as the night they had the war uptown. That brought lots of people here who aren't here usually. People who aren't already used to my sign."

"Were you picketing here between six and eight?"

"You mean when the murder happened," Robbie Yagger said. "I was around then, but I wasn't always picketing. I came in here and had a cup of coffee sometime between seven and eight o'clock. I don't remember exactly when."

"That's very interesting," Gregor Demarkian said.

"Fourteen seventeen," the woman at the cash register said.

Gregor gave her a twenty. "Would you mind having lunch with me?" he asked Robbie Yagger. "I mean, I'm only going to have this cup of coffee, but do you mind if

I join you while you're eating? You may be able to tell me something I need to know."

Robbie looked down at his full tray of food and shook his head. "I'll tell you anything you want. I haven't been able to eat like this for months."

Gregor's private opinion was that Robbie Yagger probably hadn't been eating too well before that, either, but he had to save a little of the young man's pride. Nobody ever needed pride so badly as when he was down and out.

F·I·V·E

1

For Martha van Straadt, volunteering at the Sojourner Truth Health Center was a kind of torture. The fact that it was torture she had chosen to experience, for money, didn't help any. She might have done all right if she had been assigned to some impersonal medical service. She could have survived a couple of years of cleaning bedpans or setting up lunch trays without too much mental anguish. Instead, she had been handed over to the Sisters and put to work in the Afterschool Program, day care for children in the first through fourth or fifth through eighth grades. Martha had first to fourth, along with Sister Edna and a young woman named Kerri Stahl who was studying education at SUNY Buffalo and thinking of opening a day-care center of her own when she got through. Martha wasn't too happy with Sister Edna and she couldn't abide Kerri Stahl—but she truly hated the children. The children were a nightmare come to life. Today they were making Father's Day cards and posters—except they weren't, exactly, because Father's Day didn't mean anything to most of them, they didn't have fathers. Martha had attended a very expensive college with a ferocious speech code that had effectively prevented the discussion of real life in any of its myriad forms as it existed outside of college dormitories. She had been convinced by a parade of right-thinking sociology professors that the only reason some people said that the fatherlessness of the ghetto family was a problem was racist propaganda, and sexist, too, because what difference did fathers make? Now here she was. She didn't know a single child with both a mother and a father in the house—or even a mother and a stepfather. And fathers might not matter in the long run, but in the short run the children certainly thought they did. It was crazy. It made Martha's head ache just to think about it. It made Martha want to cry every time she turned off the light in her room upstairs. She wanted desperately to be downtown in her apartment, taking a shower in the walk-in stall lined with periwinkle blue ceramic tiles, lying down in the queen-size bed under four down comforters. She wanted to be sitting in Serendipity and eating cheesecake Vesuvius. She wanted a nice, sensible job in a bookstore or an art gallery or an Off-Off Broadway theater, where she would meet only the kind of people she liked.

Now she picked up the big box of crayons Sister Edna had sent her in to the storehouse to get—there were only used crayons at the center; schools and church groups donated them when they were half their original size and embedded with flecks of dust and sand—and went back out into the play area, where a little clutch of girls was lying on the floor, drawing something that made them giggle that they wouldn't show anyone else. Martha made a face at them—first to fourth grade didn't matter; Martha knew what they were drawing; it had something to do with sex—and went across the room to where Sister was sitting at an old-fashioned teacher's desk. Sister

Edna was a tiny woman in her early sixties who wore more of a habit than any other nun at the center except Sister Kenna. Sister Edna was some kind of Dominican and had a white dress with long white flaps to the front and back and a black veil. Martha didn't like nuns any more than she liked anyone else at the center. They gave her the creeps.

Martha put the box of crayons down on Sister's desk.

"Here they are," she said. "Are you going to need me for the next five minutes?"

"I always need you," Sister Edna said, imperturbable. "Where do you want to go?"

"I want to run down and get myself a cup of coffee. I didn't get much sleep last night."

"Coffee."

"Yes, Sister."

"You should make a point of getting to sleep on the nights before you're on duty here. You're expected to be here when you're on duty here."

"Yes, Sister."

"This isn't a hobby, you know. This is a desperate necessity in the lives of these children."

"Yes, Sister."

"This is a desperate necessity in the lives of these children's parents, too. Are you sure you need this coffee?"

"Yes, Sister."

"Well, go get it, then. But hurry along. We're understaffed even when you're here."

Martha was going to say "yes, Sister" one more time, but she didn't. Nuns didn't just give her the creeps. She hated them. They made her feel as if she were ten years old again. Who was Sister Edna to tell her when she couldn't get a cup of coffee and when she could? Who

were any of these people? This wasn't some job Martha
had taken to pay the rent or further her own career. She
got paid room and board and a dollar a week. It was a
charity she was doing. She wouldn't be doing it much
longer. If it had been up to Martha, she would have
handed in her resignation to the center the day after
Grandfather was found dead in Michael Pride's office.
With Grandfather dead, there was no reason for her to
suffer under this nonsense anymore. It was Ida who had
convinced her to stay. How would it look? Ida had said,
and Martha had had to concede the point. If Martha up
and quit right after the death, the police *might* think it
was because she suspected Michael Pride and didn't
want to be around him. Then again, they might think it
was because she was guilty herself and wanted to be
away from the scene. There was no way to tell which
way the police would jump. Martha didn't want to pit
herself against Michael Pride. In the city of New York,
Michael Pride was a secular saint.

The Afterschool Program was held in the east building. Martha didn't like to cross to the west building over
the bridge because she didn't like to look at the day-care
children any more than she liked looking at the children
she was supposed to be caring for herself. She didn't like
to cross the bridge in the dark because it was spooky. She
went down to the first floor of the east building and out
the front door. The street was absolutely empty and absolutely calm. Even the damn fool with the sign had disappeared. Martha went down the east building stoop,
along the sidewalk, and up the west building stoop. The
doors there were wide open as always. Sister Augustine
only deigned to close them when the wind chill got into
the negative figures. Martha said hi to the girl at the reception desk—the girl at the reception desk was always

some local teenager, fourteen years old and very pregnant—and went on to the back to the stairs that led to the cafeteria. She didn't really want a cup of coffee. She was only here because she wanted to make sure nobody saw her anywhere else and reported her whereabouts to Sister. Why did she care?

The cafeteria was almost empty. Sister Kenna and Sister Clarice were sitting together at a table in the far corner, eating coffee and chocolate cake. Nuns ate so many sweets. Julie Enderson was sitting by herself in a table near the cash register, drinking a glass of milk and reading a thick textbook that was making her frown. Shana Malvera was sitting by herself, too, looking over a copy of the New York *Sentinel* she didn't seem to be very interested in and glancing up every once in a while to see who else had come in. Martha caught her eye and waved. Shana waved back. Martha got herself a cup of coffee, paid for it and went to sit with Shana. On her way she passed the only other table in the room that was occupied, taken up by a tall, muscular, well-padded man in a good suit and a red sweater—and the Eternal Protester, Robbie what's-his-name. Martha wondered who the well-dressed man was. The chief lawyer in charge of Right to Life Vigilantes, Inc. The president of Keep Women Down Unlimited. Somebody. Martha knew good tailoring when she saw it.

Martha put her coffee down at Shana's table and sat. "Who's the man with Robbie the Ridiculous?" she asked. "He looks like a recruiting officer for the FBI."

Shana Malvera giggled. Shana Malvera always giggled. She always rolled her eyes. She always shook her head. She always shrugged her shoulders. Shana Malvera was never still. At the age of five, it had been cute. At the age of forty-five, it was intensely annoying. People put up with it because Shana always knew everything. Shana was a one-woman compendium of gossip.

"FBI is exactly it," she now told Martha. "I'd have thought you'd know. It's all because of your grandfather that he's here. Gregor Demarkian, I mean."

"Gregor Demarkian?" The name was vaguely familiar. "He's from the FBI?"

"No, no." Shana's head-shaking was so vigorous, her eyes looked as if they were going to pop out. "He used to be with the FBI. He used to chase serial killers. You know. Like Jeffrey Dahmer. Except he's really old. I don't think he chased Dahmer himself. No, he's some kind of private detective now. The Cardinal called him in. Don't you remember all that fuss a little while ago when Donald McAdam died?"

Martha certainly did remember "all the fuss" when Donald McAdam died. There had been a lot of it. In the first place, Donald McAdam had been the lynchpin of a federal insider trading case that had touched every important financial firm on Wall Street. In the second place, he'd gone right out a penthouse apartment window onto Fifth Avenue in the Fifties.

"What did this Gregor Demarkian have to do with Donald McAdam?" Martha asked.

"He solved the case," Shana said, obviously surprised Martha didn't know. "Not right away, you know, but later, on that boat Jonathan Baird owned. I'd think your grandfather would have known Jonathan Baird."

"Maybe he did. He knew Donald McAdam."

"Well, from what I hear, the Cardinal is going crazy. With the murder being unsolved and all. So he's called in this Demarkian person to clear it up. The police are supposed to be just livid."

"I wonder what he's talking to Robbie the Ridiculous for."

"Maybe Robbie saw something pacing back and forth with his sign like that. Maybe he saw somebody come in or somebody go out. Or maybe he saw something inside the center itself. He was inside that night, you know."

"No, I didn't know."

Shana was nodding this time. It was just as violent as everything else she did. "Oh, yes. I gave him directions to the cafeteria myself. He was lost up on the first floor. It was the first time he'd come in."

"I'm surprised he does come in," Martha said. "Considering."

"Oh, Martha. He's harmless enough. He's just one person by himself and he isn't the kind who does dangerous stuff like unplug things. And he's so sad. Anyway. I found him upstairs by the examining rooms looking perfectly ready to panic, and I told him the way down here."

"And he's been coming down here ever since," Martha said musingly.

"Mmm hmm." Shana sounded happy. "You know, Martha, I don't think he's really serious about all this pro-life business. I don't think he's real about it, you know, the way somebody like the Cardinal is, or that woman who went to jail for five years because she wouldn't give her name at her trespassing trial or whatever it was down in Florida. I think he's just—lonely."

"Lonely," Martha repeated, shocked. "Shana, what are you talking about? The man's outside our doors with a picket sign twenty-four hours a day. I don't think he sleeps."

"He does. He goes away at midnight and comes back at six. I heard somebody say he lives in Brooklyn or Queens or somewhere."

"The Holly Hill Christian Fellowship. In Queens."

"Whatever. Do you think if he had a family that loved him he'd be here like this all the time? At least he wouldn't be alone. His wife would come with him once in a while."

"Maybe his wife has to stay home taking care of their seven children."

"If he had seven children he wouldn't be able to picket." Shana was definite. "No matter how bad the economy was, he'd have to find work doing something, like working in Burger King or picking up deposit bottles or even dealing dope. Trust me. He's all alone in the world."

"And you're going to make it all better?"

"I just thought I'd start talking to him, that was all. See what he's like. If he isn't too crazy, maybe there's something around here he could do."

"What? Lecture some eleven-year-old who's been knocked up by her mother's boyfriend that she'll burn in hell forever if she terminates her pregnancy? Maybe he could do double-duty by lecturing her mother on how the best thing would be to marry the boyfriend and save his soul by turning into a submissive wife."

"Oh, Martha, for God's sake. You're just so extreme. You can't listen to reason."

"Right," Martha said, glad her coffee was finished. She looked at Robbie and Gregor Demarkian again. Gregor Demarkian was bent over the table, listening intently. Robbie was wolfing down enough food for at least three people. "I don't think your precious Robbie is lonely now. Just look at him. He's got a friend in the Cardinal's detective."

"Oh, Martha," Shana said again.

Martha stood up and picked up her empty coffee cup.

It was made of that white spongy plastic material that everybody called Styrofoam, but that wasn't really Styrofoam. Martha could never remember what it was really called. Whatever it was, it was terrible for the environment. The center used it because they didn't have enough money to hire dishwashers and bus people to look after stoneware and glass.

"I've got to go," Martha said. "Sister Edna is probably having a fit. I'll see you later."

"Okay," Shana said.

"I'm supposed to be on duty at the Afterschool Program."

Shana looked shocked. Like everybody else at the center—except Martha, who was forced to be here—Shana could no more imagine stepping out for a cup of coffee when she was supposed to be on duty than she could imagine not giving the benefit of the doubt to idiots like Robbie. As far as Martha could tell, Shana didn't disapprove of the attitude Martha took to her work. Shana didn't believe it.

Martha went to the doors of the cafeteria and stopped. She turned around and looked back. Gregor Demarkian was still hunched over his table, listening to Robbie the Ridiculous. Maybe Shana was right. Maybe Robbie had seen something the night Charles van Straadt was killed. Maybe he had something very important to say that the police hadn't bothered to listen to. The police were so stupid. Then there was all that about Robbie actually being inside the Center on the night it had all happened. Yes, there was that.

Sister Edna was probably sitting over in the east building, ready to commit bodily mayhem as soon as Martha walked through the door—but Martha didn't care. This was too crucial. They had to be so careful about everything these days.

She rummaged through the pockets of her jumper, came up with a quarter, and headed for the phones.

Victor wasn't much of a solace. He didn't have the brains to wear a hat in the rain. Still, he was all she had.

And if Robbie the Ridiculous really had seen something, if he really did know something—well, they'd all have to get moving.

2

The picture was a mishandled Polaroid snapshot, made up of colors that were faded in places and overbright in others, taken in light so bright it made all the faces look washed out. According to Eamon Donleavy's informant, it had been taken the night before at the Getting Bent, an establishment on West Forty-third Street that billed itself as "a multimedia relaxation station." Eamon Donleavy had never been inside the Getting Bent, but he had heard about it. It wasn't a fly-by-night operation and it wasn't low rent. It wasn't cheap, either. Eamon wondered how Michael had ended up there. Michael might be no saint, as he always insisted—and as pictures like these seemed invented to prove—but he was an obsessive about money. Michael spent enough on himself to stay alive, and that was it. He would never have forked over the fifty-dollar cover for a night in the Getting Bent. Somebody must have forked it over for him.

Eamon Donleavy had received the picture at ten forty-five this morning. He had put it down on his desk next to the Happy Father's Day poster the children in his

First Communion class had made for him. Sister Margarita Rose had insisted on his taking the poster, because
he was the children's "spiritual father" and most of them
didn't have one of the other kind. This gave them a way
to participate in the holiday. Eamon wondered wearily
why they wanted to. Old Charlie van Straadt had been a
father and a grandfather, too, and as far as Eamon could
see, all it had gotten him was dead.

That's not fair, Eamon told himself. You don't know
that one of his grandchildren killed him. You just want to
think one of them did.

It was almost three o'clock in the afternoon. Eamon
had been down to the station to pick up Gregor
Demarkian and back again. He had been sitting at his
desk like this since he'd left Michael's first-floor office after Rosalie van Straadt had her fit. He had not been
happy then and he was not happy now. He had taken the
picture with him when he left the office to meet
Demarkian. He had put it in the back of his very thin
wallet and the wallet in the front pocket of his pants. He
had only taken the picture out again when he knew he
would be able to sit at his desk for a good long time.
None of these precautions made sense. If this picture existed, so did others. There was no way around that. He
wondered who had the other pictures. He wondered if
that person knew what he had. He wondered when the
pictures would surface.

He heard the sound of steps on the stairs and sat up
a little straighter. He had been hearing sounds on the
steps for the past hour, but always been disappointed.
The steps had reached this landing and gone on. Nobody
had even stopped in to say hello.

These new steps reached this landing and stopped.

Whoever was walking was also whistling. Eamon Donleavy stood up.

"Eamon, you in?" Michael called out.

"I'm in." Eamon picked up the picture and put it in the pocket of his jacket.

Michael reached the door of his own office and waved to Eamon across the hall. Michael's door was propped open with a rubber doorstop and he left it that way. Eamon walked across the hall and stood in the open doorway.

"Hi," Eamon said. "You got a minute?"

"Just about one," Michael told him. "I'm on duty in Emergency. Jenny needed the afternoon off."

"This will only take one. I've got something to show you."

Eamon put his hand in his pocket, got hold of the picture, took it out. He handed it over and waited. He wondered what he was waiting for. Michael looked at the image of himself for a long time, but he showed no reaction. He just handed that picture back.

"So, Eamon," he said. "What are you going to do with that? Keep it as a souvenir?"

"I'm going to burn it, of course. What did you think I was going to do with it?"

"If you're going to burn it, you'd better do it soon. We wouldn't want something like that to go wandering around the center."

"Fortunately, it's too raw to end up on the cover of the New York *Post*. Michael, for God's sake—literally, for God's sake, for your sake, for anybody's sake—Michael what do you think you're doing?"

"Eamon, for God's sake yourself. Take a good look at that picture of yours. It's perfectly obvious what I'm doing."

"Thanks a lot, Michael. Thanks a lot."

Michael's chair was pulled far away from his desk, almost to the back wall of the office. Michael pulled it in close again and sat down, putting his elbows on the pile of papers on his desktop, putting his head on his hands. Eamon thought he looked tired, but Michael always looked tired. Michael had been born tired. What was it all supposed to mean?

Michael sat back, ran his hands through his hair, looked away, looked at Eamon again, put his chin on his hands again. He was uncomfortable.

"Look," he said, "Eamon. Believe it or not, I don't do this stuff just to make you crazy."

"I know that. But Michael, no matter why you're doing it, if you keep on doing it, you're going to make yourself sick. Very sick. It's a miracle you aren't sick already. Never mind the rest of it. Like Gregor Demarkian. Like Charles van Straadt's corpse. Like the fact that if you had been any other human being in this city, the police would have booked you two weeks ago."

"I didn't kill Charlie van Straadt, Eamon."

"I know you didn't. But the entire New York City homicide division thinks you did. They think Charlie was so disgusted at the things you were doing, he was going to withdraw funding for the center. Either that, or he was going to get the *Sentinel* to pull out all the stops, really run you ragged, and force you to quit."

"Charlie knew about all that before you did," Michael said. "He knew about it for years. He knew about a lot of it without asking. Charlie was a very interesting man, Eamon."

"Yeah, well. Anyone who starts in a tenement and ends up with a billion dollars is going to be interesting.

Anyone with a billion dollars is interesting. They can't avoid it."

"Maybe not. Tell me about this Demarkian person. Do you think he's intelligent?"

"Very. He makes me nervous."

"I'm going to have dinner with him tonight. At the Four Seasons restaurant. He's buying. It's been years since I was in the Four Seasons. Do you know what the Cardinal told him? Does the Cardinal think I killed Charlie van Straadt?"

Eamon considered this. "Yes," he said at last, "I think he does. I think the Cardinal is looking for a way to cover it up."

"That's interesting." Michael nodded. "Yes, I can see that. How does he explain it to himself?"

"He hasn't explained it to me," Eamon said, "but I'd guess it goes like this. Michael Pride is brilliant but obviously mentally unbalanced. Mental imbalance is the only way to explain his sexual behavior. Therefore—"

"A sin is not a sin without full knowledge and consent of the will," Michael recited. "Yes, I see. Well, if you ever get the chance, tell your Cardinal from me that if I had killed Charlie van Straadt, I would have done it quite deliberately. In spite of what may seem to be evidence to the contrary, I do not lose control of myself."

"You just lose control of your common sense." Eamon waved the picture in the air. "I don't think Gregor Demarkian would put up with it, by the way. If you were guilty. He'd find a way to hang you."

"We have capital punishment in New York State, but it's functionally inoperative. Governor Cuomo pardons everybody."

"You know what I mean, Michael. He's a dangerous

man, Gregor Demarkian. I'd be careful at that dinner of
yours."

"Don't worry. I will be. Do you think he'll end up
solving the crime, finding out who did it?"

"If they give him half a chance, yes," Eamon said.
"They could get in his way to the point where it would
be impossible."

"Who could?"

"The police. The Cardinal. Mostly the police. I think
he could get around an ordinary person."

"What about the family? They were barely cooperating with the police, the last I heard. I can't see them cooperating with some private detective hired by the
Cardinal."

"I don't think they will." Eamon shook his head.
"He's good, this Demarkian. I looked him up. He was
the one who solved the McAdam case. And the murder
of that psychotherapist or whatever he was out in Philadelphia. I don't think he needs a lot of cooperation, from
the family or anybody else."

Michael tilted his head. "What about you, Eamon?
Do you want this murder solved?"

"It depends."

"On what? Who did it?"

"Yes," Eamon said, feeling defiant. "On who did it. I
wouldn't want it to be solved if the murderer was you—"

"I told you—"

"—I know you did. I want it to be one of the family.
Good old grand patricide. I don't want it to be any of us."

"The rumor around the center is that the murderer is
Robbie Yagger. Do you know who I'm talking about? The
little man who carries the sign accusing us of being a
death camp for performing abortions."

Eamon shook his head. "I think that's ridiculous and

so do you. He isn't the type. And why would he want to kill Charlie van Straadt?"

Michael smiled. "Get rid of the head Satan and all the little Satans will wither on the vine."

"Ridiculous," Eamon said again. "You don't really believe that, do you, Michael? Who do you think did it?"

"I don't think anybody did it," Michael said firmly. "I spend my time convincing myself nobody could have done it, providing alibis for people, providing excuses. Don't ask me why."

"You're very good-natured."

"I don't have a good nature. And I've got other things on my mind. If you know what I mean. Eamon?"

All of a sudden, Eamon Donleavy didn't want to talk anymore. He didn't want to talk at all. He wanted to walk right out of Michael Pride's office and across the hall. He wanted to go down the stairs and out the front doors and into the city. He wanted to get as far away from here as fast as he could.

Because he knew what was coming. He had been expecting it for weeks now, waiting for it, feeling it just on the edges of things, like a phantom pain in a missing limb. Eamon was sure he wasn't the only one. Augie down there in the emergency room had probably been feeling it too. It was the cliché at the end of the second act, and there was no way to avoid it.

"Eamon," Michael said, very quietly, very steadily. "Eamon, what makes you think I'm not sick?"

S·I·X

1

The only other time Gregor Demarkian had been to the Four Seasons, Bennis Hannaford had taken him. "Taken" was the right way to put it. Bennis had her American Express Gold Card in one hand and her latest contracts in the other. She had been steaming, and incomprehensible to Gregor. What Gregor remembered most was feeling out of place—big shaggy ethnic-looking men did not seem to be who this place had been made for—and the fact that his menu had no prices on it. He had no idea why he had suggested the place to Michael Pride. The Cardinal had reserved Gregor a room at the Hilton. Maybe Gregor was making some kind of subliminal connection. Seeing Michael Pride come in in his battered tweed sports jacket and a tie that looked old enough to have done service in the Eisenhower administration, Gregor thought he'd done the right thing. Michael Pride looked right here somehow, more right than Gregor looked himself.

The woman at the desk smiled at them and took them to a table in the "Pool Room." It could have been a table in any room at all, because the restaurant was nearly empty. Gregor supposed the rooms had status rankings among Manhattan regulars who kept track of that sort of thing. Because he couldn't hold on to information of that kind even when he wanted to, he didn't worry about it. The table he and Michael were seated at was on a raised platform looking out over a sea of other tables, all empty. Gregor ordered a bottle of wine and Michael ordered a Perrier water.

"I work too much, you see," Michael said, when the drinks had come and he had a menu in his hands. Gregor was interested to see that Michael wasn't much interested in the menu. He flipped through it quickly, seemed to check something he expected to be there, and put it down. "With the clinic, it's not possible to say that I'm actually off duty. If I'm around and somebody needs me, I'm on. Once every four years, I declare myself on vacation and rent a motel room on the Island for a night. Then I watch the returns from the presidential elections and get dead drunk."

"I know somebody else who drinks for presidential elections," Gregor said.

"It's necessary. Republican, Democrat. Reagan, Carter, Bush, Clinton. Nixon, for God's sake. Where do they get these guys?"

"Do you vote?"

"Absolutely. I write in James Madison."

"My friend who also drinks for elections writes in Snoopy."

"Snoopy couldn't hurt."

The waiter came with the drinks, but not with his order pad—did the waiters carry order pads in here? Gregor couldn't remember. He did remember that there were a lot of waiters, in the way that there were a lot of people on Broadway stage crews. Each waiter did one thing and no other. It was rather nice. Michael Pride took a sip of his Perrier water and looked around.

"Funny," he said. "My brother took me to this place once, right after I'd opened up uptown, trying to talk me out of it. I had a wonderful time, stuck him with a six-hundred-dollar bill, and went right back to doing what I was doing. Larry was furious."

"This was right after you opened the clinic?"

Michael shook his head. "No clinic. I never intended to open a clinic. In the beginning there was just me and a rented office suite about five blocks north of where we are now, with a sign hung out saying I'd do doctoring for anyone who wanted it for free. Believe it or not, it took a while before anybody showed up at my door. I realized later they all thought I'd had my license revoked. It wasn't until I got friendly with one of the African Methodist ministers that I got any business."

"Do you have family money?" Gregor wondered. "You must have income from someplace, to work for free. That is, if you do work for free. I'm afraid I didn't ask the Cardinal about the arrangements at the clinic. Possibly they pay you a salary."

"They quite definitely pay me a salary," Michael said. "Fifty dollars a month. And I've got my room, of course, and I can take anything I want from the cafeteria without paying for it. And no, I don't have family money. When I first went uptown, I had about twenty-two thousand dollars that I'd put away from three years as part of a medical partnership with offices off Central Park West. If I'd stuck with the partnership, I'd be a millionaire several times over by now. All the men I used to work with are into real estate."

"What did you intend to do for money after the twenty-two thousand dollars ran out?"

"I didn't let myself think about it."

"New York is full of people who didn't let themselves think about it, Dr. Pride. Bag ladies. People sleeping on the street."

"That's not how people end up sleeping on the street, Mr. Demarkian, you should know that. And it's not the same thing. People like me do not end up on park benches, not unless we take to liquor and refuse to do anything about it. People like me have something to give. If we give it, the world gives back. Which isn't to say it gives back very well. I've slept with my share of bed-bugs."

The waiter was back, except that it was a different waiter. Maybe. Gregor gave his order and then sat back to listen to Michael Pride order enough shrimp to populate an ocean. Gregor hadn't realized there were that many different kinds of shrimp on the menu. Gregor's wine was gone. He asked for a bottle of Chardonnay and the waiter disappeared.

"The wine waiter will be back to create a fuss," Michael warned him. "Where were we? Oh. At the beginning of my brilliant career."

"I think the question is why you didn't continue with your brilliant career," Gregor said. "Your credentials are very impressive. In fact, they're spectacular. You had started out with what sounds like a lucrative partnership. You're probably right, you probably could have been a millionaire several times over if you'd stuck with it. Why didn't you stick with it?"

"Why should I bother?"

"Money," Gregor suggested.

Michael Pride nodded. "I like money as well as any-body else, that's true. I like lots of shrimp in the Four Seasons and a dozen other luxuries I could name. I've had this jacket for fifteen years. I've never replaced it because I couldn't afford to replace it with anything this well made. But everybody likes money, Mr. Demarkian. Most people don't have it. As long as they're not destitute, they survive well enough. They're even happy."

"If they've got a chance of getting money, though, they usually take it."

"True." And then they're stuck with what I've always thought of as the fate worse than death."

"What's that?"

"Boredom."

"Were you bored, in that partnership of yours, Dr. Pride?"

"Very. And I would have gone on being bored. I would have had regular hours and regular days and an apartment on the Upper West Side and a house on Martha's Vineyard, and I would have lived for the two days every three years that a difficult case came up. What's worse, I would have done heart surgery after heart surgery after heart surgery. That was my specialty. Heart surgery without end."

"That kind of experience is necessary, isn't it?" Gregor asked. "Specialists specialize because it makes them better at what they do."

"Some of them specialize for that reason, yes. And the best ones do work they couldn't have done any other way and that nobody else on earth can do. Maybe I would have been one of them. But my eyes glaze over even thinking about it. And thinking about the patients I would have had to put up with is worse."

The wine steward came with the Chardonnay. He did indeed make a fuss, which Gregor endured with as much grace as possible. There were swishings and smellings Gregor didn't understand at all. There were bowings and assurances that only made him feel ridiculous. Gregor drank Chardonnay because he liked the taste of Chardonnay. He didn't know what it was supposed to go with and he couldn't tell the good stuff from the bad, except at the extreme ends of the scale. Every time the wine steward raised his voice in a question, Gregor made indecipherable grunts he hoped would suit. They apparently did. The wine steward backed off and gave a final bow. Then he disappeared into that limbo where Four Seasons waiters went until the instant they were wanted by their tables, at which point they reappeared instantaneously, like genies out of lamps.

"Told you he'd make a fuss," Michael said.

Gregor poured himself a new glass of wine. He had a new wineglass to pour it in. The Four Seasons would never have let him pour Chardonnay into a glass that had held Chablis.

"So," Gregor said, "all this is very interesting, but none of it seems discreditable to me. I can't believe this is what you meant when you said that people were deliberately withholding information about you from me."

"It isn't." Michael Pride smiled. "I think I was just trying to head you off at the pass, stop you from doing what everybody else does. I was just trying to convince you that I'm not a saint."

"With that résumé? With that résumé I could press your case in Rome, tomorrow."

"Oh, no, you couldn't. That's my point here, Mr. Demarkian, and it's a very important point. I'm not a crusader, I'm not Robin Hood, I'm not Mother Teresa—whom I've met, by the way. She came to tour our operation a couple of years ago. *There's* a saint. No, Mr. Demarkian, I'm like anybody else. It's just that I'm not afraid of the same things most people are. I'm afraid of other things."

"Boredom."

"Boredom. Waking up when I'm sixty-five years old and not being able to explain what I've done with my life, not being able to remember it. That's what happened to my father, you know. He was a brilliant surgeon, too. But by and large saints are ascetics, Mr. Demarkian, and I am no ascetic. Just watch me with the shrimp tonight. And later at dessert with the chocolate. Just what do you know about me, Mr. Demarkian, aside from what I've told you?"

"I don't know what you want me to say," Gregor said. "The Cardinal told me you were a homosexual."

"Oh, *homosexual.*" Michael waved this away. "My brother Larry is a homosexual. He'd say gay. He's living with the same lover he's been living with for the past twenty years. They bought an apartment in the West Seventies and they're more married than our parents were. Homosexual is not the point. Do you know what happened to me the night before Charles van Straadt was murdered?"

"No."

"I got arrested."

"For what?"

"I got arrested in a raid. On a gay porno theater in Times Square. It was not an upmarket porno theater. It took quarters and there were glory holes. When the police hit I was using one of the glory holes."

What, Gregor wondered, did you say to a confession like this? Especially because Michael Pride didn't look like he was confessing anything. He was using the tone of voice people use to describe minor irritating problems with their bosses or run-ins with their stepmothers.

"Isn't that dangerous?" Gregor asked him. "I don't mean because you might get arrested. I mean medically."

"I'm very careful, medically. I wasn't always, but I am now. No, Mr. Demarkian, at the moment, the chief problem I have in relation to my activities in this direction is definitely legal, although not legal in the everyday sense. I got arrested in that raid, Mr. Demarkian, but I did not get booked and I did not get charged."

"The district attorney was doing you a favor?"

"The district attorney was doing the city of New York a favor, or so he thought. Everybody seems to think the clinic will collapse if anything happens to me. Whatever. The problem was, I got arrested in that raid, and I got photographed being led out into the paddywagon, and the photographs ended up on the front pages of both the New York *Post* and the *Daily News*."

"Not on the front page of the New York *Sentinel*."

"No," Michael said. "That's what Charlie van Straadt was doing at the center on the night he died. He'd made sure that the *Sentinel* and that television station he owns kept strictly off the story of my arrest. He was a good contributor to the center and Charlie and I went back a long way. He couldn't just let it go, though, and we both knew it. He came uptown that night to talk to me."

"Yes." Gregor nodded. "That's in the Cardinal's report, not as a fact but as a conjecture. Still, everybody seems to have assumed it."

"They ought to. What nobody knows is that Charlie called me, in the afternoon, before he came up."

"He did?"

"Oh, yes, and that's the funny part. I've been thinking about it ever since and I just haven't been able to sort it out. Charlie was upset about the publicity, of course. I was upset about it, too. I may not have intended to start a clinic, but I have started one and I think the neighborhood would be in even worse shape than it is now—good God, can you imagine worse shape?—if we were forced to close. In spite of the insinuations the police made, I wasn't worried about Charlie and his money. There were never any secrets between Charlie and me. It was our position with the Archdiocese of New York that was making me antsy. We walk a tightrope with them every day."

"Because the clinic does abortions."

Michael shook his head. "Believe it or not, the abortions are a sore point only in a technical sense. Our position and the position of the Archdiocese is that the abortions are performed by the Sojourner Truth Family Planning Clinic, which is a separate corporation from the Sojourner Truth Health Center, and no nuns or recognized practicing Catholics work in family planning. Were you in favor of *Roe v. Wade*?"

"I don't think I ever thought about it," Gregor said. "It's not an issue that comes up often in my life. Abortion, I mean. The only young woman I've known in the past ten years or so who's gotten pregnant when she didn't want to be decided she did want to be in no time at all."

"Well, I was in favor of *Roe*," Michael said. "I'm still in favor of it. The black churches don't like it. They think it's a form of genocide. It's an argument that makes me uneasy sometimes. However, getting to the here and now and the Archdiocese of New York and the center's abortion practices, the fact is that making abortion safe and legal was a wonderful idea as far as I am concerned, but making abortion legal didn't exactly make it safe in the kind of neighborhoods the center serves. New York State pays for abortions for indigent women and the hospitals in the area do them, but in spite of those two things, most abortions performed in Harlem and Spanish Harlem and the less desirable neighborhoods of the Bronx are still performed by back-alley abortionists. Except now, the back-alley abortionists have offices right out in the open and there's no way to know whether you're in the wrong place until it's too late. They convicted one of these guys a couple of months ago, but he'd killed a few women before they got hold of him and his arrest isn't going to do his victims any good. Now the Archdiocese is opposed to legal abortion and I am in favor of it, but we both are opposed to the kind of butchery that goes on in the offices of these quacks. And we both know that there isn't any other way to stop it except to drain off as many clients as can be drained. The state and the city don't move in Harlem until they absolutely have to. So. The Archdiocese looks one way. I look another. The high-wire act is successful for one more day."

"But it's precarious," Gregor said.

"It is definitely precarious," Michael agreed. "Especially with this new Cardinal. People used to complain about the old one, you know, and say he was intolerant. But he wasn't, really. He was just orthodox. This one is intolerant."

"I didn't like him either." Gregor poured himself another glass of wine. "Were you worried that your arrest would give him a chance to change the Archdiocese's relationship with the center?"

Michael snorted. "Worried? No, I wasn't worried. I was scared to death. Not about the funding. I can always make up the funding elsewhere. I don't care about the money. But the nuns. Ever since my face ended up on the front page of the *Post*, I've been lying awake nights, wondering when Augie is going to walk through my office door to tell me that the Cardinal has issued a ban on clergy and religious working at the center. We couldn't survive without nuns. We couldn't survive without Augie. She can work fifteen hours straight, take fifteen minutes off for a cup of coffee, and do it all over again. And she works for less than I do. There's nothing in the world for getting work like we do done and done right than nuns."

Gregor sat back. "But the Cardinal didn't withdraw the nuns from the center," he said. "And the murder and your arrest are two weeks gone. He's not likely to withdraw them now unless something else happens."

"I know. Something else could always happen. I told you I wasn't an ascetic, Mr. Demarkian. I meant it."

"Are you at least attempting to protect yourself from being caught in raids?"

"Raids are very rare in New York, I'm thankful to say. The one I got caught in only came off because the proprietor was enmeshed in a RICO action."

"Still."

"I know. I know. That's what Eamon said. But there's more, as I said. More about the night Charlie died. I'm not worried, at the moment, about everything blowing up in my face because of my tastes in extracurricular activities. I've got some control over those. I don't worry about what I know. I worry about what I *don't* know."

"Charlie called you in the afternoon before he came down to the center," Gregor repeated. "And you didn't think the reason he wanted to see you that night was entirely concerning the publicity around your arrest."

"I know it wasn't."

"Then what was it about?"

Michael's Perrier water was gone. He picked up the glass it had come in and rolled it back and forth between his palms. Gregor thought he looked even more tired than he had when they had first come in. Relaxation had been a mistake. Now that his guard was down, Michael had nothing to keep him going. The creases in his forehead were as deep as riverbeds.

"Charlie was laughing," Michael Pride said carefully, "the way he laughed when he had something going in business. He'd call me up and tell me about real estate and loans and laugh like that. Don't ask me why, why he told me or why he laughed. I never understood half of it. This time, though, it wasn't about business. It was about people."

"What people?" Gregor asked.

"I don't know," Michael said. "Charlie told me that he'd done a brilliant thing, because he'd given someone just what he didn't want. That was the ticket. He'd told this person he was going to give him this thing, whatever it was, and the person couldn't say he didn't want it, because it would sound crazy, but the person didn't want it and it was going to cause no end of trouble. And then everything would come out, and it would all be to the advantage of the center in the end. And then he laughed even harder and said, 'Happy Father's Day, Michael, Happy Father's Day.' I'm sorry I'm not being more coherent, Mr. Demarkian, but to tell you the truth, I had my mind on other things at the time. My face was all over the New York papers. And there had been rumors all morning that we were on our way to a shoot-out sometime later in the day."

"Hmm," Gregor said.

"Here come the hors d'oeuvres. You could have done better than that, you know."

Gregor sat back and allowed one of the waiters to put a small plate of smoked salmon in front of him. The waiter put a large platter of fried shrimp in front of Michael Pride.

"Are you really going to be able to eat all this food?"

"Sure. The way you look, you ought to be able to do just as well."

"Not without gaining forty pounds," Gregor said. Actually, at this point in his life, he couldn't do that well at all. No one could do that well unless they had gone hungry for a while. Michael Pride must have gone hungry for a while. Either that, or he was at the start of being seriously ill.

Gregor nibbled on a bit of salmon and then decided to get back to business. "Let's start from the beginning," he told Michael Pride. "Maybe if we go over it all in detail, we can make it make sense."

Michael Pride was better than halfway finished with his shrimp.

2

Gregor should have known that starting at the beginning would be useless. It was the kind of thing that worked for the great detectives in the books Bennis gave him to read, but that never had worked for him. Three and a half hours after the arrival of the hors d'oeuvres, after Michael Pride had dispatched with countless shrimp, mounds of green vegetables, boatloads of rice and a dessert that had to be lit on fire before it could be eaten, Gregor was no closer than he had been to discovering what had been on Charles van Straadt's mind the afternoon before he died. Gregor had come to the conclusion that he would like to take Michael Pride back to Cavanaugh Street. Gregor knew a lot of middle-aged women whose mission in life seemed to be to feed the people around them as much food as possible. Michael

Pride would be a wonderful subject for their attentions. And they were more sophisticated on Cavanaugh Street than they used to be. They wouldn't blink an eye when they found out Michael was gay. Lida Arkmanian would just switch her efforts from trying to find Michael a nice Armenian girl to trying to find him a nice young man of the same persuasion. In Gregor's experience, those women were incorrigible on Cavanaugh Street.

It was Michael's idea that they should both go up to the Sojourner Truth Health Center and look through the things he had of Charles van Straadt's, tucked away in his third-floor office. It was after eleven o'clock, but Michael Pride quite obviously had no sense of time. This, too, Gregor should have expected.

"He used to come in and talk to me and leave debris lying everywhere," Michael said. "He'd come in and just talk and talk and talk. I have a file cabinet drawer I keep it all in. In case he ever wanted it back."

"But he never did?"

"No. It's not likely any of it is of any importance. Charlie liked props, that's all. He liked to tell me how he took revenge on people who tried to cheat him and he liked to wave things around while he did it. Have you ever noticed how rich men are obsessed with the idea of people wanting to cheat them?"

"It's probably a very practical form of paranoia. A lot of people probably are trying to cheat them."

"Maybe. That's another reason not to want to be rich."

Michael had called a cab from a restaurant phone brought directly to their table. There was no use, he assured Gregor, in trying to get an ordinary street cab to take them where they wanted to go at this time of night. The cab that drove up was a yellow medallion and not a gypsy, but its "off duty" sign was on and its meter was off. The driver was a virtual clone of Juan Valenciano, but not Juan himself. Michael spoke to the driver in rapid Spanish and was answered with a lengthy disquisition on something or the other. Michael sat back, looked at Gregor and shrugged.

"All quiet on the western front, so to speak. No big emergencies, no big accidents, no big shoot-outs uptown. We might actually have half an hour or so to talk before somebody wants me for something."

"Good."

"Ricardo here was saying this is his last week. He and his family are going to close on a candy store in Queens this coming Friday. They all get out as soon as they can, all the people up there. Not that I blame them. I just worry there's going to be nothing left some day except the junkies and the children."

"Mmm," Gregor said, because he had nothing to say to that.

The cab shot northward recklessly, seeming to catch every green light, seeming to make the lights turn green. The buildings went from imposing and solid to imposing and deteriorating to imposing and dilapidated to just plain bad. In no time at all, Gregor found himself in a landscape of broken windows, darkened street corners, scattered garbage, echoing emptiness. The street the center was on was a little better because the area immediately around the center was so well taken care of. Either the city or the center staff had decided that that small stretch of sidewalk was much too valuable to waste. The rest of the block was just as bad as the blocks around it. Gregor wondered where all the garbage came from, when all the buildings were abandoned. Nobody lived here. Who was putting cardboard and tissue paper into big green plastic bags and throwing them off the curbs?

The doors to the east building were still open. Light spilled out of the doorway and down from a powerful arch light positioned between the second and third floors of the building. The sidewalk immediately around the center's front entrances was as well lit as a movie set during filming. Michael said something to the driver and he pulled up in front of the west building. The doors there were closed, but the entrance was just as well lit.

"We'll go in the back way," Michael told Gregor. "That way nobody can stop me on the run and ask me fifteen questions."

"What if they need you for something serious?"

"I've got my beeper."

Gregor followed Michael to the west building door. Michael knocked and introduced himself to someone looking through the peephole. The cab waited until the door opened and let them inside. The woman on the other side of the west building door was the nun Gregor knew as Sister Kenna. She asked a lot of fluttery questions about where they'd been and how they felt and what they were doing on the side of the bridge, and then she was called off by a voice down the first-floor hall. Michael took Gregor to the stairwell and started to climb.

"Going this way is a little difficult in some ways," he said. "You've got to go up to five and then across the bridge and then down to three again, but it's the only way to have even a modicum of privacy. And it's only a modicum, believe me."

Gregor believed that Sister Kenna was probably on the phone right now, telling Sister Augustine that Dr. Michael Pride had done the very odd thing of bringing Gregor Demarkian into the center by the wrong door.

Gregor followed Michael up and up and up and then over a bridge with glass sides that made him dizzy and more than a little anxious. Twenty years in the FBI had had an effect on his assumptions of the world. He kept wondering what would happen to them if there was a sniper down there, or in one of the buildings across the street. Whose idea had it been to build a glass bridge like this in such a dangerous part of town?

Michael Pride didn't think anything of the bridge at all. He let Gregor into the east building and looked around.

"We have day care here from six in the morning to seven at night. Day care for infants and toddlers, I mean. Sixty kids under the age of five. Lots of volunteers. It's easy to find volunteers for projects like day care."

"What happens when the kids are five?"

"They go over to the west building to another program we have there. Actually, half the kids in this program are doing a version of Head Start. It's not Head Start itself—the center doesn't take any public money, not even Medicaid—but it's the same idea. Works pretty well, from what I've seen."

"Good."

"Two more flights. Right this way."

Gregor followed Michael again, glad to see that these last two flights were well lit and reasonably wide. He was trying to pretend he was not out of breath. Some of the floors they had passed on the way up in the other building had been essentially shut down for people to sleep. There had barely been any light at all. Michael had perked right up when they had gotten to this building. His tiredness seemed to have been almost a result of the atmosphere downtown. He went down the last two flights of stairs humming softly under his breath. Gregor recognized the song. It was "Under the Sea." For no reason at all, it suddenly occurred to Gregor that one of the two composers of that song had died of AIDS.

"Maybe Eamon will be in his office," Michael said, as they rounded the last bend in the staircase before reaching the third floor. "You should talk to him about Charlie. Eamon had more to do with Charlie than anybody else in this place but me."

Gregor didn't think Eamon Donleavy was feeling especially cooperative. He decided not to bring it up. He went barreling down the stairs after Michael, not looking where he was going. He almost ran right into Michael Pride's back.

"What's the matter?" he asked, pulling up short.

Michael was standing motionless in the middle of the third-floor hall, staring at a closed office door.

"My office," Michael said. "The door's closed."

"So what?"

"My door's never closed. The only time I ever saw it closed was when Charlie—oh, for Christ's sake. This is asinine."

Michael Pride strode ahead, grabbed the knob of his office door and yanked the door open. He was so sure that he would find nothing there but an empty office— and Gregor was so sure with him—that it took them both a long minute to assimilate what they did see.

What they saw was a woman in a short black dress, rolling around on the worn carpet on Michael Pride's office floor, bucking and spasming as if she were being electrocuted.

Rosalie van Straadt.

P·A·R·T T·W·O

The Cardinal Archbishop of New York
Is Beginning
to Lose His Patience

O·N·E

1

They tried to bring her back. They tried so hard, Gregor thought they were going to do it. He was a veteran of dozens of murder cases and an expert on poisons. He should have known better than to believe for a moment that someone in Rosalie van Straadt's condition could recover from strychnine toxicity. But he got caught up in Michael Pride's conviction. Michael Pride radiated conviction. Gregor had had hands-on experience in medical emergencies. He had once provided enough first aid to a woman who had swallowed lye so that she didn't die from it—although, lye being lye, she hadn't ended up in very good shape, either. First aid, however, was the key. Always before, when Gregor had been called on to do something about a man or woman who needed a doctor, no doctor had been available. Now the doctor was available, but Gregor's help was needed anyway. There were never enough professionals on staff at the Sojourner Truth Health Center. The first thing Michael Pride did when he got over his shock at seeing Rosalie spasming and shuddering in his office was to go for his upstairs cabinet. The second thing he did was to start issuing

Gregor orders. Gregor wanted to issue a few orders of his own. Don't touch the upstairs cabinet, he thought. The strychnine probably came from there. Don't touch the papers on your desk. The murderer might have gotten careless and left something important lying around. Watch where you step on the carpet. There could be fibers, sand, pieces of lint, anything. It was ridiculous. Gregor kept his mouth shut and followed orders.

"Pick up the phone," Michael said. "Push nine. Then push four four four."

"Who am I calling?" Gregor asked.

"Nobody and everybody."

Gregor picked up the phone, pushed nine, then pushed four four four. The Touch-Tone beeps hammered into his ear. A second later, what sounded like an air raid siren began to go off in the building. Gregor jumped. Michael went right on doing what he was doing. The siren stopped abruptly and a computerized voice said: "Code blue. Third floor. West building. Code blue. Third floor. West building."

"Like it?" Michael asked. "It's put together with spare parts and I don't know what. We had a kid here a few years ago, wealthy family in Thailand, studying to be an engineer, got religion and joined the Catholic Church and came out to volunteer. He rigged it up for us."

"Who keeps it working?"

"Other kids."

The computerized voice was going on and on. Gregor wondered what you had to do to stop it. He heard the sound of pounding on the stairs. Somebody was running up to them at full speed, probably several somebodies. Michael's door was still open. Gregor sat down on the edge of the desk and watched as a small crowd of people emerged from the stairwell and crowded in around Michael.

Sister Augustine went immediately to the phone, punched in more numbers, and shut off the computerized voice.

"What's going on around here?" she asked the air.

Michael knew better than to answer. "I need a stretcher," he said. "Does anybody have a stretcher?"

"Yes." A young man at the back of the crowd stepped forward. "We brought the folding stretcher, Dr. Pride, what do you want us to do with it?"

"We've got to get her downstairs."

Michael Pride stepped away from Rosalie van Straadt's body and let the young man come in. The young man unfolded what looked to Gregor like a battlefield carrier and motioned another young man to help him. Rosalie van Straadt was still and blue around the lips, but she was breathing—just. Michael Pride was wet with sweat and dead white.

"What did you do?" Gregor asked in astonishment. "I'd have thought she'd be dead by now. Strychnine victims die quickly."

"Strychnine?" Augie asked sharply.

"Oh, shit," somebody in the crowd said.

"Get her down to Emergency Three," Michael told the young men holding the stretcher. He turned to Augie and shook his head. "I threw dice," he said grimly. "I gave her Comprozan."

"Oh," Augie said.

"What's Comprozan?" Gregor demanded.

Michael was heading for the door behind the stretcher. "It's a hypnotic. A very powerful hypnotic. Strychnine victims don't die from strychnine poisoning. At least not technically. Strychnine makes the body hypersensitive to outside stimulus—light, sound, all of that. The sensitivity is so acute the victim is subject to violent seizures. It's the seizures that kill him. Her. Whatever. Hypnotics reduce the sensitivity of the body to outside stimulus. So—"

"That can't be standard medical procedure," Gregor said. "Why haven't I ever heard of anyone doing that before?"

"Because there's no way to know if the combination of strychnine and a hypnotic is deadly in itself." Augie was beside herself. "Michael, for God's sake. If it turns out to be absolutely contraindicated, the police will think—"

Michael wheeled around. "I know what everybody will think." He was shouting. "What did you expect me to do? Let her go on in convulsions like that? Do nothing? Augie, be rational for a minute. The woman is dying."

"They'll say you did something to make sure," Augie went on implacably. "They'll say you did something even a fool would know was lethal. They'll say she hadn't taken enough strychnine to kill her and you finished the job."

"She'd taken enough strychnine to kill her all right, Augie. Mr. Demarkian here can testify to that."

"She was like a cartoon," Gregor said. "She was jumping around like—I didn't know a body could move like that."

"Come on." Michael pulled at the sleeve of Augie's sweatshirt. "Let's get moving. That Comprozan I gave her won't last long. She's still breathing. We still have a chance."

Most of the rest of the crowd had left in the wake of the stretcher—most, but not all. Gregor thought there were just enough people around to get a good round of gossip going. Most of them seemed to be voyeurs of one kind or another. Gregor saw a couple of teenage girls, one made up clownishly in everything from undereye liner to rouge, one of them scrubbed so clean the skin of her face looked as if when you touched it it would squeak. Gregor wondered if they had come up because of the unusual location of the emergency—third floor, west building meant Michael Pride's office, or one or two others—or if they had just been on their way up or down and just found themselves caught up in the excitement. Whatever the reason, these two would have the story all over the center in the next five minutes.

Neither Michael nor Augie was paying any attention to either of the girls. They were hurrying out into the hall. The girls stepped back to let them pass. The one with the terminal makeup job looked into Michael's office and gave Gregor a cursory look-over. Michael got into the middle of the hall, seemed to think of something and turned back. He smiled wanly at Gregor and took a deep breath.

"If I were you," he said, "I'd get on the phone to Manhattan Homicide and ask for Detective Sheed. We're going to wind up with him in our laps one way or the other."

2

They didn't bring her back. Of course, it had always been impossible. Gregor had known that from the beginning. He had known it from before the beginning. In the middle of a real emergency, it was so hard to stay rational. This emergency had felt like something on television. *Res-*

cue 911. St. Elsewhere. Gregor couldn't count the number
of emergency room scenes he had been subjected to in his
lifetime—and that in spite of the fact that he had been
born and brought up well before the Age of Television
made its debut. He couldn't even count the number of
emergency room scenes he had been subjected to in the
last year. Gregor baby-sat on and off for Donna
Moradanyan's young son, Tommy. Tommy's favorite
activity—after being read to by Father Tibor Kasparian out
of a book of Greek and Roman mythology—was *Rescue
911* and all its clones, so that Donna had made him a vid-
eotape of two dozen of these shows with the commercials
taken out. The problem with those shows was that they
were rigged. The producers never seemed to pick a case
in which the victim died, where all the efforts to save the
woman on the stretcher proved futile. Gregor had real experience in the real world, which should have countered
all this rot. He found it a little embarrassing that it didn't.

Where his experience did come in handy was in the
matter of Michael Pride's office. Gregor had been with
the FBI too long not to know that he couldn't just pick
up the phone in Michael Pride's office and call the police, or leave the office unattended and call the police
from somewhere else. He didn't want to disturb anything
at all in the office. He had no way of knowing what this
Detective Sheed would find important. The two teenage
girls were still in the hall. Gregor went out to them and
directed his attention to the one with the scrubbed face.
Looking at the other one made him a little dizzy.

"Excuse me. My name is Gregor Demarkian. I was
wondering if you could do me a favor, Miss—"

"Me?" the girl said. "Oh. Enderson. Miss Enderson.
Julie Enderson."

"Miss Enderson. I was wondering if you could go

into one of the offices on this hall and get me a roll of tape."

"Tape?"

"He wants to secure the crime scene," the one in the makeup said breathlessly. "Julie, listen. This is the PI the Cardinal hired."

"Tape," Julie Enderson said again. Gregor wondered if she were stupid. She didn't look stupid. Maybe she was shell-shocked. She turned around and looked at the other side of the hall. "There might be tape in Father Donleavy's office," she said. "I could check in there."

"Not Father Donleavy's office," the other girl chided. "Julie, be sensible. Father Donleavy wouldn't have tape. Mrs. Biederson would."

"Who's Mrs. Biederson?"

The made-up girl flapped her hands. "She's head of the office staff. But she's on vacation this week. But her office is open. All the offices on this floor are always open. Give me a second and I'll get you some tape."

"Masking tape," Gregor said. "The brown kind. Not Scotch."

"In a flash," the made-up girl said, pumping off across the hall. Her heels were so high, she was almost walking *en pointe*.

Julie watched her go and sighed. "Her name is Karida. I don't think it's working out for her here. Can I ask you a question?"

"Of course," Gregor said.

"I overheard Augie tell Dr. Pride—well, that the cops were going to suspect him. Of killing that woman. Who was that woman?"

"Rosalie van Straadt. The granddaughter of Charles van Straadt, the man who died here—"

"—two weeks ago," Julie finished for him. "Are the

cops going to suspect Dr. Pride? Of killing the woman, I mean?"

"They shouldn't," Gregor said carefully. "That is, they shouldn't suspect him of killing her directly. In fact, that would have been impossible."

"I don't understand."

"Dr. Pride and I have been together continuously since seven o'clock, except for one or two trips to the bathroom. And since the trips to the bathroom took place better than sixty blocks downtown from here, they wouldn't have been long enough to allow Dr. Pride the time to get all the way up here and give Rosalie van Straadt strychnine."

"He couldn't have given it to her before he left for dinner?"

"If he had, Rosalie van Straadt would have been dead a long time ago. Strychnine acts very fast."

Julie nodded. "Good," she said. "Good. Maybe they'll think he hired someone else to do it or he had an accomplice, but if he's got a really good alibi, they'll leave him alone. They'll have to. Even the mayor gets upset when they bother Michael and there doesn't seem to be any good reason. I saw the other one, you know."

"Who?" Gregor asked, startled. "Charles van Straadt?"

Julie Enderson nodded. "I didn't know that that's who it was at the time. It must have been right before he got killed, too. It was in the middle of the shoot-out. I was going down to the emergency room to see if they'd brought my mother in."

"Your mother," Gregor repeated.

"She lives with this gang guy. She's only about thirty. She had me when she was really young. Karida and I came right down this way from the east building and when we got to this hall, there he was. This van Straadt guy. And then—"

"Tape," Karida said, clattering back. Her hands were full of spools. In spite of Gregor's instructions, she had brought a spool of Scotch tape. Fortunately, she had also brought two spools of masking tape and a spool of black electrical tape. There was a spool of duct tape in her hands, too. Gregor took the masking tape, shut Michael Pride's office door, and began to weave tape from one side of the doorframe to the other.

"Do you two have anything you have to go do right now?"

Karida and Julie shook their heads.

"Good," Gregor said. "Then you can stay here. Make sure nobody goes into Dr. Pride's office. And I mean nobody. Not Dr. Pride himself. Not Sister Augustine. Nobody."

"If somebody went into the office, they'd mess up the tape," Karida said reasonably. "You'd know."

"I might. On the other hand, somebody might be careful enough not to mess up the tape too much and to put it back when he was finished. Then I wouldn't know. Or somebody might come along and take some tape off the door but decide they'd better not go on with it, and I'd have no way of knowing if the room had been entered or not."

"This is just like a television show," Karida said. "This is wonderful!"

"Will the two of you stay?"

Julie Enderson straightened up a little. She had been staring off into the distance. Gregor hadn't thought she'd been paying attention. What is it with this girl? Now that he'd talked to her, he knew she wasn't stupid. He didn't think she was on drugs. If she was, it was on a drug he was unfamiliar with. She wasn't showing any of the obvious signs—except for this accursed spaceyness. It was as if she'd been hypnotized, or as if she were sleepwalking. Why was it, Gregor wondered, that he could never think of anything but clichés in a pinch? Still, there was something wrong with Julie Enderson. If he'd had the time, he would have found out what it was.

"All right then," Gregor said, instead of investigating. He had enough to investigate at the Sojourner Truth Health Center. "You two stay here until the police show up. And don't move. Go to the bathroom in shifts. Don't leave the door unattended for even a minute."

"We won't," Karida promised him. "Hey, Julie, this is neat. They put this guy in *People* magazine all the time. They put him in the *National Enquirer*. Maybe after he solves this case, they'll put us in there with him."

"I don't want my picture in the *National Enquirer*," Julie said.

"I've got to call the police," Gregor told them. "You two stay put."

"We will," Karida trilled. She sounded just like a bird.

Gregor called the police from Eamon Donleavy's office. Then he went downstairs. He would have felt safer if it had been Julie promising to stay put, but he had to live with what he had.

3

It was over. Gregor could feel it in the air as soon as he stepped off the service elevator onto the first floor. He knew only stretchers and their support staff were supposed to take the elevators. He even accepted the rule as necessary—usually. This, however, was an emergency. Gregor had had enough of stairs and stairwells. He was frustrated as hell with low-tech economies. The irrational part of his mind kept urging him to get back into the twentieth century. If someone ever gave him a time machine for Christmas, he would not use it to go into the past.

There were half a dozen copies of the New York *Sentinel* lying on a wheeled metal table against the wall near the Admitting desk. Gregor found the headline incomprehensible and the red banner—**WIN! FOR FATHER'S DAY!**—idiotic. He found the emergency room dead. Being in the middle of a life-and-death crisis was exhilarating. It was better than coffee for keeping you awake and alert. The aftermath was worse than a mental and physical letdown. It had a lot in common with the aftermath of being hit in the head with a cast iron skillet. Either that, or of being drained of blood. The drained-of-blood feeling was all over the emergency room now. Gregor could feel it.

There was no one at all sitting at the Admitting desk. Gregor went around it and down the hall on the other side. This one was lined with doors that said things like "oxygen" and "lead shields" and "OR supplies misc." At the far end, the hall curved around to the left again. Gregor went there and found himself where he wanted to be. This hall was very short. It ended in a pair of double doors marked "Emergency Room 3."

Just as Gregor was about to go up to the doors to look through the windows—the last thing he wanted to do was breach a sterile environment—the doors were pushed back from the inside and Augie came walking out. She was wearing OR greens over her sweatsuit and crying. She kept wiping the tears off her face with the back of her hand. Beyond her, Gregor could see a still body on a table and a clutch of men and women in hospital whites. Dr. Michael Pride was taking off his face mask. From this distance, he looked to Gregor as if he were in pain.

"Oh, Mr. Demarkian," Augie sobbed. "There you are. I forgot all about you."

"I called the police," Gregor told her.

"Oh, the police. Yes, you'd have to call the police. She died, you know."

"I guessed that."

"I don't even know if we came close. I don't know what we were doing in there."

"You were trying," Gregor told her. "There's nothing in the world wrong with trying."

"Isn't there? I've got to go get out of these things. I've got work to do. It's a good thing this is turning out to be a slow night."

Michael Pride walked up to them. He had his mask in his hand. His eyes were red and raw. He hadn't been wearing one of those caps doctors wore on television. His hair was stiff with sweat and sticking up in spikes like a punk rocker's.

"That's that," he said. "I take it you got in touch with the police."

"I didn't talk to Detective Sheed directly," Gregor said, "but I talked to a young woman who said she could get in touch with him. There are going to be a few regular police officers on the scene as well."

"Oh, yes, there would have to be—although you didn't have to make a phone call for one of those. We've got them practically parked on the premises. That's what happens when you treat a lot of knife wounds. Christ, what was she doing here? I thought she'd gone home hours ago."

"She had dinner in the cafeteria," Augie said, wiping her eyes. "I saw her there myself. With Ida and Martha and Victor. She was looking very cool."

"I'm surprised the three of them didn't beat her up," Michael said. "What was she doing in my office?"

Augie considered this. "I suppose we can ask Martha. She's supposed to be around somewhere tonight. Not on duty, of course, she took the Afterschool Program with Sister Edna this afternoon. But she's supposed to be around."

Michael snorted. "She's been around less and less often these last two weeks. She's going to quit on you, Augie, and you know it."

"Oh, I know it." She turned to Gregor. "All the van Straadt grandchildren volunteer at the center because old Charlie van Straadt insisted on it, but the only one who ever liked it was Ida. Ever since Charlie died, Martha's just been itching to quit."

"Were you talking about Rosalie van Straadt?" Sister Kenna asked, coming out of the emergency room. She had a sterile face mask hanging around her neck, but otherwise she was wearing the same modified habit she had been wearing when Gregor first met her. Gregor wondered what use they'd found for her in the emergency room.

"Isn't that a terrible thing," Sister Kenna said. "A terrible thing. I saw her, though. After dinner. Over in the east building."

"Visiting with Martha?" Augie asked.

"I don't know," Sister Kenna said. "I didn't see Martha. Rosalie was just there. On the first floor in the room with the television, you know."

"She was watching television?" Gregor was confused.

"No, no," Sister Kenna said. "The television wasn't on. She was just there. Rosalie was. She was just sitting."

"Doing what?" Augie demanded.

"Doing nothing," Sister Kenna answered. "She was just sitting there. I would have gone in to say hello, but I was busy. We needed diapers up in infant care. I'd just gone through this incredibly complicated demonstration on how to diaper a baby, and then the baby I was diapering did a—well, you know—and there weren't any extra diapers. The cupboard hadn't been restocked. So I went down to the first floor to get some more."

"What time was this?" Gregor wanted to know.

"About eight," Sister Kenna said promptly. "The infant care class starts at seven thirty and goes for an hour. It has to start that late, you see, because all our students work. And then they have to come home and get dinner and look after whoever else it is they're responsible for in their families, which usually isn't anybody but you never know. There could always be one with an invalid mother. So the class started at seven thirty and we'd been at it for a while when the—um—accident happened. The class was beginning to get restless and that always happens about eight."

"And she was just sitting there," Gregor repeated. "Doing nothing."

"That's right."

"Not watching television."

"The television wasn't on. I told you."

"Not reading a book or a magazine."

"No. There are books and magazines in that room, but Rosalie didn't have one."

"Not doing a crossword puzzle."

"Really, Mr. Demarkian, I meant exactly what I said. She was just sitting there."

"You must see Mr. Demarkian's problem," Michael Pride jumped in. "People don't 'just sit there.' It's insupportable. Whether you realized it or not, Rosalie must have been doing something."

"Oh," Gregor said. "I know what she was doing. That's not the problem. The problem is that the times are wrong."

"What are you talking about?" Augie demanded.

Gregor didn't have time to tell her. There were sounds in the emergency room again, although not the sounds Gregor associated with an emergency. There were no sirens or running footsteps. What Gregor heard was stiff walking with a march beat. It was the rhythm of uniformed men everywhere, in armies as well as police forces, in professional fire departments as well as the National Guard. Gregor had always been able to tell which of the men on his staff at the Bureau were spending their weekends with the Guard. For some reason, women didn't seem to pick up the gait in the same way.

Gregor left Michael Pride and Sister Augustine and walked back along the wraparound hallway toward the Admitting desk. He ran into three men coming the opposite way. Two of these men were uniformed police officers who looked vaguely familiar, but Gregor didn't put much credit in that. It was their uniforms that were familiar, and this situation, which Gregor had been in too many times before. The third man was a massive African-American, with *massive* being the operative word. Gregor was six feet four inches tall, but this man towered over him. Gregor was naturally broad shouldered, but this man looked as if he could have taken on the entire defensive line of the New York Giants and made it an in-

teresting match. The effect was made more pronounced
by the fact that the man didn't have a single hair on his
head. His baldness served to emphasize the fact that his
facial features were as outsized as the rest of him. Gregor
had a sudden vision of this person as a star performer in
professional wrestling. The only problem with that was
that this man looked far too serious. Professional wres-
tlers weren't supposed to really scare anybody.

The three men came to a halt. The tall African-
American looked Gregor Demarkian over from head to
foot and nodded. Gregor felt the way he'd felt standing
at attention while the troops were being reviewed by the
local general. Gregor had spent a great deal of his time
in the army standing at attention while the troops were
being reviewed by one visiting dignitary or the other.

The tall African-American held out his massive hand.
"I take it you're Gregor Demarkian," he said, in an
Oxford accent so perfect that if Gregor had had his
eyes closed, he would have thought he was watching
Brideshead Revisited.

"Yes," Gregor told him. "That's right. I'm Gregor
Demarkian."

"I'm Hector Sheed, detective first grade, New York
City Homicide. You look fatter than your picture in *People* magazine."

"Right," Gregor said. "Of course."

"Never mind." Hector Sheed sighed wearily. "Let's
see what kind of a mess Michael Pride's gotten himself
into this time."

T·W·O

1

By Thursday morning, Julie Enderson's head felt as if it were filled with tiny hand grenades, pins pulled, ready to explode. This was a feeling Julie had had often in her life. Right now there were a million things she could use to explain it. Two people had been found dead in Michael Pride's office in just over two weeks. There was nothing necessarily odd about finding dead people in the west building, but these had been the wrong kind of people to end up dead. Julie was still young enough, and had been poor long enough, to think of rich people as immortal and rich-and-famous people as more immortal still. Women with money floated up above the street on cushions of electrified air, untouchable. Nobody called them "cunt" or offered them twenty dollars to get in the back of the car. They didn't stand in front of their mirrors in the morning, wondering if the mask they were putting on would work today, wondering how long they were going to get away with hiding their awful ugliness. Julie thought about Rosalie van Straadt often. Money, looks, education. Rosalie seemed more real to Julie than Martha and Ida, who worked at the center. Ida was always too preoccupied. Martha was what Julie thought of as "a born social worker." It was not a compliment.

Then there were the reporters, who had come out of nowhere after Rosalie van Straadt died and decided to stay. Julie was used to television cameras and print reporters with stenographer's notebooks and tape recorders. Gang wars and drug busts got them uptown on a sporadic basis. She wasn't used to this crazy kind of invasion, this seige. Julie slept in a dormitory bedroom with three other girls. The room's two windows faced the street. On the mornings after Rosalie van Straadt died, she would get up early to look out. They were always there, two or three of them. Julie became convinced that they were waiting for a third death. What if there was a third death? What would happen then? The center had always seemed like such a solid place to her, like such a sure thing. Now it felt shaky at the foundations. Shudder and roar, shudder and roar, Julie thought. A breath of the wrong wind could blow it into rubble.

No matter how many things Julie had to blame the feeling on, though, the truth of it had nothing to do with Michael or murders or little gray men from the *New York Times* asking painful questions in the street. For years, Julie had felt like this all the time, day after day, minute after minute. When she'd first started whoring, the feeling would come to her as soon as she woke up. She could get rid of it by smoking a little dope or picking up a john. The johns had always worked better for her than the dope. The dope turned on her sometimes, spun her around and made her look at herself. Back in Rakey's apartment—Rakey was her first pimp, the one her mother's boyfriend sold her to, when she was eleven—Julie would stand in front of the cracked yellow mirror in the bathroom and watch the skin of her face turn into cockroaches and worms, black and dead and pulsing. That was how she saw the inside of herself. That was what she thought of the first time she went into a church and heard a priest talk about her soul. That was what she thought of the first time the social workers picked her up and put her in a program. The program had a "self-esteem workshop" all the girls had to attend, where a peppy brunette in low stack heels ordered each and every one of them to "love yourself! love yourself! loving yourself is the key to loving your life!" It wasn't until Julie met Augie that she had begun to be able to pass her reflection without revulsion, that she had begun to have days when waking up had not meant a collision with self-hatred. It was Augie who had told Julie that a true Christian looks not only at the person but at the image of Christ in every person—and oddly enough, that had worked. Julie didn't look for the image of Christ in herself, not even now, when the image of Christ in her mind looked suspiciously like Michael Pride. Christ was too much of a man to make Julie entirely comfortable with looking for images of Him. She looked for images of the Virgin Mary instead. The Virgin Mary was very important to Julie. The Virgin Mary had been poor, but she had also been untouchable. If she had also been black, she would have been perfect.

Julie kept a picture of the Virgin Mary standing on a cloud with the moon at her feet tucked into a corner of the small mirror that hung on the wall of her dormitory room at the Sojourner Truth Health Center. She used a plastic-covered bookmark with a picture of the Virgin Mary with streams of light coming out of her fingers to mark her place in her history text. On Thursday morning, days after Rosalie van Straadt's murder, neither of these pictures did any good at all. She looked in the mirror and she saw herself, that was all, not the Virgin Mary or Christ or anyone else. Julie looked down at the palms of her hands and wondered how the johns could bear to have her touch them. Didn't they see that she was dead? Any minute now, her skin would begin to slough off in ripples and folds. She was a walking, talking corpse, going to rot. The hand grenades in her head had coalesced into one big neutron bomb. It was feeling like this that had blasted her out of every other program she had been in.

It was seven o'clock in the morning. Julie's roommates lay huddled in lumps and curls under blankets and around pillows. They hadn't noticed that Julie had pulled up the shade and let in the sun. Julie pulled the shade down again. She had thrown away all her makeup. She didn't have a single thing with which she could paint on another face. The other girls had lots and lots, grocery bagfuls, that they shoplifted from five-and-ten-cent stores on Broadway. Julie could borrow a lipstick from Karida and a blusher from KelsiAnne. Neither one of them would ever notice there was anything missing, and if they did they wouldn't mind. Julie picked up her history books instead. This was a very delicate moment. This was make or break. If she put makeup on her face this morning, it was as good as over. She might stay at the center another day or week or month, but sooner or later she would be out on the street again, looking for another john, looking for another pimp. Thinking of what all that was like—of what wanting it was like—scared her, because by now there were times she did want it, even when she didn't want it, it got all confused. It was as if "normal" was feeling dead and getting beat up. Feeling alive and not getting beat up was better, but it was also terrifying, Julie didn't know why. She just knew that she

had to get past it. The rational part of her, the sane part
of her, the part of her she was actually coming to like,
didn't want to end up back on the street at all.

Julie had two history books, the textbook for the
course she was taking and a book by Oswald Patterson,
who was black and taught at Harvard University. Before
Oswald Patterson, Julie hadn't known there were any
black people at Harvard University, except maybe to
play sports. African-American, she reminded herself.
These days you were supposed to call yourself African-
American. She had a green canvas bookbag with the
words "St. Rose's Academy" and a logo printed in black
on one side. She tucked her two history books into that
and slung it over her shoulder. Then she let herself out
of the room and into the hall. There was a self-locking
door at the end of the corridor. It let girls off the floor
but wouldn't let anyone on. To get on, you had to ring the
bell and wait for someone to answer it. That way, the
girls didn't have to lock the doors to their individual
rooms all the time. Julie had a passionate ambition in her
life. She wanted to live for one full year in a place where
nobody ever locked their doors at all.

There was a dining room in the east building, for the
children who came to day care and Afterschool (the dining room served breakfast, lunch, and snacks) and for the
girls in the refuge program. It was early enough for Julie
to have been able to get breakfast there. Instead, she
went straight down to the first floor and out the front
door. Then she went up the steps to the west building.
The street around her was empty and cold. Nothing
about it called to her. She remembered nights spent
sleeping in abandoned buildings and sitting on steaming
grates. She went to the back of the building and down
the stairs. The cafeteria there was open twenty-four

hours a day. At seven o'clock in the morning, it was reasonably crowded. Julie took a tray, loaded it down with sausages and hash browns and bacon and eggs and toast, and got out her resident's card. If you had a resident's card, you could come to the cafeteria and eat anything you wanted for free.

Augie was sitting by herself at the big round table under the steam pipes, looking through a newspaper with a scowl on her face. Julie put her tray down on Augie's table and pulled out a chair. The newspaper was the New York *Sentinel*, and it was lurid. Julie caught a grainy black-and-white photograph of Rosalie van Straadt's dead body lying on a stretcher. There was another photograph of Dr. Michael Pride in a sea of uniformed policemen. It made him look as if he had been busted, even though he hadn't been. On the front of the paper there was a red banner over the masthead, announcing the Father's Day contest for the millionth time. Julie had read through the contest rules once, just to see what they were like. If she'd had a father, she would have entered.

Augie put the paper down. "Good morning," she said. "What's wrong with you?"

That was Augie, Julie thought. Straight to the point. "I'm having one of those days. I came looking for company to talk me out of it."

"Out of what?"

Julie looked up, toward the doors out of the cafeteria, toward the street.

"I'll lock you in a closet, if that's what it takes," Augie told her. "You can't be serious."

"Not really. Not exactly. I'm just—nervous."

"We're all nervous."

"I know. Augie, listen. You don't think Michael did it, do you? Killed those two people?"

"Of course not." Augie was astonished. "Julie, what are you thinking of?"

"I don't know. I mean, they were really terrible people, weren't they? The two people who died. I saw the last one, that woman, I used to run into her all over the center. I didn't know her name then. She was a real—uh—"

"Bitch," Augie said dryly.

"Right. Exactly. She was always—saying things, to people. You know. Asking Karida if it was really necessary to wear *quite* that much makeup on her face. Telling me once that she supposed I was going to get a free ride right through college, so why should I study, since nobody was going to care if I knew anything or not."

"Did she really say that to you?"

"She did. In here one night. I was with Sister Kenna and Ida Greel. Is it true that Ida is that woman's cousin?"

"Oh, yes," Augie said. "She's Martha van Straadt's cousin, too. I forget how it works, whose mother and whose father and all that, but they're all related. There's a boy, too, Victor. He volunteered here several years ago. It was before your time."

"Everything was before my time. Anyway, she said things to people. And her grandfather, that Charles van Straadt—he was the old man in Michael's office that night, I mean, he was there in person and then his body was after he died. If you know what I mean."

"Not really. If you're trying to say that Charles van Straadt spent some time in Michael's office before dying there, the answer seems to be yes. The way the police have worked it out, Charles and Rosalie got to the center at about six o'clock or a little after and went straight up to Michael's office. Then Rosalie ran around doing errands while Charles stayed in the office doing God only knows what. He made at least one phone call, over to the east building, looking for Martha. Sister Edna answered the phone. After that, nobody knows what he did. Nobody saw him anywhere else in the building. The assumption is that he stayed in Michael's office, or at least on the third floor of the west building, until he died."

"Mmmm." Julie looked down at her sausage and bacon. Her eggs seemed to be congealing into an art form. Her toast looked wet. She pushed the tray away and reached into the back pocket of her jeans for her cigarettes. The cafeteria and the emergency-room waiting area were the only places in the west building where you were allowed to smoke. In the east building, you could smoke anywhere you wanted, except in the classrooms for the Afterschool Program. The nuns had given up trying to enforce discipline.

There was a round black plastic ashtray in the middle of the table. Julie pulled it toward her and dropped in her spent match. Then she took in a deep lungful of smoke and breathed it out again.

"Augie," she asked carefully, "did you ever see Charles van Straadt anywhere except for here?"

"You mean in person?" Augie looked confused. "I don't think I have. I've seen his pictures, of course. Parties at the White House. Benefits with movie stars. Old Charlie did tend to get around."

Julie shook her head. "No, that's not what I meant. You used to work at Covenant House, didn't you?"

"I volunteered there once, years ago. Why?"

"I don't know. You never saw him there, in that neighborhood?"

"Charles van Straadt? No, of course I didn't. Why should I have? Does he contribute to Covenant House?"

"I don't know. I never went to Covenant House myself. But it's in the right neighborhood."

"Right for what?"

It was always hard to predict what nuns knew and what they didn't. When you expected them to be naive, they surprised you, but when you expected them to be hip they surprised you, too. Julie took another drag on her cigarette. Everybody else in New York knew what that neighborhood was good for. Everybody else in the world knew.

"Augie," Julie said, "do you know this man, this Gregor Demarkian, that the Cardinal hired?"

"I don't think you can actually hire him," Augie said. "I don't think he takes money."

"Do you know if he can be trusted?"

Augie shrugged. "I know he's good at his work. The Cardinal wouldn't have sent him if he weren't. What's the matter? Is there something you know about one of those deaths? You shouldn't keep it to yourself if you do. It could be dangerous."

"No," Julie said. "I don't know anything about the deaths. It isn't that."

She pulled the tray of food back toward her and looked down at the hash browns. Augie was staring at her oddly, but she couldn't help that. The hand grenades that had become the neutron bomb were now turning into fragments of shrapnel. She felt as bad as the time she'd had the flu and no place to sleep at the same time.

"Julie," Augie said.

"I'm all right," Julie told her. "I've just got an awful pain in my head."

2

Victor van Straadt had never much liked his cousin Rosalie, and he had liked her even less after it began to look as if their grandfather was going to leave Rosalie every cent of his personal fortune. Two weeks ago, he could have contemplated her death with cheerfulness. Two weeks ago, however, was two weeks ago. Two weeks ago, Grandfather had still been alive. Or was it longer than that? Victor only knew what day of the week it was because the day of the week (along with the date) was always written on a large chalkboard set up in the lobby down at work. *"Monday, January 10,"* Victor would read when he got in in the morning, and then he would know where he was. It didn't matter. The problem was this. Having Grandfather found dead in Michael Pride's office at the Sojourner Truth Health Center was one thing. That was a death that could have been caused by anyone for any reason. Having Rosalie also found dead in Michael Pride's office at the Sojourner Truth Health Center was something else again. That looked deliberate. That looked planned. In short, that looked like one of the family—in spite of the fact that now that Grandfather was dead, there was no good reason for any of them to kill Rosalie at all. Victor didn't think the police were very logical about reasons. They liked to make their arrests and hand their suspects over for trial. They liked to see their names in papers like the New York *Sentinel* so that they could send the clippings to their parents who had retired to Florida. Victor had no doubt that he would make an excellent subject for a tabloid clipping. He was scared to death.

It was ten o'clock on Thursday morning, and he was standing in the reception area of the offices of Grandison, Harcum, Slater & Cole just off Wall Street, waiting for Bartram Cole to stop blathering and lead them all back to a conference room. Today was the day that had been set for the reading of Grandfather's will, and it was going off as planned, in spite of what had happened to Rosalie. Martha and Ida had both come down from the Sojourner Truth Health Center. Martha looked pinched and angry, the way she always looked. Ida looked oddly attractive in an ugly way, dressed in jeans and a shirt and a bright red linen blazer. When they had handed out the brains in this generation, Ida and Rosalie had definitely gotten all there were. Victor knew that almost everyone thought that Martha was more intelligent than he was, but he didn't credit that. He knew Martha.

Bartram Cole was a small man made entirely out of globes. He had globular cheeks on a globular head over a globular belly. Cole made his expensive suit look as if it had come off the rack at Sears. He bounced up and down on the balls of his feet, keeping time to the rhythm of his monologue.

"Well," he said after a while. "I suppose we ought to go back there and get down to business."

"He charges three hundred and fifty dollars an hour," Ida said into Victor's ear, in a whisper so soft Victor was sure he was the only one who could hear her. "At those rates, I could learn to bore people to death for hours on end, too."

In Victor's estimation, Ida could bore people for hours on end without being allowed to charge anything for it. Ida always made him tired. Victor hated serious people. They never had any fun. His sister and his girl cousins were all serious. Ida and Rosalie were at least useful, every once in a while—at least, Rosalie had been—because they helped him with that infernal contest. Martha couldn't even do that.

Bartram Cole was leading the way back into the bowels of the office suite. The bowels of this particular office suite might as well have been lined with mink. It might have been cheaper than what it had cost to outfit them as they were. The last time Victor had been up here—which was for his twenty-first birthday—the decor had been rather drab and office-y. Now it was high-tech pink, with lots of shiny metal surfaces and tinted glass. Victor knew decorators. This was the trademark of a famous one. Victor put the price down at about a hundred and fifty thousand dollars, no structural changes included.

The office suite was not quite so pink and shiny as the rest of the suite. The big custom-carved teakwood table that had been with the firm since its founding in 1867 had been retained. It had been surrounded by what Victor put down as a Ralph Lauren Polo version of English country-house chic. It had also been decked out in too many flowers. The room smelled like perfume.

Victor sat down in one of the chairs near the head of the table—you could always tell the head of the table at Grandison, Harcum, Slater & Cole; it was the seat closest to the Sargent portrait of the founder, old William Grandison the First—and stretched his legs. Ida sat down next to him and tapped him on his arm.

"I don't see why we have to go through this," she said. "I don't see why he can't just mail each of us a letter with the particulars and that would be that."

"That's so modern," Martha said. "We're in the wrong place for modernity. They wouldn't know what to do with it around here."

"Well, they ought to find out." Ida was indignant. "I

had to get someone to cover for me this morning, and it wasn't easy. I have work to do. The days when nobody had anything more important to do than attend meetings like this one are over."

"They're not over for me," Victor said. "I intend to be as idle and indolent as I possibly can, as soon as I get my hands on some cash. I'm certainly going to quit my job. Somebody else can present the grand prize check to the lucky Father's Day winner."

"Can't you just imagine what they say about us around here when we're not around?" Martha demanded. "They've probably got an office pool going on which of us did it."

"Don't be ridiculous," Ida said. "You always exaggerate everything. Nobody thinks we did it."

Martha shrugged. "That police detective does. Sheed. And I think Gregor Demarkian agrees with him."

"Hector Sheed thinks nothing of the sort." Ida sounded ready to explode. "He thinks Michael did it. You would have realized that if you weren't always so self-absorbed. And as for Gregor Demarkian—"

"I don't think Gregor Demarkian is half as frightening as I thought he'd be," Victor put in.

The women ignored him. They always ignored him.

"Gregor Demarkian is definitely the one we have to worry about," Martha said. "He insinuates himself into places. Have you noticed that? He's everywhere."

"I don't think we have to worry about anyone," Ida said. "None of us did it. None of us is in any danger of being accused of doing it. Grandfather got killed by some stray crazy who wandered up to the third floor without anyone realizing it."

"Is that what happened to Rosalie, too?" Martha asked. "Maybe the stray crazy is hiding in somebody's closet up there. Maybe he's like the phantom of the opera, always waiting in the wings."

"Oh, stop it," Ida snapped. "Just stop it. I don't know why I put up with you."

Victor didn't know why he put up with either of them. He didn't know why he put up with sitting in this chair. The conference door opened and Bartram Cole came in, carrying a sheaf of papers in one hand and a cardboard accordion file under the other arm. He bounced and bustled to the head of the table and sat down.

"Well," Cole said. "Here we are. Pleasant news in the wake of tragedy. A deeply felt tragedy, of course, but here we are. Pleasant news nonetheless."

"It's pleasanter than it could have been," Victor agreed. "You know, now that I'm thinking of it, what happens to Rosalie's money? The money she inherits under the will, I mean?"

"Oh, Victor," Martha said.

Bartram Cole shook his head. "I'm afraid I don't know anything about that. Miss van Straadt—possibly she would have said Ms. van Straadt—wasn't a client of ours. She preferred to retain a separate firm of attorneys. Of course, we would have been more than happy to oblige her. It's so often true that one can avoid a great deal of red tape, of duplication and expense, if all of a family's affairs are under one legal roof, so to speak. But Miss van Straadt was adamant. She wanted her own firm."

"It all depends on if she made a will," Ida explained to Victor. "If she did make a will, then her money goes to whoever she willed it to. If she didn't, then it goes to her next of kin. That would probably be her mother, if she's still alive."

"I think she is." Victor sighed.

"You've got to wonder what's wrong with this family," Martha said. "People who marry into it disappear as soon as they get the chance. We must send off some kind of antiattraction signal."

"Rosalie didn't send out any antiattraction signal," Ida said. "She had so many men around, you fell over them every time you ventured through her front door."

"Maybe one of them killed her," Martha said. "Rosalie van Straadt, cut off in her prime for being the world's champion prick tease."

"Did she only tease?" Ida asked the air. "Maybe that was the trouble."

Bartram Cole cleared his throat. "Well now," he said. "I have copies of the will for each of you. If you'll just look these over for a moment." He handed out long legal-size sheets of paper. Ida took one and appeared to read it. Martha took one and turned it upside down. Victor refused to touch his. It might be catching.

"Isn't it funny," he said. "This was supposed to be Rosalie's big moment. Grandfather dead. The will being read. Now she isn't even here to be upset that Grandfather died too soon."

"Just be glad that Grandfather didn't die too late," Martha said. "Did you know about all this, Mr. Cole? That Grandfather was thinking of changing his will."

"Well, yes." Bartram Cole was nonplussed. "Your grandfather spoke to me about it just a week before he died. I've been worried about it. I've been thinking I ought to tell the police about it. Under the circumstances, you know. On the other hand, confidentiality being what it is, and the firm acting in the interests of the remaining family—"

"Oh, there's nothing confidential about this," Victor said. "Everybody on earth knows that Grandfather was only a day away of leaving everything to Rosalie. You wouldn't be telling the police anything new."

"I don't understand," Bartram Cole said.

"You ought to go right ahead and talk to the police about Grandfather's changing his will," Martha explained patiently. "It's perfectly all right with us, because it isn't really a secret. We knew all about it all along. And of course we told the police all about it, too. So you wouldn't be betraying a confidence or anything like that."

"Rats in the basement of the New York *Sentinel* building knew that Rosalie was going to get it all," Victor said gloomily. "It was pitiful."

Bartram Cole looked from one to the other of them in consternation. "I don't understand," he said again. "I really don't understand. You're right, of course, that Mr. van Straadt was considering changing his will. In fact, I would say he was determined on it. But he wasn't going to change it in favor of Rosalie van Straadt."

"He wasn't?" Victor asked. "Who was he going to change it in favor of?"

"If Mr. van Straadt had lived," Bartram Cole said carefully, "he would have signed a will drawn up by me on the morning he died, leaving his entire personal fortune of eight hundred, eighty-five million dollars to his granddaughter Ida Greel."

T·H·R·E·E

1

From what Gregor Demarkian had heard about the attitude of the New York City Police Department to Michael Pride and this case, he had expected nothing but hostility from any member of the department he might run into. On the subject of himself, he had expected something worse than hostility. Shut out of the information loop, threatened with arrest for obstructing justice, lectured endlessly on the respective provinces of amateurs and professionals—Gregor had imagined all kinds of things. He knew how he would have behaved in Hector Sheed's position. He knew how he had behaved in those few cases when, as the agent in charge of a Bureau investigation, he had been provided with the spectacle of a private investigator. Of course, Gregor told himself, technically, he wasn't a private investigator—at least, not a private detective. You had to have a license to be one of those, and Gregor had neither gotten one nor intended to get one. He had never hung out a shingle or taken money to solve a case. He had simply fallen into things, a lot of things, over and over again. He tried to count how many extracurricular murders there had been in his

life since the death of his wife, Elizabeth, had led to his
early retirement from the Federal Bureau of Investigation. There must have been at least nine. Maybe there
had been ten. It had all gone by so fast. Gregor didn't
think he had ever acknowledged the ambivalent nature of
his involvement in these cases before—or the ambivalent
nature of his attitude to them. Back on Cavanaugh Street,
Bennis Hannaford was always telling him he didn't know
what he wanted out of his life. He was always telling her
she was absurd. Here he was, a man of almost sixty. Of
course he knew what he wanted out of his life. He must
already have had it. Every time Bennis would lecture
him like that, Gregor would go down to Father Tibor
Kasparian's apartment behind Holy Trinity Church and
rant and rave for an hour, telling Tibor what an absolute
pain Bennis was getting to be. Tibor would wait until he
was through and then say, well, since you already know
what you want out of this life, maybe you should give
some consideration to what you want out of the next one.

But Hector Sheed was not hostile. He was curious.
He was so curious, he made Gregor uncomfortable, walking around and around him, looking him over back to
front, peering down into his face the way dim high
school students peer into the eyepieces of microscopes
they don't know how to use. Except that Hector Sheed
wasn't dim. He was strange, Gregor thought, but not
dim. On the other hand, maybe it wasn't so strange that
Hector Sheed was strange. What did it do to a man to
work day after day in an environment like this one? Manhattan Homicide was an interstation service. Hector
Sheed wouldn't necessarily spend all his time in Harlem
or places like it, at least not as a matter of policy. Policy
notwithstanding, Gregor was willing to bet that Hector
did, in fact, spend most of his time in Harlem or places

like it. That was the way the world worked. Gregor didn't think he could have stood it, himself. Bleak urban landscapes made him tired and depressed. He needed both color and hope to keep his mind working smoothly. Maybe everybody did.

"The problem," Hector Sheed had told Gregor that first night, after Rosalie van Straadt's body had been taken to the morgue, "is that this is New York. It's not like some other places. I can't just declare you a consultant and haul you around like a fire dog, the way that guy in Pennsylvania did with the phony psychic."

Gregor winced at the word *psychic* but was heartened by the word *phony*. Too many people believed that kind of nonsense to make him entirely happy with the mental state of the American public.

"I don't think I have to get in your way at all," Gregor told Hector Sheed. "If you'll just tell me when I'm becoming a problem, I'll accommodate. After all, I'm only here on behalf of the—"

"Of the Cardinal. I know. The Catholic Church in New York may not be what it once was, Mr. Demarkian, but it's still a political force about the size of King Kong. The city will go head to head with the Cardinal when it feels like it has to, or when there's another constituency just as powerful with closer ties to the mayor's office. The city does not pick fights with a Cardinal Archbishop for the hell of it."

"Protesting interference in this case by me would constitute picking a fight for the hell of it?"

"Of course it would. You're not interfering. You're helping the department with its investigation. What's the phrase they use in all the English murder mysteries? 'Helping the authorities with their inquiries.'"

"That means you've been arrested," Gregor said.

"Oh. Sorry. I don't really like English murder mysteries. They're not realistic. My wife reads them the way kids eat cotton candy. My line on you is that you're our conduit to all the people at the center we don't know much about. I'll find a better way to put it if I have to talk to the media about you."

"That's good. What you just said didn't make any sense to me."

"Well, don't worry about it, Mr. Demarkian. It'll all be perfectly painless. You can conduct this entire case by running around the center asking questions and meeting me for a beer at the Akareeba Restaurant to give me the answers."

Gregor was intrigued. "The Akareeba Restaurant. Is that African?"

"Nah," Hector Sheed said. "It's a steak and fries place off Central Park North. You might as well get ready to be the only white guy in the place. They won't mind."

"I'm glad to hear it."

"So ask questions I'm going to want to hear the answers to. I'll get back to you later."

Now it was bright and early on Friday morning, with the sun streaming through the plate-glass window of his sixteenth-floor room at the New York Hilton, and Gregor found himself wondering how he'd been working out. With one thing and another, he hadn't had a chance to meet Hector Sheed at the Akareeba Restaurant. Their first meeting there was supposed to be today, for lunch, at eleven thirty. Hector had apologized for the early hour. He couldn't help it. He had to get in to work. Gregor merely felt frustrated. Hector had his reasons, Gregor was sure. The murders at the Sojourner Truth Health Center would not be Hector's only responsibility. Gregor could only imagine what a detective's caseload at Manhattan Homicide was like. Gregor could make no such excuses for himself. In the time since Rosalie van Straadt had been found dying in Michael Pride's office, he seemed to be going around in circles. Talk to Michael. Talk to Augie. Talk to Father Donleavy. Talk. Talk. Talk. Nobody ever seemed to say anything important, or even sensible.

The room at the Hilton was being paid for by the Archdiocese of New York. Gregor had stayed there once or twice before, when the Bureau was paying for it. He found the rooms much too large and much too luxurious. The bathrooms were always meticulously clean and startlingly high-tech. There were never any claw tubs or visible plumbing at the Hilton. Getting out of the shower, he caught himself in the wall-long vanity mirror. He did not have the kind of body that lent itself well to being looked at in wall-size mirrors. Gregor wrapped himself in a towel. If he had still been with the Bureau, they would have sent him out to get into shape again—or tried to. From what Gregor had remembered, they had tried to, several times, and he had always been able to come up with enough work to make the project impossible. He went to his suitcase and got out a clean set of underwear and put it on. Then he went to his closet and found a pair of good gray slacks and a shirt. A few days in New York had disabused him of the notion that the city was always cold. Yesterday, sitting in the main branch of the New York Public Library, going through ten years of microfilmed magazine stories on Charles van Straadt, Gregor had been sweating in spite of the air-conditioning. Now he reached for a jacket and tie anyway. He couldn't help himself. If he wasn't on vacation, he was supposed to be in a suit.

He opened the door to his room and found his papers

waiting for him in the hall. He paged through the *Post*, the *News*, and *The New York Times* and came to rest for a moment on the *Sentinel*. The murder of Rosalie van Straadt wasn't front-page fodder for any of the papers. The *Sentinel*, however, seemed to have gone off the news beat altogether. There was another red banner over the masthead, announcing their Father's Day contest—**ONLY THREE MORE DAYS TO ENTER!!!**—and a headline that simply said, "Aww . . ." in really gigantic type. The subhead read: **"This pathetic pooch is a miracle worker. See page 17."** Gregor flipped through the other papers again. President Clinton had held a press conference on the state of the economy, which was bad. Bosnia-Herzegovina had exploded in round 2,224,667,998 of their civil war. The government of the Ukraine had voted to install a monarchy, or something very much like it. On the front page of the *Sentinel* there was a picture of a miserable looking dachshund in a baseball cap.

Gregor walked back into the center of his room, threw the papers onto his still-unmade bed, and sat down in the chair next to the desk. Then he picked up the phone there and dialed. If this had been Philadelphia, not only would the van Straadt case still have been all over the papers, he himself would have been all over them, too. He could just imagine what the *Philadelphia Inquirer* was saying about him right this minute: "The Armenian-American Hercule Poirot Takes on the Big Apple." That would be about right. It depressed Gregor mightily to be in a place where murder was so common that even the sequential killings of two members of an internationally prominent family couldn't hold the attention of the public for three days. Well, maybe that wasn't quite fair. The public was probably still interested. They just weren't interested enough to get the professionals in-

terested. What would it take to get them off their rear
ends and moving? The World Trade Center blast had
done it. Maybe they could get really involved in something like a flying saucer landing in Central Park. Or
maybe not. Maybe New Yorkers would look on Martians
as just one more set of damn tourists.

The phone was ringing and ringing in his ear. No one
was answering. Bennis must be out. Gregor hung up and
drummed his fingers against the desk. Frustration didn't
even begin to describe it. He felt bottled up.

He got up and went over to the window to look outside. The Archdiocese of New York had more clout than
the Federal Bureau of Investigation. He had a room over-
looking Sixth Avenue. Down on the street, cars were
bright colored blobs. They looked like they were having
a hell of a lot more fun than he was.

They're probably all down there hating the traffic,
Gregor told himself, but the thought wouldn't stick. He
had to get out of this room. It was driving him crazy.

He had taken his wallet and his change and his keys
out of his pants the night before and put them on the
night table next to his bed. Now he picked them up and
stuffed them into his pockets again. A walk, that was
what he needed. A walk would clear his head.

If anything could.

2

Whether Gregor Demarkian's walk cleared his head or
not was a moot point. He took a very long one, going down
Fifth Avenue to look in the windows of Bergdorf Goodman
and Saks, clucking indulgently at all the silly looking
clothes Bennis would probably buy six of and never wear.

He went west to Times Square and looked at the bright fronts of the theaters and the neon jumpiness of the adult entertainment centers. The adult entertainment centers seemed to be operating twenty-four hours a day. After a while, he began to walk slowly up Central Park West. He had gotten explicit directions to the Akareeba Restaurant from Hector Sheed. He had been a little worried about how difficult it would be to find a cab that would take him there. In New York, when you didn't know the neighborhoods, it was difficult to know what you were getting yourself into. In the end, Gregor decided not to worry. He was involved in walking. He would go on walking. He walked up past the Dakota and the San Remo and the other great apartment buildings on Central Park West, and then farther, past buildings just as large and just as grand but without the famous names. The buildings got more and more run down and the people got shabbier and shabbier the farther north he went, but the energy level actually seemed to be rising. These people were poor but not destitute, that was it. This was poverty as Gregor had known it, growing up. Here the broad sidewalk of Central Park West was cluttered with people selling from blankets and garbage bags spread across the pavement. He was offered watches and sunglasses and books and ties in the space of half a block.

"Traditional for Father's Day," a very young man with black skin and the almond eyes and fine-boned jaw line of a Thai watercolor portrait. "Ties for every occasion."

Gregor reached the Akareeba Restaurant in a much better mood than any he had been in since he had arrived from Philadelphia. He believed in the melting pot, he really did, especially since nothing was ever completely melted in it. A friend of his at the Bureau had once described the United States as a kind of pudding stone. There was a mass of glue and then a plethora of different rocks. The rocks were stuck together in the glue, but never dissolved in it.

If I go on like this, I'm going to start singing "America the Beautiful" on street corners, Gregor told himself. The Akareeba was only one block north of Central Park North. Gregor walked that block, made the right turn he had been told to, and found himself face to face with a gaudy front that took up a third of the commercial space along that side of the street. "AKAREEBA" the sign said in shiny foil letters. The letters were made up of tiny sequins in half a dozen colors that shivered and jumped in the wind. The windows were painted over with African scenes that featured large numbers of bare-breasted, monumentally well-endowed women. Gregor could just imagine what the wives and girlfriends of the men who came here said about those. He found the door, four steps down from the street, and went in through it. He found himself at the edge of a large room full of dark wood tables and presided over by a long, ebonywood bar. The bar was out of a 1930s movie. There was more glass behind it than there was in Gregor's bathroom in the Hilton. There were enough bottles and glasses and siphons and tumblers to cater a Washington political wedding. There was no hostess. Gregor moved into the gloom and looked around. It was only eleven fifteen. Maybe Hector wasn't here yet.

Hector was here. The detective came towering out of the darkness, looking shocked and a little exasperated.

"How did you get here?" he demanded. "I'm sitting right over there by the window. I didn't see a cab come into the street."

"I didn't take a cab. I walked."

"Walked?" Hector was worse than shocked. "Check your pants. Make sure you still have your wallet."

Gregor checked. He still had his wallet, as he knew he would, but he checked anyway. "I'm not a complete babe in the woods," he said dryly. "I was with the Federal Bureau of Investigation for twenty years."

"Twenty years of insulation, that's what that was," Hector said. "You can't just walk around the city like that. Especially not in this neighborhood when you're so—uh—"

"White?" Gregor suggested.

"Just come on over here." Hector led the way to the table he had staked out, a big round one pulled right up next to a window with a woman carrying fruit on her head painted on it. Gregor saw immediately what it was Hector liked about this table. The ceiling above it was significantly higher than the ceiling in the rest of the room. What quirk of architectural whimsy or haphazard remodeling had made it that way, Gregor couldn't begin to guess. He took off his jacket, hung it over the back of a chair, and sat down.

"We got the lab reports back last night," Hector said. "I tried to call you, but you must still have been up at the center. And I didn't want to talk to you there."

"I don't blame you." Gregor sighed. "I was up at the center. Getting nowhere, if you want to know the truth. I'm beginning to feel fairly useless."

"I'm beginning to feel fairly useless myself," Hector said. "The lab reports said just what we expected to say. Strychnine. Just like Charles van Straadt. And just like Charles van Straadt, nothing in the room that the strychnine could have been in."

A young woman in a black skirt and a white blouse came up to their table. Hector ordered a cup of coffee and looked quizzically at Gregor. "You want a beer or something?" he asked. "You want some lunch?"

"I'll just take a cup of coffee. Black," Gregor said. "You know, I hadn't thought of it before. What the strychnine was administered in, I mean. It completely slipped my mind. I suppose that's because strychnine is almost always given in food or drink, when it's given deliberately. Especially drink. Coffee. Alcohol. I just assumed—"

"I keep assuming the same thing." Hector finished off his own coffee. "I have the reports to force me to keep looking at it, though. We tested everything in Michael Pride's office, both when Charles van Straadt was killed and this last time, with Rosalie. There wasn't a thing in the place that any strychnine had ever been in, except the bodies."

Gregor considered this. "Did you test the things in Michael's downstairs office? In his examining room?"

"With Charles van Straadt we didn't. With this we did."

"And?"

Hector shrugged. "There's a bottle of strychnine clearly marked 'strychnine' in Michael Pride's private locked medical cabinet. Other than that, not a thing."

"That's odd," Gregor said. And it was, too. Very odd. "That doesn't make sense, does it? Did you run a stomach content analysis?"

"Of course we did. Both times."

"What about those?"

"Well," Hector said. "Charles van Straadt's stomach was empty except for coffee and strychnine. Rosalie van Straadt had had a doughnut recently enough for there to be traces of it left in her stomach—and coffee and strychnine."

"It was in the coffee, then." Gregor nodded. "It would

have had to be. Unless—you did check for hypodermic needle wounds?"

"We checked, yeah, Mr. Demarkian, but we could always be wrong. Hypodermic tracks aren't easy to find unless there are a lot of them, like with junkies. But you know, I don't think there were any to find. I mean, what would the murderer do? Tell Charles van Straadt and then Rosalie van Straadt, just a minute there, I want to give you a shot of this stuff, don't worry about it?"

"That might not be entirely out of the question if the person administering the shot was Michael Pride," Gregor pointed out. "He is a doctor. And there is another possible scenario. Maybe the killer filled a hypodermic with strychnine and used the hypodermic the way another killer would have used a knife. Wait until the victim's back is turned, stick it in to a convenient patch of uncovered skin and plunge."

"Would that have worked if the killer didn't hit a blood vessel?" Hector asked.

"I don't know," Gregor admitted. "To tell you the truth, I've never run across a case of that kind. Without something like that, though, we're back to the problem of what became of the cups the coffee was in, and why. Neither Charles van Straadt nor Rosalie was on any kind of medication?"

"Nothing prescribed."

"What about over the counter? Were either of them taking allergy pills? Did either of them have a cold they might have been taking a decongestant for? How about aspirin for a headache?"

Hector Sheed shifted in his seat. "Neither of them had a cold, and neither of them had any allergies severe enough for their doctors to know about. We've talked to the doctors, by the way. We're pretty thorough in New

York. I'll admit we didn't ask about over-the-counter allergy medication per se, but we did get complete health records. The only thing of the kind you're talking about now in either record was in Rosalie van Straadt's about ten years ago. She was taking diet pills."

"Diet pills? But she was very thin."

"She was even thinner, then. She weighed about sixty-nine pounds. She had to be hospitalized."

"Wonderful. But that doesn't help us much, does it? We're still back to the coffee cups. Or to Michael Pride. I was given to understand that you were determined to pin the killing of Charles van Straadt on Michael Pride."

"Were you?" Hector Sheed looked amused. "I'll bet you didn't hear that from Michael. No, Mr. Demarkian, I'm not intent on pinning anything on Michael Pride. In fact, I don't think Michael Pride could have committed either of these two murders. And you know why?"

"No. Why?"

"Because they're not nuts enough." Hector was adamant. "Michael Pride is probably a great man. He may even be a saint. But what he also is, no question, is a certified nutcase. I kid you not. I used to be in uniform down in Times Square. Good God."

"You ran into Michael Pride down there," Gregor suggested.

Hector snorted. "Ran into is putting it mildly. You think this glory hole business the papers made so much fuss about is a big deal? Hell, Michael must be getting old. Some of the things he used to pull—what are you supposed to make of something like this? I mean, never mind the fact that the man's tastes in sexual congress are bizarre in the extreme—I mean, what the hell, Mr. Demarkian, everybody's a little weird about sex—never mind all that, what about AIDS? The man is a doctor. The man is a good doctor. He ought to know better."

"I agree with you," Gregor said. "But he doesn't seem to care."

"If Michael Pride committed a murder," Hector said, "what he'd do is get a wheat scythe and whack his victim's head off into the fountain in front of the Plaza Hotel. Michael Pride is not an introvert. He's not even what you could call ordinarily restrained."

"Possibly," Gregor insisted, "but look at what we have here. We at least have to consider the possibility—"

"That Michael pretended to administer medication to Charles van Straadt and Rosalie van Straadt and administered strychnine instead? All right. Consider it. It won't work."

"Why not?"

"Because Rosalie van Straadt wouldn't have let him near her," Hector said triumphantly. "She had a case for Michael Pride that made Elizabeth Taylor's love for Richard Burton look weak. And Michael was Michael. Rosalie hated him. She wouldn't have let him near her."

Gregor thought about the scene in Michael Pride's examining room. The glass on the floor. The papers scattered everywhere. Rosalie in tears.

"Maybe you're right," he admitted. "But then we're back to where we began, and we have the same problem as when we began. Strychnine works quickly. It works very quickly. It couldn't have been administered to the victims in the cafeteria, say, and not taken effect until they got upstairs. There might have been a ghost of a chance of something like that if either of them had eaten a large meal right before taking the poison, but neither of them had. That means the strychnine would have to have been administered either in Michael Pride's office or somewhere else close on the third floor."

"It couldn't have been administered anywhere else in the case of Charles van Straadt," Hector pointed out. "Charles van Straadt went into Michael's office around six or so and stayed there until his body was found by Michael at eight something. You can look up the times in the report, but you see what I mean."

"I see what you mean. Did Charles van Straadt or Rosalie have some special coffee cup they always used?"

"Not that I know of. We can ask around." Hector took a little notebook and a Bic pen out of the pocket of his jacket and wrote it all down. "I don't see how that's going to help us with our problem, though. Why would the murderer take away a cup belonging to the victim? Even if it did have strychnine in it? What difference would it make?"

"I don't know."

"I just remembered something else," Hector said. "When we were questioning people right after Charles van Straadt was killed. I talked to Rosalie. She was drinking coffee out of one of those white squishy disposable cups. You know, like they give out in the cafeteria."

"Right." Gregor sighed. While they had been talking, his coffee had come, and so had more coffee for Hector, and neither of them seemed to have noticed. Gregor took a sip from his and found it good but only lukewarm. He looked around and found at least a dozen people in the restaurant who hadn't been there when he first arrived. "It seems to be getting late," he said. "I don't want to hold up your lunch."

Hector Sheed looked at his watch. "Quarter to twelve. I'd better eat something before I have to leave. I hate eating take-out at my desk. I get grease on my papers and the stuff tastes like shit anyway."

"I think I'll skip lunch until I get back to the center."

"Really?" Hector Sheed shook his head. "You're making a mistake, Mr. Demarkian. In spite of the low-rent atmosphere, this is one of the best restaurants in New York. Maybe because of the low-rent atmosphere. The food's much better here than it is in the cafeteria uptown."

"Oh, I'm sure of that," Gregor said. "It's not the food that's the point. It's that I want an excuse to buy lunch for somebody at the center."

"Who?"

"Martha van Straadt."

"Why?"

Gregor smiled. "Because of a very interesting conversation I had on the afternoon before Rosalie van Straadt died with a young man named Robbie Yagger. Go ahead and order yourself some lunch and I'll tell you all about it. I didn't think it had anything to do with the death of Charles van Straadt when I first heard it, but now I'm not so sure."

F·O·U·R

1

Sister Mary Augustine had been too well trained to have anything like a hair-trigger temper, or even what most people would call a spontaneous emotional life. She might let herself be called "Augie" and wear bright colorful sweatsuits under her tiny modern veil, but at heart she was the same sixteen-year-old girl who had left her Irish Catholic neighborhood in Boston at the end of her senior year in high school to enter her order's Rhode Island motherhouse. That had been in the days well before Vatican II, when the church and the nuns who ran so much of her believed that a religious Sister ought to be a model of discipline, a beacon of self-control. Augie had started out with a hair-trigger temper. She had spent most of her novitiate doing penance for one outburst or another, the penances always being preceded by long lectures from the novice mistress, Sister Charles Madeleine. At the time, Augie had considered Sister Charles Madeleine the eighth wonder of the world, the only body in history that was able to walk and talk and breathe after having been entirely drained of blood. After all these years, Augie hadn't changed her mind. In spite of the outfits, she wasn't really a modern nun. She had no use whatsoever for those orders that had gone whole hog into self-actualization and the fulfillment of the person. She believed wholeheartedly in the emptying of the self, in living not for her own sake but for the glory of God and the good she could do to other people. On the other hand, there was a limit. Sister Charles Madeleine was well past Augie's limit.

It was twelve o'clock noon on Friday, and Augie knew why she was thinking of Sister Charles Madeleine. Sister Charles Madeleine was like a lightning rod, the place Augie's anger went to when she was angry, the one object Augie felt perfectly comfortable being furious at. Noon on Friday was always a slow time for the emergency room. Actually, except for the death of Rosalie van Straadt, they had been having a slow week. Augie came out of the head nurse's office and looked around at the empty corridors and the admitting desk with nobody at it. She was wearing a jade green sweatsuit with "Luck of the Irish" printed across the chest. These days, everybody she knew gave her sweatsuits for Christmas and her name day. Her name day was what they celebrated in the convent instead of her birthday. She looked up and down again and then began to walk slowly toward the back of the floor. As she walked, she stooped to pick up scattered copies of the New York *Sentinel* from the floor. The New York *Sentinel* was still delivered to the center every morning in batches, intended to be given out free. Augie would have thought, with Charles van Straadt dead and gone, that the newspapers would stop coming. Maybe she had misjudged the van Straadt family—all of whom, with the exception of Ida, she considered absolutely worthless. Maybe nobody in the circulation department at the New York *Sentinel* knew that Charles van Straadt was dead.

I'm going senile, Augie thought. I'm descending into schizophrenia. I'm losing my mind.

She got to the door of Michael Pride's examining room and stopped. The door was open. Augie looked inside and saw Michael with his back to her, standing next to his desk, going through a stack of papers. There was always a lot of paperwork to be got through these days. The Manhattan City Council didn't like the Catholic Church much, or anything connected to her. They had closed down two of Mother Teresa's AIDS hospices for "zoning violations," and Augie knew they would close the Sojourner Truth Health Center if they could. They didn't push it because Michael was no self-effacing, saintly nun. He wouldn't accept defeat in meek resignation. He'd go to the newspapers and he'd get their attention, too. Still, the council felt free to harass. The center had to file document after document after document. Fire inspectors and health inspectors and other city inspectors showed up so often, Michael kept a volunteer lawyer on duty at the center at all times, to follow the inspectors around, to make sure the inspectors didn't bribe anybody or intimidate anybody into believing the inspectors had to be bribed. It was crazy. And this was what happened when the mayor and the police department and the vast majority of ordinary citizens supported the center. What would happen to them if that support was ever withdrawn?

Michael looked away from his papers and stretched. He didn't look at her. Augie came into the examining room and shut the door softly behind her. Michael turned and raised his eyebrows. It was worse than *déjà vu*. This had happened a million times before. This had been her life for over a decade now. Michael. The center. Herself.

Michael looked down at the papers he had been working on and then back at her again. He was smiling slightly. "Hello, Augie. I've been expecting you to show up. You've been banging around like a drummer all day."

"Have I been that obvious?"

"To me, you have."

"I talked to Eamon Donleavy," Augie said. "He's— let's not use the word *upset*. It's a stupid word. Upset."

There really were a lot of papers in the stack Michael had. He picked them up and carried them across the room to his file cabinet, moving deliberately, as if he were playing a part in a dramatic dance. He looked fine, Augie thought, feeling how insane this meeting was. Michael looked *fine*. He couldn't possibly have AIDS.

Michael opened the top drawer of the file cabinet, took out a nearly empty manila folder, and put the papers inside. Then he refiled the folder and closed the file cabinet drawer.

"Prescription records," he said absently. "I've been meaning to get to them for a couple of weeks."

Augie came farther into the room and sat down on the edge of the examining table. "I'm not Eamon Donleavy. I'm a nurse. I want you to tell me a few things."

"I'll tell you anything you want to know, Augie."

"Do you actually have AIDS or are you just HIV positive?"

"I've got AIDS. The Kaposi's sarcoma showed up about two weeks ago—at least, that was when I noticed."

"If you noticed it, other people might notice it. People you were . . . intimate with."

"I'm not intimate with anybody, Augie, you ought to know that. Not intimate in that way."

"You could spread it."

"I could if I wasn't careful. But I am careful, Augie, I'm very careful. I'm careful at the center and I'm careful when I'm out."

"You can't always have been careful. If you had been, you wouldn't have caught it."

"I don't know if that's true," Michael said. "We don't really know much about how people catch AIDS—oh, we know about the contact of bodily fluids and all that, but for somebody who lives the way I do—"

"You don't have to live that way," Augie said harshly. "You really don't."

Michael made an impatient gesture. "I live the way I live because I want to, Augie, you ought to know that by now. I work at the center because I want to. I've never had a single reason for doing anything in my life except that it was what I wanted to do. I'm not a religious person, Sister Augustine. You ought to know that by now, too."

Augie looked down at her hands. They were an old person's hands, wrinkled and veined. She wouldn't see the fair side of fifty again. Michael would never see fifty at all. Augie's head ached.

"I've been thinking of the City Council," she said. "Of what they could make of this. I've been thinking of the papers. I've been thinking of the center. What's going to happen to the center?"

"I don't know what's going to happen to the center, Augie. I don't even know what's going to happen to me. Maybe, when I get too sick to work, I'll just check in downstairs and have your nuns take care of me."

"I don't understand what you think you're doing with your life," Augie said, "I never have understood it. You're an attractive man. So you're gay. You're gay. You could have found somebody to settle down with."

"I didn't want to find somebody to settle down with. Augie, don't do this."

"Why shouldn't I do it? Why shouldn't I? You're one of the few people I'm close to in this world, one of the few people I've ever been close to, you're closer to me than family, and you're going to die, die, in two or three or five years, and what for? What for? Glory holes?"

"Augie—"

"Don't patronize me, Michael. I'm not some seventeen-year-old blushing virgin and I'm not some hysterical woman, either. What you've been doing doesn't make sense. It never made sense."

"I'll bet you're a virgin," Michael said.

"I told you not to patronize me." Augie hopped off the examining table onto the floor. Had this room always been so shabby? Augie couldn't remember ever having paid attention to it before. Augie couldn't remember ever having had the time. Michael was staring at her. His hands were tucked into the patch pockets of his white smock. His face was set in a serious mask. Augie had the terrible feeling that she was letting him down.

"I'm sorry," she said. "I suppose I ought to get back to work. We won't be this quiet for long. We never are. I have things to get done."

"Are you going to be all right?"

"Yes, Michael. I'm going to be fine. You're the one who's not going to be all right."

"I'm going to be physically miserable, Augie, but I still think I'm going to be all right."

"I don't understand how you could have gone on doing the things you did, knowing what the risks were."

"I never pay attention to risks, Augie, I can't. I'm a coward. If I pay attention to risks, I get scared, and then I don't do anything at all."

"I have to get out of here," Augie said.

And it was true. She did have to get out of there. She had to get through the door and back into the hall and then down the hall and then—where? She didn't know. She was just glad that Michael wasn't trying to stop her. She couldn't see anything. Sister Kenna was in the corridor. She was saying hello. Augie felt her own head nod, stiffly, the way it used to with parents she didn't like when she was working as the head nurse in the pediatrics ward at the last hospital her order had been able to run before Vatican II happened and the world fell apart. Augie was a little shocked at herself. She had never longed for the days before Vatican II. She was not an ecclesiastical Luddite. What was wrong with her?

Sister Kenna was gone. The corridor was empty. There was a big walk-in linen closet just this side of the stairs. Augie jerked the door of the linen closet open and walked inside. Then she closed the door tightly on herself and sat down on a pile of folded white sheets. She didn't want the pre–Vatican II church back. That wasn't it. She just wanted Michael. She wanted Michael. She wanted Michael not to be sick.

When Sister Mary Augustine was a very small child, the priest in her parish had been an immigrant from the old country with a head full of fire and brimstone. He had believed in delineating each of the separate flames in the fires of hell and in making his parishioners look on the terrible face of God. The face of God is in the tornado, Father Connaghie had said. The face of God is in the erupting volcano. The face of God is in the tidal wave engulfing the shore. The face of God is not comfort but power, unleashed and vast.

Sister Augustine folded her arms over her knees and put her head down on them. Every blood vessel in her body was throbbing. Her mind felt as if it had been wiped clean. Augie didn't believe in a God who would send a disease like AIDS to punish people for sex. She did believe in a God who met each and every one of his creatures face to face at the moment of death. She didn't know if that was orthodox Catholic theology or not, but it was what she had taken away from her from Father Connaghie's homilies, and what she had held fast to ever since. She tried to make herself imagine Michael standing face to face with God, but all she got was a terrible hole, an absolute emptiness, standing here next to her on earth where Michael should be.

Then she tucked her head even lower, past her arms and onto her knees, and burst into tears.

2

Ida Greel knew that ever since the reading of the will, Victor and Martha had been angry at her. To be precise, Victor had been vaguely annoyed, and Martha had been furious. Ida didn't blame them. They suspected she had known about Grandfather's intentions all along, and they were right. Ida had taken a certain amount of satisfaction in watching Grandfather string that silly twit Rosalie along. She hadn't given a thought to how Victor and Martha would feel about it. Ida had never liked Rosalie very much. She had never liked any of her relatives, even her grandfather, but she had been especially intolerant about Rosalie. When they were all growing up, Rosalie had been the perfect one, thin, pretty, not stupid like Victor. Ida would go to her grave thinking she had heard twice as much as she needed to just how cute Rosalie was in curls.

If it had been Rosalie who was angry at her, Ida wouldn't have bothered to do anything about it. She wouldn't have cared. If it had been Victor, Ida would have let it ride. Victor always came around in the end. Martha was a special case. Ida wasn't close to Martha. Nobody could be. Still, Ida relied on her. It was a relief for Ida to have somebody at the center that she could talk to without having to mentally translate everything she said. Before coming up here to work, Ida had never realized how many differences there were in simple vocabulary between rich people and poor people. Then there were the expectations. Ida had a whole list of different kinds of behavior that she considered "normal." She wasn't aware of it as a list, but it was there. When she had lunch with a large group of other people and they were going to split the check, she expected to *split* it, to divide it by the number of people at the table, to charge everyone an equal share. Up here, split checks were pored over endlessly, the charges parceled out bit by bit, each person being responsible only for what she had actually ordered. The check took half an hour to unravel and left at least one person in tears. Then there was the little matter of the coats. Ida put her winter coat anywhere, on the back of a chair, across a desk, shoved into a locker all crumpled up. If it fell on the floor, she picked it up, brushed it off, and put it out of the way again. All the other people here were very careful to hang their coats on hangers. If those coats fell on the floor, their owners cleaned and agonized and accused. Everyone got together and tried to figure out who had *caused* the coat to fall onto the floor. It drove Ida crazy. The big things were easy to take in stride. Race and class, education and politics—Ida had been astonished at how little any of these things had mattered. The small things were impossible. Ida had started to refuse invitations out to lunch and dinner from the people she worked with. She had begun to steer clear of the lockers and the racks and the other places people hung their coats. She had begun to use her cousin Martha as a tranquilizer.

Now it was fifteen minutes after twelve noon on Friday, and Ida had no one she wanted to go to lunch with. It had been a quiet morning. She had used her unusual free time to get her paperwork done and to look over the notes for her pharmacology class. Ida had something close to an eidetic memory. She could repeat her own notes back to herself verbatim, even without studying. Her mind was still on that scene in the lawyers' offices yesterday, with Victor in shock and Martha brewing steam and vitriol. She got up and walked to the door of the nurses' station and looked out. She went far to the other end of the hall, walking into what seemed to be the linen closet. She told herself she wasn't getting enough sleep and searched around in the pocket of her smock for her cough drops. Michael was in his office, free for once, but Ida didn't have anything to talk to him about. There was nobody else around.

Ida found her cough drops, popped one into her mouth, and made up her mind. There was a phone at the station desk. Ida picked it up, dialed the east building, and asked for Martha. She didn't say it was Ida calling, because Martha might refuse to answer, just the way she had refused to answer Grandfather on the night he died. Ida said she was Augie.

"Sister?" Martha asked, coming immediately on the line.

"It's not Sister Augustine," Ida said, "it's me. I want you to meet me in the cafeteria right away."

"I've got nothing to say to you," Martha said.

"I've got plenty to say to you," Ida told her. "Stop acting like a jerk. Come on downstairs."

"Why should I come downstairs? Why should I talk to you at all? You knew all about it."

"Yes, all right. I knew all about it. That's not the point."

"It's the point to me." Martha was working herself into a grand passion. "You let Victor and me make absolute fools out of ourselves. Victor. Your own brother."

"My own brother is an ass," Ida said impatiently. "Will you listen to reason for once? It doesn't matter what Grandfather intended to do. He didn't get around to doing it."

"He might have. And Victor and I were having meetings with you, getting together to formulate strategy, intending to head him off at the pass. And you never had any interest in heading him off at the pass. You were going to pick up eight hundred million dollars and—and laugh at us."

"Maybe I would have and maybe I wouldn't have. Can't you understand that that isn't what we have to be worried about now?"

"No."

"This is just what the police want, you know, Martha. The police and the Cardinal and that Demarkian. They want us fighting with each other. They want us divided."

"They don't care about us at all," Martha said. "They think Michael did it."

"Maybe they did before Rosalie died, but they don't now. And after all, Martha, I'm not the one that silly kid with the sign saw going into Michael's first-floor office just before Grandfather died."

"What?" Martha said.

There was a chair pulled up against the counter far-

ther along toward the door. Ida got it over to where she
was standing and sat down on it. She had heard the panic
in Martha's voice. It had made her feel instantaneously
better. Panic was exactly what she needed.

"What are you implying?" Martha asked now. "I was
nowhere near that examining room on the night Grandfather died."

"He says you were," Ida told Martha. "Robbie Yagger.
That's his name. The one who carries the sign about how
abortion is the same as the Holocaust. I heard him tell
Gregor Demarkian."

"Robbie Yagger is a loon," Martha said indignantly.
"And you couldn't have overheard him tell Gregor
Demarkian anything. I saw him the day he talked to
Gregor Demarkian in the cafeteria. You weren't any-
where around."

"It wasn't in the cafeteria. It was outside on the sidewalk. They were just standing there talking."

There was a pause on the other end of the line. "I
don't care who told who what," Martha said. "The only
time I was in the west building that whole night was
when Victor and I went to the cafeteria. And then later
I was there with you."

"If you came in and out by the front door the way
you are supposed to, you probably went right by Michael's examining room. I'm not denying that you didn't
go in there, Martha, I'm just telling you what Robbie
Yagger said. And I'm trying to make you understand how
it's going to sound."

"Why should I care?"

"Martha, for God's sake. Of course you have to care.
We all have to care. We're in the middle of a murder investigation."

"You don't have to care, do you?" Martha said. "You're

the one who never would have done it. Assuming you can prove you knew it was you Grandfather was going to change his will in favor of, instead of Rosalie."

Ida looked down at her nails. They were without polish, bitten to the quick. "I have a letter," she said.

"From Grandfather?"

"Yes."

"Grandfather never wrote letters."

"Well, he wrote this one to me. Martha, for God's sake. Will you please meet me in the cafeteria? For one thing, I'm starving. For another, we have to talk."

Out in the hallway there were footsteps, the brisk footsteps of a nurse, the halting ones of a patient coming in off the street. Ida looked at the clock and tapped her foot. If a real emergency exploded around this place, she would never get her lunch.

"Martha?"

"All right," Martha said. "I'll meet you downstairs. For a minute."

"For as long as it takes. Don't be stupid, Martha. Hurry up before somebody comes along and wants you to do something."

"I'll be there as soon as I can."

There was a click in Ida's ear, sharp, too sharp. She hung up and stared at the phone. Maybe she had overplayed her hand. Martha was so impossible. Maybe she shouldn't have made it sound so—definite—about what Robbie Yagger had said to Gregor Demarkian. If she were Martha and she were the murderer and she'd just heard something like that, she'd get Robbie Yagger into a safe place and do him in.

Ida got off the chair she had been sitting on, stuffed another cough drop into her mouth, and went out into the corridor again. The patient she had heard was sitting at Admitting, looking morose. He was an ancient man in tattered clothes who looked as if he hadn't had a coherent thought in years. Ida didn't understand Michael Pride. Why did he want to save these people? What was left in them worth saving?

She went to the back of the hall and down the stairs to the cafeteria.

3

Outside, at exactly one o'clock, Robbie Yagger found himself getting tired. No, he was worse than tired. He was confused. He was confused with a confusion so violent and so lawless, it was as unlike his usual state of mental chaos as a full-grown jaguar was like a domestic feline kitten. Back at the Holly Hill Christian Fellowship, they had warned him not to talk to anybody at the center except to tell them what he wanted them to hear. Back at the Holly Hill Christian Fellowship, they had warned him that talking was dangerous, because the devil could just as easily defeat you as you could defeat the devil. Now he had been defeated, not by the devil, but by a girl, and he didn't know what to do. He had been carrying his sign all morning, up and down, up and down, just like always. Instead of feeling like a soldier, Robbie felt like an absolute fool. Between six o'clock this morning and now, fewer than a dozen people had gone in and out of the center. Nobody paid attention to him. There had been no traffic on the street. Usually, deadness like that made him frustrated. It made him feel as if he were talking to dead air. Today, he had welcomed the emptiness. His sign looked odd to him. His attitude felt all wrong. He didn't know what he wanted.

The girl's name was Shana Malvera, and Robbie supposed he shouldn't call her a girl. Girls liked to be called women now, especially when they were all grown up, which he was sure Shana was. He didn't think she was much more grown up than he was, though. He couldn't be sure. She moved around a lot and talked a lot and wore a lot of jewelry. She had half a dozen charm bracelets on her left arm that made musical silver sounds when she gestured with her arm. Shana was always gesturing with her arms. Shana did not like his sign.

It was hot out here. It had been hot this morning, and it was getting hotter. Robbie could feel the sweat on his forehead and his neck. Walking past the small, square, basement level windows of the center, he could see the reflection of his scuffed shoes and his pants legs that didn't reach down far enough. He'd bought both new at a discount place in Brooklyn, but the discount didn't seem to have been worth much. He was falling apart. Why would a girl like Shana Malvera, who could afford to wear all those charm bracelets, want to talk to somebody like him?

Robbie had his jacket with him, just in case. He had a stack of leaflets stuck into one of the pockets, printed up by the Life Project Committee at Holly Hill. These had the picture of a forlorn looking young man on the cover and the words, "FATHER'S DAY IS COMING, BUT HE'S NOT CELEBRATING." Inside, it told the story of how the young man's wife had wanted to fulfill herself and didn't have time for children, so when she got pregnant she had an abortion and didn't even tell him until afterward. Robbie had cried the first time he had ever heard that story, and he wanted to cry right now just thinking about it, but then the confusion started at the back of his brain and he didn't know. Shana had told him a whole lot of stories that had made him want to cry, and they were nothing like this one. He didn't know whom to believe.

Robbie walked wearily up the front steps of the center and looked in. There was nobody around that he could see, although somebody would come out if he went inside. The door had an electric eye that rang a little bell in the back just in case all the nurses were busy. Robbie felt in the pocket of his pants and came up with fifty cents. That was just enough money for a cup of coffee in the cafeteria. If he went to the cafeteria, Shana might be there.

Down at the end of the hall, a young woman came out of one of the offices or one of the examining rooms— Robbie didn't know which was which—and hurried toward the staircase at the back. Robbie did a double-take. It was the same young woman he had seen the night Charles van Straadt died, and she was doing now what she had been doing then. She was carrying one of those paper funnels you put in coffee machines. It looked full and sopping wet.

Robbie stepped past the electric eye, heard the bong, and winced. Gregor Demarkian had to be right. There was nothing the least bit strange about a young woman carrying a funnel full of coffee grounds. It was just his imagination that made the scene seem so strange.

F·I·V·E

1

Hector Sheed ate long lunches, talking all the time in that oddly English accent of his that had nothing to do with anything Gregor had ever known about New York, talking about Michael Pride and the center and the Homicide division and the three children his wife was looking after out in Queens. By the time Hector was finished with three pastrami sandwiches on rolls with Russian dressing, two orders of french fries, two orders of cole slaw, six large garlic pickles, and a piece of chocolate pie, Gregor was getting desperate. How could the man eat like that? Why wasn't he fat? It hardly seemed fair. But Hector Sheed wasn't fat. His massiveness was all muscle and bone. His appetite wasn't accompanied by stupidity, the way it often was in movies and books. Gregor didn't think Hector noticed what he ate. He just ate.

By the time Hector was finished and ready to release Gregor into the wider world, it was after one o'clock. Hector called the waitress over and asked her to call Gregor a car. "A car" seemed to be the neighborhood euphemism for a gypsy cab.

"Gypsy cabs are supposed to be illegal," Hector explained, "but without them, half the people in this town couldn't get where they were going. Never mind the prices."

"I take it gypsy cabs are cheaper," Gregor said.

"They run to about half the cost. We're looking for a Black Dragon Enterprises car. They used to have these great streaks of red fire across their hoods, but it made them too conspicuous. They kept getting picked up. They'll be here, though. Just give it a minute."

Gregor gave it a minute. This street was still an interesting place to be. Now it was full of people, by no means all African-American or other minorities. Farther west, Central Park North was 110th Street and 110th Street was Morningside Heights, which meant Columbia University. Gregor saw dozens of young white college students in jeans and T-shirts. He saw dozens of everybody. The young man with the ties who had called out to him when he first got up here had put out a sign. The sign said,

SHOP HERE FOR ALL
YOUR FATHER'S DAY NEEDS.

The gypsy cab turned out to be a nondescript Plymouth in gunmetal gray. It looked at least half a century old. Gregor got into it and thanked Hector Sheed for his help.

"Don't mention it. I'll see you later. I want to go down to the center this afternoon anyway. I got some things I want to check. You be careful."

"I'm always careful."

"That's not what they say about you in *People* magazine."

Gregor didn't pursue a discussion about *People* magazine. The gypsy cab driver was eager to go. Gypsy cabs didn't have meters. Payment was what had been agreed on up front. That meant there was no incentive to let the customer sit at the curb talking to his friends. The only way to make any real money was to drop this fare as quickly as possible and get on to the next one.

"As quickly as possible" was the watchword here. Gregor had heard stories about lunatic New York cabbies, careening through the traffic at ninety miles an hour while reciting involved epics on their troubles with the city government, but he had never been the customer of such a cabbie until now. Lunatic was putting it mildly, and ninety miles an hour was an underestimate. They shot onto a main thoroughfare Gregor couldn't put a name to and went straight uptown. They kept doing crazy loops around lumbering buses and tailgating cyclists. The only good thing about the trip was that it was short. In no time at all, they had reentered the landscape Gregor now associated in his mind with Harlem. They were surrounded by abandoned buildings, empty lots full of rubble, blank windows that looked out on nothing and kept nothing in. The South Bronx was supposed to be worse, but Gregor didn't see how it could be. The only thing worse would be a neighborhood that had been reduced to stone and ash.

Gregor got out in front of the Sojourner Truth Health Center's front doors and looked around. The doors were open, but the sidewalk was deserted. Robbie Yagger, who could usually be found pacing up and down with his sign, was nowhere to be seen. Gregor paid the cabbie and added a nice large tip—it was a kind of blood offering, a prayer to the gods that the man would not come back to drive him again—and decided to go inside.

Maybe Robbie was in the cafeteria, nursing along a cup of coffee. That would be ideal for Gregor's purposes.

Gregor went up the steps and in through the doors. The young woman at the admitting desk looked up when she heard someone come in, saw who it was, and nodded hello. In the past days, almost everybody at the center had learned to recognize Gregor on sight. He went down the hall to the back, looking around as he walked. The nurses' station was unmanned. The open examining rooms were empty. On a bulletin board on a wall next to a room marked "PEDIATRIC EMERGENCY" there was a poster with a picture of a cloud on it with sharp-edged rays of light coming from its center. Under the cloud were the words: "ON FATHER'S DAY, REMEMBER YOUR FATHER IN HEAVEN." Gregor shook his head. What he remembered were the Sisters of Divine Grace back in Philadelphia and the way they had celebrated Mother's Day. Nuns. Nuns never changed.

Gregor went down the back stairs and across the open space to the double doors of the cafeteria. He looked inside and frowned. Robbie Yagger was not there. Not much of anybody was there. He wondered where everyone had gone. Sister Kenna was sitting by herself at a table in the corner of the room, reading intently in what Gregor thought was her Divine Office. At this distance, it was difficult to tell. The largest round table in the room, near the rail for the cafeteria line, was taken up by a crowd of very young women wearing blue smocks and volunteer staff pins. They were alternately whispering and laughing hysterically.

Gregor moved cautiously into the room. Maybe Robbie was in the men's room. Maybe he had run downtown a block or two to buy cigarettes. The trouble was, if Robbie wasn't in the cafeteria and he wasn't out picketing, Gregor had no idea of where to look for him. The idea that Robbie might simply not be at the center today struck Gregor suddenly. It was a possibility that was both logical and appalling. Gregor knew from his long lunch with Robbie Yagger that Robbie didn't have much of a life outside his self-imposed mission at the center, but he did have some life. Maybe he had gone home to live it. Did anybody know where he was from, what his address was, if he had a phone number? Would anybody be able to find him if he decided to disappear?

Gregor had had enough coffee while he was watching Hector Sheed eat lunch, but he hadn't had any lunch, and he was starving. He picked up a cafeteria tray and one of those free copies of the New York *Sentinel*, ordered himself a couple of grilled ham-and-cheese sandwiches and a side of french fries, and then virtuously took a large bottle of Perrier water to drink with them. In his head, he could hear Bennis Hannaford counting up the cholesterol, but he ignored her. He got out his wallet and paid the woman at the cash register.

He was just about to put his tray down on one of the small tables against the wall when a young woman he vaguely recognized walked up to him, looking very tense. Gregor tried to remember where he had seen her before, but couldn't. Whatever he associated her with seemed to be vaguely disturbing.

The young woman had her hands behind her back. She was shifting from one foot to the other. "Excuse me," she said. "You may not remember, but we met. My name is Julie Enderson."

"Julie Enderson," Gregor repeated. It didn't ring a bell.

"It was upstairs after Rosalie van Straadt died," Julie said. "In the hall outside Dr. Pride's office. My friend

Karida and I watched the door for you when you went down to call the police."

"I remember," Gregor said, and he did, too. Karida was the one with the makeup. This was the pretty one.

Gregor put his tray down on the table and pulled out a chair. "Would you like to sit down? I was just about to have lunch. Could I get something for you?"

"Oh, I've had lunch already, thanks. I'm not hungry. It's just—I mean, do you think you'd mind if I sat down for a while and, you know, um, well, talked to you?"

"No," Gregor said. "I wouldn't mind. Is it something important?"

"I don't know," Julie said truthfully. "I just thought I'd tell you and you could decide for yourself."

"That sounds fair enough," Gregor said. "Have a seat."

"I will."

Julie had a large, heavy book in her hands. As far as Gregor could tell, it was some kind of history textbook. Julie put it down on the table with a thump, pulled out the chair facing Gregor, and sat down.

2

It may have been true that Julie Enderson had eaten lunch, but it was not true that she was no longer hungry. Gregor wondered what it was about the people he had met up here. Did living and working in Harlem make you hungry? It didn't necessarily make you fat. Julie Enderson was thin as a rail. She had Gregor's order of french fries in front of her, covered with enough ketchup to drown a cat. She was eating her way through them as methodically as a paper shredder ate through paper.

"It isn't about Rosalie van Straadt I wanted to talk to you about," she said. "I don't know anything about that. It's about Charles van Straadt. The first one."

"I remember Charles van Straadt," Gregor assured her.

"Yeah, well, Karida was with me that night, too, except Karida wouldn't know, because Karida's never worked anywhere but uptown. I used to work down in the Square, though, when I was younger. If you're black and you get to maybe fifteen, sixteen, down there they don't have any more use for you. You know we used to be hookers? Karida and me and all the other girls in refuge?"

Gregor knew that "refuge" was what the center called their program to help hookers leave their pimps. He wondered how old Julie had been when she started hooking. Young enough, obviously, to think of fifteen or sixteen as getting old.

Julie had finished the french fries.

"That's where I first saw Michael Pride," she said. "In the Square, I mean. He didn't buy time with hookers. When all that stuff came out in the papers everybody was shocked, but I wasn't. That's how I ended up here the first time. Two years ago. He came up to me where I was standing and gave me a card with the center's name on it and the address and the number. Then he said I was smart enough to know I couldn't do what I was doing forever, and then he disappeared." Julie laughed. "I told myself he was some kind of higher-class pimp and the center was a fancy house with million-dollar clients and women dancing around in their underwear, but I didn't believe it. With Michael, I couldn't believe it. Did you know there are rumors all over the center that he's sick?"

"Sick?" Gregor was startled.

"Never mind," Julie said. "They probably aren't true. If Michael got sick, he'd tell us about it. He wouldn't just go off somewhere to die. I was going to tell you about Charles van Straadt."

"That's right."

"Well, you see, I started to tell you upstairs right after Rosalie van Straadt died. About my mother, you know, who lives with this guy in a gang, and I came down from the east building with Karida to see if she'd been hurt in the shoot-out. I don't know why, I really don't. It's not like she cares about me one way or the other. It's not like she cares about anybody. I don't know. I was worried. So I went."

"I think that's understandable."

"Yeah, well, the thing is, the stairways are all crazy in the west building, because of the way they remodeled to put in the elevators. You can't just get started on a stairwell and go down and down and down. You go down some and then you have to cross the hall and then you go down some more. When you come off the stairs from the fourth floor to the third you can pass Michael's office and Father Donleavy's. And there was a light in Michael's office, you see, so I stopped."

"Because you wanted to see Dr. Pride."

"Everybody wants to see Dr. Pride, Mr. Demarkian. Dr. Pride doesn't have time to talk. Almost ever."

Gregor nodded. "Did you go into Dr. Pride's office?"

"Oh, no," Julie said. "I'd never do that without permission. I just wanted to know what was going on in there. But I also thought it was very odd. I mean, we were in the middle of a major emergency. There had been loudspeaker announcements all evening—when there's a shoot-out or a major drug bust or something and the emergency room is going to be jammed, they put an announcement over the public address system about how we're all supposed to stay in our rooms and not go over to the west building except for a real emergency. Not even to come in here and get food. So I thought it was odd, you see, that there would be someone in Michael's office. I didn't think it really could be Michael. If he needed anything, one of the nurses or the orderlies or the volunteers would go get it for him. I didn't understand who could be in there with the light on. And there was a voice, you see, but it wasn't Michael's voice. The whole thing felt—creepy."

"Was there only one voice?" Gregor asked her. "You didn't hear two? It wasn't a conversation?"

"There was only one voice," Julie said definitely. "Maybe he was talking on the phone. I didn't see. I went down along the hall toward the door, thinking I'd look in and see who was there, and then as I was still on my way, he came out. Charles van Straadt. Except I didn't know that he was Charles van Straadt at the time. I didn't know that until the next day, when I saw the papers. I just saw this man come out of the doorway really quick, so quick he scared me, and I kind of shrieked."

"And this was Charles van Straadt?"

"Oh, definitely, Mr. Demarkian. I knew as soon as I saw the newspapers with his picture in it. He wasn't a very usual looking man."

"No," Gregor admitted. "No, he wasn't. Was he the only person you saw? Not only in the room, now. I mean on your whole trip downstairs."

"He was the only one. Until we got to the first floor, of course, because down there there were tons of people. Nurses. Doctors. Ambulance men. And that guy who carries the sign out on the sidewalk out front."

"He was in the building?"

"Oh, yes."

"What time was this?"

Julie Enderson shrugged. "I'm sorry, Mr. Demarkian, I really don't remember. I'm sure I checked, but I can't make myself hold the information. Augie always says I ought to, that I've got to learn because when I have a real job I'm going to have to, but I never do seem to remember."

"Was it closer to six? Seven?"

"Oh, it was after seven, I'd think. It took me a long time to work up the nerve to come over. It was against the rules, you know, and I don't like to break the rules. I don't want to get kicked out of the program."

Gregor thought this over. "When you got down to the first floor, did you see any of the other van Straadts? Rosalie, the one who just died? Martha? Ida Greel?"

"I saw Ida Greel," Julie said. "She was on duty in Emergency with everyone else. And later in the east building I saw the guy. You know, Ida's brother, the cute one with no brains."

"That about sums it up," Gregor said dryly.

"He was sitting in the reception room over in the east building for a while, but that was later on at night. I don't remember what time that was, either, Mr. Demarkian. Karida said she saw all three of them except Rosalie down in the cafeteria that night, but you'd have to ask Karida. I didn't have the guts to come down in here. I got my information and then I went back home."

"Had something happened to your mother?"

"Not as far as I could tell. I don't even know if she's alive, Mr. Demarkian. We've lost touch."

Julie had finished the french fries. Gregor still had a grilled ham-and-cheese sandwich. He offered her half. Julie took the half unself-consciously and began eating.

"You know," Julie said, "if this was all, I wouldn't have bothered you. I mean, this isn't much. What keeps bugging me is what I know about Charles van Straadt that nobody else seems to. I mean, I keep hinting and hinting, but nobody picks up on it." She stared at the ragged edge of her half-eaten half sandwich. "I don't know about Dr. Pride. I haven't had a chance to bring it up with him."

"I should think everybody on earth knew who Charles van Straadt was," Gregor said. "He's had one of the most spectacularly public careers in the history of capitalism."

Julie shook her head. "Some of it may be public, Mr. Demarkian, but all of it isn't. Look, when I was about twelve or thirteen years old, I used to work in this revue in the Square. It was a musical thing, you know, but this one was all kids all under fourteen, some of us as young as eight or nine, and we'd dance to things like 'Big Spender' and then we'd strip. And then later, you know, the place made private arrangements with the guys who came to see us." Julie's face broke into a big grin. "After I came here, Michael and Augie helped me set it up so that the place got raided, and half a dozen people got arrested and now they're probably going to go to jail. Of course, another place just like it probably opened up a week later and a block away, if you know what I mean, but there isn't anything I can do about that."

Surely there had to be something somebody could do about it, Gregor thought, but nobody seemed to.

"Was Charles van Straadt one of the clients?"

"Oh, no," Julie told him. "An old man like that, if I saw him on the street and I was hooking, I wouldn't even bother to ask. He just doesn't care. You can tell. No, it wasn't like that. It was this one night. A really dead night. There had been a whole lot of raids over the month before and business was slow. The cops don't really care about what goes down in the Square, and they really, really don't care about the prostitutes, but every once in a while they try to clean up the kiddie stuff because they do care about that. And they stage raids on the gay stuff, too, you know, because it gets their rocks off. Excuse my language. Augie keeps trying to teach me to talk right but I just go on and on like I was ignorant or something."

"I'm not worried about your language," Gregor said. "Keep going."

"Yes, well, the thing is, it was a slow night, as I said, but slow or not the deal was that the bar had to cash out every two hours, because we were always getting robbed, you know, if we didn't do that. I mean, everybody always says that nobody robs the Mafia, but they're wrong. Junkies do it all the time. Nobody can find them afterward, and they're half dead anyway. So, it was about ten o'clock and the bar cashed out and the bartender put the money in this black metal box that locked up and he gave the black metal box to me and told me to go up to the manager's office and get a receipt for it. So I took the box and I went. But I didn't go the way I was supposed to go. I didn't go up the back stairs. I hated the back stairs. They were dark, and sometimes you'd find johns on them, jerking off—excuse me—you know what they were doing. And if they caught you there when they were like that you didn't know what was going to happen. And they wouldn't pay you for it afterward. And then if the guys who owned the place found out they'd say you gave it away for free and beat you up. So I didn't use the back stairs. I went around to the front and up that way. Which was how I saw him."

"Charles van Straadt," Gregor said.

"Right. He was standing in the door of the manager's office when I got to the top of the stairs. He really stuck out. Nobody down there dresses like that. If they get a lot of money or they're really good at lifting stuff they go for the expensive flash. This guy's clothes were just quality. You could tell."

"Was there anything else on this floor except your manager's office? Were there other offices?"

"The place was a big production. The revue was a secret. You had to have a pass to get in and they were very careful because of the raids. But there was a bookstore they had, too, with dirty books and a video rental place and one of those peep shows that are all over down there. There were lots of offices on that floor, but they all belonged to the same company. Us. If you see what I mean. And besides, I know he was coming from my manager's office because I heard him talking."

"To your manager."

"That's right. He was saying, 'Raids or no raids, if this place doesn't bring in a profit, there's no point in keeping it going. Do something.' And my manager was all jumpy. 'Do what?' he kept asking. 'I can't go drag johns in from the street. Not for something like this.' But it was really obvious what was going on. It was really obvious who this man was. The one who turned out later to be Charles van Straadt."

"Who was he?"

"The owner, of course, or somebody connected to the owner. But I thought at the time that he had to be the owner, because of the way he was dressed and everything. And now that I know he was Charles van Straadt, I'm sure of it. Aren't you?"

"I don't know," Gregor told her.

Julie wriggled around in her seat. "I thought, you know, that it might be good news for Dr. Pride. Because a man like that, an old man that owns that kind of place, well, he knows all sorts of people who might want to murder him. People who know how to murder people, if you see what I mean."

"I think those people tend more to bullet holes in the back of the head than to strychnine."

"Those people would do anything," Julie said staunchly. "Michael wouldn't kill anybody."

Gregor was about to say that he agreed with her, he didn't think Michael Pride would kill anybody, when there was a commotion near the cash register, and like everyone else in the cafeteria he turned to look. For a moment or two it was difficult to decipher what was going on. The cafeteria had filled up a little since Gregor and Julie had first sat down. A little clutch of people with half-filled trays blocked Gregor's view of the scene of the commotion. Then one of the women moved away a little and Gregor saw. Martha van Straadt was standing next to the cash register, her back to the cashier, her arms folded across her chest. Facing her was a confused looking Robbie Yagger, holding nothing at all. Gregor looked around for a tray or a paper cup of coffee, but found nothing.

"Excuse me for a second," he told Julie Enderson. Then he got up and began to advance on the cafeteria line.

"You!" Martha van Straadt was screeching. "You. I can't believe you have the nerve to show your face here. I can't believe you have the nerve to just walk in and drink our coffee. Who do you think you are? What do you think you're doing?"

Robbie Yagger seemed to be swaying a little on his feet. "I don't feel so good," he said. "It tasted funny."

"What tasted funny?" Gregor asked, coming up next to Robbie on the other side of the rail.

Martha van Straadt was still screeching. "He doesn't feel so good. Hell. Why should I care how he feels? Why should any of us? He doesn't care how we feel. He stands out there day after day, carrying that damn sign, terrifying half the clients going into the family planning clinic, how do they know what he's going to do? How do any of us know?"

"It was the coffee." Robbie Yagger's voice was oddly distinct. "It tasted funny. It had stuff in it."

"What kind of stuff?" Gregor asked him.

Martha van Straadt advanced on them both. "I want him out of here," she said. "I want him off these premises. And I don't want to see him back until he apologizes to every woman in this center for his bigotry, his fanaticism, and his bad manners."

"For God's sake," someone in the crowd murmured. "She can't throw him out of here just because he doesn't approve of abortion. What about the nuns?"

"I'm not carrying the sign any more," Robbie Yagger said. "I changed my mind."

"She doesn't care about abortion," someone else in the crowd said. "She's just Martha van Straadt. She thinks she can run everybody else's life just the way she wants to."

Gregor ducked under the rail. Robbie's eyes were beginning to glaze over. He seemed to be petrifying in front of Gregor's eyes.

"I changed my mind," Robbie said again. "I talked to Shana. I'm not going to picket any more."

Michael Pride loomed up out of nowhere. "What's going on?" he asked.

Gregor pointed to Robbie. "What do you think? He keeps talking about the coffee tasting funny."

"It had stuff in it," Robbie said again. "Floating around. I didn't think that was right. I—"

Robbie's back began to arch and his head snapped forward. Michael Pride lunged at him and caught him around the waist.

"Oh, no," Michael said. "Not this time. Augie. Get me the Comprozan."

"Coming," Augie said.

"Meet me in Emergency Room Three."

Then Michael Pride picked Robbie Yagger up, slung him over his shoulder, and headed at a full-tilt run for the stairs.

P·A·R·T T·H·R·E·E

The Cardinal Archbishop of New York
Does Not Get the Solution
He Was Looking For

O·N·E

1

This time, Michael Pride pulled it off. Gregor didn't understand how he pulled it off—Gregor didn't have the first idea how medicine worked, or why it sometimes didn't—but the impression he got was that nobody else understood how Michael had done it, either. The surprising thing was how quick it all was. Gregor had time to call Hector Sheed. In spite of the fact that he didn't know, then, for sure, that what he had was a strychnine poisoning, Gregor thought getting Hector to the scene was only common sense. *Something* was going on. Besides, he was half sure. *People* had once called Gregor Demarkian America's foremost expert on poisons. They had been exaggerating, as usual. The real expert was a professor of pathology at the Yale Medical School. Gregor was only number two. He did, however, know poisons. He'd never seen anyone as early in the process of being poisoned by strychnine as Robbie Yagger had been in the Sojourner Truth Health Center's cafeteria, but he was willing to bet that strychnine poisoning was in fact what Robbie had had. After calling Hector Sheed, Gregor paced back and forth in the open space near the front doors in front of the Admitting desk. The emergency room seemed to be suddenly full of people, although not people with emergencies. Gregor saw dozens of volunteer staff pins, half a dozen short modern veils, a few habits. There were also people from the street, some of them old, some of them young and garish looking, all of them poor. It was as if the center were putting out messages on some kind of silent shortwave. All these people had sensed trouble. All these people were willing to help. Gregor wondered what it was any of them thought they would be able to do.

By the time Hector Sheed showed up, Michael Pride was finished with Robbie Yagger. The doctor came out of Emergency Room 3 looking so gray in the face, Gregor thought he was going to have a stroke. Augie came out behind him, looking ill. Gregor was standing still near the front doors. Michael walked up to him with his surgical mask in his hands. His hands were covered with surgical gloves—two apiece.

"Did it," Michael Pride said. He looked over Gregor's shoulder and blinked. "Hello, Hector. You got here fast."

"Demarkian said there'd been another poisoning," Hector Sheed said. "*Another* poisoning."

Michael ignored him. "The technicians took stomach samples," he told Gregor Demarkian. "I made them. They've got the samples preserved. The police can have them any time they want them. Robbie's going to be out of it for the next couple of days."

"How out of it?" Gregor asked.

Michael shrugged. "Don't expect him to talk to anybody until at least tomorrow afternoon. Even then it might be difficult. What we just did was essentially a stomach pumping operation. It wasn't just a stomach-pumping operation, but you see what I mean. And we're still worried about residual effects of the strychnine. He's heavily sedated. And he's got to be kept in a dark room with as little distraction as possible for at least ten hours."

"How do you know it was strychnine?" Hector demanded. "Nobody comes back from strychnine. It's a bitch."

Michael was peeling the surgical gloves off his hands. "It was strychnine. Ask Gregor Demarkian here. Test our samples. It was strychnine. Nothing on earth looks like it."

"For Christ's sake," Hector said.

Michael dropped both pairs of gloves into a tall wastebasket with a red lining. The red was to let everyone know that the waste the bag contained was medically hazardous, toxic, contagious. If you put a red trash bag by the side of the road, no ordinary garbage truck would pick it up. Gregor wondered why he was thinking of that and decided it was because he didn't want to think about Michael Pride's face, which was getting worse by the minute. It had gone from gray to chalk white. The eyes looked sunk into the sockets. The skin of the head didn't seem thick enough to hold in the skull. Was it really still the middle of the afternoon? Gregor wondered. But of course it was.

"I thought it all out after Charlie died," Michael said dreamily. "Thought about how there had to be a way. If you went at it logically, you had to be able to do it. Don't you see."

"No," Hector Sheed said.

Michael shrugged. "Don't worry about it. Take the samples. He was saying something about his coffee."

Michael Pride began to drift away. Hector started after him. Gregor caught Hector by the sleeve and pulled him back.

"Let him go," Gregor said. "He's not going anywhere. He's sick as hell."

"He said something about this guy's coffee."

"I know more about the coffee than Michael does. That guy in there, the one with strychnine poisoning, do you know who it is? That's the guy I wanted to talk to. The one who told me something I hadn't taken seriously before."

"Did you get a chance to talk to him?"

"No."

Gregor looked around the admitting area again. Eamon Donleavy was standing in a crowd of older women, making reassuring noises. Michael and Augie had both disappeared. Julie Enderson may never have come upstairs at all. Gregor didn't remember seeing the girl after he'd come upstairs. Over near the doors, Ida Greel and Martha van Straadt were standing with a tall, attractive, ineffectual-looking young man. Gregor had been introduced to Martha and Ida, just as he'd been introduced to everybody at the center over the last two days. He had no idea who the young man was.

"Who's that?" he asked Hector Sheed, pointing.

"That's Victor van Straadt," Hector said. "Ida's brother, Martha's and Rosalie's cousin, one of the late Charles van Straadt's grandchildren. Why? Does he look suspicious to you?"

"I didn't know who he was." Now it was Gregor's turn to be distracted. It was odd, he thought, how the very obvious thing never occurred to you until the bitter end. And yet it had been there for you all the time. Just sitting in front of your face.

"Hector," he said. "You know what the problem is here? Time."

"Time? Do you want to give me the particulars of this incident? What does time have to do with it?"

"I didn't mean this incident. I didn't mean Robbie Yagger. I meant Charles van Straadt. I take it we are in agreement that all three of these poisonings were perpetrated by the same person?"

"As long as this last one was a poisoning. Yeah. Sure."

"For the moment, it doesn't matter if this last one was a poisoning or not. Although it does in the long run, of course. In the long run, it has to be." Gregor started to pace. "Look at the problem as a puzzle now. On the night Charles van Straadt died, there was a major emergency up here, a shoot-out in a gang war. From approximately six o'clock in the evening, when Charles van Straadt showed up in the center—totally unexpectedly, according to your own reports, without having told anyone he was going to do it—from that point until after eight o'clock when Charles van Straadt's body was found, this floor was a mass of people. So far so good?"

"Yes. Fine."

"In spite of that mass of people," Gregor went on, "our murderer got hold of either Michael Pride's keys or Sister Augustine's, without whoever it was ever knowing they were missing, got into Michael Pride's private examining room and opened his private medical cabinet without anyone seeing a thing, got the strychnine, doctored the coffee—let's give the benefit of a doubt here, let's say the murderer had the cup of coffee he or she wanted to feed poor Charles van Straadt with him—anyway, doctored the coffee, got up to the third floor by the staircase, fed the poison to Charles van Straadt, and got both the coffee cup and himself out of Michael Pride's third-floor office before Michael walked in. Does that make sense to you?"

"The murderer could have taken the elevator to the second floor," Hector said. "Then he could have gone up to the third from there."

"Don't forget the emergency," Gregor warned him. "Those elevators were being used to carry stretchers. Even the doctors were using the stairs. Anyone who entered an elevator that night carrying nothing more than a cup of coffee would have been told off—and we would have heard about it."

"Maybe."

"Definitely. Seriously, Hector, think about what I just told you. Does that sound possible to you?"

"Lots of things are possible." Hector was hedging. "If you had my job, you'd know. It sounds crazy, I'll admit. But believe me, it isn't anywhere near impossible."

Gregor threw up his hands in exasperation. "Of course it's impossible," he said. "Of course it is. Nobody could have done all that on the night Charles van Straadt died without having been seen by somebody who would have mentioned it. Nobody could have gotten the strychnine out of Michael Pride's office without being caught at it except Michael Pride himself—or maybe Augie. But neither Michael Pride nor Augie could have been off this floor long enough to get to the third floor and feed poison to Charles van Straadt without half a dozen people knowing. Michael himself was in the emergency room for nearly the entire two hours nonstop."

"Augie was out of the fray for a while," Hector said. "Look at the report. She was in the head nurse's office having dinner."

"Which was brought to her by Sister Kenna, who stayed to talk for five minutes. Never mind the fact that the head nurse's office opens directly onto the corridor between Emergency Room Two and Emergency Room Three."

"Still," Hector said stubbornly.

"The times aren't right," Gregor said triumphantly. "Charles van Straadt had to have been fed that strychnine within ten minutes of the time Michael Pride found him dying—and ten minutes is making it very, very long. I didn't see anything that said Augie was missing during that time. It was earlier that she had dinner by herself in the office."

Hector Sheed looked up toward the front doors. "What about them?" he asked. "Ida, Victor, and Martha. Ida works in the emergency room, but the other two had all the time in the world."

"How would either one of them have gotten the strychnine out of Michael Pride's office without being caught in the act?"

"Maybe they were caught in the act. Maybe somebody saw one of them do it and doesn't realize how important that information is. Maybe that's what your Robbie Yagger saw that got him poisoned."

"What Robbie Yagger saw was a young woman carrying a funnel of used coffee grounds to the back of the emergency-room area," Gregor said. "And yes, that got him poisoned, but not because the young woman was coming out of Michael Pride's office. She wasn't. Nobody was. That elaborate scenario we've both been so entranced with as the most likely reconstruction of the way Charles van Straadt was murdered? Well, it's a pile of nonsense."

"Charles van Straadt is dead. That's not nonsense."

"No, it's not. But he didn't get dead by someone running around like a maniac in the middle of a full-scale crisis doing God knows what so skillfully and so well that he, or she, was no more visible than a ghost. You've got to help me with something. I want to try an experiment."

"What kind of an experiment?"

"An experiment with time. Go down to the nurses' station and ask the nun for her stopwatch. They've got a couple of them down there. They need them for cardio-vascular testing or something. Meet me back here as soon as you can."

"A stopwatch," Hector Sheed repeated.

"Go," Gregor said.

Hector seemed to hesitate, but not for long. Gregor watched him stride purposefully through what were still aimlessly milling crowds of people. Crowds parted before Hector like hair pulled by a rat-tail comb. Nobody looked at him in surprise or amazement. Hector Sheed might be big, but he was also a familiar quantity. He'd been around here much too often in the past two weeks for anybody to be surprised at his appearance.

Gregor turned his attention to the three people still standing next to the front doors, still clutched together, still talking. Martha van Straadt was looking resentful. Victor van Straadt was looking bewildered. Ida Greel was looking as if her patience were being sorely tried, but she was going to hang in there no matter what.

This, Gregor thought, was an opportunity he might never have again.

2

Even in the days when Gregor Demarkian was the second most powerful man in the Federal Bureau of Investigation, he'd had problems with rich people. The

chief problem he'd had with rich people was attitude.
There were people who said that the rich got away with
more because they had good lawyers, and that was true,
to an extent. In Gregor's experience, good lawyers only
went so far. The poor and the middle class had had long
experience in pleasing other people. They had bosses to
make happy and spouses they depended on. The habitual
criminals had a lot to prove. They struck attitudes and
looked forward eagerly to cameras in court. The rich just
didn't care. They not only knew they didn't *have* to give
out any information, they simply didn't want to. They
didn't care what the police detective thought of them.
They didn't care if the district attorney liked them or
not. It was maddening. You asked them for their cooperation, and they said no.

Working with no official connection to any established law enforcement office was worse. Gregor was always surprised at how willing people were to cooperate
with him, relying on nothing but the rather spurious reputation he had attained in popular magazines. It was incredible to him how many people were overjoyed to
spend a little time with someone they thought of as a
"celebrity." Not everyone was inclined to be that voluble,
however. Gregor had met with his share of defeat, and
more than his share of that inevitable question: *Who do
you think you are?* The question was made worse by the
fact that Gregor had no idea who he thought he was. He
hadn't known for years. It wasn't the kind of thing a man
wanted to ask himself at any stage of life.

In Martha van Straadt and Ida Greel, Gregor had so
far met with what he thought of as reluctant acquies-
cence. He had been invited here by the Cardinal Archbishop of New York and his presence had been approved
by Michael Pride. Martha and Ida were willing to put up

with him. Just. Gregor wanted more than that. He didn't think he'd have much trouble out of the young man, Ida's brother, whom he had yet to meet. Victor van Straadt looked like the kind of person who talked endlessly about himself if given half a chance.

Martha, Ida, and Victor didn't seem to be too happy with each other. They were as tense a group as Gregor had ever seen. Martha kept scowling from Ida to Victor and back again. Victor kept dropping the sheaf of papers he was carrying under one arm and rescuing them only a second before they scattered all over the floor. Gregor nodded a little to himself and made his way over to them. They were paying no attention to him at all.

"Excuse me," Gregor said, when he reached Martha van Straadt's side. "I don't know if you remember me. My name is Gregor Demarkian. I was wondering if I could ask for your help."

Victor van Straadt was the only one of the three of them that seemed to have any reaction at all to Gregor's arrival. The other two turned to look at the man who was speaking to them, but their faces were blank.

"I'm Victor van Straadt." Victor put out his hand. "We haven't met. I'm Ida's brother."

Gregor shook. Victor had a good strong handclasp, the kind that was allowed only to the hero in 1930s British books. So much for that as an indication of character, Gregor thought. He looked at the papers under Victor's arm. They were slipping again.

"Oh," Victor said. "Excuse me. That's my work. I work for the New York *Sentinel*."

"He runs their contests," Martha said sarcastically. "It's not exactly a reporting job."

"Right," Victor said. "Father's Day. That's the one we're doing now. Maybe you've seen the announcements.

We run a red banner over the masthead. It does wonders for newsstand sales."

"Oh, how would you know?" Martha said. "Really, you never do any work. You don't know the first thing about it."

"I don't think that's fair," Ida came in. "Victor has a very responsible position. He has to oversee the physical running of the contest itself, and keep an eye on the escrow account, and work with the publicity. It's not as if he were Vanna White turning letters."

"He might as well be Vanna White turning letters," Martha said sharply. "You know as well as I do that Victor never does any of that stuff. You and Rosalie and I do it all, one way or the other. I mean, my God, escrow accounts. The only reason Victor knows how to make out a check is that he left his bank card at home one day and the woman at the bank showed him how to write a check for his money instead. I mean, for God's sake. He's hopeless."

"He's no more hopeless than you are," Ida argued.

Victor was putting his papers into a tidy pile. Gregor saw that the one on the top had a red banner printed across it. It said:

FOR A FANTASTIC FATHER'S DAY! PLAY IT NOW!

Victor got the pile neat, looked up, and grinned. He was a little green around the gills.

"Well," he said. "Help. You asked us if we could help."

"That's right," Gregor said. "Hector Sheed—the detective assigned to this case from Manhattan Homicide— Hector Sheed has just gone to get a stopwatch. He'll be back in a minute. I need somebody who'll be willing to do a little running around that we could time."

"Why?" Martha van Straadt asked.

"Because we're trying to figure out how long it would have taken for someone to do what had to be done on the night your grandfather was killed," Gregor said. "I don't know if you realize it, but for the murder to have been brought off the way it was, the murderer had to do quite a lot of running around. We're having something of a hard time figuring out how long it all took, and when. If we knew how long, you see, we might be able to figure out when."

"But you know when," Ida insisted. "Strychnine is a fast-acting poison. Grandfather must have been poisoned almost immediately before Michael found him."

"Not that kind of when," Gregor explained. "It's true your grandfather must have been poisoned very close to the time he was found, but that doesn't mean the poison itself was acquired in the preceding few minutes. It could have been taken out of Michael Pride's medical cabinet an hour earlier and not been given to Charles van Straadt, but hidden instead. There's no way to know."

"I don't think we ought to do this," Martha said. "We could be incriminating ourselves."

"Of course we won't be incriminating ourselves," Ida said impatiently. "Don't be ridiculous."

"There are dozens of people around here," Martha shot back. "He could get any one of them to do it. It doesn't have to be us."

"It doesn't have to be," Gregor told her, "but it would be convenient. You're all young and healthy, so we don't have to worry about giving you a stroke asking you to race up and down stairs. And none of you seem to be on duty at the moment. Of course, Miss Greel might be called on in an emergency."

"I go on at six," Ida said. "I think this all sounds perfectly reasonable, Mr. Demarkian. I'm sure we'd all like to do anything we can to help."

"Speak for yourself," Martha said. Her face was a little red. "I'm not going to help. I'm not going to have anything to do with this."

"I think it sounds like fun," Victor said. "I haven't done any real running since I left college. I was on the rugby team."

"I should have known this was going to happen." Martha was indignant. "You're ganging up on me. Ida's got all the money and Victor thinks she'll throw him some of it, so they're closing ranks against me. I should have realized."

"Oh, Martha," Ida said. "For God's sake."

Victor looked confused. "I'm not closing ranks on anyone. I just think it would be fun to run around for a while."

"It was supposed to be Rosalie who got all the money." Martha swung around to Gregor Demarkian. "That's what Rosalie thought and that's what I thought too, but it wasn't true. It was Ida."

"I didn't get all the money," Ida said angrily. "Martha, I mean it, for God's sake. Grandfather died before he could change his will."

"And you're trying to make it look like I killed him," Martha snapped. "You're trying to make it look like I fed him a lot of poison so he wouldn't have a chance to change it."

"And then you poisoned Rosalie," Ida said, "and this Robbie Yagger. What for? Obviously there's some kind of maniac running around."

"I don't care who you think is running around." Martha had a full head of steam now. Gregor had seen cartoons where furious characters shot smoke through their ears. He had never before seen a living human being who seemed capable of replicating the feat. Martha seemed to be going feral. Her left foot was stamping rhythmically against the floor. It reminded Gregor of something large and shaggy pawing the ground.

"I don't care what either of you say," Martha bit out at them. "Family solidarity. Family solidarity my foot. This family has as much solidarity as Bosnia-Herzegovina. You two do anything you goddamn well want, but don't expect to drag me into it. I'm going to go out and hire my own attorneys."

"*Martha.*" Ida was near tears.

Martha wasn't listening. She pounded her foot one last time onto the hard floor, glared at Gregor Demarkian, and spun away. Then she marched straight to the front doors and out of them, out of sight. She didn't turn around once. Ida, Victor, and Gregor watched her go. Hector Sheed watched her go, too. The detective had come up to the group with the stopwatch in his hands just moments before Martha started her last speech. Now he stared after her in astonishment.

"What was that?" he demanded. "What was the matter with her?"

"She didn't want to help with the experiment," Victor said nervously.

"So what?" Hector was still bewildered. "She didn't want to help, all she had to do was say so. What's going on around here? What's all this about? Gregor?"

Gregor Demarkian was thinking. He was thinking as hard as he had since he first got to New York on this trip, and for once it was doing him some good. What was it

Sherlock Holmes always said? "Eliminate the impossible, and what you have left, however improbable, will be the truth." Gregor didn't know if that was the exact quote, but it would do. Not that he put much stock in silly fictional characters like Sherlock Holmes. He was too much of a professional for that. But still. You had to take your good advice where you could find it. Anywhere.

They were all staring at him. Hector Sheed was being especially intense. Gregor forced himself into the present.

"Miss Greel," he said. "Miss van Straadt just now said something about the money. About how Rosalie was supposed to 'get it all,' I think she put it, but instead it was you."

Ida looked at Victor and then at her feet. "Yes. Yes, she did. Grandfather had made arrangements to change his will."

"To leave everything to you?"

"To leave the bulk of his personal fortune to me, yes."

"Which amounts to about eight hundred million dollars. Do you actually know for a fact that your grandfather was going to change his will in this particular way?"

"Oh, yes," Ida said. "He'd contacted the lawyers. Mr. Cole had already had the new will drawn up. If Grandfather had lived another day, he would have signed it."

"Meaning that if your grandfather had lived, you would be a much richer young woman than you are now."

"That's right, Mr. Demarkian. But I don't see that that matters much. I'm a very rich young woman now."

"Oh, yes." Gregor nodded thoughtfully. "Did you know about this change?"

"Yes," Ida said firmly. "Yes, I did."

"Can you prove that you did?"

"I think I can. Grandfather wrote me a letter about it. I have the letter. I have the envelope it came in, too."

"Do you have it here?"

"Yes, I do. I have a room here, on the staff floor. The letter is there."

"Good," Gregor said. "Very good. Would you do me a favor, Miss Greel? Would you go get that letter and let Mr. Sheed and I take a look at it?"

"Right now?"

"Right now."

"All right," Ida Greel said. "Certainly. Just give me a minute or two. I'll have to use the stairs."

"We'll be on the stairs ourselves," Gregor told her. "We'll be using your brother here to get our times straightened out."

"Of course."

Ida Greel seemed to hesitate, then shrugged her shoulders and walked away from them, in the opposite direction to the one Martha had gone. Gregor and Hector and Victor watched her disappear into the people near the back of the hall.

Hector Sheed blew out a long stream of air. "What was *that* all about?" he demanded. "I'm gone for five minutes and everybody goes absolutely crazy. Are you sure you know what you're doing?"

"Of course I know what I'm doing," Gregor told him. "In fact, I know what I'm doing for the first time since I got here. Mr. van Straadt, I'd like you to do some running up and down the stairs."

"No problem," Victor said, but he looked confused again.

Gregor Demarkian thought Victor van Straadt would always look confused, but that was all right.

Gregor himself no longer was.

T·W·O

1

Eamon Donleavy was too good a Catholic, and too much of a rationalist, to believe in precognition, or telepathy, or auras. Nevertheless, walking into his office after the emergency-room crisis with Robbie Yagger, Eamon knew his phone was going to ring before it rang. He also knew who would be on the other end of it before he picked it up. For a split second, he considered not picking it up. To say that Eamon Donleavy was having a bad day was ludicrous. Eamon Donleavy was having a bad year. Ever since he had first heard that Michael Pride was sick, he had been in a walking coma. He did all the things he was supposed to do. He said Mass at six o'clock every morning at St. Martin Porres Roman Catholic Church three blocks downtown, for the nuns from the center and anyone else who wanted to show up. He visited the sick. He did his paperwork. He spoke to the First Communion classes and the Confirmation classes and the Interfaith Sunday School classes that were held in the east building. He just couldn't make any of it mean anything. He had become deaf, dumb, and blind. He kept coming to in the middle of rooms and hallways, utterly unable to explain how he had gotten where he was, utterly unable to explain what he was doing there. Sometimes he found himself thinking it wasn't Michael who was sick. Sometimes he found himself hoping that he would die first.

Today, coming up from all that fuss in the emergency room, Eamon Donleavy was not in a walking coma. He knew where he was and where he was going. He knew what he intended to tell people if they asked him what he was doing. He passed Victor van Straadt running up the stairs—what was Demarkian up to now?—and went into his office. The surface of his desk was absolutely clear except for a maroon felt desk blotter and a little stack of lined notebook sheets held down by a crystal paperweight. In the center of the paperweight there was a tiny statue of St. Joseph and a plastic plaque with the words: "**St. Joseph, Foster Father of Jesus.**" On the lined notebook sheets were letters written by Sister Angelique's fourth-grade Afterschool Program class, thanking Eamon for being their spiritual father. Eamon sat down and looked at all of it. In the old days, his desk had never been so clean. It didn't seem possible that "the old days" were only the beginning of this week. He had cleaned his office out, putting his affairs in order. He had begun to eat aspirins the way children eat Pez, battling a headache that wouldn't go away.

Up on the wall next to his door, Eamon Donleavy had a crucifix. It had a brass corpus on a walnut cross. On the other side of the door, he had the framed print of the Constantinople Madonna that had hung next to his bed all the years he was growing up. Both these things seemed to be connected to the phone. The phone is going to ring, Eamon thought, and it did. The man on the other end is going to be that son of a bitch from the Chancery.

Eamon Donleavy had never used the words *son of a bitch* in his life. He had never even thought them before.

He picked up the phone and said, "Hello?"

There must have been something in his voice. There was hesitation on the other end of the line. There was coughing. Finally, the Cardinal Archbishop said, "Father Donleavy? Please excuse me if I've disturbed you at work. I hadn't heard from you for quite some time."

There's been nothing to hear, Eamon Donleavy wanted to say, but he couldn't. That boy was downstairs, poisoned. The world was falling apart.

"We've been very busy here," he said. "We all have been."

"I got a call a little while ago, Father Donleavy. I was told there had been another—attack."

"There seems to have been another poisoning, Your Eminence, yes. The victim was a member of the Holly Hill Christian Fellowship. You know those people. He came to the center every day and carried a protest sign."

"A pro-life protest sign."

"Yes, Your Eminence."

"Have you talked to Gregor Demarkian in the last day or two? I haven't talked to him at all."

"He's been here almost continuously, Your Eminence." Eamon Donleavy didn't like Gregor Demarkian, but if he had to choose between his Cardinal Archbishop and anybody, he almost always chose anybody. "He's been very busy. And he's managed to gain the cooperation of the police."

"Is that good?"

"I think it is, Your Eminence, yes. It saves a lot of

trouble. And it gives him access to information he couldn't get otherwise. It gives us access, too."

"I don't like the way this is going," the Cardinal said. "Demarkian's been here almost a week. I thought it would be settled by now. When he went up to Maryville for John O'Bannion, he had the whole mess cleared up in three days."

"When he went up to Colchester for John O'Bannion, the mess took two weeks. I don't think you can put time limits on murder like that, Your Eminence. It's not a calf-roping contest."

"I know that."

"Besides, I think he's close to a solution. He's out in the stairwell with Detective Sheed, making Victor van Straadt run up and down and up and down, over and over again. I think it has something to do with establishing the times."

"For Charles van Straadt's death?"

"Yes."

"Demarkian suspects Victor van Straadt?"

"I don't know that he does. He asked Victor to help him out. That's all I'm sure of."

"He doesn't suspect Michael Pride?"

"I don't think so."

"Or you?"

"Why would he suspect me, Your Eminence?"

"This is New York, Father Donleavy. If they can pin it on the Catholic Church, they will. You know they will."

No, he didn't. "I suppose so, Your Eminence. Your Eminence, I'm sorry to cut this short, but with all the trouble we've had around here lately, I'm a little backed up. I'm late for an appointment."

"Of course, Father Donleavy. I'll let you go."

"If there's any news here, I'll call you, Your Eminence."

"That will be a novelty, Father Donleavy. But don't strain yourself. I'll call you."

Eamon Donleavy heard a click in his ear, as sharp and lethal as a gunshot. He put the phone receiver back in its cradle and stared at it. Why bother to call the Cardinal Archbishop? The Cardinal Archbishop had spies. The Cardinal Archbishop knew everything. The Cardinal Archbishop probably had the whole damn building bugged.

Eamon got out of his chair, and went into the hall. Victor was still on the stairs, running up and down. The voices of Gregor Demarkian and Hector Sheed drifted up through the well. Eamon got the impression of calm and deliberation, but no actual words. He crossed the hall and looked into Michael's office.

Michael's office looked the way it always looked. There was mess. There was clutter. There was no religion. Michael didn't keep crucifixes on his wall. He didn't keep prayer wheels or mezzuzahs. He didn't have plastic statues of the Virgin on his file cabinets or a copy of the Koran tucked away on a bookshelf somewhere. Michael always said he was a man without God, and tried to mean it. What confused Eamon Donleavy was that what Michael meant by being without God was not what all the other atheists meant by it. With Michael, nothing came out right, nothing was the way it was supposed to be. With Michael, when you signed on for the ride, you never knew where you were going to end up.

Suddenly, Eamon Donleavy spun around and slammed the door of Michael Pride's office shut. It was too much for him, it really was. All the things he had tried so hard to hold back from himself for years were

coming at him in waves. Just when he thought he was
going to have a chance to breathe, they hit him again.
No, Eamon thought, not *them*. Never *them*. Just *it*. One
single sentence. Four short words. Enough to kill him as
surely as strychnine had killed Charles and Rosalie van
Straadt.

Oh, Christ, Eamon thought, doubling over, nause-
ated, in so much pain he felt as if he had needles in his
bones.

Oh Christ, oh Christ, oh Christ.

I love this man.

2

Every person in residence at the Sojourner Truth
Health Center for more than two weeks on a nonmedical
matter was supposed to take housekeeping duty if they
were asked, and since Julie Enderson had been resident
at the center for months now, she was often asked. She
was asked especially often because the nuns knew she
was reliable. Housekeeping duty was one of those things
that was very important in the aggregate but not very important piece by piece. Seeing that the laundry was
folded and put away in the linen closets, dusting the stair
railings and the furniture in the common rooms, making
sure the flatware was properly sorted—if any one of
those things hadn't managed to get done on any one particular day, it wouldn't have mattered, but if all of them
had been consistently left unfinished, the whole place
would have gone to pot. Julie Enderson knew about
places going to pot. Her mother had had a kind of genius
for them, so that any apartment Steeva Enderson so
much as looked at instantly became a repository of litter

and peeling paint. Julie didn't mind cleaning. The really important cleaning—meaning what had to be done in the west building in the medical facilities—was taken care of by a professional service. The service protected the center from the kind of nasty surprises health inspectors could bring. Julie was assigned only those duties directly relating either to the east building itself, or to the cafeteria and basement of the west building. Even the west building offices were taken care of by the service. In practice, Julie was assigned to sort clothes in the laundry and to sort flatware. Those two things could be accomplished while studying. Julie didn't mind that either. She wanted the time for studying. She wanted to study and study and study until her brain fell out of her head. She was convinced that if she worked as hard as she could and then harder, she would get beyond the place where she saw worms and maggots in the mirror. She would get home.

Today, she was sitting on a high stool at the table in the laundry, folding pillowcases. It was six thirty in the evening, hours after All That had happened, but she was still shaken. She had her history book open to the start of the chapter on the abolitionist movement. She had even read a paragraph or two. She hadn't been able to retain anything. It was a good thing the qualifying test for the academy wasn't due to be held for another month. The way things had been going around here, Julie was surprised she had been able to concentrate at all. She looked at the photograph of Harriet Beecher Stowe and the reprint of the illustration from the original *Uncle Tom's Cabin*. The illustration showed a tiny black girl on her knees, praying to heaven in agony. It was not the first nineteenth-century illustration Julie had seen that had black people in it. All such illustrations made her won-

der. Maybe black people had changed between the time
these illustrations were drawn and now. Maybe black
people were different. Certainly no black person Julie
had ever met looked anything at all like the black people
in these pictures.

Julie took a yellow pillowcase out of the pile, folded
it, and put it on the stack of yellow pillowcases. She took
out a blue one, folded it, and put it on the stack of blue
pillowcases. Folding pillowcases was a terrible thing to
do when you couldn't study. The nuns didn't believe in
watching television, so there was only one set in the east
building, in the common room upstairs. Julie hadn't
thought to bring a novel or a magazine. She didn't have
the money for novels or magazines anyway. She put another folded yellow pillowcase on the stack of yellow pillowcases and listened, hard. The laundry room was in the
basement of the east building. Julie was down here by
herself. There was nothing for her to hear but the sound
of herself folding pillowcases and the soft scurry of rats
and mice in the walls. The nuns tried and tried, but it
was no use. This was New York. If you had a basement,
you had rats and mice in the walls. Period.

Julie had folded five more pillowcases before she
heard the sounds of footsteps on the basement stairs. The
pile of pillowcases was half transformed into folded piles.
Most of what was left was Julie's least favorite color,
white. She slipped off the stool and went to the door of
the laundry room. There were definitely footsteps on the
stairs. The rest of the basement looked dark and empty.
Julie reminded herself that the door to the basement was
locked. It locked automatically and could not be left unlocked without resort to burglar's tools. The lock had
been fine when Julie had used Sister Kenna's keys to
come downstairs. She stood in the doorway and looked at

the dimly lighted sweep of stairway going up. She saw a man's good brown shoes come into sight and then the crease on a pair of pants. For a second, Julie couldn't remember who, connected to the center, could be dressed like that—except maybe for Charles van Straadt, and Charles van Straadt was dead. She ran a terrible movie through her head that had to do with ghosts in drag and corpses walking in the night, and then the rest of the man came into view, and she saw that it was Gregor Demarkian. Julie Enderson half relaxed, although she told herself she had relaxed completely. The truth of it was, Julie Enderson would never in her life feel entirely comfortable being alone in a room with a man. Any man. Even the Risen Christ himself.

Gregor Demarkian came the rest of the way down the stairs and saw her standing in the laundry room doorway.

"Hello," he said. "Sister Kenna said I'd find you here. Do you have a moment to talk?"

Julie Enderson looked back at the history textbook lying open on the table. Half an hour, and she hadn't turned a single page.

"Sure," she said. "Can I fold pillowcases while I talk? I think Sister Kenna is in a hurry."

"It sounds all right by me."

Julie retreated to her stool. When he came into the laundry room, she was holding a pillowcase in the air in front of her body. She got it folded and put it on the stack and quickly reached for another one. Gregor Demarkian got another stool, pulled it up to the sorting table, and sat.

"Robbie is going to be all right," Julie babbled. "I heard Augie and Sister Kenna talking. Everybody is saying Michael did something with him that nobody's ever done before, and now Michael will be in all the medical journals again, like that time a couple of years ago. I don't know what he did a couple of years ago, just that it was important."

"I think this was important, too," Gregor Demarkian said, "but I probably know less about medicine than you do. All that happened with Robbie interrupted our talk."

"Yes," Julie said. "Yes, it did. I hope I wasn't wasting your time."

"You weren't wasting my time."

"It's not the kind of thing everybody would think was important. People uptown, men I guess I mean, maybe even some women, I don't think they think things like that matter. You know, that a man like Charles van Straadt owned a place like that. It would matter more to them that he was rich and that he owned the *Sentinel* and a radio station and had a lot of houses with rooms he didn't use."

"I think it would matter to quite a few people," Gregor told her. "It mattered to me. It—solidified something I was thinking."

Julie was curious. "Solidified? What does that mean? Do you mean you're solid now about who committed the murders?"

"Oh, I was pretty solid about that even before I talked to you this afternoon, but it was what you'd call an aesthetic solution. I knew who the killer was because I knew who the killer had to be. Given the personalities of the other people involved and the setup, there was only one possible solution. I just wasn't too sure how it had been done."

"And now you know? Did sending Mr. van Straadt— the young one, Victor?—did making him run up and down the way you did tell you how it was done?" Julie blushed. "We all heard you. I mean, it was all over the center."

"I'm sure it was. Making Victor van Straadt run up and down the stairs told me how it hadn't been done. I'm hoping to get something of the same kind of help from you."

Julie cocked her head. She must have trusted Gregor Demarkian more than she thought she did. Her folding had slowed. She was no longer being meticulously careful to keep an open pillowcase in front of her body. She picked up a white pillowcase and shook it out.

"I don't understand," she said finally. "Do you mean that all that I had to say about Charles van Straadt and the place in Times Square makes something impossible? I thought it would make a lot of things possible. I thought that was the point. That a man like that would have so many people who wanted to kill him, it wouldn't make any sense to go looking into Michael Pride."

"Don't worry about Michael Pride," Gregor told her. "At least, not on this score. No, it's not the things you told me about the place in Times Square I want to talk about now. It's about the things you did on the night of the murder. About the time after you saw Charles van Straadt."

"We talked about that already," Julie said quickly. "In the cafeteria. I didn't kill Charles van Straadt, Mr. Demarkian."

"I didn't think you did, Julie. It's what happened when you got to the first floor that I want to get straight here. You said you saw Ida Greel."

"That's right. Ida was on duty."

"What was she doing?"

Julie frowned. "She was just walking around, in the hallway."

"Was she near Dr. Pride's examining room?"

"Oh, no." Julie's face cleared. "Mr. Demarkian, nobody could have gotten near Michael's examining room, not then. And not for a whole while later, either. I know. Remember how I said I was trying to find out if my mother had been caught in the fight?"

"I remember."

"Well, that was where I went. Down to Michael's examining room. Because it was really late, you see, and the nuns were using it as an extra emergency room. They were using all the offices and examining rooms. I mean, if you've got someone bleeding on the floor, you can't stand on ceremony. Or go by the rules. I'm not sure what I mean."

"I am. Now let me get this straight. When you came downstairs after seeing Charles van Straadt on the third floor, the first floor of the west building was so full of patients that Michael Pride's examining room was being used to see cases. Was Michael Pride himself there, by the way?"

"I don't think so. Everybody said he was in the operating room."

"All right. What about Sister Augustine?"

Julie shook her head. "Augie was in the operating room, too. At least she was when I was first there. I saw her come out about the time I decided to go back to the east building. I don't think she saw me. She would have dissed me out."

"Perfect." Gregor nodded. He reached for a white pillowcase and began to fold it. "Perfect. The examining room was occupied that way for as long as you were in the west building that night?"

"As far as I know."

"At no time was the area cleared for any reason whatsoever?"

Julie laughed. "You've never been around here in the middle of an emergency. Cleared how? And to where? There wouldn't be anyplace for people to go except out in the street, and the people here are very big on how they never put anybody out in the street. In the winter when the homeless people come around, Augie won't even call the city vans. She just gets a bunch of blankets and lets them bed down on the old furniture in the basement space off the cafeteria. That's when they started getting exterminators out here and putting down rat poison. Augie said you couldn't let people sleep in the basement if they were going to get bitten, and she wasn't going to stop letting people sleep in the basement."

"Perfect," Gregor Demarkian said again. He put the folded pillowcase on the pile. He got off his stool and put it back into the corner it had come from. He seemed to be bouncing a little on the balls of his feet. "Thank you very much, Miss Enderson. You've been a great deal of help."

"Ms.," Julie said automatically.

"Ms. Enderson," Gregor Demarkian repeated.

"Have I really been of help? It doesn't seem that I told you much of anything."

"You helped me to cut off the avenues of escape," Gregor said. "Law enforcement has changed since I entered it, Ms. Enderson. It used to be that all you had to do was prove a positive case. Now you have to make sure you haven't left any gates lying open a good lawyer could drive a defense through. Now you not only have to prove that the defendant committed the crime, you have to prove as far as possible that there was no other way the crime could have been committed. If you don't do that, the lawyers scream 'reasonable doubt,' and half the time the jury buys it, and off walks your murderer, free."

"Oh," Julie said.

"Thank you again," Gregor Demarkian said.

He backed up to the doorway, nodded to her happily, and then disappeared into the gloom. Julie stared into the space where he had gone with perplexity. In the world in which Julie Enderson lived, defendants were almost never let off by juries on grounds of reasonable doubt. Defendants were almost never let off by juries. That's why so few of the people Julie knew who had been arrested had ever had a trial. They just got themselves lawyers from the Legal Aid Society to cut them a plea bargain. Sometimes they were guilty and sometimes they were not, but it hardly seemed to matter. Surely they had been guilty of something somewhere. Almost always they had been dealing drugs. One way or the other, they had been expecting to land in jail ever since they knew what jail was.

Oh, well, Julie thought now. Maybe it was different for people downtown. Everything else was.

For some reason she couldn't pin down, she was much calmer now than she had been before she talked to Gregor Demarkian. She could almost concentrate. She didn't want to concentrate on the abolitionists, though. Julie leaned across the table and flipped through the history text until she came to the page with the colored boxed article on her favorite person in American history.

Sojourner Truth.

3

Downstairs on the second floor, in a room only three feet from the nurses' station, Robbie Yagger was lying in a white-sheeted hospital bed, limp. Next to him in a green plastic molded chair was Shana Malvera, fretting. Shana had been there for nearly an hour now, ever since she had heard what had happened to Robbie and where they had taken him, and she expected to be there for a couple of hours more. Shana believed implicitly in the healing power of human connection. She had said so now at least five times. Every time she did, Robbie felt all warm and light. He was supposed to be unconscious, but he wasn't, not quite. He was floating in something like twilight. He could hear, very clearly, everything that Shana said. He thought he might be able to see, if he could just get his eyes open. His eyes felt weighted down by lead. Mostly what he could do was remember, but it was a strange sort of remembering. Nothing was in order. Nothing was worrisome. Nothing was frightening. Nothing was at all important except the sound of Shana Malvera's voice.

"Dr. Pride says you're going to be in bed for about three days," Shana was saying, "and then you're going to be able to get up and around a bit. If we thought you had somewhere decent to go, we'd send you home, but we're worried about you, Robbie, yes we are. We're very worried about you. So what Augie decided was, when it was time for you to do your convalescence, you could come over to the east building and do it there. You'll like it. Just wait and see. Lots of women to wait on you. Lots of good things to eat. Dr. Pride says you haven't been eating anywhere near as well as you should."

I don't want a lot of women, Robbie Yagger thought. Women make me nervous. I just want you.

Of course I haven't been eating enough, Robbie Yagger thought. I haven't had any money for food. I haven't had any money for anything.

The sheets on the bed were warm, warm, warm. The pillow was soft. Shana's voice was soft, too, and very soothing. Robbie thought about himself looking down into his cup of coffee and about the things floating in it and how he hated it that way and how he hadn't wanted to drink it, but the coffee had been a gift, he remembered that, it had been free and he had wanted to be polite. Who had given it to him? He couldn't remember.

"Stuff," Robbie tried to say, but there was something in his throat, one of those tubes, and he couldn't.

Shana got up and leaned over the bed to listen to him breathing.

"Did you try to say something?" Shana asked him. "You shouldn't try to say anything. You have to rest now."

Yes, Robbie thought, I have to rest now. But I wish I could explain.

The problem was, at the moment, he couldn't even explain it to himself. He wished Gregor Demarkian would come to visit him. Gregor Demarkian would know. Gregor Demarkian could stand here and explain it all to him, while Shana sat in her chair and held Robbie's hand.

T·H·R·E·E

1

"You can't just walk into a New York City newspaper and start asking questions," Hector Sheed said, when he heard what Gregor Demarkian wanted to do. "They'll make you get a court order. They won't talk to you. And it's Friday night, for God's sake. Nobody you want to talk to will be there. What do you think you're going to accomplish?"

Actually, Gregor thought he had already accomplished a good deal. After talking to Julie Enderson, he had made a series of phone calls. Some of them had not worked out as well as he had hoped. It *was* Friday night. A good many of the people he needed confirmations from had gone home. A good many others were in no mood to discuss this matter before Monday. If Gregor had been the police commissioner or still with the Bureau, he might have been able to force the issue. If he had been able to, he probably would have. Now he thought it might be just as well. It wasn't as if he wouldn't be able to get the information he needed tonight, right away. If he had any luck at all—and any right to call himself both an intelligent man and a detective—he would. What would be the point of upsetting the weekend plans of so many people, when they wouldn't be definitively needed until the case came to trial? Assuming the case ever did come to trial. Gregor tried to think his way into the mind of this murderer and couldn't do it. He could never do it. He couldn't count the books he had read where the Great Detective closes his eyes and *becomes* the man he is stalking. Gregor had never understood those books. If he could become one of the people he stalked, he would be one of the people he stalked. It was one thing to try to think yourself into the mind of a man or woman who had killed in anger or fear, on the spur of the moment, impulsively. Anybody could end up in that position. Gregor even understood the battered-woman defense. If someone four inches taller than you are and fifty pounds heavier beats you bloody every time he's drunk, and you can't get a police officer or a judge to do anything about it, then it made perfect sense to Gregor that you would be in enough of a panic when the man was drunk that you'd blow his head off. This was not a battered-woman murder or an impulsive one. This murder had been planned and carried out by a cool head. That Gregor didn't understand at all.

Hector Sheed had an unmarked police car parked at the curb at the front of the center. Gregor led him out to it, down the front stoop and into the darkness of the street. There were two street lamps directly in front of the center's two buildings that worked, but the street lamps on the rest of the block were broken. The unmarked police car was surrounded by marked ones. Uniformed patrolmen were leaning against the hoods, waiting to be told what to do.

"The people we want to talk to will be there," Gregor said, "because I called ahead. We're going to see Dave Geraldino, the editor-in-chief, and Lisa Hasserdorf. Lisa Hasserdorf edits something called the Lifestyles page."

"The Lifestyles page," Hector muttered. "Gregor, what good is this going to do us? What difference does it make?"

"Listen," Gregor said. They were at Hector's unmarked car. Gregor opened the door to the passenger side and got in. Then he waved Hector around in a gesture that made it clear he wanted Hector to get in behind the wheel. Hector didn't move. He stood leaning over Gregor, keeping Gregor's door opened. Gregor sighed.

"Listen," Gregor said again. "If you look at the death of Charles van Straadt—and that's the one you have to look at; the death of Rosalie van Straadt and the poisoning of Robbie Yagger—"

"Assuming it was a poisoning."

"It was a poisoning," Gregor said confidently. "Those two cases are much more difficult. The times are too loose. Anything could have happened. But with Charles van Straadt, it's different. The murder of Charles van Straadt—given when and where and how it was committed—was a very difficult thing to pull off. Hasn't it occurred to you that it was very odd that Charles van Straadt was killed that night at all?"

"Odd? I wouldn't call it odd."

"I would. Look. What have we established up front? Charles van Straadt showed up unexpectedly at the Sojourner Truth Health Center that night. Nobody expected him to come. Therefore, the murderer, seeing Charles van Straadt at the center, decided to take that opportunity to do him in. Right?"

"Right."

"Right as far as it goes," Gregor said, "but it doesn't go far enough. What else do we know about this case? We know that the murder was committed with strychnine. The only strychnine unaccounted for at the Sojourner Truth Health Center came from Michael Pride's personal, locked medical cabinet in his private examining room. We also know that it is highly unlikely that strychnine or anything else could have been removed from that cabinet after Charles van Straadt was known to be in the center on the night in question except by Michael Pride himself or Sister Augustine. So here's your first solution. Either Michael Pride or Sister Augustine killed Charles van Straadt."

"I don't believe it," Hector said. "Neither do you. A couple of hours ago, you went through the times convincing me that that wasn't the way it happened."

"I know I did. I didn't believe it either. But once you've eliminated those two people as suspects, you've got a serious problem. In the first place, you've got strychnine and you don't know where it came from."

"It could have been acquired earlier," Hector pointed out. "Maybe even days earlier."

"And then what?" Gregor demanded. "Carried around in a pocket, night and day, even when the murderer had no use for it? What for? What would happen if the murderer put his hand in his pocket and pulled it out again and there was a little package of poison—"

"It wouldn't necessarily be recognized as poison."

"No, it wouldn't, but nobody could be a hundred percent sure that it wouldn't. Of course, staff and volunteers have rooms at the center, but those rooms are all above the third floor in the east and west buildings and they're mostly in the east building. The times still won't add up. There was no time during that two-hour period when any member of the staff could have run up to the fourth or fifth or sixth floor of either of those buildings and got hold of the strychnine, without their absence being noticed.

No, Hector, the strychnine from Michael Pride's medical cabinet was not used to kill Charles van Straadt. It wasn't even missing at the time Charles van Straadt was murdered. It wasn't taken until much later."

"Later?" Hector was indignant. "When later? We were all over that place later."

"Hector, be reasonable. Not that much later. First Michael Pride finds Charles van Straadt dying. Then a half dozen people arrive at his office—I saw it happen when Rosalie van Straadt died. People came from everywhere. Well, when Charles van Straadt died, they probably came too. You can check it out, but it has to be true. And that left the emergency room, and especially Michael Pride's examining room, unattended."

"Relatively."

"Relatively was all that was necessary."

"What about the keys?"

"Michael Pride keeps his keys in his desk in his office on the third floor. The murderer started off in Michael Pride's office on the third floor. All the murderer had to do was—"

"Get the keys. Get downstairs when everybody else was going up. Dump some strychnine out of Michael Pride's supply. Go back upstairs when everybody was coming down. Put the keys back again."

"Entire operation, fifteen to twenty minutes," Gregor said, "and the police are still a good five to ten minutes from showing up at the door."

"But where did the strychnine that killed Charles van Straadt come from? Did the murderer bring it in from the outside?"

"That has the same problems as having the murderer steal it from Michael Pride's supply a few days in advance. Nobody in his right mind carries a batch of strychnine around on his person for days, not even knowing when he's going to get a chance to use it. I mean, Hector, think about it. Think about the possibility of accident. You're carrying strychnine in your pocket. You've got your mind on something else. You reach for what you think is your packet of aspirin or you've got the strychnine in the same pocket with your gum and the packages of both are breached, or—"

"Never mind," Hector said.

"Listen," Gregor told him. "The trick here is twofold. One, the strychnine was not difficult to get. It was easy. Two, the only reason Charles van Straadt was killed on the night he was killed was *because the murderer couldn't afford to wait any longer.* If Charles van Straadt hadn't shown up at the center that night, bumping into his murderer accidentally, his murderer would have come looking for him. His murderer would have had to. If that wasn't the case, Charles van Straadt would not have died on the night he did under the circumstances he did. Any other explanation is nonsensical. The timing of that murder was nonsensical."

Hector Sheed straightened up. "You think it was one of them, don't you? Victor or Martha? One of them trying to make sure the old man didn't have time to change his will."

Gregor leaned over and pulled his car door shut. The window was cranked all the way open.

"Get in and drive," he said to Hector Sheed. "I told Dave Geraldino we'd be there right away. It's Friday night."

"Eight hundred million dollars." Hector Sheed was shaking his head. "Money. That's the best motive anywhere. Ninety percent of the cases we get in Homicide, everything from drug killings to women who off their husbands, it's money money money and nothing else."

Gregor Demarkian had spent ten years of his life chasing serial killers. In his experience, ninety percent of the time it was sex sex sex and nothing else. This did not seem to be a point worth arguing about at the moment.

"Get into the car," Gregor told Hector Sheed again. "Get into the car and drive."

Hector Sheed gave the car roof a great slapping whack with the palm of his hand and then ran around the front to the driver's side.

When he got in behind the wheel, Gregor heard that he was humming.

2

The New York *Sentinel* had its own building off Times Square on Forty-third Street, a tall gray and brown edifice with windows that looked as if they hadn't been cleaned since the administration of Franklin Delano Roosevelt and a carved stone frieze surrounding its glass front doors that couldn't have been replicated now at any price. It also had security. Gregor had known Secret Service operations that had provided less security. The glass front doors were locked and covered at this time of night by an inside metal grate. To get in, a visitor had to ring the bell, stand back on the pavement to be clearly seen on the security camera over the door, and wait to be opened up for. When he was opened up for, he found that the "doorman" was armed. In fact, he was armed like a cowboy, with a belt holster and a .45, and he wasn't the only one. Gregor counted four other men walking in or through the lobby who were carrying visible weapons.

The street outside might be crowded with junkies and juvenile delinquents, street people, and crazies, but everything was safe in here. It would take a small armed force to breach this place.

The "doorman" let Gregor and Hector Sheed inside, nodding at a list he held on a clipboard in his left hand.

"Demarkian and Sheed," he said. "Mr. Geraldino's office. Up to the forty-second floor."

Gregor looked around at all the guns. "Is this stuff legal?" he asked Hector.

Hector shrugged. "It is if they've got permits for the weapons."

"Do they?"

"How the hell should I know?"

"Forty-second floor," the "doorman" said again, more pointedly this time.

No, Gregor thought. You really wouldn't want to mess with this man, or with any of the others, either. Charles van Straadt did not hire amateurs. Gregor's real question was whether Charles van Straadt hired mercenaries. And where did he get them?

There were half a dozen elevator doors lined up on the far wall, marked everything from "1 to 10" to "Express to 22—22 to 42." As far as Gregor could tell, no single elevator would allow you to stop at each and every floor on the way up or down. Gregor remembered the days when only military installations had elevators like these. Maybe a military installation was what this was.

The elevator was manned. The elevator operator had a holster and a .45 just like everybody else working in the lobby. Gregor got into the elevator car, asked for the forty-second floor, got checked off on another clipboard, and sighed. Hector Sheed was taking it all in stride.

Gregor didn't know what to make of it. Were New Yorkers becoming used to living in an armed camp?

The elevator shot up so fast, Gregor's ears rang. When it came to a stop at the forty-second floor, it bounced a little and rattled. Gregor didn't like elevators. He couldn't keep himself from imagining terrible things happening to them. Cords breaking. Safety systems disintegrating into dust. Once, at the FBI training school at Quantico, an instructor had described in detail the mess that had resulted when an elevator car, broken free of its cables by a small explosion, had dropped thirty stories in its shaft with twenty people inside. Gregor Demarkian had a very vivid imagination. It was so vivid, he could still recall the exact picture that had been emblazoned into his brain with this instructor's description. He could still see himself lying bleeding in the wreckage. He didn't like what this building was doing to him. It was making him remind himself of Bennis.

When the door opened on the forty-second floor, they were met again. This man had a clipboard but no visible gun. Gregor did a quick check for weapons bulges and didn't find any. The man with the clipboard nodded at his list and said, "Mr. Geraldino's office. Come this way, please."

Hector Sheed heaved an enormous sigh. "It would be easier to get in to see the president of the United States," he said, "than it is to get in to see Mr. Dave Geraldino."

The man with the clipboard didn't see any humor in this at all. His face remained perfectly blank.

"Mr. Geraldino is a very important man," he said solemnly. "Come this way, please."

Gregor and Hector both decided to come this way. It was easier than arguing.

Gregor caught a glimpse through a doorway of the reporters' bullpen, fully staffed even at this hour on a Friday night. In the middle of the bullpen, a rickety tripod held a blown-up, grainy, black-and-white photograph of Charles van Straadt.

3

Fortunately for Gregor's equilibrium, Dave Geraldino was considerably less pompous, portentous, and self-important than his security staff. In fact, it would have been difficult for Dave Geraldino to be pompous at all. He was a small muscular man, barely five feet two, who looked like the second lead in a prize-fighter movie from the 1930s. When the man with the clipboard ushered Gregor and Hector Sheed into his office, Dave Geraldino leapt up from the chair behind his desk, hurried to the door, and shook both their hands. Then he pulled chairs from their resting places and placed them close to his desk. Dave Geraldino's office was the kind with glass walls. The walls looked out on the bullpen. His desk held a copy of the New York *Sentinel* logo carved into crystal for a paperweight. Gregor recognized it as the kind of thing owners give their chief operating officers after a particularly good year.

Dave Geraldino had been taken aback for a moment at the sight of Hector Sheed, but only for a moment. Now he was waving them both into the chairs.

"Sit down, sit down," he said. "Lisa will be here in just a minute. Mr. Demarkian, you don't know how glad I am to meet you at last. I already know so much about you. At least, I know so much about your professional life."

Gregor tried to remember what the *Sentinel* had had

to say about the Baird case, or any of the other cases he had taken on since he had retired from the Bureau, but he couldn't. He supposed the *Sentinel* had said something. All the papers had.

"I'm very glad to meet you, too," Gregor said. "This is Hector Sheed, detective first grade—"

"Manhattan Homicide." Dave Geraldino was pacing around and around the perimeter of the office. "In charge of the van Straadt case. I know. I know. I do read my own paper."

"Good," Hector rumbled.

"You don't know how thrilled we are that you have agreed to this interview," Dave Geraldino continued. "An interview like this in the middle of a case is an extraordinary thing for a paper to have. An extraordinary thing. Especially from you, Mr. Demarkian. You have such a reputation for refusing to give interviews at all."

"Interview," Hector Sheed said slowly.

Gregor shot him a look. "Leave it alone," he said. "It's getting us what we want."

"What is it we do want?" Hector asked.

There was a rattle at the door of the office. Dave Geraldino stopped his pacing long enough to open up. Gregor and Hector stared at the woman coming inside. That she was very young was attested to by the condition of her skin. It was so soft and unlined, it looked newborn. That young did not mean naive or innocent was attested to by the look in her eyes. Gregor's first impression was that here was a woman who could have reported on the bombing of Hiroshima firsthand and not even blinked.

Dave Geraldino waved the young woman inside. "Lisa," he said enthusiastically, "Lisa, come right in. This

is Mr. Demarkian and Mr. Sheed. This is Lisa Hasserdorf, our Lifestyles page editor."

"Not for long." Lisa Hasserdorf sat down on the edge
of Dave Geraldino's desk. She had long black hair to her
waist and big black eyes. The lipstick she was wearing
was bloodred.

"So," she said, after she had looked them both over.
"You want to know how our contests are run."

"Gregor?" Hector asked.

Gregor was smiling pleasantly. "That's right. Specifi-
cally, I want to know how your Father's Day contest is
being run and about any other contests that have been
run the same way."

"Any others? But Mr. Demarkian, there have been
hundreds. Going back years. From well before my time."

"You're in charge of the contests?"

"Not in charge, no. Victor van Straadt is in charge, at
the moment. But he's in charge under me, if you see
what I mean."

"Not exactly," Gregor said. "What do you do? Do you
check on his work? Do you oversee the money— There
is money involved, isn't there? A hundred thousand dollars?"

"That's right. And no, I don't do any of those things.
I just make sure Victor has what he's supposed to have
when he's supposed to have it. Right now, I'm constantly
making sure that he has his copy written, and that he's
keeping the entries that come in in the glass jar in the
storeroom and that he's logged them in before he puts
them in there. He had a computer program to log them
in on. The Father's Day contest is a lottery kind of thing,
you see, where people have to send in the right numbers.
Sometimes we run straightforward drawings. Those are
easier."

Gregor considered this. "Let's back up a little. You say this Father's Day contest is a lottery kind of thing. Do you mean that people send in their numbers and then you pick balls out of a bowl with numbers on them?"

"No," Lisa Hasserdorf said, "although we've done it that way once or twice. What we've found, though, is that people like to do puzzles. They like to feel that they've really figured something out. And if they win, you know, it gives them a kick to tell their friends that they're one of the smartest people in New York. Although these days, you wouldn't think that would take much. Anyway, what we've got going this time is a quiz about the most famous fathers in history, and what you're supposed to do is guess the year they were born. We don't give the exact names, you understand. We don't say William Tell, for instance. We say, 'This father was forced by an evil government official to shoot an apple off his son's head with an arrow.' Then you're supposed to figure out who that is, write the name down and write the year he was born. There are ten of those."

"So you have to know both things," Gregor said.

"That's right."

"What happens next?"

"Well, next, Victor looks into his computer at the end of the time period, you know, after all the entries have to be in, and he finds out how many people got the right answers and who they are—"

"Are there always more than one?"

"Usually, yes. Anyway, he double-checks those entries and then he gives the winners a call, and they come down here for a drawing. We put all their names in a drum and pull out one and that one gets the hundred thousand. We usually have five or six people in at the end."

"What if they can't come down here? Do they forfeit their right to be in the drawing?"

"Oh, no." Lisa Hasserdorf looked very disapproving. "We couldn't do that. Many of the people who enter these contests are homebound or disabled. We often have people who can't come down here. We put their names in the drum anyway. Then, if they win, we send a photographer out to their house and get their picture for the paper. That is, if they'll let us photograph them, of course. It's illegal in New York State to insist on cooperation with publicity as a condition for winning a contest like this one."

Gregor thought it over. Carefully. "Do you often have people who don't want to be photographed?"

Lisa Hasserdorf shrugged. "It runs two to one in favor of getting your picture in the paper. But it's not unusual for someone not to want to be photographed. Of course, we do put their names in the paper, and their boroughs. It isn't illegal in New York State to insist on that."

"How long has Victor van Straadt been running these contests?" Gregor asked. "Is this his first one?"

"Oh, no," Lisa said. "Victor's been with the paper two years now, and quite frankly, we put him on the contests right away, right after the secretary who used to handle them quit. Victor had been with us about six months then. He's really hopeless."

"Lisa," Dave Geraldino scolded.

"Well, he is," Lisa said. "In fact, *hopeless* may not be a strong enough word. I know he's a van Straadt, but really. He didn't inherit any of his grandfather's talent for newspaper work. I don't even know if he reads newspapers. We couldn't fire him, considering who he was, but we couldn't leave him running around loose, either. So we gave him the contests. Any idiot could do what he does. It doesn't matter if he doesn't have the brains God gave a donkey. In fact, the contests just don't matter."

"It would matter if there were any irregularities, wouldn't it?" Gregor asked. "Most states have very strict laws about that kind of thing."

"That would matter, yes," Lisa agreed. "But Victor isn't dishonest, Mr. Demarkian. He's just stupid. And in my opinion, he's much too stupid to devise any— irregularities—that wouldn't be picked up immediately by one of the rest of us."

"All right," Gregor said. He certainly couldn't argue that Victor van Straadt was not stupid. That would be like arguing that the ocean wasn't wet. "Just one more thing. How many of these contests would you say Victor van Straadt has run?"

"Nine," Lisa answered promptly. "We do six a year."

"Of this nine, how many would you say have involved winners who have not wanted to be photographed for the paper?"

Lisa frowned. "I don't know. It's not the kind of thing I keep track of. Is it really important that you know?"

"Yes, I think it is." Gregor nodded slowly. "It would also help if I knew who among the winners had and who had not shown up for the drawings and the names and addresses of the winners who had not been photographed for the paper. Do you think you could get me all that?"

Lisa Hasserdorf was bewildered. "Yes, of course I could. It's all on the computer. But Mr. Demarkian, I just don't understand. How is all that going to help solve the murder of Charles van Straadt?"

"That's the question I've got, too," Hector Sheed said. "You got an answer to it, Gregor?"

Gregor stood up to stretch and looked reproachfully at Hector Sheed in the process.

"The murder of Charles van Straadt is solved, Hector. That was the easy part. Now is when the real work has to be done."

"Oh, marvelous," Dave Geraldino said gleefully. "Just the way they described it in *People* magazine."

F·O·U·R

1

It was Martha van Straadt's idea that her brother Victor should go down to the offices of the New York *Sentinel* after Gregor Demarkian and Hector Sheed to find out what they were up to, and it was Martha van Straadt who waited at the door of the east building hour after hour until Victor came back. Actually, it was only about an hour and forty-five minutes. It just felt as if it were taking forever. The wait was made worse by the fact that Martha had been left utterly alone. Ida had agreed with this project, in principle, when Martha had first brought it up. Ida had behaved the way Ida always behaved, deliberating calmly, coming to reasoned conclusions. Martha hated Ida's reasonableness the way she hated Robbie Yagger's conversion. Martha liked change only in the abstract. She liked Social Change, which to her meant reaching the point where all the stupid people in the world who believed things Martha found anathema would be forced to recognize both their own stupidity and Martha's dazzling advancedness. In her daily life, she preferred routine, predictability, assurance. Martha remembered Ida as a child, volatile and spiteful, imperious and volcanic. In Martha's mind, Ida should have stayed the way she had begun, the way Victor had.

Ida's excuse was that she had work to do. She was on duty in the emergency room. It was Friday night. What did Martha expect? Martha expected a great deal more than she got. Unlike the doors to the west building, which were almost always kept open, the doors to the east building were almost always kept locked. Martha had to stand in the long thin window next to the door and look out that way, or go into the reception room and look out the windows there. Martha preferred the long thin window. The reception room was too public. People saw you there and thought you were available for conversation. Martha didn't want to talk to anybody. She watched the moving shadows in the street and listened to the low sharp voices coming out of the darkness. It happened every Friday night. The street was full of people again. The people were invisible, uncatchable, out of sight—but they were there. Martha had no idea where they came from. What she could see was a big black pit of nothing, crowded in by hulking outlines in brick and stone. The pools of light at the entrances to the east and west buildings were empty.

By the time Victor came back, Martha was agitated beyond belief, hopping up and down, angry-frantic, the way she got when her anxieties got out of control. It didn't help that Ida had undoubtedly been right about how busy she was going to be. In the twenty minutes before Victor's car arrived at the entrance to the east building, Martha had seen two dozen people climbing the steps to the west building, and four ambulances coming in to the doors around the side. Dear God, Martha hated life in Harlem. She didn't think anybody should have to do the kind of things she did in this place or witness the kind of things she witnessed. In a perfect world, the government would take care of all of this, and people like Martha wouldn't even have to think about it.

Victor got out of his car only after his driver had come around to open his door. That was the drill they had when the neighborhood felt too jumpy, so that Victor wouldn't get mugged. As soon as Victor got out on the sidewalk, Martha opened the door to the east building and went out on the stoop. She held the door open with her foot and waited for Victor to climb the stairs. If she let the door shut, it would lock automatically. She would have to ring the bell to be let inside again, and she didn't want that. Victor came up to her, smiled vaguely, and passed her. Martha followed him inside, letting the door hiss shut on its cylinder. Victor looked tired. Martha didn't care.

"Well?" she said.

"Well what?" Victor looked around. The entry hall was empty. The reception room was empty, too. He motioned through the archway and said, "I'm going to go sit down. I'm tired."

"I don't care if you're tired, Victor. I want to know what happened. Did you see them? Did you find out what they wanted?"

"I overheard them talking to Dave Geraldino," Victor said.

There were two worn sofas in the reception room. There were three large club chairs with patched arms and sagging springs. There were a couple of hard chairs with wooden backs. He chose one of the club chairs and sat down. Martha couldn't bear the thought of sitting. She had to pace.

"Well?" she said again. "What was it about? What did you overhear?"

"It was about the contest," Victor said.

Martha drew a blank. "What contest?"

"The Father's Day contest down at the paper. You know, what I do on my job. It was about that."

"It was about it how?"

Victor shrugged. "Well, you know. How do the contests run. What happens with the winners. That kind of thing. Lisa was there, too. Lisa Hasserdorf. My boss."

This was like swimming through mud. This was really awful. Martha hated talking to Victor.

"Look," she said. "Try to make sense. Demarkian and Sheed went all the way downtown just to talk to Dave Geraldino and Lisa Hasserdorf about the contest? Doesn't that seem strange to you?"

"It wasn't just this contest. It was all the contests that I've run. And no. It doesn't seem strange to me."

"It doesn't?"

"No. And it shouldn't seem strange to you, either."

"Oh, Victor, for God's sake. Make sense. Nobody cares about those contests. Even the paper doesn't care about them. They're just something Grandfather liked to do because that sort of thing works so well in other places."

Victor shifted in his chair. The line of his leg was elegant. The cut of his suit was beyond belief. He had a dreamy smile on his face. Was Martha crazy, or was he even vaguer and stranger than usual? There was something Martha definitely didn't like in this attitude of Victor's. There was something menacing under the surface. Had it always been there? Martha walked quickly away from Victor's chair and went to look out the window.

"You're not making sense," she said again. "If you've got some idea why Demarkian and Sheed are doing what they're doing, I wish you'd tell me. I don't like the way things are going. I keep expecting one of us to be arrested at any moment. It's making me physically ill."

"They got the names of the people who wouldn't let themselves be photographed," Victor told her placidly. "The one from the supercontest last year, with the quarter million payoff. Mrs. Esther Stancowycz from Brooklyn. I love the name Esther Stancowycz, don't you?"

"I don't know." Martha's voice had a wild note to it. She could hear it. "Why should I like it?"

"They got the name of that woman in Queens who won the Presidents' Day contest in February, too. Miss Sharon Cortez. All the names they got were names of women. Of course, they had to be women."

"Why?" Martha asked desperately.

Victor stood up. "We ought to go over and get Ida, don't you think? She's going to want to know about this as much as you do. We're going to have to fill her in."

"Ida's on duty in the emergency room," Martha said uncertainly.

"I think I'll go down and tell her I'm here anyway. Then I think I'll go down to the cafeteria and drink some coffee and read the papers. I'm going to find that very interesting. And it will be the last time. The last time for anything is always interesting."

All of a sudden it hit Martha, in a wave, that she knew what was going on here. She felt poisoned. Sickness rose in her stomach and spread into her veins.

"Victor," she said, "did you kill Grandfather?"

"No."

"No? Just like that?"

"What other way is there to say no? No. No. No. No. But I'll tell you a secret. I'm going to get arrested for killing him and I'm going to get tried for killing him and I'm going to get convicted of killing him. I'll even go to jail for killing him. I don't think the state of New York would take too well to a request for alternative community service in a case like this, do you? Not even for somebody with a name like van Straadt."

Victor's lost his mind, Martha thought, but she didn't say anything. She didn't want to say anything. She was just glad Victor knew so little about the center. He had volunteered here, of course, just like the rest of them, but he hadn't really taken to it. He didn't know his way around. Martha knew half a dozen ways to get to Ida before he could. Martha had to get to Ida. Martha had to warn her.

There was a framed photograph of Michael Pride on the wall of the reception room. Victor stopped in front of it, straightened it unnecessarily, and smiled.

"Saint Michael Pride," he said.

And then he burst out laughing.

2

Down in the emergency room, Sister Augustine was counting sodium pentathol doses on a long metal tray. The doses had already been counted twice, once by Sister Kenna and once by Sister Mary Grace. The counts had come up wrong both times. Augie could see now that the counts were going to come up wrong again. The tray had been left out. That was the problem. The situation had gotten bad—not as bad as it had been two weeks ago, on the night when Charles van Straadt had died, but bad—and somebody had gotten careless. If Augie went to work at it, she could figure out just whose responsibility it had been. She never did bother to go to work at it in these cases, because doing that was stupid. She just took responsibility for it herself. There wasn't a single member of this staff that hadn't gotten careless at least once because of lack of sleep or lack of food or lack of something else. Except Michael, of course, but Michael didn't count. Michael was the exception to all the rules in the universe except one.

The count came out wrong. Augie pushed the tray away and looked up at Sister Kenna and Sister Mary Grace. Both looked haggard. It was horrible when the counts came out wrong. You always knew what had happened when you were short a dose. The junkies would take anything if they were far enough gone. You always wondered if your carelessness had killed somebody. Mixing drugs was not the safest thing to do.

"It's all right," Augie said. "I'll have to report it, but it's all right. It's only three doses."

"Only three," Mary Grace repeated miserably. "Three is enough."

"For a veteran junkie, three is barely an appetizer."

The tray was lying on the lower level of the counter at the nurses' station. From there Augie could see the front doors and the people coming in and out. Most of the people tonight looked damaged. There was nothing hidden about their pain. Then a flutter of excitement seemed to rise from the darkness just outside the door. The people milling around the entrance stood back. Augie saw Gregor Demarkian and Hector Sheed come in one right after the other. They stopped near the front to talk, Augie didn't know to whom.

"It's the detectives," she said to Sister Kenna and Sister Mary Grace. "With the kind of night we've been having, I'd almost forgotten they were here."

"They haven't been here," Sister Mary Grace said.

"They've been out. I know because Michael was looking for them earlier, and I couldn't find them for him."

"They went down to the New York *Sentinel*," Ida Greel said, coming up to the nurses' station with her white smock open and a red smear of Mercurochrome across her cheek. "Victor and Martha and I heard them talking before they left. I don't know what it was about."

"The New York *Sentinel*." Sister Kenna brightened. "That's a new tack, isn't it? Maybe they don't think those murders had anything to do with the center. Wouldn't that be a relief?"

"No," Ida said.

Sister Kenna shot Ida a remorseful look.

Gregor Demarkian and Hector Sheed had finished talking to whoever it was they were talking to. Augie watched them detach themselves from the crowd that had gathered around them and begin to work their way to the back of the hall. The crowd drifted in their direction, but not for long. Everybody wanted to be close to the action, to know what was going on—but not too close. Getting too close could be a jinx. The police could pin anything on you if they wanted to. Augie was surprised at how much of the ordinary attitudes of this neighborhood she had taken for her own. She wouldn't have thought that way about the police when she first came here.

"I hate to be callous," she said, "but I don't really care what they're doing as long as they're not being a threat to Michael."

"I don't think they were ever a threat to Michael," Ida said. "I think that was just our paranoia."

"Somebody's a threat to somebody," Sister Kenna said. "I'm glad Robbie Yagger didn't die, in spite of all the trouble he's caused us. I don't think I could have stood to have somebody else die around here—I mean—"

"I know what you mean," Augie said.

"Is Robbie Yagger doing well?" Ida asked. "I was on duty in Family Planning when all that happened. Later somebody told me that Michael had committed another miracle, and done something nobody had ever done before. Doesn't Michael always?"

"Robbie's doing all right," Augie told her. "Michael's saying he should be sitting up and talking in a couple of days. There's something going on now about making sure he stays absolutely still because there might still be some strychnine in his body."

"I'll have to tell Julie Enderson about that." Ida touched the red smear on her cheek. "She was all worked up about it. I'm going down to the cafeteria right now. Maybe I'll run into her."

"Are you taking a break?" Augie asked.

Sister Kenna nudged Augie in the ribs. "Look. They're coming right this way. I think they're going to stop and talk to us."

"Why shouldn't they stop and talk to us?" Augie demanded. "We can talk to them any time we want to. Or at least we can talk to Mr. Demarkian. That's why he's here."

"Oh, Augie," Sister Kenna said.

Hector Sheed and Gregor Demarkian were only a couple of yards away. Augie hated to admit it, but she knew what Sister Kenna was getting at. This morning, she had felt as if she could command Gregor Demarkian's attention any time she wanted it. Now she didn't. Robbie Yagger's near-death had caused a psychological shift Rosalie van Straadt's murder hadn't. That probably means they're close to knowing the answer, Augie thought. And then she shivered.

"If I wasn't a nun, I'd think Hector Sheed was cute," Sister Mary Grace said.

Augie hated waiting for things to happen to her. She stepped around the side of the nurses' station counter and said, "Mr. Demarkian? Mr. Sheed? Can I speak to you for a moment?"

The two men came to a stop when there were less than six inches left between them and Augie. Augie backed up a little. She had been trained in the days when nuns had been careful to keep a safe space between themselves and seculars at all times. She didn't like to get too close.

She also didn't know what she wanted to say. "Mr. Demarkian," she tried, ignoring Hector Sheed completely. "We've heard—that is, there's a rumor going around—there's some talk that you might have the answer. That the police might be close to an arrest."

There was, of course, no such rumor. Augie was telling a lie. She didn't care.

Hector Sheed was looking impatient. "The police are close to losing their tempers," he said pointedly.

Gregor Demarkian ignored him. "I think it's a little soon to talk about arrests," he explained to Sister Augustine. "Right now, I need a word with Dr. Pride."

Augie tensed. "With Michael? But you can't have a word with Michael. It's Friday night."

Gregor Demarkian's eyebrows rose up his forehead. Augie flushed.

"It's Friday night," she repeated. "We're inundated. We're always drowning in emergencies on Friday night."

"What are you talking about?" Ida Greel asked. "We're

busy, but we're not drowning. Actually, we're doing pretty well for a Friday night."

"Shut up," Augie told her fiercely. "Michael's *busy*."

"I just want to ask him a couple of questions," Gregor said gently. "I'm not going to slap him into handcuffs and haul him off to the Tombs. I don't have the authority."

"He does." Augie pointed at Hector Sheed.

"Oh, Augie," Ida Greel said. She turned to Gregor Demarkian and Hector Sheed, looking a little helpless. Augie felt anger welling up inside herself and turned away. "Michael's in his examining room," Ida continued. "I think he's alone. He did a job in OR about ten minutes ago and when he came out there was nothing immediately waiting. Of course, it's early in the night."

"Thank you," Gregor Demarkian said.

Gregor Demarkian and Hector Sheed started to walk away. They knew where Michael's examining room was. Every single reader of the New York City newspapers knew where Michael's examining room was. Augie could feel the fury mounting up inside her like steam in a pressure cooker. She spun around on Ida and hissed, "What did you think you were doing? What did you think you were doing? Do you want to destroy him?"

"Destroy him?" Ida was shell-shocked. "Augie, what are you talking about?"

"None of you thinks for a minute about him," Augie raged. "None of you thinks for a minute. You treat him like he's some kind of machine."

Sister Kenna and Sister Mary Grace were looking at each other.

"Augie," Sister Kenna said tentatively, "I think you're a little tired. You're overreacting."

"Of course I'm not overreacting," Augie exploded. "Oh, you're all such babes in the woods. None of you understand anything. You don't realize how dangerous this situation is."

"Dangerous," Sister Mary Grace repeated in bewilderment.

But of course, Augie knew she was overreacting. She knew she had been overreacting for days. She couldn't help herself.

What she could do was get out of there, and that she did. She picked up the tray of sodium pentathol doses and sailed off down the hall to put them away in the drugs cupboard.

3

Through the open door of his examining room, Michael Pride had seen Gregor Demarkian and Hector Sheed and then Augie, having one of her epiphanies of sense. Now he sat on the corner of his desk and waited, tired, for the two men to get to him. He had gone on working without so much as a nod in the direction of his condition, at the same intensity, at the same hours, with just as little food or rest. It hadn't mattered until tonight. That was the real problem with cancer, Kaposi's sarcoma or any other kind. Your body spent so much time fighting a war it couldn't hope to win, there was nothing left over for your ordinary life. Half an hour ago, Michael had been standing in the operating room, extracting four .38-caliber bullets from the bone marrow of a boy no more than fourteen years old. Michael had stayed awake and alert throughout the procedure, but in the end he had done it only by an effort of will. In a week or two, he knew the effort of will would not be enough. With proper care and careful management, he could expect to go on working for months, or even for years—but he could not expect to go on working like this. The twenty-hour days, the six operations back to back, the endless marathons that constituted his part in the gang warfare of the ghettos of New York City: All that was going to have to come to an end. Michael rubbed his face and told himself that all that had already come to an end, just now, it was over, he was never going to be able to do it again. He needed somebody to lean on and there was no-body here. Eamon and Augie were falling apart. They reached out to him and he gave them what help he could, because he always had. What was he going to do next? Michael Pride had always been a man alone. He had always wanted to be a man alone. He wanted to be that now. He just wanted to rest.

There was a gentle tap on his open door. In the hall, Gregor Demarkian and Hector Sheed waited politely. Michael stood, said, "Come in," and walked around the desk to take a seat in the chair.

"There was some discussion outside that you might be busy," Gregor Demarkian said. "If we're interrupting something, we could wait a few minutes until you had time."

"I've got time." Michael waved them into the two seats in front of the desk. The chairs looked much too small for such big men. "If I didn't have time, waiting a few minutes wouldn't be much help. Sometimes it seems to me that what we do around here is either everything or nothing. We're either frantic or dead."

"And now you're dead?"

"Not quite," Michael said. "No such luck on a Friday night. We just aren't frantic quite yet. Could I get any-thing for the two of you? Coffee? Augie always keeps a pot of the stuff in here, in one of those drip machines. She says I run on caffeine."

Hector Sheed cleared his throat. "No, thank you," he said. "Not for me, anyway. Although that's funny, about the coffee."

"Funny?" Michael asked. "Why?"

"Because that's what Mr. Demarkian is here to talk to you about," Hector Sheed said. "Coffee."

"Don't pay any attention to him," Gregor Demarkian said. "And I don't need any coffee now, either. What I want to talk to you about is Robbie Yagger."

Michael nodded. "Robbie's all right. If everything goes the way it's been going, he should be fine in about a week. Will that solve all our problems here? Will he be able to tell us who tried to kill him?"

"Maybe." Gregor nodded. "We can't know for sure now if he saw who tried to kill him. When I saw him, he was saying something about there being 'stuff' in his coffee."

"I heard that, too." Michael nodded vigorously. "Shana Malvera heard it, too. Shana is a friend of his. She's been keeping him company in his room as much as she can. She told me just before dinner that Robbie keeps trying to talk through his tubes, and what he seems to be saying is that there was 'stuff' in his coffee."

"I wish I knew what that 'stuff' was," Hector Sheed said.

Gregor brushed it away. "I know. It's not the stuff. It's the who. And the coffee cup, of course. I don't know if you realize it, Dr. Pride, but the police made a very thorough search for the cup from which Robbie Yagger drank his coffee. They didn't find it."

"He didn't have a cup," Michael said. "Not when I saw him."

"He didn't have a cup when I saw him, either," Gregor agreed. "When did you first see him?"

"We came into the cafeteria together. Down at the tray and flatware end of the line. If he was sick then, I didn't notice it. What am I talking about? Of course he was sick then. He would have had to be. I must have been thinking about something else."

"He wasn't carrying a coffee cup when you saw him."

"No, he wasn't. He wasn't carrying anything. He didn't even pick up a tray. He just walked on through and started looking around. I assumed he was meeting somebody."

"Yes," Gregor said. "I thought the same thing myself. Would that be Shana Malvera?"

"She wasn't in the cafeteria. You could ask her, though. Maybe she was supposed to be and she got tied up."

"Is she up in Robbie Yagger's room now?"

"Yes, she is. She's got somebody to cover for her over in the east building and she's going to spend the night sitting in the chair next to Robbie's bed and keeping him company. Shana's wonderful, really. She's one of our staff volunteers next door. She's not too bright, but she's got all the right instincts. Just what Robbie needs to pull him through."

"Yes," Gregor said. "I can see that. She can't spend all night in that chair, can she? She would have to use the bathroom from time to time at least."

"The bathroom's right next door to Robbie's room. We don't have space for private bathrooms upstairs, but we do our best to make what we've got convenient. The nuns will bring Shana her food. They'll even keep her supplied with coffee and magazines. I don't see what else she would need."

"I don't either," Gregor said. Then he gave Hector Sheed a long look that made Hector squirm.

Michael Pride looked from the face of one man to the face of the other. He might be in terrible pain. He might be exhausted to the point of collapse. But he hadn't turned into a mental defective. Something was definitely going on.

"Maybe one of you two could tell me what's going on," Michael said pleasantly. "Just so I'd know. Because I'm supposed to be head of this center, for instance."

Michael expected to get an argument. He was a little shocked at what he got instead.

"Of course we'll tell you what's going on," Gregor Demarkian told him. "In fact, we need your help. If we don't do something right away, there's going to be another murder."

F·I·V·E

1

Usually, Gregor Demarkian was given to understatement, not overstatement. Ten years of chasing men who killed their victims and hung them on meat hooks, killed their victims and stuffed them in store windows, killed their victims and sent them to Honolulu in packing crates, had left Gregor with very little taste for exaggeration. Even the kind of hyperbole he was used to being handed on Cavanaugh Street made him uncomfortable. The Church Roof Fund was a worthy and necessary cause, but the four asphalt shingles that had fallen from the top of Holy Trinity Church to the pavement below didn't constitute *a crisis, a veritable crisis*, no matter what Lida Arkmanian said. The afterschool program in Armenian language and culture that was being held every Tuesday and Thursday afternoon in the church basement was a nice idea and fun for the children who attended, but it did not constitute *an eleventh hour rescue mission to snatch the flame of Armenian history from oblivion*, and Gregor had told Howard Kashinian so. No, Gregor was definitely one of the tribe that called full-scale tornadoes "windstorms" and major blizzards "a fair amount of snow." He exaggerated in this case only because he felt he had to. He didn't really know that there was about to be another murder. If he was right about what had happened at the Sojourner Truth Health Center—and Gregor was right; he could feel it—what happened next depended on a variable he had no way of determining for sure. Had Robbie seen the person who had handed him his last cup of coffee? Had that person been the same person who filled that coffee with "stuff"? The single impossibility was that the coffee had been handed to a third party with instructions to turn it over to Robbie. The third party would have come forward. That left Gregor with two avenues of investigation. Robbie could have gotten his own coffee, run into his murderer, and been slipped the "stuff" when he wasn't looking. Robbie often wasn't looking. Gregor had talked to him at length. Robbie was one of those people who seem to be perpetually distracted, with no attention span. Robbie couldn't watch out for himself or anything else, for that matter. The more likely scenario was that the murderer had come right up and handed Robbie his coffee, "stuff" and all. This was especially likely because Robbie never had any money. That day Gregor had bought Robbie lunch had been no different from any other. Robbie was trying to live on unemployment benefits that were quickly running out. For someone whose job had been minimum wage and who had no assets to speak of—no house, no bank account, no property— those benefits had been inadequate to begin with. Robbie was always so grateful when somebody gave him something to eat or drink for free. He was always so hungry and so parched. Gregor thought he was on the verge of being homeless, too. Robbie couldn't be paying the rent on a New York City apartment, even an apartment in one of the outer boroughs, on what he was getting in unemployment. How many months was he in arrears? How long did he have before he would be out on the street? Maybe Robbie's church would take care of him then, Gregor didn't know. What Gregor did know was that Robbie had had an air of desperation about him. It would be the easiest thing in the world for someone to walk up to Robbie Yagger, hand him a cup of coffee laced with strychnine, and stand by while Robbie took a great big gulp of it. Then it would only be a matter of a little subterfuge—jogging Robbie's elbow, dropping something and offering to hold the coffee cup while Robbie picked it up—to get the cup back and whisk it away. A minute or two later, and it should all be over. The murder of Robbie Yagger should have been a much easier proposition than the murder of Charles van Straadt. It was worse than ironic that the murder of Charles van Straadt had come off without a hitch and the murder of Robbie Yagger had failed to come off at all.

Gregor was still standing in the middle of Michael Pride's examining room. Michael Pride and Hector Sheed were staring at him. Gregor had the uneasy feeling that they had been staring at him for a very long time. Gregor shifted on his feet. How long had he been drifting around inside his head, thinking it all out? How long did they have? They not only had the murderer of Robbie Yagger to worry about. They had all of Harlem. As Gregor had heard from half a dozen people, this was Friday night. Friday nights got crazy at places like the Sojourner Truth Health Center.

"It was the strychnine," Gregor told them as clearly as he could. "That's when I first realized we were looking at this thing backward. It was the strychnine that couldn't have come from Michael Pride's cabinet."

Michael Pride perked up. "You mean the strychnine wasn't mine? This didn't all happen due to my own criminal carelessness?"

"Have you been careful since Charles van Straadt died?" Gregor asked him.

"I've been a fanatic."

"There now. And there has been another murder *and* a murder attempt."

"A lot of strychnine was gone from that cabinet," Hector Sheed put in. "More than enough to kill three people."

"If you go at it that way, you get back to where we were in our discussion before," Gregor told him. "You have a murderer carrying strychnine around on his or her person for days at a time, or hiding it in his or her room, or whatever. No, you see, your problem, my problem, all of our problems in thinking about the strychnine center on the phrase *accounted for*. When I first came here, Eamon Donleavy said that all the strychnine in the building had been 'accounted for' except for the strychnine that was missing from Michael Pride's cabinet."

"That's right," Hector Sheed said. "It was accounted for."

"Augie did the accounting," Michael Pride said. There was an edge in his voice. "Are you trying to tell us that Augie is dishonest?"

"No, no," Gregor told them. "But think about it? What does *accounted for* mean? It means you know where that strychnine is, right?"

"Right," Hector Sheed said.

"Wrong," Gregor countered. "At least some of that accounted for strychnine was the strychnine in the rat poison the nuns were using in the basement. Most rat poisons are principally strychnine and whoever did the investigation here was smart enough to realize that. The stores of rat poison were checked, and they were not depleted. But you see, they didn't have to be. What is it that you do with rat poison?"

"Kill rats," Michael Pride said.

"How?" Gregor asked him.

"You spread the poison out in the corners or on the floor and— Oh," Hector Sheed said.

Gregor nodded in satisfaction. "Exactly. You wouldn't spread the poison out on the floors in the middle of the center, but down in the basements and subbasements where nobody goes, why not? You'd sprinkle the stuff here and there, maybe mix it in with a little cheese or a little garbage or some warm wet coffee grounds—"

"Oh, shit," Hector Sheed said.

"Don't worry," Gregor consoled him. "I don't think it's that bad. I don't think they're making a practice here of using coffee grounds to mix rat poison in. Are they, Dr. Pride?"

"I don't know," Michael Pride said. "They use whatever's to hand, I guess. I've never asked."

"It doesn't really matter," Gregor went on, "because even if what it was mixed with was a little cheese, the cheese would have been present in the poison in what amounted to microscopic quantities. There would be no reason for it to show up in the stomach content analysis when Charles van Straadt was killed. And even if it did, it didn't matter. So Charles van Straadt ate some cheese? So what? There might have been some trouble if cheese also showed up in the stomach content analysis when Rosalie van Straadt was murdered, but it didn't. And that's not surprising. When you're mixing rat poison with garbage, you use whatever garbage comes to hand. It differs from day to day or week to week. It probably differs from one side of the room to the other."

"But what about the poison missing from my cabinet?" Michael asked. "It really is missing, Mr. Demarkian. It ought to be there and it isn't."

"It's probably down in the basement with the rat poison by now," Gregor said. "It was only taken to incriminate you. Because by incriminating you two things were accomplished. In the first place, the first murder—of Charles van Straadt—was made to look incredibly difficult, a matter of expert timing and cool nerves, when it was really quite simple. That had us running around in circles, looking for a master criminal who doesn't exist. The second thing it did was to direct suspicion to the two people least likely to have been able to commit this particular crime. Michael Pride and Sister Augustine."

"I suppose at the same time it directed suspicion off someone else," Michael said. "It wasn't so impossible that I could have committed that murder. I figured it out on my own, after it happened. I could have done it when I first came up to the third floor and only said that I found Charlie already poisoned when I got there."

"It's just possible," Gregor agreed, "but we're back to master criminals again. The timing would have been brutal. Of course, you are the only person around here with the brains to be a master criminal. There is that."

"Thanks a lot." Michael's tone was dry.

"Really, though," Gregor went on, "it makes much more sense to go on working out how the murder of Charles von Straadt could have been committed simply. Most murders are committed simply. Even murders in this little subcategory of murders. It isn't only street criminals who are lazy. The simple fact is that there was no reason for the murderer to involve himself in a lot of

complicated nonsense if he wanted to kill Charles van
Straadt, even if the murderer wanted to kill Charles
van Straadt at the center and do it on that particular
night. Of course, that particular night was crucial. It was
going to be done then or not at all—"

"Because of the will change," Hector put in.

"That's right," Gregor told him, "but look here. All
the murderer had to do was to get hold of a cup of
coffee—possible in half a dozen places on this floor and
down in the cafeteria and I don't know where else; this
place runs on coffee—go down to the basement, pick up
some of the rat poison—"

"With his bare hands?" Hector demanded.

"No," Gregor said. "Not with his bare hands. With
coffee grounds."

"Coffee grounds," Michael Pride repeated. "I don't
understand."

"I didn't either, for a while," Gregor said. "That was
why I thought Robbie Yagger wasn't telling me anything
important when he said he'd seen someone leaving this
examining room on the night Charles van Straadt died
carrying one off those paper funnels full of coffee
grounds. That's something else there's more than enough
of around here. Coffee grounds. The murderer took the
coffee grounds into the basement, pressed them into the
rat poison, and dumped the whole mess, coffee grounds
and all, into a cup of coffee."

"Stuff." Michael Pride sat bolt upright. "That's what
Robbie was talking about when he said his coffee was full
of stuff."

"Absolutely. Oh, by the way. Coffee grounds have another virtue. I've been assuming that the murderer acquired the cup of coffee first, before the strychnine, but
that wasn't necessary. It doesn't take a lot of strychnine to

kill a person, not even a large man like Charles van Straadt. If you want to commit a murder in this way and you don't want to carry a cup of coffee to the basement and back, all you have to do is palm some coffee grounds, use them to pick up the strychnine you need, and carry the grounds to wherever the coffee is. That would be messy, but it would certainly be feasible."

Hector Sheed was nodding. "That's why the coffee cups always disappeared. They were full of coffee grounds. You never find grounds in coffee when it's been made in the kind of automatic machines they use around here. If we had found them, it would have made us suspicious."

"It might have made you think about rat poison," Gregor said, "and that was insupportable."

"Why didn't the victims get suspicious that their coffee was full of grounds?" Michael asked. "Why didn't they just get grossed out and demand a different cup?"

"I think Robbie Yagger had a lot more grounds in his coffee than the other two had," Gregor said. "By the time it was Robbie Yagger's turn to die, our murderer was getting very impatient. And exasperated. It was never supposed to get this involved."

Hector Sheed stirred uneasily. "Gregor," he said, "if Robbie Yagger was a candidate for murder before he was poisoned this afternoon, isn't he an even more likely candidate now? He must have seen the person who handed him that coffee."

"Not must," Gregor said. "I worked it out. But I agree it's most likely that he saw the murderer."

"Well, nobody is going to be able to poison him with coffee tonight," Michael said. "He isn't going to be able to swallow anything for days."

"There are other ways to kill somebody," Hector

pointed out. "Especially in a place like this. Somebody could just go into that room and rip his tubes out."

Michael shook his head. "That wouldn't work. The only way Robbie could die from that is by dehydration, and one of the nurses would find him long before he dehydrated. Or Shana Malvera would."

"I'm more worried about something nasty like a little strychnine injected into his IV bag," Gregor said. "When I first started thinking about this, I told myself Robbie was only in danger if he had seen the person who doctored his coffee, but I realize now that that's not true. He's in danger for the same reason he was in danger before. Because he saw that person carrying those coffee grounds. He's in *worse* danger than he was before, because the murderer must know that after everything that's happened, we're going to be taking anything he says much more seriously than we did before. I don't think it would make any sense for this murderer to allow Robbie to wake all the way up."

"All right," Michael Pride said. "Then what am I supposed to do? You said before that there was some way I could help with this."

"There is. Hector Sheed and I are going to go upstairs now. We're going to ask this young woman, this Shana Malvera, to leave Robbie Yagger's room, and we're going to hide ourselves inside. Is there room for us to hide ourselves inside?"

"There's room for one of you in the closet. The other one of you will have to use the closet across the hall. I mean, you two aren't clones of Tinkerbell."

Gregor let that pass. "That will be fine. What I want you to do is, first, wait about three minutes after we've gone, to make sure we're well on our way. Then I want you to go downstairs to the cafeteria. My guess is that you'll find Victor van Straadt at a table down there, wasting time."

"Victor?" Michael was doubtful. "What would Victor be doing there? I saw him leave the building hours ago."

"He came back. Don't ask me how I know. I know. If Victor isn't in the cafeteria, go for Martha or Ida, but Victor would be best. I don't want you to talk to him. I want you to talk near to him. I want you to run into one of the nuns or take Augie downstairs with you or whatever, and I want you to say in a very loud voice, loud enough for Victor to hear, that you've just given Shana Malvera strict orders to go to her room and lie down for an hour no matter what. Do you think you can do that?"

"What if none of the van Straadts is in the cafeteria?"

"Find a van Straadt and stage that scene somewhere else," Gregor said. "The important point is to stage that scene somewhere and to do it right away. All right?"

"All right." Michael Pride sighed. "But if you don't mind, I think I will bring Augie with me. If I start accosting stray nuns in the cafeteria with odd conversations delivered in a loud voice, they're going to think I've finally had a breakdown."

2

Later, upstairs, it was Hector Sheed who got the closet in Robbie Yagger's room—not because he was an official New York City policeman, but because he couldn't fit into the linen closet in the hall. Gregor could barely fit into the linen closet himself, but with a little folding and twisting he managed. The sheets and pillowcases that surrounded him smelled clean but acrid, nothing at all like the linens the cleaning woman put on his

own bed back on Cavanaugh Street. Outside in the hall,
the air smelled of disinfectant, the way hospital air always did. The floors had been meticulously swept and
the doors to the rooms and closets had been polished.
This was a convalescent ward. Aside from Robbie, there
was only one old woman in residence and it was no secret what she was in residence for. She had no place else
to go. Gregor tried to check his watch and couldn't in the
darkness. It was very, very dark. There was a single small
security light burning in this hall, and a light above the
desk but under the counter of the nurses' station. All the
other lights had been turned off. Gregor and Hector had
made sure of that as soon as they got upstairs. Gregor
had expected the nun who served as head nurse on this
floor to protest, but she hadn't. She had merely given the
two of them a very odd look and decided to take a break.

"I'll be in the nurses' lounge at the end of the corridor," she had said, "with the door closed. You will find a
buzzer next to every patient bed. If I'm needed, all you
have to do is ring."

Then she had disappeared, the way only a nun can
disappear.

Gregor tried to look at his watch again and failed
again. There was a sharp corner of something sticking
into his back. Gregor twisted around in an attempt to
avoid it and gave himself a cramp in his side. This was
taking forever. He was getting very nervous. What if he
were wrong? Gregor Demarkian was almost never
wrong, especially in cases like this, but almost wasn't always. What if he had misread all the signals? He wasn't
wrong about the identity of this murderer. He had that
much nailed down tight. He might be wrong about the
way the murderer's mind worked. This was the part he
had always hated most about work when he was with

the Bureau. This was why he had given up kidnapping detail as soon as he possibly could. He hated stake-outs with the kind of passion Serbs brought to their relationships with Muslims. Back on Cavanaugh Street, Bennis Hannaford gave him books to read, and Gregor's favorites were about a Great Detective named Nero Wolfe. Nero Wolfe was the only human being Gregor had ever heard of who managed to chase criminals without ever venturing out of his easy chair, except to advance on the dining room for lunch.

Gregor stretched, twisted, rubbed his temples. He reminded himself that waiting in the dark was never anything but interminable. He wished he were in a position to hear Robbie Yagger breathing. He opened the linen closet just another crack and stared out into the hall. Nothing, he thought. Nothing, nothing, nothing—

—except there was.

It started way down on the other end of the hall, the end that opened not onto the elevator doors and the nurses' lounge, but the end that led to the back stairs. The door down there, like all the doors on the wards, was a firebreak. It was a heavy green thing on a pneumatic delay with a window at eye level. The window was a double pane of glass sandwiching in a thin net of wire. For a second, Gregor thought he saw a flash of light behind that window. It was gone so quickly, he couldn't be sure. The door swung open slowly and steadily and then began to swing shut again. It took Gregor a moment to see that someone had come in down there.

"Someone" was as close to an identification as Gregor could get. In spite of the fact that he knew who this had to be, he couldn't really recognize anything but a tall shapeless mass, moving toward him. He pulled back into the linen closet and held his breath. The figure was walking oddly, in jerky movements. The sound of shoes on floor was unnaturally loud. Gregor held himself against the sheets and waited. The figure came closer and closer. It was moving very slowly. It was being very careful.

Trench coat, Gregor said to himself, when the figure got close enough. That was all he could make out clearly in the shadows. A trench coat and a pair of long white pants, the kind the orderlies wore. The collar of the trench coat was pulled way up, over the back of the figure's head. Gregor couldn't even make out the color of the figure's hair. That was odd, but he didn't have time to think about it, not now. The figure was advancing on the door of Robbie Yagger's room. It was going inside. Gregor let the door of the linen closet begin to swing slowly open.

Inside Robbie Yagger's room, everything was in absolute darkness. Gregor and Hector had been careful to turn out even the small nightlight that was supposed to glow perpetually over the emergency buzzer. Robbie Yagger wasn't going to buzz anybody by himself. He wasn't going to turn over on his side until well after lunch tomorrow. What was important was making sure that Hector could not be seen by anybody.

The trick was to move without giving yourself away. Gregor had never been good at it. He got out of the linen closet without making any noise, but it took him forever. He got across the hall to the wall next to Robbie Yagger's doorway, but he must have done something wrong. In the middle of the room, the figure hesitated. It looked up and around. It was suspicious. Gregor flattened himself against the wall and held his breath.

The things he'd done must have been sufficient. He heard the figure beginning to move again. He moved forward, twisted with aching slowness, and put himself in a position to look in through the door. He must have done it all right, because the figure continued to move. It walked up to Robbie Yagger's bed and picked up the IV line. It put the IV line down and reached into the pocket of its trench coat. The nightlight next to Robbie Yagger's bed was still off, but Gregor and Hector hadn't incapacitated it. The figure leaned over and turned it on. Surgical gloves, Gregor told himself, straining to see in the shifting shadows. A stocking over the head. Idiot.

Now that there was a light on in the room, the figure in the trench coat seemed to pick up a sense of urgency. It stuck its hand into its pocket and came up with a syringe. It stuck its hand into its other pocket and came up with what looked like a small perfume bottle. Gregor would bet anything that what was in that perfume bottle was strychnine dissolved in water. Murderers were so damned lazy, and so unoriginal. They wanted to do the same thing over and over again. They didn't want to have to think.

The figure put the syringe and the perfume bottle down on the rolling tray at the side of Robbie Yagger's bed. There wasn't much time now. A real nurse engaged in giving a real medicine through injection would have to be careful. She'd want to make sure there wasn't a bubble of air in the syringe. This dim figure would want only to make sure that it was fast. In and out as quickly as possible was the only advantage it had.

There was no need to go on being careful. Nothing could come of staying hidden now but Robbie Yagger's murder. Gregor started toward the open doorway and the dim figure in the trench coat. He wondered what was keeping Hector from moving. He was just about to go through the door when he collided with the nun.

"Excuse me," the nun said, in a very loud voice. She

was the nun who had been on duty at the nurses' station when Gregor and Hector came up to this floor, but beyond that, she was not a nun Gregor knew. She was small and old and she had a voice like frozen arrowheads.

"Excuse me," she said again.

Then she marched past a stunned Gregor into Robbie Yagger's room and right up to the figure in the trench coat. The figure had frozen, syringe in the air. Now a shudder seemed to pass through its body; the syringe dropped on the floor. The nun got a grip on the figure's wrist and refused to let go.

"What do you think you're doing?" she demanded. "What are you doing with those shoes? Those are Karida Johnson's shoes."

Gregor looked down at the shoes. They were hidden under the long white pants, but what he could see was the thick bottom of a high platform, the kind of thing the whores wore to make themselves look five or six inches taller. Gregor himself had seen Karida Johnson in those shoes.

"Take that silly thing off your head," the nun said, pulling at the stocking. "I know who you are."

That was when Hector Sheed decided to join the festivities. The huge detective stumbled out of the closet, tripping over the equipment that came cascading after him like a metallic waterfall.

"That trench coat," Hector said. "Where did he get that trench coat?"

"It's not a he," the nun replied with contempt. "It's a she, of course. *Anybody* could tell."

The small nun tugged at the stocking mask again, and now the figure decided it was time to bolt. It crouched into a ball and swiftly shot up again, knocking the Sister backward. Then it spun around and sprinted for the door.

This was definitely not Gregor Demarkian's strong suit. He not only couldn't sprint, he could barely walk at what Bennis Hannaford called "a normal pace." Still, what had to be done had to be done. He couldn't just let this person go sailing out of here before they'd had time to make a positive identification. He reached out as the figure sped by.

It worked. Gregor Demarkian had no idea how it worked, but it worked. He caught hold of the trench coat's sleeve. Unbalanced, the figure tottered on her high platform heels and began to fall sideways. Then Hector Sheed was there, pulling the stocking mask apart.

"Goddamn it," he bellowed. "I've had enough of this, I really have. I've had enough of this."

"I've had enough of this, too," Victor van Straadt said, appearing in Robbie Yagger's doorway. "Is it over now? Doesn't she get away with it this time?"

"Who is she?" Hector Sheed exploded.

Gregor would have told him, but he didn't have to. The stocking mask Hector had been ripping at gave way. It tore into pieces and fell back off the figure's head.

At that point, everybody could see that the woman in the trench coat and the platform heels was Ida Greel.

E·P·I·L·O·G·U·E

**The Cardinal Archbishop of New York
Is in a Very Bad Mood
on Father's Day Morning**

1

That year, Father's Day came on the twentieth of June, and the twentieth of June was hot. Gregor Demarkian got up early and stood at the window of his living room, looking down on Cavanaugh Street and watching it start to happen. Father's Day was not as big a holiday as Mother's Day on Cavanaugh Street—nothing was as big a holiday as Mother's Day on Cavanaugh Street—but Donna Moradanyan had done her best. In fact, in the week and a half that Gregor had been in New York, Donna had exploded in a riot of creativity, strewing ribbons here, blowing up balloons there, wrapping Lida Arkmanian's town house up in crepe paper and paper foil until it looked like the principal present at a surprise birthday party. Not that Lida was there to see it. Lida was out in California somewhere, on vacation. It was the second vacation she had taken since Valentine's Day. It had Gregor a little worried. Was Lida sick? It was the only reason he could think of that she would take so many vacations.

Bennis Hannaford sat cross-legged on Gregor's couch, wearing a shawl in defense against his air-conditioning and paging through the *People* magazine story on the murders of Charles and Rosalie van Straadt. There was a picture of the Cardinal Archbishop of New York there, too, and she had stopped to look at it.

"Tibor doesn't like him," she said, meaning the Cardinal Archbishop. Tibor was Father Tibor Kasparian, priest at Holy Trinity Church and Gregor's best friend on Cavanaugh Street. "Tibor says he's a very learned man, but very cold. Can you imagine Tibor calling someone cold?"

"I didn't like him either," Gregor said. "I'd gotten so used to John Cardinal O'Bannion, I thought that was what a Cardinal was like. He called here this morning, by the way."

"Who? John O'Bannion?"

"No. The Cardinal Archbishop of New York. He wasn't in a very good mood. I'd done it all wrong, you see. The murderer wasn't supposed to have turned out to be a relative of the van Straadts'."

"Do you mean he brought you in hoping to see the arrest of Michael Pride?"

"I think he brought me in hoping I'd give him an excuse to end the Archdiocese's involvement with the Sojourner Truth Health Center. Michael Pride or anybody else in authority over there, even one of his own nuns, and he could have pulled his funding and his permissions and washed his hands of the whole thing. He can't do that now, of course. It would look as if he were kicking Michael Pride when he was down."

"That's exactly what it would be, too. You look cute in this picture, Gregor. Very tousled and hot. But you're gaining weight again."

"I'm going to go get myself some coffee. Some black

coffee. While I'm in the kitchen, I think I'll eat an entire plate of *loukoumia*."

"Do you have an entire plate of *loukoumia*?"

"That and a whole pile of *banirov halvah*. Sofie Oumoudian came to visit me yesterday. I think she wants to turn me into her term paper for her civics class. Crime, punishment, and criminal investigations in the American urban jungle."

"Get me a couple of pieces of *loukoumia* while you're there. I want to read the article in *USA Today* before I go downstairs to change for church."

"You ought to convert to the Armenian Church," Gregor told her. "That way you could receive communion and all the rest of it, instead of being a kind of non-participant observer every Sunday."

"If I converted, I'd have to show up every Sunday whether I wanted to or not," Bennis told him. "Get me some *loukoumia*. I'm absolutely starving."

Bennis was always starving. Gregor went into his kitchen, filled his kettle full of water, and took the jar of instant coffee off his counter. The *loukoumia* was on a plate on the kitchen table. The *banirov halvah* was in the refrigerator, in spite of the fact that it was supposed to be eaten warm. That was what microwaves were for. Gregor looked at his wall calendar and saw the square for next Sunday marked over in green and red. "*DINNER AT TIBOR'S,*" said the green, and the red said, "*BRING SKATEBOARD.*" Life was back to normal.

The water in the kettle boiled. Gregor got a coffee mug, filled it full of water, and dumped in instant coffee. He dumped in too much. He always dumped in too much. He could never remember how much he was supposed to use. He got a paper plate out of the cabinet next to his sink and piled it high with pieces of *loukoumia*. Then he felt like an idiot. Why had he bothered with the paper plate? He should be bringing all the *loukoumia* he had into the living room, right on the original plate. He and Bennis were going to eat it all anyway.

Gregor went back into the living room, coffee in one hand, *loukoumia* in the other. Bennis had passed *USA Today* and gone on to the *Philadelphia Inquirer*. The *Inquirer* had a Sunday supplement special titled,

DEMARKIAN IN MANHATTAN:
Philadelphia's Armenian-American Hercule Poirot Goes to the Big Apple.

Gregor put the *loukoumia* down on top of it and walked back to the window. Bennis started eating.

"You know what I don't understand," she said after a while. "It's this business with Charles van Straadt changing his will. Why didn't Ida just wait a day and let him change it?"

"Because he wouldn't have changed it in her favor," Gregor said. "This is the tricky part, I know. It's giving the New York DA's office migraines. But it's perfectly reasonable once you understand what was really going on. Charles van Straadt was going to change his will the next day, yes, but he wasn't going to change it in Ida's favor. He was going to cut her out of it."

"Out?"

"Okay," Gregor said. "Start from the beginning. Victor van Straadt is not too bright. He's never been too bright. All he's ever wanted to do is to keep out of trouble, make his grandfather at least not annoyed with him, and go to a lot of parties. So, he graduates from college and he needs a job. His grandfather wants him to go to work on the New York *Sentinel*. He goes to work on the New York

Sentinel. It doesn't take any time at all for the editors there to realize that Victor is hopeless as a newspaperman. They look for something to keep him busy and they find—"

"The contests," Bennis said. "Yes, I know that, but—"

"No buts. Wait. The thing about Victor is, he's not only not too bright, he's not too energetic. In fact, he's lazy as hell. He takes a look at the contest setups and he's confused as hell. He could probably figure it all out if he wanted to take the time and make the effort, but he doesn't want to do either. Instead, he does what he has always done. He goes for help to the women of his generation, to Rosalie who is good with money, and to Ida, his sister, who has always been good at everything. Who has always made a point of being good at everything."

"Made a point of it," Bennis said. "That's important. You said that in two of the interviews."

"Yes, I did. And it is important. It was Ida's primary motivation for just about everything. Victor is exceptionally good looking. So was Rosalie. Martha is rather plain, but her personality tends toward the phlegmatic. She's never looking to make a splash. Ida, though, Ida is different. Ida likes to be the center of attention. It's very noticeable when you meet her. She likes to set herself apart. She has, however, always had one handicap. She's very plain. She has never had any of the physical qualities, the appearance of femininity, that young women in her position can trade on for notice and esteem. Instead, she's had to compensate, and she's compensated very well. I don't know how often I was told, by her cousin Martha especially, that it was unbelievable that Ida was going to medical school. In the beginning I thought that meant that Martha found it unbelievable that anybody would go to medical school, but that wasn't it. What was unbelievable was that *Ida* would go to medical school. Medicine wasn't enjoyable for her. Medicine isn't enjoyable for a lot of doctors, of course, but those doctors have other motivations, most often money. Ida didn't need money. Why would she do it? Well, she did it for the same reason she did everything else. To show off the one thing she did have to offer. Her intelligence. Ida Greel is a very intelligent woman."

"I don't call killing two people and trying to kill a third intelligent," Bennis said. "I mean, for goodness sake, Gregor. There's no way to avoid an investigation in a situation like this. And there's no way to know how an investigation will turn out."

"Yes, Bennis, I know. But Ida Greel never intended to murder anybody. She got forced by circumstances into that. No, what Ida Greel set out to do, when Victor first came to her with those contests, was to pull an underhanded little trick on her grandfather and pay him back for the attention he was paying to Rosalie. And to get away with it, of course. That was key. Ida didn't want to steal a lot of money from the New York *Sentinel* and wave it around in the air in front of her grandfather and go *nyah, nyah, nyah*. Charles van Straadt was never supposed to know."

"But he did."

"Oh, yes, he did," Gregor said, "eventually. But only eventually. Before Charles van Straadt found out what was going on, Ida had rigged five separate contests and defrauded the New York *Sentinel* of six hundred and fifty thousand dollars. All of it tax free, by the way. The Manhattan District Attorney's office found the stuff last week, down in the Cayman Islands. She was gearing up to rig the Father's Day contest, too, until Charles van Straadt found out what she was doing. Her method was really very simple. She never worked the straight drawings. Lottery fraud is really very difficult and easy to detect. She worked the contests where people had to answer questions and only the ones with the perfect scores would be a part of a drawing at the end. On two of those contests, she devised the questions in such a way that no one could answer them but herself. On the President's Day quiz, for example, there was a question about a president who never existed. Ida submitted an entry in the name of Miss Sharon Cortez from Queens, and of course Sharon Cortez won. She had to. Sharon Cortez also decided that she didn't want to be photographed for publicity purposes, and the check was mailed to her. The New York police checked out the address. It was an accommodation house. You know, one of those places nobody lives, but everybody gets mail."

"Nice," Bennis said.

"Ida fixes a couple of small drawings, too," Gregor went on, "but that was a lot easier to do than fixing a lottery number pick. Her big coup was what the paper called the Christmas Supercontest last year. The payoff was a quarter of a million dollars. The qualifying puzzles were masterpieces of convolution and deception. The winner was Mrs. Esther Stancowycz from Brooklyn, whom nobody from the paper ever saw. The phony winners were always women, by the way, because Ida liked to take care of business by herself. Ida would set herself with a fake identity and open a bank account about three weeks to a month before the contest went off. Then she would deposit the check, wait for it to clear, and deposit the cash in the Cayman Islands. Then she would close the bank account and start again somewhere else. Different banks, different boroughs, different names. Middle-aged ethnic ladies. That was her specialty. She was good at it."

"She must have been," Bennis said. "But Gregor, how do you know that Charles van Straadt knew that Ida was stealing from the paper?"

"Because he told Michael Pride. Not in so many words, of course, but he did tell him. I took Michael Pride to dinner, when I first came to New York. He told me that on the afternoon before the night on which Charles van Straadt died, Charles called him up, ostensibly to talk about some trouble Michael had been having—"

"I've read about that."

"The population of the United States has read about that by now, Bennis. The point is, Charles van Straadt got off the subject fairly quickly. He told Michael Pride that somebody had been trying to cheat him and that he had that somebody caught. He said that he had the perfect revenge, too. He was going to give this person something that this person didn't want, but this person was not going to be able to say he didn't want it, because it would sound crazy."

"Meaning all the money," Bennis said.

"Well, he was at least going to float the rumor that he was going to leave Ida all the money. I don't think he would actually have changed his will in that direction, in spite of what he told his lawyers. After all, he hadn't signed anything yet. I think he was just trying to make his game look believable."

"But why? Why would he want to do that?"

"For the same reason that *Ida* started the rumor that he was going to change his will to leave all his money to

Rosalie," Gregor said. "She had Martha and Victor convinced, by the way. She had them holding strategy meetings and I don't know what else. And do you know what they did? They cut Rosalie off. They stopped talking to her completely."

"So they would have stopped talking to Ida."

"Yes, they would have. And at that point everything would have started to unravel. Victor may be stupid. Martha and Rosalie were not. Once Ida was separated from that contest and Martha and Rosalie had to take charge of it, all the little discrepancies would start to come out. I don't know if Ida knew at the end her grandfather was only toying with her or if she thought he was serious. It didn't matter. She couldn't allow him to change his will in her favor or even to convince her cousins that he was going to change his will in her favor. She didn't dare take the chance of finding out what he would do if he did—or had—found out about those contests."

"What would he have done?" Bennis asked. "Would he have prosecuted her?"

Gregor shrugged. "I don't know. He would have exposed her, I'm sure of that. That would probably have been enough."

"What about Rosalie? Would Rosalie have exposed Ida, too?"

"My guess is that Rosalie, like Robbie Yagger, saw Ida someplace she shouldn't have been. Fortunately for Ida, Rosalie was so obsessed with Michael Pride, she wasn't much interested in any other solution to her grandfather's death. Do yourself a favor and never fall in love with a man who hasn't fallen in love with you first. That kind of thing causes women a lot of trouble."

"It would cause anybody a lot of trouble. I don't fall in love with anybody."

"Donna Moradanyan has." Gregor pressed his face against the living room window. Down the street, he could see Donna Moradanyan and her young son, Tommy. They were sitting on the stoop of Lida Arkmanian's town house and holding hands. Standing in front of them was a Philadelphia plainclothes police office named Russell Donahue. Russell Donahue had been visiting Donna Moradanyan's apartment upstairs on a regular basis for several months now.

"Are you keeping track of that?" Gregor asked Bennis. "Is he treating her well? Is he responsible? Does he drink?"

"He drinks a glass of wine every night with dinner if he isn't on duty. He loves Tommy to pieces. He brings Donna a single rose every Sunday night. Things are fine."

"That's nice. How are things with you?"

"Don't ask questions you don't want the answers to."

"You ate all the food," Gregor Demarkian said.

The paper plate with the *loukoumia* on it was empty. Bennis glanced at it, shrugged her shoulders and stood up. Gregor watched her leave the living room and go into the kitchen, the shawl slipping down her back like a sheet of cashmere snow.

Investigating extracurricular murders was all well and good, Gregor thought, but he was always very glad to be home.

And if he stayed home long enough, Bennis and Tibor and Donna and Lida and Hannah and old George and Howard Kashinian would drive him crazy enough so that he would be chomping at the bit for another problem to investigate, anywhere in the world but here.

If people ever started to make sense, Gregor Demarkian thought, the universe would have a nervous
breakdown.

2

Up in Harlem, staring out at the brilliant sunshine of
Father's Day morning and the children from the east
building walking off hand in hand to church, Michael
Pride was having his worst day yet. He had a terrible
feeling it was only going to deteriorate from here. He
couldn't afford to go upstairs to rest. Both of the doctors
who spelled him were off this morning, taking their ease
after a particularly bad Saturday night. One of them
would have stayed if he had asked them to, but Michael
hadn't wanted that. They had looked so wrung out. They
had looked so discouraged. They didn't have what he had
to fall back on, that thing inside, that nameless thing that
had brought him here to begin with.

Michael Pride was sitting in one of the plastic chairs in
the emergency-room waiting area in the west building. He
had collapsed there after a trip to the men's room. Now he
thought about getting up and getting moving, about going
down to his examining room, about finding a nun to get
him a cup of coffee. He didn't want Augie to find him here.
Augie got so—irrational—about his condition.

Michael had just managed to get himself upright,
holding on to the back of the chair, when the woman
walked in the front doors and stopped uncertainly in
front of the admitting desk. She was a white woman
with bright red hair and a slight frame. She was
dressed in very expensive clothes and wearing the kind
of delicate gold watch sold for Christmas presents in

places like Tiffany's. The expensive clothes were casual in an Upper East Side kind of way, fawn-colored slacks made of silk, a white silk T-shirt that had cost at least a hundred and fifty dollars at Bendel's. Michael wondered how she'd made it all the way up here without getting mugged.

The woman looked around, saw him, and paused uncertainly. Then she walked over to his chair. Michael had sat down in it again. It was too much of an effort to stand up.

"Excuse me," the woman said. "I'm looking for Dr. Michael Pride."

She's in her early to mid-thirties, Michael thought to himself. She looks younger. Then he held out his hand to her and said, "I'm Michael Pride. Who are you?"

More hesitation, more uncertainty. The woman took his hand. "My name is Marianne Kempner," she said. "I quit my job last Friday."

"Quit your job?"

"I shouldn't put it like that. It wasn't what people usually mean by a job. I'm a doctor. I had a private practice down on East Sixty-fourth Street."

"Had?"

"Well, yes. I guess *had*. The building where my offices were was sold, you see, and I had until Friday to sign on to keep the suite. And I was going to. There was no reason I shouldn't. But I didn't."

"Do you have a new suite elsewhere?"

"No. No, I don't."

"Do you have partners?"

"I used to have a partner," Marianne Kempner said. "My father. I took over his practice after he died. That was—eight months ago. He'd been in that same suite for twenty-four years."

"And now it's gone."

"Yes it is. I have to be out by the end of the month."

"What are you going to do?"

"I don't know," Marianne Kempner told him. "I know this is going to sound nuts, but that's why I'm here. I think I've been thinking about it for months now. I know I've been thinking about it all weekend. I want to work here."

"We don't pay much," Michael said. "We don't pay hardly anything at all."

"Oh, I wouldn't need any money, not right away, at any rate. Didn't I read somewhere that everyone on staff here lives here? They have rooms right at the center?"

"They do. That's what we pay, mostly. Room and board. Fifty dollars a month in spending money for the doctors."

"That'll be fine. I own an apartment, you see, downtown, but I'm not happy there. I haven't been happy there since I bought it. I could sell it and live here until I find another place. And I have a lot of money put by, you know, and my loans are paid off. I should be very happy, really, it's just that I'm not. I'm . . . bored."

"I know exactly what you mean."

"Do you? All the way up here this morning, I've been telling myself I'm crazy. I must be crazy. I made three hundred thousand dollars last year. But it isn't right, is it?"

"What isn't?"

"What I see on the news. The way people live up here."

"No, it isn't right."

"I keep pacing around my apartment, making myself sick with it, and I don't know why. I'm thirty-four years old. I'm a reasonably intelligent woman. I've known about the way the world is forever."

Michael cocked his head. "When I first came up here, I used to walk around the streets sure that I had to be dreaming. It couldn't be real. I knew it couldn't be real. Even though I was standing in the middle of it."

"I really have very good credentials," Marianne Kempner said. "I got my BA at Brown and my MD at Johns Hopkins. And I did my residency at Mass General. In internal medicine."

"Surgery?"

"Oh, yes. Yes, of course. I could get you all my papers tomorrow. And you could check the AMA and the licensing people and all that. I really—there's nothing wrong. I'm not in any kind of trouble or anything."

"I didn't think you were."

"I would think it if I were you. Somebody like me coming up here like this. It's what all my friends are going to think. Either that, or that I've had a nervous breakdown."

"That's what all my friends thought, too," Michael said. "You keep forgetting I did the same thing once. I did something worse. There was no center for me to go to then."

"Oh, well," Marianne Kempner said. "That's something different. You're some kind of a saint."

Michael Pride held out his arm. "Help me up," he told Marianne Kempner. "I have AIDS, and I'm having a bad day. Get me to my office and we'll do a little more talking."

"All right."

"Do you know what you just reminded me of? The

only phrase I ever really liked from the Bible. The essence of Christianity."

"I'm Jewish," Marianne said.

"In this case, I don't think it matters. 'If you would be perfect as your Father in Heaven is perfect, then go, sell what thou hast, and give it to the poor, and come, follow me.'"

"Follow who?" Marianne asked. "I'm not following anybody. I'm not even walking a straight line."

Marianne Kempner was slight, but she was strong. Michael was leaning his full weight on her left shoulder and she wasn't even dipping to the side. He let her lead him carefully down the corridor, moving slowly, without complaint. There were so many things he wanted to tell her that he knew he couldn't tell her, so many things he already knew that she would have to find out for herself. It wasn't a question of passion or self-sacrifice. It wasn't a matter of turning oneself into a saint. It wasn't a life of renunciation or deprivation or pious punctilious giving up. Michael Pride had never been happier in his life than in the time he had spent in Harlem. He had never had a moment of regret for any of the things he was supposed to have given up. He had never for a moment believed that he was dedicating himself to a cause or going on a crusade to make the world a better place. Michael Pride was here because he wanted to be—and he wanted to be here much more than any of his partners had ever wanted to be playing golf in Scotland or lying on the beach for the season on the Costa del Sol. Actually, the idea of both of those things left Michael Pride cold.

Michael let Marianne Kempner deposit him in the first chair she came to after they got into the examining room. Then he let her get him a cup of water. He could see that she was concerned for him, but he was not concerned for himself. This was temporary. It would be months before the real pain started, the consistent pain that he would not be able to work through. That ought to be just enough time.

"Now," he said, taking a sip of water. "You'd better get yourself a chair and listen hard, because I'm going to tell you what we're going to make you do. There's a lot of work around here."

"Right," Marianne Kempner said.

She grabbed a chair and sat down, and Michael Pride smiled.

He had been worrying a lot lately, but he shouldn't have been.

He should have known that the person he needed was bound to show up.

about the author

JANE HADDAM is the author of eleven Gregor Demarkian holiday mysteries. *Not a Creature Was Stirring*, the first in the series, was nominated for both an Anthony and the Mystery Writers of America's Edgar awards. *A Stillness in Bethlehem, Precious Blood, Act of Darkness, Quoth the Raven, A Great Day for the Deadly, A Feast of Murder, Murder Superior, Festival of Deaths, Dear Old Dead,* and *Bleeding Hearts* are her other books. She lives in Litchfield County, Connecticut, with her husband, her son, and her cat, where she is at work on a New Year's Day mystery, *Fountain of Death*.

BANTAM MYSTERY COLLECTION

____57258-X **THE LAST SUPPERS** Davidson • • • • • • • • • • $5.50

____56859-0 **A FAR AND DEADLY CRY** Peitso • • • • • • • • $4.99

____57235-0 **MURDER AT MONTICELLO** Brown • • • • • • • • $5.99

____29484-9 **RUFFLY SPEAKING** Conant • • • • • • • • • • $4.99

____29684-1 **FEMMES FATAL** Cannell • • • • • • • • • • • $4.99

____56936-8 **BLEEDING HEARTS** Haddam • • • • • • • • • $4.99

____56532-X **MORTAL MEMORY** Cook • • • • • • • • • • • $5.99

____56020-4 **THE LESSON OF HER DEATH** Deaver • • • • • • $5.99

____56239-8 **REST IN PIECES** Brown • • • • • • • • • • • $5.50

____56537-0 **SCANDAL IN FAIR HAVEN** Hart • • • • • • • • $4.99

____56272-X **ONE LAST KISS** Kelman • • • • • • • • • • $5.99

____57399-3 **A GRAVE TALENT** King • • • • • • • • • • • $5.50

____57251-2 **PLAYING FOR THE ASHES** George • • • • • • • $6.50

____57172-9 **THE RED SCREAM** Walker • • • • • • • • • • $5.50

____56954-6 **FAMILY STALKER** Katz • • • • • • • • • • • $4.99

____56805-1 **THE CURIOUS EAT THEMSELVES** Straley • • • • • $5.50

____56840-X **THE SEDUCTION** Wallace • • • • • • • • • • $5.50

____56877-9 **WILD KAT** Kijewski • • • • • • • • • • • • $5.50

____56931-7 **DEATH IN THE COUNTRY** Green • • • • • • • • $4.99

____56172-3 **BURNING TIME** Glass • • • • • • • • • • • • $3.99

- -

Ask for these books at your local bookstore or use this page to order.

Please send me the books I have checked above. I am enclosing $____ (add $2.50 to cover postage and handling). Send check or money order, no cash or C.O.D.'s, please.

Name _____

Address _____

City/State/Zip _____

Send order to: Bantam Books, Dept. MC, 2451 S. Wolf Rd., Des Plaines, IL 60018
Allow four to six weeks for delivery.
Prices and availability subject to change without notice.   MC 12/95

Bantam Offers the Finest in Classic and Modern British Murder Mysteries

Dorothy Cannell

____56951-1	How to Murder Your Mother-In-Law	$4.99/$6.50
____29195-5	The Thin Woman	$4.99/$5.99
____27794-4	The Widows Club	$4.99/$5.99
____29684-1	Femmes Fatal	$4.99/$5.99
____28686-2	Mum's the Word	$4.99/$5.99

Colin Dexter

____29120-3	The Wench Is Dead	$4.99/NCR
____28003-1	Last Seen Wearing	$4.99/NCR
____27363-9	The Riddle of the Third Mile	$5.99/NCR
____27238-1	The Silent World of Nicholas Quinn	$4.99/NCR
____27549-6	The Secret of Annexe 3	$4.99/NCR

Christine Green

____56931-7	Death in the Country	$4.99/NCR
____56932-5	Die in My Dreams	$4.99/NCR

Ask for these books at your local bookstore or use this page to order.

Please send me the books I have checked above. I am enclosing $____ (add $2.50 to cover postage and handling). Send check or money order, no cash or C.O.D.'s, please.

Name _____

Address _____

City/State/Zip _____

Send order to: Bantam Books, Dept. MC 6, 2451 S. Wolf Rd., Des Plaines, IL 60018
Allow four to six weeks for delivery.
Prices and availability subject to change without notice.   MC 6 12/95